JANE THE QUENE

BOOK ONE OF THE SEYMOUR SAGA

JANET WERTMAN

Printed in the United States of America
First printing 2016

ISBN 978-0-9971338-0-6 (Kindle edition)
ISBN 978-0-9971338-2-0 (E-pub edition)
ISBN 978-0-9971338-1-3 (Paperback edition)

Library of Congress Control Number: 2016905613

Cover designed by Jennifer Quinlan of Historical Editorial
Formatting by Sweet 'N Spicy Designs

CONTENTS

PROLOGUE   1
June 9, 1525 ... 10:30 p.m.   1

PART ONE: COMMONER

CHAPTER ONE – 1535   9
Spring
May 24, 1535 ... 11 a.m.   9
June 5, 1535 ... 1:30 p.m.   17

CHAPTER TWO – 1535   31
Summer
July 9, 1535 ... 11 a.m.   31
July 15, 1535 ... 4 p.m.   40

CHAPTER THREE – 1535   49
Wolf Hall
September 4, 1535 ... 3 p.m.   49
September 6, 1535 ... 4 p.m.   57
September 8, 1535 ... 10 a.m.   70
September 10, 1535 ... Noon   76

PART TWO: SCHEMER

CHAPTER FOUR – 1535   85
Back at Court
October 28, 1535 ... 5 p.m.   85
October 29, 1535 ... 10 p.m.   89
November 13, 1535 ... 2 p.m.   93
November 15, 1535 ... 4 p.m.   97
December 1, 1535 ... 3 p.m.   100
December 16, 1535 ... 3 p.m.   109
December 20, 1535 ... 5 p.m.   112

CHAPTER FIVE – 1536   119
January/February
January 1, 1536 ... 1 p.m.   119
January 8, 1536 ... 2 p.m.   123
January 24, 1536 ... 1 p.m.   125
January 29, 1536 ... 1 p.m.   130
February 15, 1536 ... 3 p.m.   135
March 11, 1536 ... 10 a.m.   141

CHAPTER SIX – 1536   145
Spring
March 21, 1536 ... 11 a.m.   145
April 5, 1536 ... 1 p.m.   150
April 18, 1536...1 p.m.   156
April 23, 1536 ... 3 p.m.   167
April 30, 1536 ... 10 a.m.   175

CHAPTER SEVEN – 1536   180
May
May 7, 1536 ... 6 p.m.   180
May 19, 1536 ... 9 a.m.   185

PART THREE: QUEEN

CHAPTER EIGHT – 1536   197
Summer
May 30, 1536 ... 7 a.m.   197
May 31, 1536 ... 4 a.m.   205
June 4, 1536 ... 9 a.m.   208
June 14, 1536 ... 3 p.m.   214
July 6, 1536 ... 2 p.m.   220
July 8, 1536 ... 2 p.m.   223
September 1, 1536 ... 3 p.m.   229
September 28, 1536 ... 10 p.m.   233

CHAPTER NINE – 1536   237
Fall/Winter
October 3, 1536 ... 1 a.m.   237
October 21, 1536 ... 6 p.m.   241
November 1, 1536 ... 11 a.m.   248
December 23, 1536 ... 3:30 p.m.   252

February 1, 1537 ... 4 p.m.   257
February 25, 1537 ... 2:30 p.m.   259

CHAPTER TEN – 1537   264
Spring/Summer
March 20, 1537 ... 11 a.m.   264
April 10, 1537 ... 2 p.m.   270
May 27, 1537 ... 10 a.m.   274
July 1, 1537 ... 11 p.m.   276

CHAPTER ELEVEN – 1537   278
Edward
September 16, 1537 ... 7 p.m.   278
October 12, 1537 ... 1 a.m.   280
October 12, 1537 ... 2 a.m.   283
October 13, 1537 ... Midnight   288
October 13, 1537 ... 2 a.m.   292
October 18, 1537 ... 10 a.m.   295
October 20, 1537 ... 7 p.m.   297
October 20, 1537 ... 11 p.m.   299
October 24, 1537 ... 10 p.m.   301

READ ON

CHAPTER ONE   307

AUTHOR'S NOTE   315

For Adlai, in thanks for a life that lets me live my dreams.

PROLOGUE

June 9, 1525 ... 10:30 p.m.

*E*ighteen-year-old Jane Seymour paused at the entrance to the Queen's Presence Chamber, the formal public room in the royal suite of apartments. She breathed a quick prayer and smoothed the kirtle that peeked out from the red damask gown onto which she had painstakingly sewn two-dozen seed pearls. It was the most opulent dress she'd known, and its beauty soothed her nerves. Finally she nodded to her brother Edward, who signaled the page to open the double doors so Jane could be formally presented to her new mistress and begin the charmed life of a woman of the court.

The quiet dark of the hallway gave way to bustling light. The scene before Jane was grander than anything she had ever seen. She had arrived at court too late in the night before to get any kind of tour, something that would have prepared her for this moment. Now, the sights, sounds, and smells assailed her. Soaring leaded windows, carved wood paneling, and gilt edging surrounded her; incense and a heavy medley of perfumes stung her nostrils; and two musicians plucked at her nerves with each note of the soft hymn they strummed on their lutes.

Catherine of Aragon, saintly wife of Henry VIII of England, was in the center of the room, glowing on a raised chair of estate upholstered in rich arras. Seeing her there in quiet command calmed Jane, reassured her of order amid the madness. Like an oak among mushrooms, the Queen was surrounded by women on footstools who sat in small groups chatting among themselves. *That will be me soon,* Jane told herself. Her family had secured her a place in the Queen's household, as one of several companions who attended to Her Majesty's every need and saw to her every diversion. For now, Jane would be a simple maid of honor, happily living at the mercy of the Queen. Once Jane found a husband, which hopefully would happen soon, she would rise to the level of lady-in-waiting with far greater status and freedom.

The page rapped his stave and announced them. "Edward Seymour and Jane Seymour."

The Queen turned her attention to the door and inclined her head for them to proceed. She looked to be covered entirely in gold, from the cloth of her elaborately embroidered gown to the thick strands of her heavy rope necklace, to the solid frame of her tall gable hood. She was magnificent, and Jane was filled with a sense of inadequacy over her own gown that suddenly seemed far too simple.

Jane forced her legs to move forward despite their trembling. As she walked with Edward, she fixed her gaze on the Queen, whose own eyes were kind but lined and tired. Jane immediately thought of the cilice, the punishing haircloth shirt which the Queen, like Carthusian monks, was known to wear under her rich clothes; pain would certainly explain such a look. Edward, unkindly, had gossiped that it was to atone for whatever sin had caused God to withhold a son from her. Jane preferred to think it was a noble antidote to the ostentation of the Queen's life.

Three paces before the dais, Edward stopped and Jane did

likewise. "My sister Jane, Your Majesty," Edward said as he bowed.

The Queen smiled. "You may greet us, Mistress Jane," she said in a voice tinged with her heritage as a proud princess of Spain.

Jane sank to the ground with a reverence she had practiced more than a thousand times. "Thank you for accepting me," she said. "I am honored."

"Rise, my child," said the Queen. "You are welcome."

"Thank you."

The Queen settled back and resumed her needlework. It was an altar cloth, and Jane could see even from her distance that the stitching was exquisite. Jane had always been proud of her own skill at embroidery, but again she felt inadequate against this unexpected new standard.

"You will join your cousins, I believe." Catherine waved her needle in the direction of Anne and Mary Boleyn, who bobbed a quick curtsy to Jane.

Jane looked over at the familiar faces of her second cousins, so different from each other – one slim and dark and exotic, the other soft and blonde and voluptuous. She was not thrilled to see them. The Boleyn girls had always been flighty things who thought themselves so much better than Jane. Now they were both in disgrace and Jane did not want to be too closely associated with them.

Jane turned back to the Queen, and was about to voice additional thanks when she saw the Queen's face light up. Jane turned to see what had caused that reaction.

A girl of around ten had just entered the Presence Chamber. She had flowing auburn tresses and was dressed almost as richly as the Queen. Jane knew immediately this was the Princess Mary, the royal couple's only surviving child. Mary would be heir to the throne unless she were supplanted by a brother, an unlikely event since the Queen was over forty and seven years past her last pregnancy. Indeed, Mary had been named Princess of Wales to reflect her status, and before the end of the year would leave for Wales to practice the art of governing.

Edward grabbed Jane's arm and pulled her to the side so Mary could approach her mother. The girl flashed them a sweet smile of thanks as she advanced with confidence. With impeccable decorum she paused before the Queen, curtsied, then spoke. "His Majesty has sent me to request your presence in his library. He is meeting with the Spanish Ambassador, who begs to greet you."

"I should be glad to attend."

Catherine rose and placed her needlework on her chair, descended the three steps of her dais, and gave her hand to Jane to kiss. "You will take your oath of office when I return. For now, your cousins will acquaint you with my apartments, and your brother will escort me to the King."

Edward bowed and Jane followed his lead with a curtsy. She stood in her spot as the rest of the room emptied out, then turned to the two sisters, who did not look happy with the turn of events. "I thank you both for your kindness," said Jane.

"The Queen ordered it," Anne replied.

"And truthfully, it was more a punishment for us than a kindness for you," said Mary. "She doesn't want to let me anywhere near the King. Not that she can stop me."

Jane said nothing, though of course she knew of the affair. And tried not to revel overmuch in Mary's disgrace.

All Jane's life, her mother had measured Jane against her similarly-aged Boleyn cousins. And found Jane wanting. Jane's resentment had reached its peak when Sir Thomas Boleyn managed to place both his daughters in the household of the French Queen, but jealousy faded as Mary developed the reputation of *una grandissima ribalda, infame sopra tutte,* "a great whore, infamous above all others." Then Anne had returned to England, and had tried to marry above her station by seducing Henry Percy, heir to the Earldom of Northumberland. She had been cut down and shamed for that by Cardinal Wolsey himself.

Which had turned a vindicated Jane into the cousin to emulate. Finally.

Jane tried to imagine Lady Boleyn saying "Be more like Jane" to her own daughters. It strained Jane's imagination, but it was a lovely scene.

"Would that someone could," said Anne, and her voice was sharp.

"Stop pretending that I have a choice. You cannot refuse a king, and why would you want to?"

"It's about time you refused someone," said Anne.

Jane kept her face impassive. Mary and Anne had a long history of jealous rivalry and Jane did not want to get in the middle of their argument. She just wanted to get along with them as best as she could. And largely ignore them.

Jane had big plans for herself, after all.

She had been brought up to be just like Queen Catherine: sober and discreet, pious and pure. The ideal woman. It should be everything Jane needed to shine at this court.

She took a deep breath. Life was wonderful. She might be starting late, but that would just make her reward all the more sweet.

She was sure of it.

PART ONE: COMMONER

CHAPTER ONE – 1535

SPRING

May 24, 1535 … 11 a.m.

*T*homas Cromwell gave a perfunctory genuflection as he entered Henry VIII's private oratory at Hampton Court Palace. It was the smallest room in the King's suite of apartments, but the most ornamented. The walls and the altar were a matching Siena marble with deep-purple veins, while the statuary was an almost translucent Pentelic marble, mined in Greece. All chosen carefully to give the greatest glory to God.

The Mass had already begun, so Cromwell quietly took his place on the bench behind the King and waited, closing his mind against the scent of incense that was particularly strong this day.

On holy days and feast days, the King heard Mass in the Chapel Royal with the rest of his court. But most days he heard Mass alone in his Privy Chamber, and used the fact he was stuck in place for an hour as an opportunity to conduct business. For his ministers, this habit was a blessing since privacy was assured and interruptions limited. Thomas Cromwell made sure to be there for at least one of the King's three Masses every single day.

Cromwell felt a tickle rise in his throat and worked carefully to stifle any cough. He didn't want to sound like he was trying to rush things. Cromwell knew his place. While he had risen to dizzying heights – he was Chancellor of the Exchequer, Secretary of State, and Master of the Rolls – he was still the son of a blacksmith and lower born than anyone at court. But he was secure as long as he continued not only to satisfy his master's urges but also to anticipate them.

Finally the King spoke. "Have you anything for me?"

"There is news from the Bishop of Rome."

The Bishop of Rome. The title for the Pope since the day the King had broken from the Catholic Church two years ago.

The King's ears reddened. "Yes?" he asked without moving.

"He has named Fisher a cardinal. My guess is to dissuade you from executing him."

The King turned around to look at his minister. "What?"

Most other men would have been too cowed by the threat in the steely blue eyes to continue. Not Cromwell – at least not when the anger was directed at someone else. "A cardinal, Sire. They are sending him his red hat."

John Fisher, Bishop of Rochester, was being held in the Tower of London for refusing to recognize the authority of the Church of England and the King as its head. Fisher believed only the Pope could annul the King's marriage to Catherine of Aragon, and therefore refused to accept Anne Boleyn as queen and her daughter, Elizabeth, as heir to the throne. This was high treason.

"I can save them the trouble. I'll send his head to Rome; they can put the hat on it there."

Cromwell nodded. "So we proceed?"

"With all speed," the King answered, and turned back to the Mass.

Cromwell waited a moment, then leaned forward to ask the more important question. Or at least the one with the less certain answer. "What about More?"

The King bowed his head before he answered. The King had

always loved More, but the love had never really been returned. "It is time to bring him to trial as well. But even now I would be glad to pardon him. All he has to do is revoke his willful, obstinate opinion."

Cromwell kept his face impassive. "I pray he will do so, Your Majesty."

Thomas More had been more blessed than he deserved. A simple lawyer who had somehow built an international reputation for honesty and risen to the post of Lord Chancellor of England. An idiot who was too bound to Catherine of Aragon by his orthodox Catholicism to swear the Oath of Succession promising fealty to Elizabeth. Catherine and More were so much alike, with their perverse delight in their haircloth shirts – infernal contraptions that equated pain with piety. Ridiculous trappings of the superstitious Catholic Church. Cromwell had no use for such a man.

"He should be tried before we leave for the summer progress," said the King.

Each year, the King took advantage of the lazy summer days to visit his country and connect with his people. He was right that there should be no clouds on the horizon during this quiet time.

"It shall be done, Your Majesty," said Cromwell.

"When will that be?" asked the King.

"We have not yet published the geist, but it looks like you will leave Windsor for Reading Abbey on July tenth."

The King blinked. "That is quite early."

"I'd have you leave tomorrow, if I could."

"Aye."

There was too much unrest in the land. The King needed to get out among his subjects and remind them how much they loved him. He also needed to drum up support for his religious reforms and his daughter. In that spirit, this year's progress would be the longest of the King's reign, starting early and ending late. The King and Queen would visit the West Country and meet with local dignitaries and officials in almost every town Their Majesties passed. They would give largesse and be feted with pageants. And hopefully the process would work the magic they needed. If anyone could pull this off, Henry VIII could.

Cromwell had spent his youth abroad, serving as a soldier in the French army, then as an accountant and merchant in Italy. He had observed many rulers, from generals to heads of duchies, but had never seen any who commanded love and respect and awe the way this man did. Henry's enthusiasm for spectacle and his unflagging energy combined to make every person on the road feel a personal connection just from having witnessed his magnetism. Truly it was a gift. One he needed to put to use this summer.

"I need a son," the King suddenly shouted as he brought his fist down on the armrest of his prie-dieu. The priest flinched and paused until the King waved his hand, a clear sign to resume. "I need a son," Henry repeated, but softly this time.

"You have a healthy daughter. By the grace of God, sons will follow," Cromwell answered. He tried to be soothing, but the words were almost automatic. They had been spoken many times before.

The King needed a son – a legitimate son. He had Henry FitzRoy, but a bastard could not inherit the throne. And so Henry had torn his kingdom asunder to put aside his wife of twenty years, the aunt of Holy Roman Emperor Charles V of Spain, to marry Anne Boleyn. But she was having no better luck than her predecessor.

"My wife just miscarried another child; this marriage is a mirror of my last one. Except now the world is against me, and my friends – the ones I have left – mock me. Thomas More was one who said he loved me. Surely he will not choose a traitor's death?"

The King might wish all he wanted, but there was no question More sought martyrdom. "Thomas More is no one's friend," was all Cromwell said.

The bell rang and brought them back to the Mass. The consecration was beginning, so their conversation would have to wait. But the King fidgeted during the elevation then meditated only briefly after communion, sure signs he was still brooding. Indeed, he stood and walked a few steps away to continue his conversation with Cromwell in private, leaving the priest to intone the concluding rites alone.

Cromwell followed His Majesty. "Why would God deny me a son?" the King asked, his eyes piercing.

Cromwell held the King's gaze but did not answer. The King had left Catherine of Aragon after asking this very same question. That time the answer had been easy: for six months she had been wed to his elder brother, Arthur, who quickly died. England wanted to keep the alliance with Spain that Catherine personified, and so the new couple had consecrated their marriage despite the clear warning in Leviticus: "If a man uncovers his brother's nakedness, it is an unclean thing and he shall be childless." Twenty years later, the lack of a son clearly showed God's judgment on the matter.

But now this second wife had also delivered nothing more than a girl, suggesting God was not any happier with this marriage than with the old one.

"I think it's because I made the same mistake," Henry continued.

Cromwell stifled a groan. The King had first raised that possibility last January, suggesting Leviticus might not set forth the full extent of the prohibition, that it might be equally wrong to uncover a sister's nakedness – such that Henry's affair with Anne's sister, Mary Boleyn, was as much of an impediment to Henry's second marriage as Catherine's laying with Arthur had been to his first. He had claimed then he wanted to leave Anne Boleyn, but not even two weeks later had decided to have a medal struck to honor his beloved wife.

"Your Majesty is young. You have—"

With the palms of his hands, the King struck Cromwell's shoulders. Forced violently backwards, Cromwell only just managed to catch himself and right his balance. When he saw the anger and contempt in his sovereign's face, an icy fear gripped Cromwell's belly and he threw himself to his knees to speak.

"I have had extensive discussions with the Archbishop of Canterbury on this issue. He fears, as I do, that we are still at a stage where using this argument would risk the very foundation of your Church, *and* the basis of your annulment from Aragon. It would encourage your people to turn back to the Bishop of Rome as arbiter of religious issues."

The King walked over to the side table and poured himself a goblet of wine, which he downed quickly before answering. "Get up," the King motioned as he himself took a seat. Cromwell bowed his head in thanks for his reprieve. The King ignored the gesture. "When will things change?"

Cromwell scrambled to his feet. "Once every able-bodied man in the country has sworn the Oath of Succession, you will be free to rule as you will."

Cromwell was particularly proud of the Oath and the far-reaching scheme it represented. If Anne Boleyn had birthed a son, the country would easily have embraced the change in wife and heir. But with only a daughter, something more was needed to displace Catherine's daughter, Mary, from the people's hearts and loyalty. Cromwell had carefully constructed the Oath to root out dissention: everyone was required to embrace the Church of England as the true religion and Henry VIII as its head.

"But they are refusing. Your strategy is flawed," the King said.

"Nay, Sire. We have seen remarkable success."

"You see success in the execution of an order of Carthusian monks? And soon Bishop Fisher? And even perhaps Thomas More?"

"The people refusing are almost all priests, and not even

many of them. Their punishments have set a fearful example of the consequences of a refusal. We have met with almost no lay dissention."

"How much is 'almost no'?"

"So far, a single farmer in Tintagel, and he tried to recant at the stake."

The King whistled tunelessly. "Out of how many?"

"Only five hundred, but we will accelerate the pace. I am confident we will finish canvassing the entire country before the first snowfall of the year."

"So I must be patient."

"Yes, Sire, but only for six months. Then you will be free to take any steps you need to follow your conscience. After all, Queen Anne has no allies, no one to stand up for her. This would be a relatively quick process. If it comes to that of course – the Lord may bless you both well before then."

"And you are no longer worried that if I put aside a second queen, my first marriage would be magically resurrected in my subjects' eyes? I seem to recall you used that argument against me last year."

Cromwell swallowed. "No, because we are in the process of identifying and punishing all the doubters who see you as still married to the Princess Dowager. Moreover, the woman has been ill of late. With luck, she will die soon. That would solve many problems."

"She has been ill for years."

"True, but now she coughs constantly and has trouble breathing. It is said this is more serious than it ever has been."

Cromwell held the King's gaze, ready as always for the quiet instruction that never came. Rumors of poison plots had swirled for years, but Cromwell was in the ultimate position to know the King had never done anything to validate them. Smart man, to understand the importance of keeping everything legal.

The King finally looked away. He rose and walked to the window to gaze out over the fields. His face must have been clearly visible from below, as women's voices called to him from the garden. "Your Majesty."

The King waved and opened the window. Cromwell approached to see what was going on. The Queen was in the parterre surrounded by her ladies, a colorful and vivacious group except for one awkward outlier: the eldest Seymour girl, Jane. Still unmarried, she was in the unenviable position of having a lady-in-waiting's age with only a maid of honor's rank. She stood apart from the others, with a blank look on her plain face. It was a remarkable thing she was still at court, though it was clear the girl didn't have other options.

"Your Majesty," the Queen called again. She pointed at one of the paths in the Privy Garden. "The Pond Garden is at its peak right now, husband."

Cromwell could picture in his mind's eye the Pond Garden, the small, enclosed space just beyond the Privy Garden. Its privacy made it the destination of choice for dalliances, both licit and otherwise.

The King smiled broadly and leaned out the window to respond. "Lady, I will walk with you now."

A large smile broke onto her face, and she and her ladies curtsied up to him. The King took a final gulp of his wine then strode out, handing the goblet to Cromwell.

Cromwell's knees buckled. Alone in the room, he sat down and finished the wine still remaining in the cup. Could the King really mean to leave Anne Boleyn? Against all odds, Henry VIII had spent more than seven years obsessed with the idea of possessing her. It was impossible to believe such a passion could have burned out after less than three years of marriage. Especially since all she had to do was shake her hips at him to get him to come running. Could Cromwell really trust the King's doubts?

It was so much more likely that whatever this was would just blow over as it had the last time. The summer progress was soon to begin, a relaxed, romantic time – the perfect chance for him to get her with child and let events play out as they would. Six months from now they would revisit the issue. Cromwell would be better prepared then. He'd begin soon to formulate a discreet plan.

He would do whatever the King wanted. If only Cromwell could know for certain what that was.

June 5, 1535 ... 1:30 p.m.

Jane Seymour savored the heat of the sun on her shoulders and the crunch of gravel under her feet. She was walking in the gardens at Greenwich Palace with Queen Anne and her other ladies, as they did every day following the midday dinner. As always, the chatter flew, though Jane rarely joined in.

"Norris will marry me soon enough," Madge Shelton said. "He's simply having too much fun courting me."

Her confident words turned Jane's stomach. Another woman about to be wed. Not that Jane was terribly surprised: Madge's position as a maid of honor to the Queen offered high visibility and access to every young man of good birth and ambition in the land. It was a sure route to a marriage proposal.

So why was Jane still alone?

Jane was twenty-eight, and had never even had an admirer. She had sat through hundreds of interminable dinners and suppers and dances and amusements, watching while everyone around her flirted and gossiped. And ignored her. Still, she had to hope. It would happen soon. It *had* to happen soon. Please, God, what was wrong with her that it hadn't happened already?

She flushed. She knew what everyone else said. "Jane is too pale, too plain, too shy." And if they didn't think she was listening, they added a whispered, "and too simple."

Jane had been raised to aspire to the feminine ideal of Arthurian legend: demure, obedient, and industrious. Unfortunately, ideals had changed drastically when Anne Boleyn caught the King's eye almost ten years ago. Anne Boleyn had black hair and arresting brown eyes. She had bold French manners and a sense of style that every court lady copied. She was confident, educated, and witty. And Jane's strawberry blonde hair and eyelashes, her white skin, her quiet calm and placid acceptance – once real assets – were now outmoded, even ridiculous. Now even Jane's family – especially Jane's family – talked down to her. Except when they needed something. Then they conveniently remembered her capabilities and her worth.

Suddenly the Queen stopped. "I have had enough. I would take some rest," she announced.

Jane looked at the Queen, then at the others, then around the garden, trying to determine the reason for the abrupt change. Her eyes fell on the King in the distance. There was no mistaking his figure, more than six feet tall and athletic, with broad shoulders and a fine calf. He would be a magnificent figure even without the cloth of gold, glinting with jewels, that adorned him from his cap to his shoes. He was walking on a quiet path, alone with a young woman who was in service to the Duchess of Norfolk. He was whispering into the girl's ear and nuzzling her temple, an arm around her waist. Jane bit her lip. *Of course.*

One by one, the other ladies looked toward the garden, then quietly down at their shoes. No one wanted to be the one to provoke the Queen into confronting her husband over this, not after that time he'd told her to shut her eyes as her betters had done. Anne Boleyn was learning the King had reached his limit after a decade of bowing to her every whim and tantrum. Now that he no longer had to chase her love, and especially now that she had disappointed him by birthing a daughter, his patience had evaporated. Now when his wife quarreled with him, he raged back and shamed her. Loudly and publicly.

The Queen swept off and Anne Stanhope Seymour, Jane's sister-in-law and a proud woman determined to advance herself, was the first to fall in behind her. The other ladies jostled for position, but Jane held back, wanting to be as far from the Queen as possible at such a time. Jane's sister Elizabeth must have agreed, or perhaps she was just being kind, since she hung back to walk next to Jane.

The Queen refused to speak so the ten women all walked back in silence. Only when they reached the royal apartments did she open her mouth. "Lady Rochford, stay with me. The rest of you, please return in an hour."

Most of the other women dashed out the door, likely headed to flirt and gossip with the King's attendants who would be similarly unoccupied, leaving behind Elizabeth, Anne, and Jane. Anne nodded her head toward the space the Queen had designated for her ladies-in-waiting to use when they weren't serving her, a small sitting room right outside her Presence Chamber. And while technically it was a cul-de-sac in the hallway, its rich appointments created a careful aura of splendor that constantly reminded Jane of her own lack of style and substance. The walls and ceiling were carved wood, hardened by the angular corners of the marble fireplace yet tempered by the soft green hue of the hanging tapestries. Lit candles on tall iron stands brightened each corner.

Although the gift of the room was probably a discreet way to control the ladies' comings and goings, the space was a godsend when someone needed a brief rest or a quiet corner. They had barely seated themselves before Jane's brother Edward strode in. His thirty-five years as the oldest child and eldest son had given him a natural confidence and authority he used often and well. But now he looked vaguely nervous – his face was missing the aloof sneer he called a smile.

"I saw you out the window," he said to Anne. "Given the anger on the Queen's face, I thought you might be free."

Elizabeth raised an eyebrow in a sarcastic expression at odds with the angelic shape of her face, and grabbed at Jane's arm. "Would you like us to leave so you may speak with your wife?" she asked.

"No, actually," he said, "Jane is the one I want to see."

That was strange. Ah, well, he must want something. "What can I do for you?" she asked.

"Yes, well," he began, then took a deep breath. "You know there have been a number of matches announced in the past month. This is an auspicious time."

Jane's heart soared. He must have found someone for her. She smiled. "Yes?"

"I was thinking," he said, and dropped his eyes. "I hoped...I thought..."

Jane tilted her head. Edward was rarely at a loss for words, and certainly not when it involved such a happy topic.

He stopped, took another deep breath, and looked her straight in the eye. "I want you to let Dorothy take your place at court. She is seventeen, the perfect age to find a husband, and I've just had an inquiry. It is her time."

Jane heard Edward's words as if from a distance. The walls of the room closed in on her. Leave court? Give up her position so another sister might marry before Jane got her chance?

Jane was the eldest girl; she should have been married first. Instead, that honor had gone to Elizabeth when the doddering fifty-year-old Sir Anthony Ughtred had agreed to forego a dowry if he could take the younger, prettier, cleverer sister as his bride. Elizabeth had borne him two children before he died; now she was back at court, an honored twenty-year-old widow with none of the pressure faced by Jane.

Pressure that mounted with each passing year as suitors approached every woman but her. For a time, she'd consoled herself with the fact that none of the men seemed terribly appealing, but at this point she would be happy with anyone. Jane could no longer be choosy in her quest to fulfill her obligations as a Christian woman and satisfy the expectations of her family. She also could not give up this position – her one source of pride and success, her one chance to attract the husband she needed.

She looked over at Anne, who was picking at her fingernails, then at Elizabeth whose wide doe eyes showed her to be as astonished as Jane. *Good, Elizabeth wasn't a part of this.* Jane turned back to Edward. "What have I done to warrant such a sacrifice?" she asked.

"It's not what you've done as much as what you haven't. You haven't attracted any interest. You haven't represented us as you could have; you haven't advanced our family. You were sent here to make alliances, you know that."

"In what way have I failed?"

"You make no effort. And when you do, it doesn't work. I think it is time to give up and let me make a match for your sister."

"Why can't you make a match for me?"

"No one asks about you. When Dorothy arrives, the entire court will make its way to our door. I already know who will be there."

Jane narrowed her eyes. "You know which families are looking for brides? Then why have you not spoken to them about me? You seem to be good at broaching difficult topics."

A fleeting look of embarrassment passed across Edward's face but he continued stubbornly. "Dorothy is a lovely young thing. She'll soon be married off."

He spoke in the clipped manner some called efficient but which Jane found annoyingly self-important. "And once she settles down, you can come back and try again."

Suddenly Jane was transported to what her life would be at Wolf Hall. Living under her father's roof again would be bad enough. But now she would be trapped in the life of a spinster expected to run a house that wasn't hers. Presiding over a nursery for children she hadn't borne. Looking from the outside in at the life she craved.

Jane's teeth and hands clenched as heat built from her very core. It hurt her that Edward expected Dorothy to marry so quickly when Jane had tried for years. It infuriated her to think he might be right. Dorothy had an easy, light personality, developed because she was born the year Edward had left the house and had grown up without him constantly telling her what to do. Dorothy hadn't been taught to doubt herself and her every instinct.

Elizabeth stood, her hands on her hips. "Edward, how could you? You should have asked me. I should be the one to cede my place."

That silenced Edward, who just gaped at their sister. Annoyed at his reaction, Jane dropped her eyes to pick at a knot in her rich brocade overskirt and silently thanked Elizabeth's kind heart.

"Your time is better spent here," Edward finally said. "Your prospects are better than Jane's."

His callous assessment caused the resentment and hurt that had been building all of Jane's life to finally spill over. Edward didn't see her qualities, and there was no one to save her from the consequences of that judgment. Their father had abdicated all responsibility to Edward, and their mother thought his every action brilliant. They would not help her. Elizabeth might try – she just had – but she could never change anything. Jane needed to fight for herself. "No," she declared for the first time she could remember. "No."

"Jane, Jane. Mother needs your help running Wolf Hall. You are the expert there. Think of your duty."

"I visit often enough to know it is perfectly fine without me. And my duty is always before my eyes."

It was true. All her life, Jane Seymour had done what was expected of her. All her life, she had done the right thing, confident this was the path to success. All her life, she had appeased the harsh voices around her by rushing to do every impossible task thrown at her. But although this may have earned her praise in her earliest days, now it only seemed to encourage people to ignore or take advantage of her. No more.

"Always," she repeated, more bitterly than before.

"Anne tells me the Queen excludes you more and more from

the amusements she plans," Edward said in yet another attack. "Retiring for a time would improve your lot when you return."

The tears mounted to Jane's eyes. She poured herself some ale and actually felt the flagon mock her. Drinks were rationed. Everyone at court was entitled to a gallon of beer and ale each day, and the Queen's ladies had a share of wine as well. Still, Jane always quietly denied herself to make sure they didn't exceed their allotment. Another act of service no one ever noticed. She took a deep drink before answering. "I may not feature in her silly tableaux as much as some of the others, but the Queen knows me to be reliable and hardworking."

Edward wagged his finger. "To this queen, style is more important than substance. Admit it, she doesn't like you. She never has."

Jane bit at a cuticle until it bled, a small red splotch screaming out against her ghostly white skin. He was right. The Seymours and the Boleyns were second cousins and of similar ages. They had been thrown together many times growing up and had never truly gotten along, much as Jane had always tried to deny that. She pressed her thin lips together and leveled her gray-blue eyes at the brother who had always been too blunt for her taste. "Fine. She doesn't like me. But she doesn't like anyone."

"She likes Anne. She loves Elizabeth. Dorothy will fare well."

Jane's eyes flashed again and her words spit out of her mouth. "Stop it. I need a husband. Find me one, and I will happily retire from court to run his household. If you want to clear a path for Dorothy, all you have to do is get me wed."

Before Edward could answer, the door flew open and Thomas Seymour strode in. At twenty-nine, he was far more handsome than Edward, far more reckless than Jane, and far less caring than Elizabeth. As always, his smile held a smirk. "Ah, just the people I was looking for—"

"Tom, stop," scolded Anne. "Your brother is in the middle of something."

"No time to wait, Mistress. I have news." He rocked back on his heels. "Big news."

"What?" Edward asked, his voice sharp.

Tom's news was always much bigger in his own mind. His good looks gave him far more confidence than his intelligence warranted.

"You will have to be nicer than that."

"Tom, please," Elizabeth broke in.

Tom bowed with a flourish. "I just convinced Thomas Wrio-thesley to share the geist with me before anyone else. Ready?"

Jane rolled her eyes. Each summer, the King brought his entire court to different houses, happily enjoying the hospitality of his subjects. Hospitality that varied significantly in comfort for all but the highest peers. Jane had always hated the ordeal, most courtiers did. *Maybe it wouldn't be so terrible to let Dorothy take her place during the progress.*

Without waiting for an answer, Tom continued. "Well, it appears the King is eager to hunt Savernake Forest, so he has given us the opportunity to host him this year. He will—"

Edward practically leaped out of his shoes. Jane was too stunned to breathe. "They are coming to Wolf Hall?" they asked in unison.

"In September. They will stay with us for five days."

"Five days?" Jane gasped. "We will need to feed them. We will need amusements, decorations." She jumped up from her chair as if to begin, but all she could do was pace.

Edward staggered but held himself upright, eyes wide and shining. Jane could not tell if his face registered terror or thanks. "The King always defers to his hosts, learns to trust their counsel. I might be able to parlay this into an appointment to the Privy Council."

"Assuming we don't make a mess of things," Tom warned.

All eyes snapped to Jane. Jane had always been the one to

organize the banquets and hunts and celebrations, while the rest of them pretended to help but truly did little more than watch.

"We need you, Jane," Edward said quietly. "We need you to manage this for us. Now it is vital you return to Wolf Hall. Everything must be perfect, and you are the only person who could make that so."

In that instant, Jane suddenly realized the enormous advantage the royal visit conferred upon her. Not ten minutes ago she had begun to fight for herself and her rights, and now the Lord had given her the means to enforce that decision. This was her opportunity to change her future, change herself. She could ask Edward for anything right now, and he would have to say yes. The frustration that had built during their conversation hardened into firm resolve. "We are in agreement on this point, Edward. You need me desperately," she said.

Edward relaxed, turned to Tom and began to speak. It was clear he had taken Jane's words as her usual submission.

Jane interrupted him, her voice deliberately challenging. "But if you want me to do this, you must meet my demand."

She felt more than heard his sharp intake of breath, and it made her smile. She poured herself a second flagon of ale before speaking. The golden liquid caught the sun, strengthened her and spurred her on. "You must find me a husband. I want you to swear to make the search your top priority."

She felt an icy calm as she forced herself to wait for his response. She could not leave any slack in this rope. She knew how this game was played, far better than he thought she did.

"Get me on the Privy Council and I will get you wed."

Anger rose in her again: he clearly did not intend to change. "I've helped you rise for a long time," she snapped. "It is my turn now and I expect more than what you have done so far."

Edward paused. The old Jane would have quickly jumped in to staunch the uncomfortable silence with a concession; this new Jane kept silent and took another sip of ale.

"Fine. You have my word," he told her before turning to Tom. "We need to tell Father right away. Will you go?"

Tom didn't answer. Since the conversation had not been about him, he had turned his focus to a stain on his doublet. Tom cared a great deal about his clothes, had them tailored carefully to flatter his build. This one was short and tight and made of gray damask with slashes not only on the sleeves but also the chest and back. It was a very different style than Edward or Jane would choose; they both favored less showy, more serviceable shapes, but richer fabrics like brocade.

"Tom, will you go tell Father?" Edward repeated. "And Mother."

"Damnation, this is my favorite jacket," Tom said before looking up. "Why me and not you?"

Jane saw Edward's lip curl. Tom noticed too, and understanding flooded his now-sheepish face. Elizabeth and Anne looked down.

"You are better spared. Besides, I avoid the place," Edward said between clenched teeth. "I cannot have a civil conversation with our father, so you must do that for me. For all of us."

The next question hung mute in the air until Jane forced herself to ask it. "Will you be able to stay with him for the week the court is there?"

"I can handle him in a group," Edward said. "I know how to do that."

"Well, then, what about Jane?" Tom tried. "Or even Elizabeth."

"Stop trying to get out of work, Tom," Elizabeth said.

Jane clenched her jaw. She avoided their father as much as Edward, but she managed to be more discreet about it. "You will be able to make the trip in a single day of hard riding, where it will take me three or four. They need to know right away."

"They could wait a bit," Edward began. "You could—"

"It must be quick," Jane insisted. "I cannot leave right away. I first need to meet with the Lord Chamberlain and the Lord

Steward to settle details of the visit. That must be done here and it will take some time."

"How long?" Edward asked.

"I will stay at court for the next three weeks or so." She was happy to hear her voice was firm.

Edward looked at her levelly. "Will that give you enough time at home?"

"It will," she answered with forced calm.

"Fine, but I want to turn around the next day," Tom said, bringing the conversation back to himself. "Before Mother turns from pride over hosting a royal visit to self-pity that her own children didn't turn out as well as her cousin's."

"She's never far from that," said Edward with a wry smile. "But truly, I don't care how long you stay. I just cannot go myself."

"You should plan on staying for a few days," Jane said. "Enough so that you can bring Dorothy back with you so she can take my place at court while I'm gone. It won't be for long, but it will give her a chance to be known."

Edward looked at her, surprise on his face. "Thank you."

Jane smiled back placidly. She could be magnanimous here. "I'll speak with the Queen to arrange it. Surely she can't refuse."

Edward nodded and turned his attention to Tom. "Let's get you horsed."

"So quickly?" asked Anne. "I will see to provisions for him from the kitchens." And the three of them swept out without looking back.

The sudden retreat of her two brothers hit Jane hard. She felt like that time when she was seven and had bested Edward in some argument. The second their parents' backs were turned, Edward had punched her in the stomach. The air had left her body for that moment, and when it returned she quickly ran away.

He had never hit her again, but it established his dominance forever. All her life Edward had told her what to do, all her life she had let him. She lived as a supplicant. With him, with every-one. And it had gotten her nothing. Now suddenly she had grown up, taken control of her destiny. She had finally punched him back, and it was both freeing and terrifying.

Jane walked over to the window and looked out over the gardens. This royal visit was no less than a gift from God. Nothing short of such an event would have served to utterly change her power in the family, and force Edward's hand. That certainty calmed her. And excited her.

I can do this, she thought. *I must do this. Beginning now.* Her mind churned with plans, and she grabbed at objects on the table in front of her and arranged them into an imaginary map of Wolf Hall. The panel she'd been embroidering with Tudor roses to represent the house, the candle from the candlestick for the kitchens, and a pair of the Queen's marble dice for the hunts in Savernake Forest.

In the middle of Jane's reveries, her sister's voice broke in. "How can I help?"

Jane smiled at her sister, loving her dearly for not being the least bit annoyed that Jane had completely forgotten Elizabeth was there. "Thank you, but I will be fine. Managing this visit will be so much easier for me than managing Edward or the Queen."

Elizabeth giggled. "Oh, Jane," she declared. "You are brilliant."

Jane stopped. She shook her head slowly and forced the words over a sudden lump in her throat. "Not in a way that counts."

Elizabeth looked puzzled. "What do you mean?"

Jane was silent for a moment, head shaking. When the deeply buried explanation emerged, the words came out in a rush. "Our queen does not value such humble talent. All Anne Boleyn cares about – all she has ever cared about – is art, music, poetry. And of course she excels at them. My household skills mean little to her." Jane paused. "She thinks me simple, and I suppose I am.

The difference is that she sees simplicity as a vice and I hold it as a virtue."

Elizabeth bowed her head in sympathy.

Jane took a deep breath. "Though it was wonderful when my efficiency pleased Queen Catherine."

Elizabeth's eyes darted around the room. "Hush. You mustn't use that title."

The King had issued a formal declaration that anyone who referred to his first wife as Queen would incur "great pains and penalties," and several people already had spent a night in the Tower for their mistake. She was to be called the Princess of Aragon, as she was born, or the Dowager Princess of Wales, as widow of Henry VIII's elder brother.

"I know, I know. I was just overcome with missing that time." Jane patted Elizabeth's hand to reassure her. "And I know we are alone."

Jane stood quickly, propelled by the need to escape from the intensity of the memory of the wonderful days when she was the shining example of the path to tread. She poured herself some ale, her third flagon of the day, though she didn't drink it.

Elizabeth touched Jane's shoulder. "You are still the wise one, whether the Queen sees it or not."

"I would rather be the married one," Jane said as tears filled her eyes.

Elizabeth's eyes widened and she hugged her sister hard. "Jane, it will happen. Especially now that Edward has promised to work harder on your behalf. It is a blessing from the Lord that we found out about the King's visit just now."

"I too thought that."

Elizabeth's voice was firm. "Do not waver. This is your chance to prove you can be as graceful under pressure as anyone at court. It will help you make a good match."

"I hope so."

The two women nodded. "So how can I help you in this

process?" Elizabeth asked. "I offered before, let me offer again. Give me something to do."

Jane smiled. "You will be dealing with the Queen and helping Dorothy to get acclimated. That, truly, is all I need. That and for you to continue to be your gentle self."

Elizabeth didn't look convinced. Jane thought a moment as to how best to explain what she meant, and the words came to her easily. "You have always believed in me and supported me, and I have always depended on that a great deal. Thank you."

Elizabeth held wide her arms and Jane happily nestled in for the embrace.

CHAPTER TWO – 1535

SUMMER

July 9, 1535 ... 11 a.m.

*I*t was the closing dinner, the last one before the court began its summer progress the next day. Everyone was going on holiday – either with the King and Queen or to their own homes for the grass season, when the hay was being cut, other work was minimal, and the hunting ideal. Jane was one of the few doing both – she would go with the progress for its first visit, then move on to Wolf Hall from there. She would have preferred to leave directly for Wolf Hall but the Lord Chamberlain needed more time to approve the plans she'd proposed. Jane worked to swallow her annoyance and enjoy the general air of anticipation and good cheer.

It was neither Lent nor one of the weekly fast days, so there was a wonderful range of meats and food. Beef, mutton, bacon, hens and capons, supplemented by custards and fritters. Even a leafy salad with raw and cooked vegetables, dressed with oil, vinegar, and sugar. Best of all, Jane spied quail and cherries on the trenchers, her two favorite foods. A celebration indeed.

Jane looked around and sighed with contentment. She loved

Windsor Castle, everything about it. It was so much older than the King's other palaces, its stone fortifications so much more traditional than the Italian Renaissance décor that characterized the construction work the King usually commissioned. It felt safer too, having withstood countless sieges over the centuries. And as the birthplace of the Order of the Garter, it was the very symbol of knightly chivalry.

Just then, the Queen's voice rang out and startled Jane back to the present. "This would greatly amuse His Majesty."

Anne Boleyn faced her husband's table, her glass raised. Jane stiffened as she realized the King hadn't heard a word.

"My Lord," the Queen called again.

His continuing lack of reaction made it obvious he was entirely fixated on the décolletage of the woman next to him.

"My Lord," the Queen shouted sharply.

This time he heard. Still leaning toward the now-blushing lady who squirmed and drew as far away from him as she could, he looked up at his wife and waited.

She continued in a honeyed tone, but her eyes were flat and flinty. "My Lord, my brother has an amusement for you."

The King was not cowed. "I shall enjoy it later, wife."

"I pray it will keep for you, husband."

With that, Anne looked back to her table and everyone quickly fixed their eyes on their plates. The Queen hadn't quite turned her back on the King, but she had clearly disentangled herself from the exchange, against protocol. The silence that followed sucked all movement out of the room.

Out of the corner of her lowered eyes, Jane could see George Boleyn, Lord Rochford, meet his sister's gaze and stroke her arm before he leaned in to whisper to her. Still it wasn't safe to move yet. Not until the King himself had turned away did any of them exhale and look up to resume quiet conversations.

What a drama this all was, this stark reminder of how God meted out His judgment, and how clear that judgment was. It was sobering to watch that proud woman experience how it felt to have her husband pay attention to and even bed other women after ten years at the center of the court's universe. Worse for Anne, many of those women served as her own ladies, women she should have been able to trust. Anne had to interact with her rivals every day, allow them to watch her disrobe and sleep, her only revenge coming from having them carry the bowl away after she'd shit in it. But it wasn't so long ago that Anne had been the rival and the watcher, torturing poor Catherine of Aragon. Catherine had been well aware that Anne was carrying on with the King, but had still been forced to accept her hypocritical services for seven years.

Jane crossed herself surreptitiously at the perfect symmetry of Anne's punishment, so clear given Jane's front-row vantage point to both nightmares. Such were the terrifying ways of the Lord. *For all they that take the sword shall perish with the sword.* Anne had been convinced her actions were justified, that she had been chosen to bear the heir the country needed. But that didn't free her from fault. There were still consequences to sin. There were always consequences to sin.

"Some mutton, Mistress??"

Jane looked up into the smiling eyes of William Dormer, a rising star in Cromwell's household. Dormer carried a plate piled high with the treat.

"What is this?" she asked, delighted to be sought out. "Has our lord Cromwell added table service to your duties?"

She hoped her tone was properly flirtatious. In only a month of trying, Edward had actually come through with the miracle she had craved for ages: a good man from a respectable family had taken an active interest in her. William Dormer was courting her while his father negotiated with Edward; he had already walked with her three days ago and danced with her the night before. Jane finally felt a real part of things, finally felt her life might work out as she hoped. She liked this man, could envision herself cleaving to him. He was not quite the man of her dreams, but he was not the man of her nightmares either. He was a bit childlike, but surely he would mature. And his looks, though less than classically handsome, were enhanced by his wit and potential.

"Because the court is leaving, there was only one trencher of mutton, and the King sent it to my lord Cromwell after he took his fill." William set down his plate next to hers. "I knew it wouldn't make it all the way to you and I didn't want you to miss the dish."

Jane smiled but reached instead for the tray she had worked hard to position right in front of her. "Thank you, but for me mutton cannot compare to quail," she said and popped a piece into her mouth.

She bit her lip when she saw his face fall. She needed to get better at basic repartee. *Say something else,* her insides shouted. "But thank you for bringing it," she added.

The inanity only made him wince. "The mutton is my own favorite, as it is for so many, and I thought…"

"Oh, yes," she answered brightly. Too brightly. She sounded like a fool.

"Well, more for me," he finally said, and squeezed onto the bench next to her. Quickly she twisted to face him, jostling the gentleman to the other side of her, who turned to glare at them both. The old Jane would have been mortified, but William's rolled eyes and conspiratorial smile made up for a mistake that wasn't so terrible in the first place.

"My lord Cromwell has been closeted for most of the day, so I am free for the afternoon," William said. "Might the Queen release you from your duties for a time? We could walk the Flower Garden, which I hear is at its prime right now."

The Flower Garden? The very name sent Jane into a panic. The Flower Garden was a small, enclosed garden just beyond the Privy Garden and was usually spoken of in snickers. It was the destination of choice for loose women and the men who sought to seduce them. But it was currently at the height of its beauty and Jane was known to love plantings. What was his purpose? What should she do? Was her mouth open right now?

"I'm not sure what you hope to see. I don't think—"

"Oh, sweet Christ."

William's whispered curse was urgent as he jumped up and away. Had she offended him? Had she done something wrong? Jane reached after him, and realized William was reacting to the messenger who knelt before the King. The King scowled and gripped his goblet as if he would break it in two. The faces around him were pale. Jane's stomach turned over, the quail leaden in her belly.

The King stood suddenly and walked in silence over to his wife. The Queen didn't see him coming, and cringed suddenly when she felt his hulking presence behind her. She turned to look up at him as he leaned his face down to hers. Jane had to strain to hear his low voice, but nothing could mask the wildness in his eyes.

"Never reproach me for not doing enough for you," he snarled before he stormed out of the Great Hall, pages and gentlemen following at a silent trot.

All around the tables, people silently mouthed, "Sir Thomas More." Of course. More had been scheduled to be executed this week for his refusal to swear the Oath of Succession, and the messenger must have brought the report of its doing. Indeed, with the King gone, the whispers of fascination spread on all sides. More's last words –"I die the King's good servant, but God's first" – were on everyone's lips. Sir Thomas More: claiming martyrdom rather than admit his treason.

Jane pursed her lips in annoyance, even though she herself had experienced deep trepidation right after swearing the Oath. It had been frightening to turn her back on the religion she had grown up with. But it had been the right thing to do. No matter how much admiration and love someone might have for Catherine or her daughter, England needed a male heir and the

King had to do whatever he needed to get one. The Pope, or rather "the Bishop of Rome," had ruled against the annulment of the King's first marriage only because Catherine's nephew Charles had an army surrounding him. The Pope's decision had been bought, therefore it should not be heeded. To Jane, this more than anything else justified the Church of England. And made men like Thomas More doubly wrong for denying its authority.

Jane was about to cross herself automatically, just like half the table guests, but it was as if they all suddenly realized their mistake at the same time and pretended to scratch their heads. This was not the time for an overt showing of religious faith. *So many pitfalls,* Jane thought, and found herself again relieved she would not be traveling with the court during the progress. She would be much happier at Wolf Hall, preparing for their visit.

Suddenly Jane's attention – and the attention of the entire room – was captured when the Queen stood abruptly then froze. Anne Boleyn's head was high. She surveyed the room from above her raised nose, as if daring anyone to speak or even move. Cromwell looked at her steadily, as did the Duke of Suffolk, Sir Nicholas Carew, and Sir Francis Bryan. Most everyone else tried to look without staring, like cowed dogs. Satisfied, the Queen put out a hand. Her brother George rose immediately to slide his underneath it. At that signal, two of the Queen's ladies, the ones closest to her, jumped up to accompany her out. As she passed through the room, Jane and her other ladies fell quickly into line. *So much for that walk with William,* Jane thought.

Jane entered the Queen's Presence Chamber, the room that fed into her private apartments, her Privy lodging. Jane had to sidle around the Queen and her brother who stood facing each other, speaking volumes with their eyes.

Finally all the women were in the room and the outer door closed.

The Queen turned to them. "You all, stay here. See to your sewing," she ordered. "They say the Duchess of Norfolk's household clothed twenty villagers last month. I cannot have my ladies so far behind. George, attend me."

George followed his sister into her bedchamber. Jane Rochford, George's wife, made to join them but George firmly closed the door against her. At the sound of the latch, she sighed loudly.

Madge Shelton sighed next. "I think we packed all the needlework already. We just need to find the right chest."

That's when the rest of them sighed. There were some ten chests around the Queen's room that contained the things they had packed for the progress, plus five more that would continue to decorate the space in the court's absence. All the trunks were heavy wood, carefully carved with intricate designs, but with no feet or legs, to make it easier to transport them. They were also of varying heights, so they could be used as tables, as benches, even as beds in the houses to be visited. They were important supplements to ensure the Queen's rooms were always appropriately furnished. Jane already knew where every one of them would fit at Wolf Hall.

As the ladies opened lids, Jane instead went for the master list as the best authority. She skipped over the listings for the cedar chests: those were reserved for gowns. The needlework wasn't on the sheet for the first oak chest, but by the time Jane saw the notation in the second, Anne Seymour was already calling out, "I've found them!"

They all grabbed their work and cushions, then arranged themselves on the surrounding seats. Lady Rochford took the most comfortable spot, then turned around to look at the rest of them with a savage look on her face. Madge Shelton grabbed a perch on an adjoining bench and patted the spaces on either side of her. "Nan, Liz, sit with me," she said, leaving the other ladies to fan out around them.

Madge's use of nicknames reminded Jane to worry about Dorothy. This was a huge potential pitfall for her: so many names to keep straight. Three of the ladies were named

Margaret (one Madge and one Margery), four were Elizabeth (one Liz). There were also three Annes (two Nans) and two Janes (for which there was no relaxed alternative). Dorothy would never be able to keep them all straight. Dorothy should focus on all the formal titles, then ask questions if any other name were used.

As the women settled in, Madge Shelton initiated the chatter, intended mainly for Nan Zouche and Liz Worcester. Those three were the main gossips. They were also the Queen's favorites. Jane and the others rarely contributed, just kept their heads down and got their work done despite the ridiculous prattle.

"How upsetting was it to walk through the crowd like that? Did you see how everyone's eyes burned?"

"I couldn't have done that; it was hard enough just to follow her. I would have crawled under the table to stop them looking at me like that."

"I'm sure she's curled up under her blankets right now, doing just that."

"Still, she deserves credit for leaving the room with majesty."

"She didn't quite have a choice, did she?"

"No," Lady Rochford added. "But she had the same look on her face as when the peasant women came to kill her."

Jane hadn't been there when that happened, but the vivid description had been burned into her memory as if she had. It had been early on, when the King had still hoped the Pope would allow him to put Catherine aside. A line of bedraggled hags, like witches from fairy tales, brandishing rolling pins and brooms and even pitchforks, had snaked along the road from the village toward the manor where Anne Boleyn was staying. They made their presence known with wild shouts and taunts of "We'll have no Nan Bullen for our queen." Anne ran out the back of the grounds to the safety of the river, where she commandeered the only ferryman and boat around. By the time the hags reached the dock she was safely away from shore watching them, staring at them without flinching, head held high as the boat pulled farther away.

"It looked like her husband would be the one to kill her this time. Did you see the look in his eyes?"

Anne Seymour broke in, a clear attempt to ingratiate herself. "I think you're making too much of this. Not three weeks ago he laughed at a play that mocked the deaths of Bishop John Fisher and the other clergy members. He drank and sat bareheaded without his crown. He didn't blame the Queen then; I don't believe he does now. He just deeply loved Sir Thomas More, a very long time ago."

Jane noticed the three favorites share sideways glances with each other, resenting the correction. If Anne wanted to join in the conversation, she would do better to agree with them, not school them. Jane would not miss these women when she left court to help her new mother-in-law run the Dormer estate. She would love that life. *Please, Lord.*

"Well, I just wish she would get a son. He never would have been so angry if she had given him an heir."

Lady Rochford's face twisted into a sly grimace. "She needs to be well and properly bedded to have a son and he has been too…angry of late."

Nan nodded. "Well, she does yell at him a great deal. When she honeys him like she used to, he is putty in her hands."

"Unfortunately, you are right about the putty part." Even Jane could hear the heavy innuendo in Rochford's voice. Eleven needles hovered over hoops.

"What?"

Rochford continued. "That's precisely the problem. He is no longer interested and doesn't respond." She paused and glanced over her shoulder to make sure the Queen's bedchamber door was still closed. "He is having…trouble."

"Trouble?"

"It has happened several times now. They begin, but the King…can't always finish."

"What?"

"*Ni vertu ni puissance* when the mood is upon him," Rochford blurted. "Neither skill nor virility."

Jane's cheeks burned and she kept her eyes on her sewing as if it were the most important design she had ever worked. She was mortified for the King. How could the Queen betray her husband so by telling such secrets? And how could Lady Rochford repeat them?

"Well, he wasn't like that with me," Madge declared. "He was as lusty as I could imagine."

Jane looked up briefly to exchange a silent glance with her sister Elizabeth. Madge Shelton had been the King's mistress for a time, but he had quickly tired of her. The Queen had never resented her for it. Indeed, some claimed she was the one who had pushed him into it. That's what Edward believed. Edward had tried to explain that Madge was a safe choice for a dalliance, a silly enough girl who would never pose a threat. Middling looks, middling intelligence, and she loved the Queen.

Jane bent back over her sewing and allowed the useless gossip to wash over her. As Jane's needle worked her cloth, she found herself once again wishing she were going directly to Wolf Hall from Windsor and missing this difficult time. She had enough to do without the added commotion the start of the progress would inevitably produce. Not that she would ever admit that to Edward.

July 15, 1535 ... 4 p.m.

Reading Abbey was a monastery founded in the twelfth century, one of the richest religious houses in England. It was an easy destination for a court's progress, exactly a day's ride from Windsor. The abbot's house had luxurious guest quarters set aside for the King and Queen and their attendants, and there was a nearby town eager to serve any members of court who could not be accommodated at the abbey itself. Jane wondered to herself what would happen to the place. A year ago, the King – Cromwell, really – had begun investigating rumors of corruption in England's religious houses: priests making fake relics to bilk the poor, nuns acting as whores. Apparently evil practices were so widespread that many houses would be closed for good rather than reformed. Jane prayed that Reading was not such a house. It certainly was rich enough that its honesty might be suspect, but the abbot seemed such a good man. Jane felt holy on these grounds, wandering the stone cloisters and the herb gardens they enclosed. The monks couldn't be corrupt.

Right now it was raining, so outdoor activities had been reluctantly curtailed. The King and his men were relaxing in the refectory, the massive communal dining room where the monks gathered in silence twice a day and which had been commandeered to serve as the Great Hall. The Queen had decided to retire for a nap, so her ladies had some time to themselves. This would have been a perfect time to seek out William Dormer and try to find some more common interests, but he had eschewed the entire progress. Lucky man.

Jane sighed. She already felt empty without him. Even though they'd only had three conversations, it was still more attention than she'd ever received from a man. It was amazing how a love interest could change life for the better, even a love interest she wasn't really in love with. Yet. She would be, once they were actually married. It was promised by scripture, after all. Even her sister Elizabeth had come to love her husband, Sir Anthony, despite the fact that he had been almost forty years older and stank of decay.

Jane decided to use the time to find Edward, to urge him to conclude this negotiation while her star was still rising. This was the time, after all, and it didn't make sense to take so long to haggle over her as if she were a horse or a goat. Too, he might have final instructions for her before she left the following morning for Wolf Hall.

Jane entered the refectory. It was magnificent, with stone

walls stretching up some twenty feet to where thirty-six large glazed widows let in a holy light. The King sat on a chair on the raised platform at the end of the room that was reserved for honored dignitaries, candles lit around him. They made him glow, made him even more magnificent than he usually was. He was inspiring. Generous, religious, charismatic. Also tall and good looking. And warm, though Jane had never experienced that magic, that moment other ladies described when he focused on you to the exclusion of all others.

Right now he was surrounded by about fifteen of his men. The group was being entertained by the King's new fool, Will Somers.

Somers was a simple man with a natural talent for merry prate that cut to the real truth of things. The King had taken an immediate liking to Will and his savage humor. In the fewer than six weeks that Somers had held the post, he had spared no one. He had also earned a reputation for honesty, refusing the bribes that some courtiers tried to give him to secure kinder treatment. Right now he was commenting on how the King had just sent off a messenger to follow up on property that should have been conveyed to the Crown months ago. "Your Majesty has so many people trying to get your money. Frauditors, conveyors, and deceivers," he said, instead of "auditors, surveyors, and receivers."

"Ah, Will, you speak the truth," the King agreed.

Jane looked around the room at the now-empty long tables with their matching benches, and saw Edward apart from the group, lounging against one of the columns with Tom and Sir Nicholas Carew. Carew had been one of Henry's friends from boyhood, and currently served as his Master of the Horse. This showed him to good advantage, since riding was his strongest skill, and gave him special access to the King's good moods. A good connection for Edward to have made, even if Carew had fallen somewhat out of favor.

The three of them had their eyes fixed on Somers, and they

all looked eager, expectant. When Jane approached, Edward hushed her and pulled her to the side so she wouldn't block his view. Suppressing her annoyance, she joined them in their unexplained vigil.

"Henry Norris is following your lead, Your Majesty. He moons after Madge Shelton's skirts."

The King leered. "There are far worse places Norris could choose to seek out," he said, teasing.

"There are indeed, Sire," the fool agreed. "And such a pastime would put him in a better mood than the one he's been in."

A general titter ran through the crowd: Norris had been on edge lately.

"Actually, if we were looking for people whose mood needs improving, Thomas Cromwell would head the list," said the fool.

Now people snickered. The mention of Thomas Cromwell tended to bring out the worst in people. Although he was a courtly man with a fine wit, there was something too intense about him. His beady eyes and saturnine features gave the impression that every expression hid a dark meaning.

"Now, Will." The King wagged his finger, but his face still bore a smile.

"Now, Sire," Will answered in the same tone, "you have to admit, the man rarely bears good tidings."

The King rolled his eyes, but Will continued. "And he espouses such highly unpopular positions. After all, your whole country has kind words for your first wife. That should tell you something."

The King's face turned grim, but Will ignored the warning. "They call your second a ribald. That should tell you even more." Somers bowed after he said this, jingling the bells on his cap. This gesture accompanied outlandish statements whose truth might be difficult for the King to bear. Hooting and laughter followed, though the King remained stone faced and silent.

"What's that, Sire? Did you not know that men name the

Princess Elizabeth a bastard in every tavern in your land even though they accept her as your heir?" Another deep bow, and more laughter.

Jane could barely keep up with what happened next. The King leaped to his feet and lunged at Somers, then both hands were around the fool's neck. Somers' head was buffeted back and forth and his knees buckled, but still the King remained resolute. The King's men surrounded the pair and tried to pry the King's hands from the fool's neck to save him. Finally the King released his grip with a violent push. "Get that knave out of my sight," he yelled before storming off.

When Jane could speak again, she turned to Edward. "That was monstrous."

"Have you never seen the King rage?" asked Sir Nicholas.

"Not the King," Jane answered. "How could the fool have said such a thing?"

Edward shook his head, but Tom guffawed. "T'was Sir Nicholas who put him up to it."

Jane turned to Carew, her eyes wide. "Why would you do that?"

"Hush," Edward replied in his place, waving his hand dismissively. "Can you blame the man for trying?"

"Trying? Trying what? To insult and anger the King?"

"Of course not," answered Carew. "But the King must learn how many people hate his wife. Otherwise nothing will change."

Sir Nicholas Carew was one of the many people who hated Queen Anne and resented the new religion she represented. But instead of accepting the inevitable reality, he fought against it. It was a dangerous path to tread, since the chief hope of the extremists – to discredit the Queen and see her replaced – bordered on treason.

Before Jane could answer, Will Somers stood before them. "Well, I did as you said and the King almost killed me. What do I do now? Where can I go?"

"You can stay at my house in Beddington Park for as long as you need," said Carew. "I will not abandon such a good friend."

"I may need forever," was Somers' glum reply.

"Go get your things," Carew instructed him. "Then come to my rooms." Turning to Edward, he continued. "Shall we all repair there?"

Edward motioned to Tom and Jane to follow the man.

ENTERING THE APARTMENTS, JANE SCANNED HER SURROUNDINGS and noticed that Edward – despite a careful air of nonchalance – was doing the same. Edward always thought he was the one who had taught her to conduct mental inventories of people's furnishings, but the truth was Jane was simply better at not letting people see her do it. If read correctly, the location of a courtier's rooms and the value of its decorations were shockingly accurate indicators of his or her position. *If* read correctly. Many might have dismissed Carew's influence because his rooms at Greenwich and Windsor were relatively far from the King's own apartments and slightly smaller than average – but that would be a mistake. Here, the fact that Carew was lodged in the abbey and not in the village bespoke favor.

Carew poured some wine and handed it to Edward without asking if he wanted it. He did the same for Tom and Jane, then took one for himself. The cups were gilt, fine workmanship. Clearly gifts from the King, either to Carew or his wife: Lady Elizabeth Carew had been a royal mistress once upon a time, and had received an abundance of rich jewels and expensive plate.

Edward quickly broke the silence. "So what now? If we are to help Somers, we must calm the King from his current rage."

"We cannot admit any involvement, that would be fatal," Tom said.

"Of course not." Edward was dismissive.

"But then how will you help Master Somers?" asked Jane.

"Once the King calms down, Somers will be fine," said

Carew. "The King likes that Somers speaks for the common man, understands that England hates his current wife. This too shall pass."

Jane shook her head. "Men are put to death for such talk. Master Somers must take care. You must take care."

"I feel quite safe," Carew said smugly. Indeed, Sir Nicholas Carew's open sympathy to Catherine and Mary's cause had lowered his influence with the King for almost a decade, and led to his wife's dismissal from Queen Anne's service. But now the Queen's hold over the King had loosened and Carew had begun to recover. And he was growing bolder.

Tom broke in, his voice tentative. "Don't you find it curious that the King reacted so strongly? Maybe Will struck a chord? Might the many hints be finally bearing some fruit?"

Edward's face twisted. "The King will never return to Aragon."

"No, no, of course not," said Carew. "But, Tom, you may be right that this means he tires of the Night Crow. Normally I would expect Great Harry to just roll his eyes and deliver a stern warning at such jokes."

Edward looked at Carew as if had grown a second head. "My lord, they were not totally at his wife's expense; they reached to the succession. He has never had much of a sense of humor about that, as the executions show."

Carew shrugged and exchanged glances with Tom. "If we really wanted to put him in a good mood, we'd find him a pretty wench," Carew said. "Even better – a new wife."

"Hah!" Tom exclaimed. "You are so right, but the only women who seem to attract him are friends to the Queen. Like that Shelton slut. We need someone new. Margaret Douglas would be the perfect choice, if she weren't his niece. She resents the Boleyn, and would pour some good poison into his ear."

"How about Nan Gainsford?"

"Lady Zouche? She is married and there is talk she might be with child. Nan Cobham would be better."

"A thin face and a flat chest. We need someone more beautiful than the Queen."

The three men threw themselves into a ribald discussion about the women of the court, as if Jane were not present. They assessed every woman's strengths and shortcomings, with one glaring exception. Finally, Edward turned to Jane. "What do you think, Jane? Can you guess which of these women might appeal to the King?"

Jane told herself they meant nothing by it, that these men were her friends, two were her brothers. This was why they hadn't considered her. It wasn't that she wanted to be put forth as a possible mistress for the King – the terms of her marriage were being negotiated for goodness' sake – but at least they could consider her, if only for a moment. What was so wrong with her that she did not warrant a single thought? She could feel her cheeks burn. "No," she said, keeping her eyes down.

"Ah, see, you've embarrassed her," Tom exclaimed. "Despite her age, my sister's an innocent. Look how she blushes at such talk."

Carew was unfazed. "Ah, innocence. That's what we need. Above all, the King loves the chase."

Jane felt herself mollified. Finally, she was valued. Now she could step aside gracefully. She was about to reply but Carew cut her off. "Your sister Dorothy," he said to Edward. "Might she be such a one as to tempt our King?"

Edward launched into his response without pausing, as if he had already considered it. "She has a sweet face, but not the beauty we need. Also, she's never been to court, so she won't have the grace the King will expect."

"You would act as a pander to our sister?" Jane asked, trying to keep a tremor out of her voice, born as much from jealousy as protection. "And ruin her chances of a good marriage?"

"Mistress Jane," Carew stepped in. "This is the King. Any woman he takes an interest in will find herself admired and desired. Your sister would be lucky if that happened."

"As was Mary Boleyn?" Jane snapped.

"She asked for nothing," Edward answered quickly.

"And she received it," Jane retorted. "In abundance."

Mary had received no gifts from the King during her tenure as royal mistress, and the King's sudden infatuation with her sister had prevented the family from suggesting to the King that Mary deserved some jewelry or property as consolation for the end of the affair.

"Mary prides herself that she has always acted for love alone," Tom said with grudging respect.

Love. That was one word for it, but far too polite to Jane's mind. Mary was loose, always had been. The epitome of female sin. She had given her gifts freely, not only to the King but to the entire French court. And now Tom was ready to admire her?

"Mary is a fool," said Jane, shaking her head. She didn't want to be here anymore. "Gentlemen, enjoy the progress. I will see you at Wolf Hall."

"Wait," Edward said. "We should talk."

"You have something to say?" She could not keep the sneer out of her voice.

Edward shrugged. "Go with God." The other men echoed the sentiment, and Jane dropped a quick curtsy in response.

And she left.

CHAPTER THREE – 1535
WOLF HALL

September 4, 1535 ... 3 p.m.

*J*ane glanced out one of the great windows that flanked the southern side of Wolf Hall's second story, to check the position of the sun. It would be about three hours past noon now. She took a deep breath to calm herself. The King and Queen – and the two hundred attendants and servants who had been permitted to travel with the progress – would arrive in the next hour. From then on, the Seymours had five days in which either to impress deeply with their forethought and loyalty, or offend with mistakes, however accidental.

Jane had been on enough of these progresses to be able to visualize exactly what was happening right now. The King and Queen would be riding at the head of the procession, just behind the red-jacketed guards who trumpeted so villagers could run out to wave as the cortege passed. The King always rode horseback instead of closing himself in a carriage, so that he could wave back and even accept a bouquet or two or toss some coins in thanks. Moments that his people cherished forever. Since the first days of his reign he had insisted that showing himself to the masses increased their love and loyalty. Certainly the blessings they shouted made him seem right about this, and the spectacle always amazed any ambassador fortunate enough to experience it.

Because Wolf Hall was the destination, Edward and Tom would be permitted to ride with the King and Queen. The brothers would be two or three paces behind – far enough for protocol, but close enough for conversation. Edward would do most of the talking, but Tom's easy manner would help smooth over any awkward silences. Jane wondered whether Anne Seymour would be permitted to ride with them as well, or Elizabeth or Dorothy. It was more likely, though, that the Queen would insist that her brother join them, and choose Jane Rochford as her only attendant. She often did that to avoid sharing attention.

"Jane?"

It was her father's voice behind her, and Jane whirled around. As always, his face, with its bushy eyebrows and long, unkempt beard highlighting piercing eyes, made her nervous, then annoyed. She took a deep breath. "Yes?"

"I just want to thank you. Wolf Hall is clearly ready for this, and it is your doing. Your mother and I appreciate your industriousness."

Jane flushed at the compliment, so unusual for him. Sir John had grown kinder in recent years, but little of that had affected Jane. After he had been caught in a monstrous betrayal – an affair with Edward's first wife that lasted long enough for the elder Seymour to father her two children – shame and guilt had forced him to shed the skin of the stern and self-righteous ruler he had worn when Jane was younger. But he still inspired the same initial fear in her, a fear that unkind words too often justified.

"Thank you."

"Edward will appreciate it too."

That was the other piece of it. Father's grief had caused him to demonstrate a childlike dependence on his eldest son, considering his opinion on every subject as if this new focus could lead to forgiveness. It hadn't worked yet.

But still, Jane was pleased her father appreciated her efforts. Finally. Hosting the court – even the smaller, traveling version that made up a progress – had taken gargantuan effort. Preparations had begun with Jane attending interminable meetings with the Lord Chamberlain (who was responsible for maintaining the splendor of the court) and the Lord Steward (who was responsible for the practical running of the court). Together they had created a list of the rooms and halls and facilities available, and detailed the new ones that would be required. They had made lists of the gentry living in the area, to make sure that everyone of importance received an invitation to greet their sovereign. They had created sample schedules for each day of the visit, which they cross-referenced with inventories of furniture and plate and equipment. Did they want to plan for a round of archery, at which the King excelled? If so, the Queen would require a canopy to shelter her from the sun while she watched the competition, and its lining should be either satin or taffeta.

Luckily, the main attraction was to be Savernake Forest, famous for its hunting – the King's favorite pastime. Luckily too, Jane was remarkably familiar with every last detail of the running of Wolf Hall. As the eldest daughter, it had always fallen on her to help her mother in the management of the household. Jane had a full working knowledge of Wolf Hall's bakehouse, kitchen, buttery, cellar, and galleries. She even knew how much meat the boiling house could process in a day, which allowed her to persuade the Lord Chamberlain and the Lord Steward that dinners and suppers on the hunt days should feature the game the King had himself killed – a touch she knew he would appreciate (it also helped that she knew how much food their larder held, so they had a back-up plan if the hunt proved unsuccessful). She even knew that linens and plate were traditionally supplied to the hosting household, and she was not shy about asking for other provisions she knew they needed. Over the five hours the first meeting had consumed, and the endless sequels, she had surprised everyone with her efficiency and intelligence. Another way her star was on the rise. It felt good.

"The last time the King visited, we bagged six deer and three boars. Quite a day!" Sir John continued. "Hopefully he will be as successful again. Did you speak to the gamekeeper?"

"Of course I did," Jane said, trying not to sound exasperated. *As many times as you've asked me that question.*

"The King bragged about that day for months, years actually. He will expect as much this time."

Jane nodded. "We have done what we could."

"And Edward will be right there next to him."

"He will indeed," Jane agreed. Indulging her father was the easiest path.

"I thought I saw riders in the distance," he continued, off topic. "They may arrive soon. Will you find your mother?"

Jane bit back her annoyance. "Of course," she said. "I'll try upstairs." That at least would let her take one final tour of the manor. She had done four – or five – already, stopping in every room and glancing around. It relieved her anxiety to see how few tasks remained undone, how few last-minute orders she had to issue. Despite her innate nervousness, she was confident they were in excellent shape for the visit. They were as ready as was possible for anyone to be, and still making improvements with every moment left to them. The bustle inspired her, like the thrum of a beehive. Jane actually felt her insides vibrate with power, and she thanked providence once again for the faithful servants who had helped to create such a state of preparedness.

Jane checked the King's suite first. It consisted of a Presence Chamber that led to a bedchamber, study, and garderobes, and had been formed by joining Jane's parents' rooms with Edward's and Tom's. Jane, Elizabeth, and Dorothy had contributed their rooms to form the Queen's suite. There had been no complaints about this, it was expected: royalty required the best of everything. And of course Jane had made sure all the Seymours were well accommodated in the east wing of the house, a far better position than many of the court who were lodged at nearby homes or even inns in the local town.

Entering the Presence Chamber, she was again struck by how completely she had transformed the usually stiff space. Her father's imposing tapestries, featuring harsh biblical scenes, now hung in the barn to elevate it for the banquet and other events to be held there. The biblical scenes had been replaced by hangings supplied by the Lord Chamberlain's stores, which featured hunting parties happily galloping through parklands teaming with wildlife. A much more calming and comfortable setting for a king seeking relaxation.

The central bouquet drew her eyes. A mesmerizing arrangement of purplish water mint and yellow iris mixed with branches of variegated leaves, it was a combination that soothed and amazed without preening – a perfect complement to the tapestries. The smaller, more intimate, vases that dotted his bedchamber and study were equally wonderful, filled with heady sprigs of the roses for which Wolf Hall was famous throughout Wiltshire. The bushes had been carefully grafted when Henry Tudor had ascended the throne as Henry VII and married Elizabeth of York: the red rose that symbolized the house of Lancaster united with the white rose of the house of York. Pink roses had been ubiquitous then, but the gardeners at Wolf Hall had outdone everyone with a flower that featured both red and white highlights. Perfection.

Just then Jane's gaze fell on the gilt bowl of oranges on the side buffet, and her stomach plunged from its height of smugness. Over the past month Jane had examined every facet of the house and grounds. Every emblem, flower, badge, and color had been carefully considered, its message of political loyalty – or disloyalty – measured. All references to the King, however oblique, had been intensified: portraits of him and his line dominated all the main rooms, hawthorn bushes dominated the garden. All references to Aragon had been obliterated: anything bearing a pomegranate had been reworked or sold, pink cushions had been recovered in the Boleyn green. Only the citrus plants that Catherine had introduced to English gardens had been spared, thanks to the King's well-known love of the sweet fruits. But the full bowl of oranges created an unacceptable dynastic statement by their placement next to the Tudor roses.

All those weeks of preparation. Which servant had made this mistake? Not that it mattered right now. Jane quickly called for other fruits to be added to the bowl and shook her head over how close they had come to calling into question their hospitality, their loyalty, their grace, their everything. What other mistakes had they made?

A sudden thought came to her, and she wondered how well the servants had cleared the gardens after bringing in the flowers and fruit. People would be walking there; it would not do to have tools strewn around as they had been over the last few days. Fear surged in her and she ran out to check, quickly relieved by the sight of clear, even raked, paths. She took a deep breath and relaxed. All was well.

Walking calmly back to the house, she felt the thunder of horses' hooves. She looked up and saw her brother Tom approaching at a quick gallop, waving his hat to get her attention. He had a friend just behind him, whom she couldn't quite see, and one of the King's guards trailing in the distance. They must all be racing. God bless Tom for this advance warning, though she didn't need it. Wolf Hall was ready. She waved back confidently. *Let it begin.*

"The King arrives. Prepare for His Majesty," Tom yelled.

Jane suddenly realized she had never warned her mother as promised to her father. Jane turned around and let out a fish-wife's bellow in the hope of somehow being heard inside the manor house. "Mother!"

Tom's horse shied from the sound, which made Jane jump. Her headdress slipped, too far to simply push back into place, so she tore it off. She saw Tom's reaction, his face amused but wide-eyed, and it spurred her on. She streamed her waist length hair behind her like a strawberry-blond curtain and wiggled her entire body in triumph and glee. It was an uncharacteristically wild gesture and, even as she made it, she had no idea why except that she felt it had somehow been earned. "Let him come," she called to Tom. "We will dazzle him."

The horses were upon her now, and the two men reined them in. The one who was not Tom looked down at her with a wide smile and spoke. "Dazzle me," he challenged.

Suddenly Jane realized what she had just done. This was the King before her. He had seen her act crazy, even wanton. She shoved her cap back onto her head and hid her hair under it as modesty demanded. The King dismounted from his horse in a single graceful gesture and threw his reins to the servants who had raced from the barns. He walked toward her, grabbed her two shoulders almost as if to shake her – or hold her up. His nearness took away what little breath she had left.

"But what I am saying is that you already have," he said. "And now your smile is further reward."

The one thing Jane knew right then was that the look on her face was anything but a smile. She folded her knees into a deep, long curtsy. As she stammered an apology, she heard her mother's voice behind her. Lady Margery Seymour, her face aglow with pride, addressed the King. "Your Majesty, we had no idea you had arrived. Welcome."

As the King moved into a happy conversation with Lady Seymour and Tom, Jane managed to remain standing. The rest of her family gathered around while the servants – a sea of charcoal and white, the Seymour livery – lined up excitedly at the entrance to formally greet the court. Jane kept silent and smoothed her skirt carefully as greetings were exchanged and introductions made. Thankfully, Father took charge of the conversation.

"I know we have arranged for you to have your own falcons

but I hope you will try some of our hawks while you are here," he said. "Our mews are known for their excellence."

"A longstanding reputation," agreed the King, and commenced the reminiscing.

In the middle of it, the King glanced at her, a curious look on his face. *Oh, God, what must he think of me?* Her constant effort to show herself a sober, modest gentlewoman of good upbringing was gone – a lifetime of restraint erased in a single moment. *Edward will kill me,* she thought. *No, I'll beat him to that.* All of a sudden she was an awkward young girl again. Gone was the capable woman who was happily anticipating the praise she had earned from her singlehanded preparation of this entire visit, who was preparing to take a place of pride among the courtiers. In her place was this shy shell of a girl who spent most of her time studying people's shoes as a way of occupying her down-cast eyes when she was ignored in a conversation.

The trumpets blared, and the Queen rode into the courtyard ahead of the procession. Edward accompanied her, as did her brother George and his wife.

They all turned around to welcome the new arrivals. The King took a wide stance, his arms outstretched. The others all bowed and curtsied. Jane noticed the King glance at her again. She forced a smile onto her face and kept her eyes high: she didn't want to call any more attention to her mistake. Out of the corner of her eye, Jane could see her father's face, shining with affection as he welcomed Edward. Edward carefully averted his gaze, a stern look on his face. The brief embrace that followed was the first one of the year. Edward avoided Wolf Hall well.

Jane got a bit of a reprieve as the other carriages began to arrive. One after another, groups of passengers emerged, laughing and chattering and complimenting all at once. Anne, Elizabeth, and Dorothy all arrived together, and Edward and Jane went immediately over to welcome them and bring them to the center of the assembly.

The group was large and jovial now; stories were exchanged

and introductions made. No one seemed to want to move from the courtyard, but Jane had planned for that. Several maids were already passing out goblets of wine and water to the guests, while the other maids remained lined up on either side of the main entrance, shining with excitement and awe, and bursting with pride and terror – waiting for the instructions that would commence the process of showing the guests to their rooms. Almost every servant's hand was in front of her mouth, trying to hide panicked whispers: each had been assigned to a specific person or group and they worked to identify their charges based on the descriptions that had been given them.

Edward grabbed a glass from a tray passing by, took a deep breath and began. "You do us such honor by your presence," he boomed to capture everyone's attention. "Thank you for allowing us to try to fulfill your every pleasure during these next few days. To the King and Queen! Long may they reign."

And may the angels watch over us, Jane silently added as she quaffed her drink.

September 6, 1535 … 4 p.m.

The gardens of Wolf Hall aspired to great beauty and achieved it in certain spots. The Italian Garden, a park designed by Lady Seymour more for show than for contemplation, featured a pompous fountain at its center, and two classical statues carefully posed among straight rows of trees and knots of flowering bushes. It fed into the Rose Garden that showcased more than a hundred rose bushes – including the famous Tudor Rose – and fully half a dozen porticoes to provide places for people to enjoy the heady aroma that surrounded them. The Rose Garden in turn fed into the Kitchen Garden through an arched wooden door that was almost obscured by the wild fig vines that covered the stone wall. Walking through the opening, the Kitchen Garden seemed another nod to the Italianate influence, an enclosed *giardino secreto,* or "secret garden." Walking farther, and around a corner, the garden suddenly opened to the manor for easy access to the extensive variety of herbs for cooking and healing.

This was where Jane was working. This, more than the pretentious floral beds of the Italian Garden, was her favorite spot, especially this time of year. She loved the simple vine-covered walls and the unassuming pebbled paths that framed the raised beds. She also delighted in the smell of dirt and the way it amplified the scent of the blossoms. This was her domain, enough that the gardeners still knew to humor her rules about what went where. Jane sat back and surveyed the bed of bee balm in front of her, a satisfied smile on her face. She had done her work well, cutting blooms carefully enough that she had not left any ugly gaps in the magnificent display. Of course, Edward would still likely scold her – he would have insisted she send a servant to do such work. But the Queen and her ladies were rest-ing, and the King and his men were playing cards, so there was no way Jane would miss anything of importance. Besides, the servants had been called into duty either in the Great Hall to set the supper tables, or in the kitchens to prepare the five courses of food that would feed some two hundred fifty people. This was not the time to interrupt the nearly flawless job they were doing. And more importantly, the work gave Jane strength. She needed that. She deserved that.

She heard a crunch on the path behind her. That would be Agnes, her maid, warning Jane to get back to the Queen. Jane pushed herself slowly up to standing and turned. It wasn't Agnes.

The King was before her, grinning broadly, her brother Tom two paces behind. How much worse could it get? She was caught working. By the King. Her dress dirtied. What must he think of her? Despite her lifetime of sobriety, she had somehow managed once again to give God's anointed the opposite impression. Somehow the thought triggered laughter that quickly mounted and took her over completely so that her curtsy looked more like a bow. Thankfully, he laughed too – and Tom with him. They were all merry together for a moment, and Jane was relieved that everything was just fine. She felt safe somehow.

"I apologize that I am not better prepared to greet you," she said. "Again," she added with a quick curtsy.

The King grinned. "I am glad to see you recovered from the other day. You seemed happy at the hunt this morning too. The active life suits you."

Jane nodded. He was right. "Ah, I do love the hunt," she said. "Especially such a successful one." Four deer and two boars. Not quite as good as the King's last visit, but enough to satisfy.

"Much more so than Anne, Edward's wife, as you may have noticed," said Tom.

The King snorted, amused. He had clearly seen that Anne Stanhope Seymour had a face that seemed sour – even more than usual – on horseback. Was it disloyal to joke like this?

"Not everyone is blessed with grace," the King said. "And speaking of grace, it is wonderful to see you smile, Mistress Jane. I enjoyed your dance the other day, as I appreciate your industry now. You have made me and my entire court feel very welcome here, and I am nothing but grateful to you and your family."

Jane looked up at him with a rueful smile and curtsied a thank you. "I still wish I hadn't given Your Majesty quite so much amusement as I did."

"Ah but you did. And now you must tell me what you are working on."

"I came out to fetch herbs for a tincture, then decided to cut some bee balm to freshen the floral arrangements," she said. "But you, what are you doing here? This is more of a working garden than a contemplative one."

"What kind of tincture?" the King asked quickly.

"An external one, more a poultice really. One of the stable boys twisted his ankle."

"What do you plan on giving him?"

"Well…," Jane began, uncertain as to how detailed he wanted her to be. This was the King after all, and he was likely just being polite.

"Really, I am interested," he said as if he'd read her mind. "I've always been fascinated with herbs and the remedies they offer. It's how I've kept myself safe from the sweating sickness and the plague – I have parsley all through my rooms."

Jane laughed easily. "If I'd known, I would have added a vase myself." She turned to scold her brother. "Tom, why did you not tell me this?"

Tom bowed. "Apologies to you both that I had no idea. What does parsley look like?"

Jane shot him a look – she never could understand how so few people shared her interest in herbs. She caught the King roll his eyes at her, and realized they shared the same thought.

"It's the lacy green plant you'll see in the King's rooms from now on," she said to Tom before turning to continue her conversation with the King. "Marsh mallow and wall pennywort as a base, with as much rosemary as I can find. Maybe some dead nettle for the swelling. And of course cowbane against the pain. I might add some Solomon's seal, or rocket, from my stores."

"But you have mint in your basket."

Jane giggled. "Caught again. Mint makes the potion smell fresh and strong, it makes people confident it will work. It's just for comfort, really. I deliver it as a poultice so the warmth can relax and soothe the muscles."

"My own approach would have been to include fennel – to stave off fever and because fear always seems to go to the stomach. It is my own little trick – I toss fennel into everything."

"Like me and my mint!"

"Exactly." He looked around briefly, then clapped Tom on the shoulder. "I want my own basket. Will you go get me one?"

Tom bowed and, just like that, off he went. As his figure retreated, it occurred to Jane that she was now alone with the

King. It was entirely up to her to entertain him – the King, for goodness' sake – until Tom returned. Though, truth be told, His Majesty had been surprisingly easy to talk to up until now. He wasn't sardonic, as he so often was with the people around him. He wasn't at all risqué. He was easier to talk to than Will Dormer.

It suddenly hit Jane how far she had come since the start of summer. She had finally acted the way she felt inside – strong, capable – instead of showing the shy, quiet face the world knew. The change had come about with the preparations for this visit, and now look at her. Praise God. She was the person she always wanted to be. The person she always believed she was. "I may steal your fennel trick for my own remedies…assuming I can find some," she said with pride. "Hopefully there will be a few straggling plants left."

The King pointed suddenly. "There are some," he said and strode over to the telltale row of wispy green leaves and rings of powdery yellow flowers. He took off his doublet and knelt down, rolling up his sleeves to reveal muscled arms. It made Jane blush, though she couldn't say why.

"Join me," he said and she hurried to kneel beside him. They worked together for a time, the King pointing at promising shoots and Jane cutting them carefully. Every time their elbows bumped Jane was struck by the nearness of him. It was all she could think of.

Suddenly the King broke the comfortable silence. "I have to tell you again, I quite enjoy your private face, your true face. No one ever shows that side of themselves to me – I only see the calculated front they present to get something out of me." His voice was soft, almost husky. "So thank you indeed."

While she loved the praise, it upset her too. She didn't deserve it. "Oh, dear," she breathed. "You give me too much credit. The truth is, I never act like that. I always hold myself tightly in control. I don't understand why I chose that moment to let loose. All I can think is that I was just so confident that everything around me was well prepared – so happy my test was finally arriving – that I...I...I don't know."

She glanced up at him and was transfixed by the crinkling of his eyes and nose. He looked so benevolent.

"Perhaps it is your real face," he said gently. "You say you were confident; you should be so always. In any event, as I said, it gave me much joy."

Warm gratitude melted Jane's heart and she closed her eyes.

"And now," he continued, more matter-of-factly, "you will give me even more joy if you let me help you prepare this remedy and then let me share some of it."

He needed a remedy? Oh, no! "Are you hurt? Can I get you anything?"

"Nay, nay. Just that one of my men complained earlier about a sore leg and I would love to bring him something that might soothe. It is all part of the responsibility that comes with power."

"Then prepare it you shall. I am here to serve," said Jane.

"Excellent. Take me to your stores."

"Oh, no," she said. "I'll have everything brought to your rooms."

"Don't be silly. I'll work where you do."

Jane shook her head. That would not do. "My work room is off the kitchens." She couldn't bring the King of England to the kitchens. Goodness, she couldn't even promise that the scullions were wearing their shirts, despite all the scolding she had delivered these past three months. The King had ordinances about that for his own kitchens. It was harder to enforce such rules in a country manor. "It would be much better to work in your rooms."

"Why would that be?" His smile was genuine. "I would love to visit your kitchens. It would remind me of my youth."

Jane allowed a skeptical look to show on her face. It made the King laugh. "No, 'tis true," he said. "Wolf Hall looks a great deal like Eltham, where I lived with my mother and sisters while my father taught my older brother to run the country. It's configured the same, with similar staircases and gardens. I have to see if the kitchens are quite as alike as well."

"You remember the kitchens?" She didn't want to be arch, but she couldn't resist teasing him about this.

"You recall, I was the second son back then and could wander freely where I would."

Jane brought her hand up to cover her quick laugh. "Of course. People treat you more formally now. I apologize if I have been remiss."

He smiled broadly, and it put her at ease. "You are blameless in this, Mistress Jane. It has all been at my insistence. And now I insist on seeing where you work." He paused. He looked like he was trying to put on a serious face but the side of his mouth kept twitching. "It will tell me how true a herbalist you are."

It seemed the most natural thing in the world to smile and give a quick curtsy. "I will take up that gauntlet. Follow me." Jane put up her hand for him to cover it with his. When he did, she led him down the stairs, knowing this was crazy but also feeling completely free. No one could reproach her right now. No one could question her actions. It felt amazing.

The Wolf Hall kitchens bustled with activity. Serving boys squatted on both sides of the open fireplace in the main room, turning the spit racks to roast the meat – and thankfully both were wearing shirts. Cooks were lined up at one of the three massive trestle tables in front. Younger apprentices chopped, ground, sieved, and mixed, while the more senior ones assembled the savory pies and pasty dishes to be brought to the thatch-roofed bake shed. Jane glanced over at the King and motioned for him to follow her into her small room before anyone was the wiser.

"This is lovely," he said, and she had to agree. It was a delightful spot between the main kitchen and the boiling house. Carefully labeled dried herbs, some already beaten into powder, lined the shelves that flanked the window, and more bunches hung from every roof beam. Best of all, this room had been spared the general chaos that claimed the rest of the manor.

She set her basket on the worktable and handed the King a small stone mortar and pestle, then placed a cutting board in front of him. "Here you go," she said. "What else can I get you?"

"This is perfect for now," he said, reaching into Jane's basket. "You said marsh mallow and pennywort for the base?"

Jane nodded. He withdrew a handful of the pennywort and dropped it into the bowl to begin.

Jane decided to begin with a fine chop of the cowbane. She took a bunch from one of the window jars then grabbed another board and installed herself next to the King. The two worked together in silence for a bit. The King seemed happy, humming a tune under his breath.

Suddenly one of the cooks appeared, cursing behind them, and she pounded the King's back with her fist. "Barnabas Sheffield, you scurvy knave! How did you work your way into such an easy job? Did you not tell the mistress you were to be fetching firewood?"

Jane's stomach contracted. The King glanced at her, winked, then turned around wearing a playful smile. When the cook saw his face, her expression changed and she screamed. Then her knees buckled and the King had to grab her by the shoulders just as he had Jane the other day.

"F-forgive me, Your Majesty," the cook stammered. "I had no idea. I never thought to see you in your shirt...I thought..."

The head cook and some of the servants, drawn by the commotion, came running. More shouts of surprise as new arrivals realized the King was in their midst. They bobbed up and down, they poked each other in the ribs, they widened their eyes and let their mouths gape.

The King took it all in easily, his broad smile showing him to be clearly at ease with his people and even more clearly enjoying the fuss. "My dear woman, I bear you no ill will for thinking me much younger than I am," he said kindly to the cook who had hit him. "Good people, I thank you all for your welcome. I am helping to prepare a remedy for one of my men and I beg you all to go about your business without worry."

More bobs, then one of the men called out, "God save Your Majesty." That got all of them saying something of the sort, "God save the King" and "God bless you" being equally represented. The sea of voices was touching in its spontaneity, and Jane was proud of her servants and inspired by their love and loyalty.

After the crowd had dispersed and Jane and the King were alone again, Jane turned to him. "That was wonderful to watch." Then the humor of the situation overtook her. "I am a bit relieved not to find myself the only one who failed to recognize you this week. It seems to be an epidemic at Wolf Hall."

"One of the only epidemics I have ever thoroughly enjoyed. Though I have to say, I used to love going out among my people disguised and then unmasking myself. When I was young, Brandon, Compton, Norris, Carew and I snuck out whenever we could."

"A large band! You stopped when you became King?"

"Actually, I resumed when I became King. For a time, anyway."

"What?" Jane was puzzled.

"I was ten when my brother Arthur died and I lost the carefree status of the spare son intended for the Church."

A sudden insight flooded Jane and she looked away. *Had Arthur lived, Henry might have become Pope.*

"What?" asked the King. He must have noticed her change in expression.

"Actually…," she began, then faltered. She took a deep breath. "Actually, since you are head of the Church now you could say that your original destiny was fulfilled."

"I have thought that myself," he said, and Jane couldn't tell if his voice was smug or wistful.

Either way, she was vastly relieved by his reaction. She had been afraid that he would think her sacrilegious or sycophantic. Or both. They were silent for a time, chopping pensively. Then Jane continued. "You were saying? You were ten when your brother died?"

"Ah, yes. When that happened, my parents tried to conceive another child, but the baby killed my mother. Childbed fever."

"My mother told me about that. Such a tragedy. For you and all of England."

He nodded briefly, dismissing the comment as if he had heard it too many times before. "When that happened, my father had me come live with him to keep me under close watch and train me in statecraft."

"Well, he seems to have done an excellent job." *I sound so simpering.*

"Perhaps." He paused and screwed up his face as if he was weighing his answer. "Unfortunately, he mistrusted everyone. Only my almoners were allowed to speak to me outside of his presence. I was closely guarded, my rooms accessible only through his. It was a lonely, sad time."

His words were light but there was deep pain behind his eyes. Jane lowered her face into her hands. "I've made a terrible muddle. I am so sorry."

"Why?" the King asked, and his confusion sounded genuine.

Jane looked up at him. "I've made you talk about sadder and sadder things. You were so happy when we first entered the room."

"I still am."

"How can that be?"

The King grabbed one of her hands and brought it to his lips. "You have shown me a place that reminds me of innocent times. I was so free in my youth, my mother was so caring. I feel free again now."

Jane was discomfited by the gesture, the first time she had experienced it outside of the ritual of court dancing. His lips were soft, dry. She felt a hint of a scratch from invisible stubble.

She grabbed her hand back as soon as she could. His eyes flickered.

"I meant no disrespect, Mistress Jane."

Her heart sank. Of course he meant nothing by it, it was unthinkable that he would. Not him. Not with her. He had been open and honest and she had not been able to accept that. She had to correct her mistake. She had to be equally open, or she would insult his kindness.

"Forgive me, Sire. I know that. I just have little experience with such gallantry."

"It is a gesture I use often. If we are to be friends, you must accept it better than that."

Friends. A smile crept across her face and she quickly looked down and resumed her chopping. His words came back to her, and she decided to continue their conversation. "My own youth was lonely and sad too, because of my father. I know how important it is to cling to happy thoughts."

"Your father was difficult?"

The question surprised her. She hadn't expected him to delve deeper like that. She took a deep breath. *In for a penny, in for a pound.* "Nothing I ever did was good enough for him. Father ignored me unless I was quarreling with Edward or otherwise misbehaving, and then I was heavily punished for the sake of my soul. He was always quoting scripture at us, always warning us that our actions would damn us to hell."

She sensed rather than saw the King's glance and she felt the heat creep across her face. He must know, everyone did, that Jane's father's morality was in fact the height of hypocrisy. His mortal sin with his own son's wife far eclipsed any of Jane's childish transgressions. The gossip had torn their family apart, shamed them all. She flushed deeply and fell silent.

The King gently covered her hand with his own. Another touch she did not know how to respond to. This time, at least, she pulled it back gently.

"My grandmother Beaufort did likewise," he said. "Her

Welsh blood made her demanding. I never felt that I lived up to her standards."

"It's not the same," she said quietly.

"No," he agreed. "Of course, I never acted light in front of her as you did with me."

His tone was merry and clearly joking but Jane's insides tensed. He was still thinking of that moment, would always see her as that crazy girl.

She looked up at him wildly, about to cry. His smile quickly faded and he rushed to continue. "That was a joke. A poor one, but I hoped to lighten the mood."

She nodded, eyes down, but tears still stung her eyes. He grabbed her shoulders to catch her eyes. "I meant no criticism. Please believe me."

His sincerity and heartfelt pain touched her. She couldn't let herself be upset, for his sake. She smiled ruefully. "I just feel so very foolish."

"Why?"

"It is so unlike me, but now that is how you know me. I have always been the serious one, the responsible one, and I let myself look ridiculous. I can't imagine what you must think of me."

"I think you were justifiably proud of yourself and let your enthusiasm show. Everyone does so. I have done so. Would you fault me?"

Her eyes narrowed. "You?"

"Of course. No one is always sober, Mistress Jane. No one of any worth, anyway."

His gentle reassurance was comforting, and she smiled. "Thank you. Really," she said.

"It goes back to what I was saying before, about how I enjoyed interacting with people while in disguise."

"Ah, yes," she answered quickly. "But I don't understand why," she admitted.

He smiled slowly before replying. "I could have honest conversations with good men, or lusty conversations with saucy wenches. I learned, in a way I never could, their real feelings. About their king, about their world. About everything. Then I revealed myself and gave them largesse to fix whatever problems they'd shared with me."

"That does sounds like fun. Why did you stop?"

"I became too recognizable. My face is on every coin in the realm, after all."

Jane laughed. Of course. "Though you could still get into mischief with your old friends."

"Ah, no, my old friends don't like my wife. Which is why I need new ones."

Another sore point, or was he talking about her? "I am sorry," Jane whispered.

"No reason," the King declared and clapped his hands together, changing the subject. "Now where is the marsh mallow?"

They worked together, silent again but awkward this time. Jane's discomfort faded, though, when they needed to cooperate to mix the poultice. She ran over to the kitchen to fetch a small pitcher of warm olive oil. When she returned, the King had already taken a new bowl from the shelf. They measured out the herbs, then mixed them together before adding the oil to make their paste. The process brought them back to the easy camaraderie they had shared, and Jane could have sworn that even the sun shone brighter when that happened.

Then suddenly Tom appeared, basket and royal doublet in hand. He reached over to put them on the table, but it was covered with their work, so he put them on a counter on the side before he bowed, a look of confusion on his face. "Your Majesty?"

"Ah, Tom," the King replied. "Do you always take so long at a task?"

"I...I...came back to the garden and you were gone. I looked for you in the house, but then heard from a servant that you were here. In the kitchens. I didn't believe him but I…I came to check."

"Well, I am here."

"Your men were looking for you too. Thomas Cromwell just arrived and hopes to speak with you."

"Ah yes. I had promised." He turned to Jane. "Well, Mistress, I will take a dose of our preparation and then I will be off. I thank you for a wonderful experience."

Jane poured some of the mixture into a small jug and handed it to him along with a soft cloth. He bowed and left, and Jane poured the rest into another jug for the stable boy. She reached a hand to clear the table before she left, then decided to leave it as it was. She wasn't yet ready to destroy the evidence of this time together. Still, she realized that someone else might, so she grabbed a sprig of parsley and tucked it away on a shelf as a small, permanent memento.

September 8, 1535 … 10 a.m.

Thomas Cromwell was calm for the first time in weeks, waiting for the King to return from the morning's hunt. Cromwell had come to Wolf Hall to get the King to focus on important matters. The King had been enjoying himself too much on this progress to pay attention to the business that was still being conducted by the skeleton staff left behind. He kept putting off Cromwell's letters "until the morrow," which never arrived. But in eighteen days they would consecrate three new bishops of the Church of England in a lavish ceremony planned for Winchester Cathedral, and none of the necessary papers had been signed. The three good men – Edward Fox, John Hilsey, and Hugh Latimer – still needed to be formally appointed by the King so proper announcements could be made and plans finalized. And so Thomas Cromwell had come to join the progress.

He planned to stay, too – he wanted to be at Winchester. These would be the first bishops consecrated with full pageantry

– not quietly in the night – by the fledgling Church. It was an important step. It was also exciting that Edward Seymour had suggested a nice addition to the pomp: a public signing of the appointment papers with a banquet to follow. It would not entail a large change in plans or a scramble for guests: local dignitaries had already been invited for a feast so this merely enhanced the ceremonial aspect. That was an astute political suggestion. Edward Seymour was a smart man.

Cromwell stretched and looked around the small Presence Chamber that had been created for the King at Wolf Hall. Whoever designed it had done their work well. It was probably that Seymour girl: she was clearly the one in charge of the house. She had even included a vase of parsley, a trick not many people would have thought of. The King was petrified of sickness and death, though he was careful to hide the extent of that fear. People loved their Bluff King Hal, and they had hated his cautious father.

Cromwell was glad to be here: it was a comfortable place. He should send for his son, Gregory, to join him. This would be a good way to introduce the boy to court life, this combination of informality and grand celebration.

"Master Cromwell, welcome," came a voice from behind him. It was Edward Seymour with a wry smile on his thin lips that passed for warmth in the man. Much more serious and hardworking than his younger brother Tom, Edward inspired much more confidence. Even if Tom was more fun to be around.

"Ah, Master Seymour, thank you," Cromwell replied. "It is a pleasure to accept your hospitality."

"It is so much more modest than our old patron's, but no less genuine."

Cromwell smiled. He and Edward had both worked in Cardinal Wolsey's household for a time. Another smart move by Seymour, reminding him of their bond. "I am told the King is quite pleased. Is he coming now?"

"The King returned early from the hunt and is already inspecting the space my sister Jane arranged for the signing."

"Oh?" Cromwell frowned. "There was no reason to trouble His Majesty. I planned to take care of that for him."

"The King insisted on seeing the barn himself. He is there now."

"The...barn?" Cromwell croaked. The informality of such a structure would make a mockery of the entire event. Was this Seymour's plan? Was he an enemy to Reformation after all?

"May I take you there now?"

Cromwell swallowed his concern. He had not heard any indignant bellows through the open window, so the King was clearly not raging. Still, he could be quietly stewing. Cromwell would see soon enough. "Please."

Given his nervousness, Cromwell could not bring himself to his usual level of affability, so the walk over was quiet. His heart fluttered when he saw the massive brick building that could have been another manor house. And the moment he walked in, all his concerns were allayed. First he sniffed to confirm that there was no telltale animal odor. Then he allowed himself to examine the setting. The interior was impressive, at least 175 feet long by 26 feet wide, crowned by a ceiling of soaring arch-braced trusses, and the space had been carefully prepared to provide the pomp of any Great Hall. The walls were covered with silk tapestries as rich as those that hung in the house – and featuring biblical themes that were perfect for the occasion. A raised dais had been added at one end, with a trestle table on which shone a large, ornate silver cross – probably from the local church. Well done. Behind the table, and arranged at an inviting angle, a large chair covered in rich arras awaited the King. A half dozen smaller seats were arrayed in a half circle behind. Also well done. Praise God.

His heart comforted, Cromwell glanced around for the King. Cromwell had to look back and forth twice before noticing the King's figure through the open door on the opposite side of the structure. He was strolling in the garden, the Seymour girl on his arm. Nodding to Edward to follow him, Cromwell walked over to the couple.

"Ah, Thomas, is this not perfect?" asked the King when they arrived. "Another layer to the glory of the Church. And all thanks to Mistress Jane." He took the girl's hand in his and brought it to his lips. The chivalry colored her ashen features with a deep red blush. She was clearly not used to that kind of attention: there was not a whiff of scandal or intrigue attached to her name, other than that unfortunate family affair. A pale slip of a thing, she had spent years at court without anything to recommend her. She wasn't the type to stand out on account of her beauty or grace – she was not a woman you would ever notice at a ball. But here she was in her element, charming with her efficiency and quiet wit. She was turning out to be an unexpected asset of the Seymour family.

"Your Majesty!" Tom Seymour called out as he approached with Sir Francis Bryan, Henry Norris, William Brereton, and several others of the King's gentlemen. They all looked like they had coordinated their clothes as carefully as the Queen's women were known to do. Perhaps they had.

"Ah, Tom," the King called back.

"We were waiting for you at the house," Tom said. "We didn't realize you would tarry here, else we would have come with you."

"Cromwell joined me and that changed my plans," said Henry.

Cromwell carefully stifled any visible reaction to those words. Henry had just lied to Thomas Seymour. Not that Cromwell cared a single whit that the King had lied. Of course he had lied; he often did. The only thing troubling Thomas Cromwell was the fact that he couldn't figure out quite *why* the King had lied. Which courtier was out of favor right now such that the King wanted to avoid them? And what had they done?

"What say Your Majesty to a dance duel at the banquet? Masters Norris and Brereton are spoiling for a fight," Tom said.

"Now, Tom, we are on Church business this afternoon," said the King. "Maybe tonight."

"The Queen has offered to judge it, though I daresay she hopes you will join in," added Henry Norris. He was always focused on the Queen. And on Madge Shelton of course.

"Tonight," repeated the King.

"I think the Queen has something else planned as well," continued Norris. He turned to Jane. "You should probably be serving her right now, Mistress."

Cromwell saw Jane open her mouth, but the voice came from the King.

"Mistress Jane is tending to the needs of the court during this visit, not to the needs of the Queen. She will be the one to arrange your duel, Norris, so you need to show her the proper respect."

"Ah, so that is why you are not hard at work now," Sir Francis Bryan said. "You are lucky for that – I hear the Queen is a demanding taskmistress when the mood is upon her."

Again Cromwell kept his face impassive. Bryan was another one of those who was no friend to the Queen.

"She is not unkind, Sir Francis," said Jane. "She is a good mistress."

Interesting. The Seymour wench defending the Queen like that. Of course, her sister owed much to the Boleyn's influence. Were the Seymours allied with the Queen then? Nah, George Boleyn disliked Edward Seymour...

"She is kind to you?" Bryan asked, his voice dripping with irony. "I heard she wanted to send you back to Wolf Hall."

"Actually, that was my brother Edward," said Jane.

"What?" The King, clearly alarmed, turned to Edward Seymour. "Explain yourself."

Seymour began to stammer, and Jane broke in. "He wanted

to give our youngest sister, Dorothy, the chance to make a name for herself."

"I wanted to give Dorothy a chance to make herself known, so that it would be easier to make a match for her. I was right."

"Oh?" The King arched an eyebrow.

"Yes, Your Majesty. During Dorothy's brief service to the Queen this summer she quickly captured the heart of Sir Clement Smythe."

Clement Smythe. Cromwell's mind calculated the details like the abacus that sat in his office, a souvenir from his time in Italy. The Smythes were comfortable: they held a handsome manor house, complete with park and warren. They also were hangers-on at court – the father had been headmaster at both Winchester and Eaton, then managed to parlay that into service to the King in small diplomatic missions. The Seymour connection was a good one for them. Enough that they would not quibble about a dowry.

"You could have made such a match without sending Mistress Jane home."

Jane's face broke into a triumphant smile at the King's words. Edward shot her a look.

"Your Majesty, the Smythe family wanted to see Dorothy's beauty and industry for themselves," said Edward. "I cannot say this was an unreasonable request."

Cromwell stifled a smile. That was a kind way of saying the family wanted to make sure she was prettier than Jane. Cromwell couldn't say that he blamed them.

"And thankfully the timing worked out well – Jane was happy to go and prepare your visit," Edward continued. At the King's stony look, Edward turned to his sister. "Isn't that right, Jane?"

Cromwell could hear the plea hidden under the words. Seymour clearly hoped to avoid further chastising, as anyone would. He felt Seymour's deep relief when Jane relented.

"I was indeed happy to go," she agreed. "As I shall be to

return. Especially since Edward has promised never to do that again."

"He shall have me to deal with if he tries," the King said. "Your place is with us, Mistress."

The girl blushed and looked away. She actually seemed to shrink into herself at the attention. Interestingly, her shyness affected the King, who turned quickly to his men and changed the topic back to the plans for that night. But he looked over at the girl now and then during the conversation, and Cromwell was struck by how different the King's expression was when he looked at her from when he looked at any other woman. It was neither sarcastic nor impatient, but rather gentle, kind. There was no cynicism there. He looked like the idealistic scamp he used to be.

What sort of woman was this, to elicit such a response?

September 10, 1535 ... Noon

This is it, thought Jane. The court was preparing to move on to the next stop on the progress; they would leave within the hour. The visit had gone beautifully, and Jane would not change a moment of it, even her initial embarrassing display. She said a silent prayer, then decided to see if one of her sisters needed her help. They were too kind and shy, so the other ladies often took advantage of them. Unlike Edward's wife Anne, who never wasted an opportunity to pass on work.

Jane walked into the Queen's suite and was immediately overwhelmed by the chaos. Dresses lay scattered all over the floor, and Elizabeth and Lady Rochford knelt in the sea of silks and satins, almost in tears.

"She's still choosing her outfit, just dropping discards behind her as she always does. We'll never get them into the proper trunks in time."

Jane reached down for the closest dress and automatically folded it. "What can I do to help? Where is everyone else?"

"Anne and Maggie ran off to check that the kitchen was packing the proper lunch. Dorothy and Nan went to the stables to check on the saddles. Liz and Madge are tending to the Queen's hair."

It took ten minutes of diligent work, but finally all the dresses were in the proper trunks, and Elizabeth and Lady Rochford shed their panicked expressions. They almost smiled below eyes that were still slightly dazed.

"Done. I need to check on the rest of the preparations, but I will send servants to bring the other ladies back here to help with any last changes," said Jane.

"Ah, Mistress Jane, you are truly a paragon," said Lady Rochford.

Jane gave a friendly bob and set off in search of the next urgent problem. The King stepped out of his Presence Chamber as she reached the top landing of the main staircase; Edward was a single pace behind him, head turned back to bark instructions at the men following. The King smiled at Jane and she gave a quick curtsy.

"I hope your preparations for departure are going well," she said. Then, in a mischievous tone, she continued, "Edward looks like he has things well under control."

"I do indeed," Edward blandly agreed, not rising to the bait. "As do you."

"You both have impressed me with your efficiency and hospitality this week. I shall be sad to leave," said the King.

Tom and the other men emerged from the room. The King motioned to the stairs, and held out his hand for Jane to lay hers on top. "Shall we?" he asked.

Side by side the two of them descended the wide wooden steps, Edward carefully protecting his place just behind the King but still ahead of the other gentlemen. Jane had never felt so grand, and had to resist the temptation to look back to see her brother's face. She fought an inexplicable desire to stick her tongue out at him: that would be taking her newfound confidence a bit too far.

At the landing that marked the grand staircase's half turn, they saw Sir John and Lady Seymour waiting in the foyer at the bottom of the stairs, next to the imposing circular table with its massive floral arrangement. Several servants were already lined up along the wall, and more were arriving, faces beaming. The King led Jane directly to her parents, giving a smiling wave on the way to the cook who'd hit him. The poor woman sucked in her lower lip in equal measures of pride and embarrassment, and bobbed another curtsy.

"Sir John," the King boomed. "I envy your life and I thank you for sharing it with us."

Jane's father stammered his thanks and polite conversation began. Jane smiled to herself as the King absentmindedly plucked a sprig of the parsley she'd added to the bouquet and twirled it in his fingers.

Abruptly Madge Shelton captured their attention as she rushed down the stairs, alone. She reached the group, gave a quick bob to all of them, and began immediately to talk directly to the King. Jane was irritated at how Madge had dispensed with all the polite niceties, though a part of Jane envied such confidence. Ah, to be so sure of a welcome reception.

"The Queen will be down in a moment. She is putting the final touches on her toilette."

"Thank you," the King said, and it was clearly a dismissal. Madge seemed confused. Jane had to admit it was strange not to see the man exchange ironic double entendres with his former mistress. Such flirtation was how he tended to deal with Madge, indeed with many of the Queen's ladies.

The King continued his conversation with Jane's parents, and Madge shifted uncertainly as if deciding whether to return to the Queen. The decision was made for her when Anne Boleyn appeared on the landing, trailed by the rest of her ladies. She had chosen a gown of purple silk atop a crimson kirtle, and a French hood without a veil to cover her hair. A heavy gold chain adorned her neck, matching the girdle belt from which hung an intricately worked pomander. She looked every inch the queen, though the regal purple muddied her sallow complexion. In her youth, Anne Boleyn had carefully chosen every article of clothing to enhance her looks, but now she dressed to trumpet her position.

The Queen paused to wait for the company below to turn and look at her; once satisfied, she majestically swept down the stairs. It was a typical move for her – as it was for the King, as it had been for Catherine of Aragon – but it struck Jane how the King had abandoned much of that formality and show while he was at Wolf Hall. He had treated them like family, Jane like a little sister. It was so gratifying.

The Queen joined the King, and it was her turn to greet their hosts. "We thank you for your hospitality," the Queen declared to Sir John and Lady Seymour. "You showed us a fine time."

"We were honored to have you, Your Majesty," said Sir John. "We will treasure the memory for years to come."

"As will we, Sir John," said the Queen. "And special thanks to you, Mistress Jane, for tending to us so well."

Jane gave a low curtsy, heart swelling at the attention and respect shown to her.

"But now you must return to court, Mistress," the King broke in. "We will count the days until we see you again, and can create new remedies together."

Jane smiled broadly, but before she could answer she noticed the Queen looking speculatively at the King, eyes slightly narrowed. It was Tom's booming voice that replied. "Ah, Your Majesty, I am afraid I have already shared all that I know of cures."

"As you have of baskets," was the King's quick response.

Before the laughter had even the chance to erupt, the Queen broke in. "My Lord, I am tired. I think I will take the litter instead of my horse. My brother will ride with me."

Madge Shelton, never the best horsewoman, piped up quickly. "Shall we join you?"

"My brother's wife can join us, but the rest of you will ride your horses for the procession. If I am to sleep comfortably I will need the extra room."

A look of annoyance passed over the King's face. "But we are about to depart. All the arrangements have been made. We'll need..."

"Oh, Sire, there is no trouble at all," Jane interjected, glancing at her brother.

Edward bowed to the King. "It will take no time to make the change. It will be done before we even get outside." He narrowed his eyes at a servant, who took off at a run toward the stables.

Jane smiled at the King and Queen. The King smiled back and turned to his wife. "See, my Lady, your wishes are fulfilled."

"I serve the Queen as best I can, Your Majesty," Jane said. "And you as well."

"Of course," the Queen said, drawing her lips together as if she had tasted something bad.

Jane looked at the King with dismay. She was relieved to see his conspiratorial grin, and when he winked at her she giggled. All the attention snapped onto her, and she pretended to sneeze. She curtsied and was relieved when the Queen sharply turned her skirts to stalk into the courtyard. The King leaned over to kiss Jane's hand as he followed his wife.

"Sorry about that," he said in a low voice. He was no stranger to the Queen's sudden storms. Edward rushed after him, throwing Jane a silent warning.

Right before turning to mount her horse and ride off with the group, Elizabeth hugged Jane. "Praise God that trial is over."

Jane knew she should feel equally relieved, but instead she felt forlorn. This had been her big triumph, and now it was over. She was not looking forward to the process of undoing the strands of her Herculean preparations. She just wanted to get back to court, and pray that she could preserve some of this newfound royal favor and attention. It would surely impress the Dormer family, and assure her marriage to young Will. *Focus on that,* she told herself.

Though truth be told, the thought of Will Dormer had lost much of its luster. The time she had spent with the King had spoiled her, and Will's average looks and awkward demeanor now made him seem vaguely ridiculous. Even so, this match was her big chance at a real future, the only one she had ever had. She needed to resign herself to a fate that was so much better than the one that threatened her at the start of the summer, and be grateful for it. It would get easier, she was sure of that.

PART TWO: SCHEMER

CHAPTER FOUR – 1535

BACK AT COURT

October 28, 1535 ... 5 p.m.

*T*he summer's progress was finally over. The already lengthy route had been extended and now autumn had fully descended on the country, with trees and hillsides ablaze in reds and oranges. The journey had been a success, the rains abating somewhat and the harvests not as dismal as expected. The King had solidified the support of his people, and he and the Queen had honored reformist gentry at every stop to make clear that such was the way to royal favor. Now they were back, retuned to Windsor the day before.

Jane of course had expected them back earlier. She had arrived at Windsor two weeks ago to resume her duties with the Queen. It had been a quiet time with almost no one around. Eerie in its emptiness. Now it was bustling again, with lords and ladies strolling in the galleries, pages rushing down hallways, musicians gathered in corners. Now everything had changed. She had turned her heart back to Will Dormer only to find out they weren't affianced after all. Instead, he was to marry Lady Mary Sidney, if he hadn't already. The Sidneys were a prominent, rich family, better placed and better off than the Seymours, and the Dormers had jumped at the chance to ally themselves to a well-connected heiress. That left Jane further away from her dreams than ever. Edward had made no other arrangements for her – though he had paired Dorothy off with Clement Smythe quickly enough. And Edward had this crazy idea that Jane's not-quite flirtation with the King was more than it was. Right now, she sat in Sir Nicholas Carew's apartments, enduring a conference in which Edward, Carew, and Tom purported to give her instructions about how to deal with the King.

"She represents the ultimate contrast to the Queen. Pale where she is dark, meek where she is bold," Carew said. "That must be the source of his interest. She must carry that through, and be innocent where the Queen is knowing."

"That will not be difficult. She is priggish by nature," Edward said.

Jane bit her lip. It was so difficult to sit there while they discussed her. It was beyond her how they could be so insulting even while they were begging for her help.

"Ah, but priggish will not do. She needs to suggest the pleasure of her surrender. He needs to know she will be woman enough to conceive," answered Carew. "Wistfulness, that's the attitude she needs to wear."

"Yes, wistful," Tom agreed. "She must refuse him firmly, but show reluctance at having to."

"Thank you, gentlemen," Jane broke in. "I appreciate your advice, but it is premature. The King has never displayed anything beyond friendship to me, no matter how I try to interpret his actions."

"Our king is a romantic," Carew declared firmly. "He loves to pretend that a woman is beyond conquest, whether or not he is assured of the outcome. Hell, he played the game of courtly love with the Princess Dowager for years after their wedding."

"That is my point. He has never done or said anything to suggest he would like to play at being my knight. He has never sighed or moped or called me beautiful. He has never wooed me with songs or worn my colors. He has never begged for favors or tried to steal kisses. All he has done is speak to me of herbs and proclaim himself my friend."

"It's how he began with Queen Anne," Edward said.

"It's not. You forget that I served the Princess Dowager when the King fell in love with Anne Boleyn. I watched every single step of that courtship. I saw every move the King made and all of Anne's responses. None of which apply here."

"You must be mistaken," said Carew.

Jane sighed. She couldn't tell that she was hoping for a sign that the King's friendship was any more than that – and devastated that she was unable to find the proof she craved. "I wish I were," was all she said.

"Impossible." Carew was adamant.

Tom shrugged. "Perhaps she's right. Do you really see her attracting such a one as the King?"

Edward shook his head. "No. But I also don't think she has the experience to recognize when someone is attracted."

Jane jumped to her feet, ready to leave. "I'll thank you to stop talking about me like this."

Carew shook his head and put a hand on her shoulder, though Jane couldn't tell whether it was an apology or an attempt to force her back down. "Nay, nay. I just know the King, and I know he is not the man to be satisfied with mere friendship."

That was the one bit of hope that Jane clung to. If anyone was in a position to know the King's mind, it was Sir Nicholas. He had joined the King's household as a boy, to share his education and to accept the beatings the teachers could not in good conscience administer to a prince of the realm. From whipping boy he had quickly graduated to accomplice when his royal friend wanted to sneak out of one palace or another to seduce local village girls…yes, he had been at the King's side for many such forays.

Edward held up his glass in a toast. "May the Lord give truth to your words."

Carew held up his own in response before draining it. "Whatever is going on, the longer she draws things out, the better the chance she can unseat the Queen. The King loves the chase far more than he values the conquest. Especially given the high value he places on virtue."

The three men looked at each other, then at Jane. Carew let out a deep sigh. "Maybe I am overly hopeful…"

His voice trailed off and it was clear to Jane what they all thought. She was too plain, too simple, to be able to pull this off. Well, they were getting far too ahead of themselves.

"It doesn't matter if Jane is the one to finish the job, as long as she starts it," Carew continued. "She can join the growing chorus of people telling the King how his people abominate his marriage. And she can talk specifically of the Queen's meanness, pass on little stories, plant ideas in his mind to help him see the Boleyn for what she is and maybe make her a little more uneasy in her seat. And she can tell him how wonderful we three are, smooth the path to friendship."

Tom broke out in laughter. "Unfortunately, the stories she has so far told are quite the opposite. She has praised the Queen and denigrated us to the King."

"What?"

"Did Sir Francis Bryan not tell you the story? Jane told the King how Edward threatened to give her place to Dorothy. The King scolded Edward roundly for that. Edward managed to wiggle out, just barely."

Edward rolled his eyes with renewed annoyance. But Carew seemed to like it. "Ah, that is perfect. There is nothing more satisfying to the King than coming to a fair maiden's rescue… even if it is only from her brother."

"Yes, but now I have been styled an ogre from whom she needs protection. This does not bode well for me," Edward sulked.

"Just the opposite. Now every time you praise your sister, the King will pride himself on his intervention and love you all the more for it. And hopefully her."

"And hopefully her," Edward agreed.

Carew suddenly broke out into a happy chortle and clapped Edward on the shoulder. "See here, this is all good news. Even if Jane is right and there is nothing more here than some innocent conversations, I still praise the Lord for every moment the King spends away from the Boleyn's influence. The truth is, his carnal interest would end all too soon. His friendship will last far longer. Let us celebrate that he has no further designs – and let us come up with better instructions as to what Mistress Jane should say during their friendly chats."

October 29, 1535 ... 10 p.m.

It was a chilly night but the Queen's bedchamber provided a comfortable refuge. While the court was away, the light summer curtains had been changed to heavy velvet drapes meant to keep out the winter air. Now they formed a floor-to-ceiling wall that reflected the heat from the roaring fire back into the room where the Queen knelt at her prie-dieu in the corner and her ladies sat quietly with their needlework. Well, most of them anyway. Madge Shelton busily studied her cuticles while her work sat in her lap; Liz Worcester stared off blankly. They were definitely the flighty ones.

Jane looked back down to her needlework, impatient for the Queen to finish her prayers so they could begin the dozens of steps involved in formally putting her to bed. They would undress her, redress her, brush and braid her hair, warm her sheets...then right before they turned out the lights, three ladies would bring their pallets to the foot of her bed to sleep in her room, in case she needed anything during the night. Thank goodness this was not one of Jane's nights, as she could not bear it if it were. She just wanted the day to be over. William Dormer had visited court today, and Jane had come face to face with him for the first time since he'd jilted her for Mary Sidney. Jane had been running an errand from the Queen, and when Jane turned a corner quickly she almost crashed into William. The look on his face changed from annoyance to nervousness. For a moment it seemed as if he might try to walk on and disregard her completely, but then his eyes cast up as a look of resignation took over and he bowed to her.

"Mistress Seymour. I trust you are well."

Jane's lip curled as ice flooded her veins. She drew herself up to her full height and looked down her nose at him coldly. "Master Dormer. I hear congratulations are in order." Relief flooded his face, and it fueled her anger. "I wish you well," she said tersely. "But now I must be off."

She strode off with all the dignity she could summon, frozen inside. But it only worsened when she returned to the Queen's apartments. Mary Sidney was there, busily gossiping with them all. Jane's stomach turned over but she collected herself. Her entrance drew scant attention, and Mary continued to prattle about her oh-so-considerate husband. Jane sat with her needlework, happy to have an excuse to keep her eyes down and face hidden. Little by little her queasiness wore off, and she was able to sit calmly through stories of William's plans for the manor house Mary's father had given them. Jane was fully numb by the time Mary began sharing unending details of his romantically gallant courtship, and simpering descriptions of the depth of their great love for each other. *All affection is false,* Jane told herself. William had only ever sought wealth. He had never loved Jane. Though, truth be told, she had never loved him either.

A knock from the antechamber drew their attention – it was from the door that connected the Queen's apartments to the King's. Nan Gainsford leaped out of her seat to open it.

"Good evening, Lady Zouche." It was William Brereton's voice. "I bring His Majesty's message that he will arrive shortly to visit Her Majesty."

"Good evening, Master Brereton," Nan Gainsford replied. "The Queen is at her prayers right now, but I shall let her know as soon as she is done. I am sure that she will be most pleased to receive His Majesty."

Brereton bowed. Nan gave a prim curtsy and closed the door as he left. At the distinct click of the lockset, the Queen crossed herself and turned around to look at them all. "I shall indeed be most pleased to receive His Majesty," she said.

That set the women to clucking and giggling, and launched a flurry of activity. Liz Worcester and Nan Gainsford ran over to the bed to turn it down to its most inviting state. Anne Seymour and Mary Scroge moved the candle stands closer to the bed. Madge Shelton and Jane Rochford raced to the trunk that held the Queen's nightgowns, and rummaged through it for the most diaphanous specimens. The Queen joined them, and Elizabeth followed after her to unpin the slashed foresleeves from her day dress.

Meanwhile, Jane felt frozen, unsure what to do. She had been through this exercise many times in the past, but now she was stymied. She knew her role was to help the Queen appear irresistible to her husband, but Jane honestly didn't know how best to contribute to this goal beyond what everyone else was already doing.

She was strangely disoriented by the fact that the King was about to bed his wife. Jane well knew it was a frequent occurrence, but things were different now that Edward and Carew had put the crazy notion into her head that the King might have feelings for her. This was the first time she was confronted with such a stark reminder of how little those feelings really meant. Jane's heart was pounding, her mouth dry over the idea that she would be in the room to receive the King when he arrived. But this wasn't the time to dwell on that; she had a job to do. If only she could concentrate enough to figure out what that was. All she wanted to do was flee.

Finally she decided to focus on returning order to the room.

The King enjoyed a calm environment, that she knew about him. Would he guess this was her contribution? She put that out of her mind to concentrate on the task at hand. As she began to rearrange the seating, she heard the Queen call out to her. "Mistress Jane."

Jane turned to look at her. Anne Boleyn was wearing her chosen nightgown – a green silk shift that set her skin aglow and highlighted her loose black hair. She sat in front of her mirror. The wild gleam in her sharp brown eyes stood in dark contrast to the soft purr in her voice.

"Yes, Your Majesty?"

"Mistress Jane, brush my hair so it gleams in the light when the King comes."

Jane was transported back to when Catherine had been queen, when the King was in love with Anne Boleyn yet still visited Catherine's bed. As one of Catherine's ladies, Anne had to help her prepare for these encounters. As another of Catherine's ladies, Jane had been a witness to these power struggles. For of course Catherine had taunted Anne the same way. *Mistress Anne, brush my hair so it gleams in the light when the King comes.*

Jane cringed, struck to her core by how different things had been then. The King had fully declared himself to Anne. He had begged her favors, sworn his devotion, made her promises. He had done no such thing with Jane. All he had done was make a potion with her and tell her stories. Such a fuss Edward was making over little more than basic human kindness. For the second time that day Jane's stomach turned over, but she rushed over to do as she was told.

The scent of ambergris suffused the air as Jane measured two drops of the precious oil. As she brushed, Jane kept her eyes on the comb in her hand. Out of the corner of her eye she caught the Boleyn staring at her reflection in the mirror. It took all Jane's strength not to yank Anne's long black hair.

"Enough," the Queen finally snapped.

Jane opened her mouth to speak, but voices rose from the hallway followed by a knock at the connecting door. Madge giggled and ran to let the King and three of his men into the antechamber. The Queen's other women filed out of her inner sanctum, but Jane hung back to delay the inevitable. She was embarrassed at the idea of seeing him here, now. She was afraid of his reaction: she certainly didn't want any more attention called to herself after the Queen's display. Jane slipped into the room while Nan Gainsford and Madge Shelton – their knowing giggles almost shrill – joked with the men. The others joined in with simple nods and coos, but Jane was too uncomfortable for even that. Still, she held a smile carefully painted on her face.

"Don't get into any trouble out here," the King said laughingly as he broke away from the group and walked into the room. "In fact, you may leave as I plan to spend the night." He gave a start when he saw Jane, then collected himself. "Mistress," he said with a curt nod of his head. He brushed past her and shut the door behind him.

Jane felt as if the air had been sucked out of the room. That was a clear dismissal. For the second time that day, she had been cruelly reminded of her lack of importance. She was tired of confronting how little she mattered in this world. *Get me out of here,* she thought bitterly.

November 13, 1535 ... 2 p.m.

It was a warm day at Windsor, and the rainy weather made the air muggy and heavy. Still, it was beautiful in the King's library with its soaring windows with open panes on two sides. Jane was so much happier to be there than in the Queen's Presence Chamber, where the ill-tempered Boleyn, desperate for distraction, had set her lap dogs to fight against each other.

Jane had been rescued from that scene, summoned to settle an argument between the King and Edward. This had become a regular occurrence, and she found that she loved these appeals to her extraordinary recall. There was no acrimony remaining from that other night, there could not be: God and country commanded the King to bed his wife. Jane would show no more disappointment than prim avoidance.

"I say we brought down six deer at Wolf Hall this last visit, and four the time before, but your brother ventures it was the opposite. We trust you will know the real facts."

"Unfortunately, Edward is right," she said. "It was only four deer this time." The King's face fell, so Jane hastened to continue. "I'm sorry, but it's not something we could easily forget – our father wanted you to have greater success this visit than you had last one. He was so convinced we had disappointed you that it is truly a relief to hear you remembered thusly."

He visibly brightened at her words. "I am glad you understand that my mistake reflects how happy I was at Wolf Hall."

"Of course, Sire," she said.

He paused, and it lent more weight to his next words. "And with you."

Jane froze and looked down.

The King settled back in his chair. "There was not a moment of the visit that was not well considered and planned," he said in a tone that, while still warm, was more proper. "That was your doing, Mistress. Though your brother Edward will take the credit."

The compliment was gratifying and she smiled up at the King. Edward hastened to insert himself into the conversation. "Perhaps it helped that you also bagged so many boars. And of course enough rabbits to collar the coats of our entire household," he said. They all laughed.

The two men bantered easily between themselves, and Jane settled back in her chair. She kept a smile on her face and nodded occasionally, even as she lost some of the conversational threads here and there. She was just happy to be part of a good-natured discussion without being expected to lead it, or even join in. The King was kind to her that way, and she appreciated it.

She felt a tickle on her forehead. A small bead of sweat was making a slow journey down her temple. She wiped it away as discreetly as she could and hoped no one had noticed.

"It is quite warm in here," said the King directly to her.

Caught.

"Yes, Sire," she answered in a squeak, trying to ignore Edward's glare.

A broad smile broke out on the King's face and he leaped to his feet. "I have just the thing."

He walked over to the wall and rummaged around one of its cabinets before emerging with an ornate fan. White and orange feathers extended from ivory ribs held together by an intricately carved *boleta* and finished by a jeweled handle. He presented it to her with a bow and a flourish. "This was a gift from the Spanish Ambassador. I would be grateful if you now accepted it from me."

Out of the corner of her eye, Jane could see Edward struggle to keep from reacting to the gift. He was successful with all but a single eyebrow that arched up his forehead.

"Oh, Sire," she said. "Señor Chapuys would be upset to see his gift not enjoyed."

"Nonsense. I will enjoy his gift far more for seeing you use it."

She looked down at the fan. It was the perfect, thoughtful gift for an uncomfortably warm day. So courtly. Chivalrous even.

She flushed. That was precisely what Edward was saying, that the King wanted to be her knight. Edward and Carew had spent hours discussing strategy, which always seemed to involve seeing Jane as a deer that should somehow want to be hunted…

She shook off the labyrinthine thinking required to follow their arguments and returned to the present where she found it ironic that, despite all that planning and instruction, no one had thought to counsel her how to react to an expensive gift. The first gift from a gentleman in her life. Was she supposed to refuse it?

She looked down at the fan again. It was ridiculous to think that accepting it was immodest. It was stunning, and she wanted to possess it more than she cared to admit. *Who cared what Edward thought?*

"Thank you, Sire," she said softly and took the proffered gift. She batted it back and forth several times, smiling as the air stirred around her. It was a wonderful feeling.

She rested it in her lap for a moment to look at it and smile. The King took that opportunity to point at the *boleta.* "You see? It was destined for you," he said as he leaned down over her shoulder to touch the handle with his finger.

His hand brushed against hers and stayed there. He was so close it was hard to breathe. She was careful not to flinch as she had back at Wolf Hall, but it grew harder as the touch continued and the heat intensified in her cheeks.

"See?" he repeated.

She forced herself to ignore the intimacy in his manner and voice, and to look where his finger directed her. One of the lions carved into the handle resembled a panther, the Seymour family crest. "Indeed," she whispered. "Thank you."

As soon as she said that, he stood, a proud smile on his face. *That was quite impressive,* she thought, *that he remembered the panther.*

Now that he wasn't so close, she could breathe again. She quickly began to fan herself, afraid to stop.

"For you, Edward, something different." He went back to the cabinet to rummage around again. This time he pulled out a hat. A deep blue silk that brought to Jane's mind childhood days spent in the dyeing room at Wolf Hall, her mother scolding the housemaids to stir the pot harder and keep the water hotter so the dye would hold better and turn the fabric darker than it wanted to be. No matter how hard they tried, they had never obtained such a hue.

The cap's crown was encircled by a blue ribbon so dark as to be almost black, and which matched a jaunty ostrich feather. The combination would have been somber except for the strand of small white pearls sewn onto the band as a biliment. The hat was magnificent in its simplicity. It also showed her how silly she was to question whether to accept her gift. You accepted gifts from the King. Everyone did.

The King presented the hat to Edward with a flourish that Jane noticed was as enthusiastic as the one he'd used with her. And he walked over with Edward to the mirror and stood behind him as close as he'd stood to Jane.

Jane's shoulders sagged and she hoped the gesture was not noticeable. *Had she imagined the intimacy?*

Probably. She had been so affected by the idea that the King was giving her a gift, the only tangible sign she had of his alleged courtship. Both Edward and his wife, Anne, claimed that the mere fact he sought her out and cared what she said was evidence enough, but Jane disagreed. She had to. He had done nothing to convince her that he was interested in anything more than the simple friendship he'd offered.

Jane squared her shoulders. That friendship had already transformed her life, changed the way she saw herself, altered her treatment in general. She should be happy with that, and she was. But it also made her so very sad. "I should get back," she said suddenly, standing to leave.

Both the King and Edward looked surprised. Jane immediately regretted her outburst, but it was too late. She dropped a quick curtsy and smiled as kindly as she could on the King when she rose. "Thank you," she said.

He smiled back, but hesitantly. She raised her precious gift and fanned her face for a second. "I shall treasure this," she said and was happy to see his smile broaden. She bobbed again and ran off.

November 15, 1535 ... 4 p.m.

The Queen was preparing a tableau for the masque that night. She and several ladies directed the decoration of a platform upon which the three Graces would stand while three of the King's gentlemen wooed them with sketches, poetry, and music. The Queen did not believe Jane exemplified charm, beauty, or creativity – or could even contribute to their staging – so Jane had been dismissed and left to her own devices for the time. So much the better.

Jane took two large cushions and settled into the window seat in the Queen's sitting room. She picked up her needlework and sighed with contentment. While she served the Queen, Jane was expected to sew shirts for the poor; while Jane was on her own, she was free to embroider the bodice for the new gown she was planning. Edward had insisted that she spend twice as much as she ever had. The King still showed friendship toward her, walking in the gardens with her almost every day. She shouldn't always wear the same dress, even though she was able to make it look somewhat different by varying the sleeves and underskirt.

Glancing around to make sure she was alone, she reached down for the fan that hung on a gold chain from her girdle, and closed her fingers slowly around its jeweled handle. She had worn it every day since the King had given it to her. She didn't want to ever take it off. Jane had never owned anything so perfect and delicate. It made her feel like a queen.

She flinched at the thought and looked around again, afraid that someone might have heard it. Especially Edward – she kept denying to Edward that anything was afoot. She wasn't ready to admit anything to him now. She wasn't even ready to admit it to herself. She still had no proof.

When the King had pursued Anne Boleyn, there had never been any question about his intentions, even at the very beginning. There had been no mistaking his desire, evidenced in attention and gifts and a thousand other large and obvious clues, not the least of which were the letters he wrote about his intense desire to kiss her breasts – which he called her "pretty dukkys" – when next they were together. Quite a difference from the quiet discretion he displayed with Jane. Jane just didn't want to get too hopeful. All her life Jane had watched one dream after another melt into muddy puddles like wet snow in the spring. She had learned to curb her dreams.

And so Jane quietly clutched at this one gift and the handful of tiny incidents that she outwardly dismissed but secretly cherished and relived over and over. The way his eyes softened when he looked at her, the way he remembered everything she said to him and brought it up again in later conversations, the way his arm "accidentally" brushed hers...

Stop it, she told herself. *Don't do this.*

She didn't want to go down that path, she couldn't. If she did, then the Queen would have Jane banished from court the minute the King's interest waned, as punishment for her conceit. She would be stuck at Wolf Hall, unlikely to marry. God help her in that case.

Suddenly the door swung open and Madge Shelton and Margery Horsman raced in, each chattering excitedly over the other in an effort to be the one to tell the news. "The Queen just vomited," said Madge.

"She laughed afterwards, and her brother hugged her for it," added Margery. "He even asked if she had a furious desire for apples."

"She must be with child," was the next breathless statement. "That was exactly how she announced her first pregnancy."

Jane remembered it well. It was when the marriage was still meant to be a secret, when disclosure would force the King's hand. Apples. Again.

"Might it have happened at Wolf Hall? He spent many nights in her room there."

"There will be such celebrating over this. The court will be an exciting place these next few weeks."

Jane smiled gamely as the girls babbled on. The Queen was with child. The King would never marry Jane now. She felt like she had just been rudely awoken from a wonderful dream, grasping desperately at the fabric of a quickly retreating fantasy.

She tightened her grip on the gilded fan. When she could feel it about to snap in two, she forced herself to relax and stroke its soft feathers. The ladies were still talking. Jane had stopped listening.

December 1, 1535 ... 3 p.m.

"This must be done, gentlemen, for the good of my country and the salvation of my people. I ask your help in taking this important step."

Thomas Cromwell glanced around the room to gauge the effect the King was having on his Privy Council. It was good to see the lords were paying rapt attention, a notable departure from their usual grim faces. Even the Duke of Norfolk was focused, not cleaning his fingernails with his knife. Henry was sharing news of the terrible corruption that had been found in religious houses throughout the land. More importantly, he was sharing his plans to correct it.

Cromwell glanced out the arched window, looking to the view to give him strength as it always did. The Palace of Whitehall had been built just before a curve on the River Thames, and so the water seemed to stretch on forever. The sight had captivated Cromwell for years, begun when he had been a clerk for Cardinal Wolsey, and the palace had been called York Place and had belonged to the Holy See of York. How fitting that this meeting was happening here, a reminder of the King's long history of taking Church property.

And take Church property he would. A lot of it. Another benefit of reform.

It had begun simply. First, the Church of England had claimed its right to all the monies the priests remitted to Rome. Then the King had imposed a new tax of ten percent on the income from Church lands. To properly assess the tax, Cromwell had undertaken an exhaustive survey of all Church property and revenues, hiring investigators who examined every estate book at the eight hundred or so religious houses throughout the country.

The result was twenty-two volumes of reports compiled into the *Valor Ecclesiasticus*, which detailed the extent of the Church's landed properties and the profits earned from rent and tithes and even from mining and fishing interests. Last week, Cromwell had presented the King with his own illuminated summary of the *Valor*; the preliminary figures, which Cromwell had shared right before the court left on progress, had surpassed all expectations – the Church owned more than a third of the land in England! Cromwell's team had spent the last six months studying the numbers and devising a plan to seize that vast wealth. The immediate plan was to close the smallest houses, the ones earning less than two hundred pounds a year. These were the ones that did the least, so they were the ones people would miss the least.

Thomas Boleyn, the Earl of Wiltshire and the Queen's father, looked cautiously puzzled. "Your Majesty, I understand what you're saying, but I don't grasp why you chose this group to close. Why not punish just those abbeys found to be corrupt?"

"I said the same thing," said the King. "Cromwell, will you be so good as to explain our reasoning to Sir Thomas."

Cromwell nodded and turned to Wiltshire, who was near the opposite end of the long table from him. Perfect. Cromwell could address all the others at the same time. He paused. His logic was simple: they were playing the country the way a knave seduced an innocent girl. Begin slowly and progress slowly; patience would deliver the prize. But he could never tell them that, though some might have guessed. "The smaller houses showed the most corruption, while the larger abbeys were more observant. That was an important factor. We will close fewer than three hundred abbeys under the bill, and they will serve as a fearful warning to the six hundred or so that will remain."

The Duke of Norfolk broke in. He had been happy enough with religious reform when it had placed his niece on the throne of England; now, with no further personal advantage, he dragged his feet. "Was the corruption really so terrible?"

"Sadly, yes, my Lord," Cromwell answered. "We found example after example of criminality, decay, and depravity." He hefted a large folder, the words *Comperta Monastica* on its cover, to make his point. "Some of the stories are shocking. West Acre Priory, not far from you in Norfolk, pawn relics, even one they claimed to be a piece of St. Andrew's finger. And at Hailes Abbey in Gloucestershire, the monks claim to have a vial of Christ's own blood. As it turns out, the blood is drained weekly from a freshly killed duck. They bilk the gullible of much gold with this blasphemous excuse for a relic. Though I find myself more offended by the monasteries that melt their plate to mint coins."

Norfolk harrumphed, but before he could say anything, Cromwell continued. "That is stealing from the Church and the Crown. Vile traitors, they hold nothing sacred."

The King pursed his lips in distaste. "Even worse is how they use the stolen money," he argued. "Monks entertain mistresses, nuns support bastard children. These are the real perversions."

"Aye," Norfolk agreed indignantly, as if he didn't flaunt *his* mistress to the world.

The King had always been priggish. And Cromwell had employed the perfect investigator to feed the monarch's disgust for such transgressions. Dr. John London had come to Cromwell's attention after nuns at the first few houses London visited accused him of trying to seduce them in the course of his investigation. He was summoned to answer the charges, and defended himself brilliantly. He quickly admitted to everything – but explained that his actions were merely a ruse to probe the depth of the nuns' virtue. And then he brandished a ledger that described each encounter, their exact words and corresponding facial expressions, page after page of stirring detail. Some sisters requested payment for their sexual services, and he paid – listing the charges and the services received – so as to add prostitution to their list of offenses. He even sought reimbursement of those sums. Such thorough methods and utter candor warmed Cromwell's heart. More importantly, they would also sway the Councilors and Parliament.

"Wantonness was everywhere." Cromwell leafed through the book. "For example, when the commissioners arrived at the house of the Crossed Friars in London, they found the prior naked in bed with his whore. Abandoning futile attempts at explanations, the friar leaped out of bed, knelt before the officials and offered them thirty pounds to turn a blind eye."

Norfolk tried one last time. "Surely there must have been some who were honest."

"My Lord," Cromwell replied, "I have to say, even the evidence of their religious natures was far from comforting. As in that story from years ago, about the prior of a religious house who hired a band of cutthroats to commit murder for him."

"That's right, that's right," Wiltshire agreed with a laugh. "He ordered a mortal sin but had the murderers pray with him in his cell before they left to do the deed."

"So we close the small houses," Norfolk reluctantly conceded. "What will happen to the monks and nuns?"

Cromwell suppressed a smile. "We will let it be known that anyone may transfer to a larger establishment. Though I don't expect many will since those who don't will receive small pensions."

"Are there funds for that?" Wiltshire asked.

"The pensions will not be extravagant: we don't want to discourage anyone from working. The monks can become priests, teachers, apothecaries. The nuns will be allowed to return to their families."

The King broke in. "But I must repeat the Duke of Norfolk's question: is this not a reason to be more cautious? To reform rather than to destroy?"

Cromwell saw a smug smile cross Norfolk's face, as if he might have swayed the King. *Fool.* This was part of the pretense.

Too many people were opposed to closing the monasteries; the King needed to show reluctance. He needed to seem to be persuaded to this position by overwhelming evidence. Even the people closest to him needed to be fooled.

It was a credible stance. Henry VIII had been very religious in his youth. As a younger son, he was destined for the Church – a good way for his parents to assure him a rich and powerful position that would support, not threaten, his elder brother. When Martin Luther had posted his ninety-five theses on the door of the All Saints' Church in Wittenberg, Henry was incensed enough to pen a response, *In Defense of the Seven Sacraments*, that earned him the title Defender of the Faith from the Bishop of Rome. The Church of England had arisen from frustration with the Pope, not the King's rejection of Catholic principles. He disagreed violently with many of Luther's ideas, as did most of his realm.

But the dissolution of the monasteries was not just about religion, it was also about money. Cromwell knew his master. When Cromwell had originally proposed investigating the monasteries, the King had stopped breathing for a moment. Cromwell had seen him quickly hood the sudden glitter in his eyes. He could tell Henry's buttocks were twitching over the vast wealth that would come into his hands. Such greed would ensure the success of this venture, carefully cloaked in piety.

Cromwell looked straight into Henry's eyes and spoke firmly. "Nay, Sire. Just the opposite. Your investigators found dishonesty and vice in more than ninety percent of the houses. If you close the smaller ones, you send a strong message throughout the land that these deplorable conditions will not be tolerated. You say you want to save the abbeys; this is the only way."

"Here, here," bellowed Lord Rochford, and many of the men pounded fists on the table in support.

"Of course," Cromwell added, "Your Majesty can decide to exempt certain well-chosen houses from any law enacted.

Provided they prove in some way they are loyal to you and not to the Bishop of Rome."

"This should be part of the bill." Norfolk again.

"Excellent, Your Majesty," said Cromwell. "I shall make sure it is when I present a draft. You shall have it within the week." The bill had already been drafted, but there was no reason to divulge that.

"Does this mean you will support the bill when it is introduced to Parliament?" The King's voice was silky.

"I'll want to see it first," Norfolk answered. "But in principle, yes, I will."

"Er...," stammered the Duke of Suffolk. "What will happen to the houses once they are closed? What will be done with them?"

Cromwell smirked inwardly. The sly grabs for property had begun.

"Many of the houses will simply be shut. We will take their plate of course, also their furniture and other goods. Their chattels, the bells and lead from the buildings. Some of the properties will be sold outright."

"Will we be allowed to purchase them?"

Cromwell gestured toward the King to indicate that this was his prerogative.

Henry looked around the table, locking eyes with each man in turn. "In good time, my loyal friends, you will find that I have plans for each of you. But it would be unseemly to discuss these private arrangements now."

The men sat back in their seats, clearly dazzled by the prospect of their own imminent windfalls. They would support the bill in Parliament, they would get others to do the same. Even the most Catholic among them would not stand up to this.

What fools. Thomas Cromwell was one of the few at the table whose greed and conscience were perfectly aligned right now. Cromwell believed in Luther's teachings. He believed in man's personal connection to God, one that did not depend on the prayers of a corrupt priest . Relics had no magical properties, even real ones had no power to save a soul. That men were ignorant enough to love and trust the monastics didn't matter. In the end, people did what they were told to do. It was the responsibility of a ruler to instruct them well.

Thomas Cromwell took a deep breath to dissolve the religious zeal that had welled up in him. Passion was not right for now. Passion would distract him from the work to be done. He needed a cool head or he could ruin everything. *Never attach to the plan,* he reminded himself. *Remember the ultimate goal.*

The King stood and the rest of the table hurried to their feet. "Thank you, gentlemen," the King said before striding out of the room. He called over his shoulder, "Cromwell, attend me."

THE MOMENT THEY WERE ALONE IN HIS STUDY, THE KING ASKED the question that Cromwell knew burned in His Majesty's mind. "How do you think it went?"

"I think they will support the bill."

The King nodded. "I think so too." Then he shook his head, his upper lip curled. "Especially after they extort properties from me in the name of friendship and loyalty. I am surrounded by serpents."

Cromwell was silent. It was not his place to respond to truths.

"You'll give them the draft next week?"

Cromwell nodded.

"Then I must speak to each of them beforehand. You say you have suggested lists for me?"

"I have lists of all monastic properties that could be consolidated with any of theirs. I also have suggestions about properties they own that you might consider trading with them. This way you won't have to give too much away outright."

The King clapped him on his shoulder. "Good man. Now what is your request?"

"I have none," Cromwell said. "At least not now."

Henry looked at him sideways and waited for the explanation.

"If this is successful, then when we dissolve the next round I would ask to be allowed to purchase Austin Friars. I rent a small house there now. I would love to own the whole of it."

Cromwell kept his voice soft in a show of sincerity. His request was modest, to set himself apart from the wolves that would be too obvious in their greed. It should impress Henry, prompt him to be far more generous than he might otherwise be. Truth be told, Austin Friars should be given to Cromwell outright. He had certainly earned it, and more. He deserved to be made a peer too, a real one. Henry had given him lordships – three small ones, in fact – but those didn't confer real nobility. Cromwell wanted a barony. "Baron Cromwell" had a nice ring to it.

Henry nodded and strode over to look out the window, as if checking for something. Cromwell shifted his gaze to the high arch that framed the King. The craftsmen had done their work well on the carved stone. They should be rewarded with more work – and there would be a lot of that. The King loved to build and remodel palaces. It was one of the reasons the treasury was as empty as it was.

"Now all we have to do is to stop the people from speaking out against me." Henry turned back and slumped in his chair. He crossed his left leg over his right and rubbed his calf.

Cromwell narrowed his eyes, trying to gauge the amount of pain behind the King's eyes. Too much pain might cause him to rage, something Cromwell always hoped to avoid. "That is an issue," Cromwell agreed.

"That is treason."

"Not quite. The clerics preach against the reforms of your Church – not your position as its head. The peasants see God's judgment in the bad harvests – but they blame Queen Anne, not you."

"Which is treason," Henry said. His voice was sharp and angry.

"Yes…" Cromwell drew out the word in a way that managed to convey doubt. "But they would stoutly deny they meant any such harm. These are men who have all sworn the Oath of Succession; they do not attack your rightful power. They merely complain more loudly and more widely than before. Our friend Chapuys has alerted the Emperor to this – the Ambassador's secret letters suggest that as much as two thirds of the country might rise up in support of a Spanish invasion for the Princess Dowager. I believe this is a vast exaggeration."

"Damn Chapuys and his spying! And damn the Emperor and his meddling in my affairs. If only Catherine would die, we could be friends with Spain again."

"Certainly once the Princess Dowager is dead, the Emperor will have no cause to insist you return to her. But we need not wait for that happy day."

Henry narrowed his eyes and cast a sidelong glance at his minister. "So…?"

"I want to spread the news throughout the land that Queen Anne is with child. That will silence all those who speak of God's judgment. It will more than silence them – it will join them to your cause if the Emperor is stupid enough to invade." Cromwell paused to let that sink in. "Then in a few months we will be able to use the wealth from the Church properties to finance the largest army ever seen. That way Rome will solve the very problem it created in the first place."

"When will this be done?"

"You will formally open Parliament right after the Christmas festivities. You will use that opportunity to tell them of the bill and discuss it with them before one of your lords formally introduces it. I'd give them all two or three weeks to debate. You should have the approval by early February."

The King looked at him levelly. "And?"

"A messenger will inform me the moment the vote has been

cast, before all the seals are even affixed, so that we can begin seizures immediately. Assume two months to dismantle a home and transfer its wealth to your treasury. Your coffers will begin to swell by the end of April.

Henry nodded. "Good. We should celebrate. I would go riding. Send for Edward and Tom Seymour – they should come too. And Dudley, and your clerk Wriothesley should join us. I have been enjoying their company of late."

The Seymours. Dudley. Wriothesley. New favorites. For so long the King had relied almost exclusively on George Boleyn and Henry Norris. This did not bode well for the Queen if she failed this time.

"Right away, Your Majesty."

As Cromwell bowed and left, he was careful to hide the smirk he felt. Once again, the lessons of Niccolo Machiavelli had served him well: "Of mankind we may say in general they are fickle, hypocritical, and greedy of gain." How true. Once again, Cromwell blessed the training he had received in his youth, the professions and locations that had exposed him to all the wisdom of the world. Wisdom he used constantly. Wisdom that would make him a peer.

December 16, 1535 ... 3 p.m.

Cromwell was in the King's study at Richmond Palace, along with the King and several artisans expert in plate and jewels. Two tables were loaded with magnificent valuables, part of the process of finalizing the Gift Roll, the list of all the presents the King would give during the New Year's celebration at Greenwich. Every important person at court would give the King a gift and receive one in return. From gilt cups from dukes, to embroidered shirts and crafts from people of lesser ranks, each person would try to enhance their relationship with their sovereign. Then they would analyze the gifts they received to gauge their relative standing with the King.

The King was expected to be generous. It was part of the royal mystique. The people around him benefitted from his openhandedness all year long – small gifts were a constant – but at Christmas time the process was formalized to include everyone in the royal largesse. Cromwell had already prepared a draft with his suggestions, which would get most of the gifts out of the way quickly. The ones for the men mostly involved plate – chalices, flagons, serving pieces – while women, for the most part, received jewels. The size and value of each gift was based primarily on the recipient's rank, a system that minimized resentment. The King approved every gift, and some he insisted on choosing himself. He also specified their value. Cromwell smiled to himself. The world thought him greedy – everyone blamed him if their gifts weren't as rich as they'd hoped – but it was all the King, whose ostentatious generosity hid a private parsimony.

"May I suggest these for the Queen?" said the royal jeweler. He held a tray with polished gemstones, including five stunning diamonds mounted into the shape of a heart. "Or perhaps these golden buttons."

The King shook his head dismissively but leaned forward to examine the tray. With one hand he picked out two heavy gold bracelets with diamonds and pearls, then with the other he selected a fine emerald. "These will be for Mistress Jane," he said with a broad smile. "But hold them aside; I will give them to her privately."

Cromwell made a note on his list as a servant came to collect and file the treasures.

Henry pointed to a dish of pearls. "Do you have any a little smaller? I want to give each of the Queen's ladies three of them to sew into their hoods or dresses. Or perhaps five would be better. Cromwell?"

"Either would be most generous, Your Majesty."

"If they are small enough, I will make it five. For all seven attendants."

"Actually eight, Sire, by my list. Unless you are not including Mistress Jane because of her other gifts."

Henry frowned. "No, I do not want Mistress Jane singled out. Make it four each." He glanced over at the silversmith who held a tray of serving pieces. "Ah, you, let me see those wine flagons. Yes, that's more like it. And those carved basins and ewers. Where are the pieces from Sir William Compton's estate? The gilt plate. The Queen shall have some of those."

"Yes, Your Majesty."

Cromwell stifled a smirk. In previous years, the King had poured on the romance with Anne Boleyn. In 1529 he had given her nineteen diamonds for her head, in recognition of how she wove jewels into her long hair when she wanted to make a special impact. He had also given her two bracelets set with ten diamonds and eight pearls; two diamonds on two hearts for her head; twenty-one rubies artfully arranged into gold shaped like a rose; two borders of cloth of gold for the sleeves of a new gown, trimmed with ten diamonds and eight pearls…yet now he gave her plate. Yes, it helped her achieve the magnificence expected from a queen, but it was so much less personal.

Indeed, Henry's attitude toward Anne Boleyn had altered. Where he had once been the gallant knight completely focused on his lady, he was now the bored husband wanting little to do with his wife. Over-explaining when she asked questions. Offhand where he had once been enthusiastic. Now her fits of pique annoyed him, as well they should. And he spent more time with people who disliked her. A new coalition was forming. Edward Seymour was becoming a confidant of the King, and Seymour's friends were tagging along. Cromwell, of course, was careful to remain one of those friends. It was not terribly hard. They had a history together after all, and had always been on good terms.

"But those crystal-handled forks – yes, that set – put those aside for Edward Seymour and his wife."

Seymour was definitely on the rise. Thanks to his sister.

"Oh, and that gold chalice. Cromwell, that is perfect for you."

Cromwell blinked to avoid showing any reaction. "Sire, I believe that was my gift to you last year."

Henry's eyes narrowed and he turned back to the artisan. "Then give that one to the Duke of Norfolk. Find me another one, a larger one, for Cromwell."

Cromwell bowed. He prayed the gifts would be given together so the good Duke would see that he had been snubbed.

December 20, 1535 ... 5 p.m.

It was late afternoon, shortly before the evening meal, and Jane was as carefree as it was possible to be. The King had managed to spirit her away from her official duties for some quiet time together, a walk in the gardens. It was easy enough for him to do: all he had to do was to send a page for her – that was how he had handled matters when Catherine was his wife and he wanted to see Anne. Now, thankfully, he was more discreet and sent Edward to pretend that a family matter required her presence. Truth be told, though, Anne surely knew the truth. But because of the thousand tiny punishments the Queen inflicted on Jane, she no longer cared how the Queen felt.

As Jane paused at the small staircase that swept down to the formal grounds, she took in the expanse. Gardens were very different in winter than in summer. The plants were cut to the ground; only the outlines of the beds and the spines of the bushes remained to charm. These were the bones of the garden, where its real beauty was seen. This was the time of year that the edging showed off, that the stones on the path gleamed. In the summer they were taken for granted and ignored but in the winter they ruled.

Jane loved this time. The time when true beauty won out over temporary flash. It was her time of year.

She took a deep breath, enjoying the hint of peat in the smell of the chilled earth, and sighed happily. As she walked along the path with the King, it felt like everything was precisely where it was supposed to be.

"What?" he asked.

"Nothing," she answered, embarrassed to be caught so content.

"Mistress, please tell me."

"I was just enjoying this weather. However cold it may get, it is glorious when the sun shines."

He looked at her, then turned his face up to the warmth. "It is indeed." He paused like that for a moment, eyes closed, then took a breath and shook off his trance. "Once again, Mistress, you have reminded me of the pleasure involved in simple things. Thank you."

Jane smiled to herself. The King liked simple things. That was something that Edward and Carew found difficult to grasp. After Henry had acceded to the throne and inherited the vast wealth his father had bled from the land, Henry had gradually abandoned restraint. His overdid opulence reached its apogee during his courtship of Anne Boleyn, when he engaged in expansive – and expensive – building projects. Now he looked to Jane to lead him back to the pleasures of his youth, a simpler time. An innocent time. Jane was the perfect foil to Anne Boleyn, on every level. It was hard not to believe that God had planned this. And smiled upon it.

Still, Jane shook her head. "You always attribute such wonderful thoughts to me, and yet I don't deserve it. I thought to keep that from you because I didn't want you to think me light or foolish."

"You need to stop doubting yourself, Mistress."

She resumed walking, looking down.

He continued. "Like when we hunt. Why do you hang back? You are a better horsewoman than anyone there. You should have the confidence to be next to me always."

Jane smiled up at him. "Your Majesty forgets such a thing

as protocol. Would you have me shove the Duke of Norfolk out of my way, then? I think not." She paused. "And I thank you not to try to force me to stand out. It makes me uncomfortable."

The King laughed. "I know it does, and I shall stop. Not completely, but I will try. But you must do the same." He paused, drawing a package out from inside his doublet. "I ask you to take this token as a visible reminder of our promises."

It was a pair of riding gloves, magnificently embroidered with silk and metal thread, and worked with seed pearls. They were still warm from the heat of his body.

The perfection of the gesture and the moment ceded quickly to doubt. "Another present, and I have given you nothing in return. I shouldn't…," she began.

"Christmas is coming; you will give me a gift then. This is just a small token." Changing tones, he added playfully, "You cannot think I hoped to buy your affection with them. Do you think me so ungallant as to seek to dishonor you for so small a reward?"

Her eyes opened wide and she looked him full in the face. The great amusement in his expression spurred the same reaction in her. She laughed and curtsied. "I cannot argue with that reasoning."

"I would never seek to dishonor you. I ask nothing more than to serve you, to be your knight."

I ask nothing more than to be your knight. Jane felt a savage triumph at his words. Finally he had declared himself, and it had been as Edward and Carew had surmised, as a chivalric knight. He loved her, on her terms.

She felt powerful. She could do this. She could navigate this path. Anne Boleyn herself had shown the way.

That thought brought reality. Anne Boleyn was with child. The King would never leave her if she bore him a son. Jane had to be careful not to get her hopes up. She had to leave it all to God. If the baby were a boy, so be it. If the Queen miscarried as she had before, or if she birthed another girl, Jane had a chance. All she had to do was wait and see.

Jane closed her eyes. Anne had held the King off for more than seven years. Jane only had to hold him off for seven months. It was a good strategy. Especially since it would set her up either way. Edward had already agreed that if the Queen had a son, Jane might become the King's mistress but condition her surrender on his promise to see her well married. That way she would not care about being banished after the affair had run its course; she would have an honorable life no matter what.

One way or another, I will have my life's dream within the year.

The thought was not completely comforting. Who could ever compare to the King? How could she ever cleave to another after this? But the choice was not hers...

"May I serve you?" he asked, and he looked uncertain. "It will be our secret, I swear."

She kept her eyes down and nodded.

They walked without speaking for a time and took turns sneaking glances at each other. Finally the King broke the silence. "This is one of my favorite times of the year," he declared. "I love everything about it – I am even enjoying my fast right now."

It was a relief to be back to innocent enthusiasm. "You don't miss your cheese?" she asked, incredulous. "I crave it every morning, and then again late at night."

"I crave it as much as you do, Mistress. The trick is to relish the virtue of your pain."

Jane lowered her eyes. The huskiness of his voice made it clear that he was talking about more than just the cheese...

"And it will make it all the sweeter when you finally indulge, don't you agree?" he added.

She forced mild distress into her eyes before she raised them. It was a pattern of theirs, like the thrust and parry of a sword fight. The King would say something provocative, then draw back immediately once Jane showed herself to be spooked. Carew and Edward had noticed the tendency, and had worked with Jane to reinforce her reaction – as a way to force the King into the position of protecting the very virtue he hoped to assault.

Indeed, he returned to innocuous banter. "I love best when they come into my rooms in the morning with toasted cheese – I love the texture of the melted wedge with the butter and crispy bread below..." His words trailed off and she looked over at him. His head was back slightly, his eyes were closed but his mouth was open. He was a picture of ecstasy, whether over the thought of the cheese or the virtue of his sacrifice. She cast her eyes down to ignore his pleasure, again blessing Sir Nicholas Carew and even her meddlesome brothers for their insights into the King's character that kept him putty in her hands.

Again he recovered himself and continued in a voice far more matter-of-fact. "I have asked often enough that they now know to add bits of cured bacon – so I can break the entire fast in a single dish."

"Would that your wife have such a palate! She prefers sweets, so our Christmas break-fast is usually *pain-perdu*. Though, last year, it went perfectly with the special treat we had: a sparkling wine devised by Benedictine monks in Carcassonne; they called it Blanquette de Limoux. The French Ambassador sent it to her – it was heavenly."

"He sent some to me as well. My men adored it, so I let them have most of it."

"Ah, you are a kind master." She let her eyes shine at him. She liked the effect it had on him, how it softened his features and put a wistful smile on his face.

"I can be," he said. "Though I am told I insist too much on perfection. I want people to do what I tell them to do, and get angry when tasks are done poorly."

"Well, of course," Jane agreed. "For me, I panic when things are left undone, when people around me don't take things as seriously as I do." She paused, in case he wanted to break in, but when he stayed silent she continued. "I had a difficult few days right before you and the court arrived at Wolf Hall, and I must admit I held my breath the entire time. I didn't want the Seymour name forever to be associated with some accident, like the Duke of Norfolk breaking his arm hunting or playing tennis. Worse, I was terrified we would run out of food. I had visions of bands of rogue courtiers sneaking into town to beg some bread from the locals."

The King threw his head back and roared. When he could breathe again, he answered. "Out of respect for you, I would not have gone with them...though I confess in my youth I might have."

"Yes, from what Father says you might well have."

"Your father? And what does he say?"

"Father has always been impressed with your boldness; he says it is the true mark of royalty. He pointed it out to us often, as a trait he wanted us all to emulate. He was always giving Edward speeches about how great men behave, how they act."

"Not you too?"

"No, I only ever received the mirror version, the list of terrible traits to avoid." Jane laughed. "Only Edward got the helpful speeches, and it was because of what Father called his 'great responsibility' as heir to Wolf Hall. Edward would give me and Tom all the details afterwards."

They were both silent, and then Jane remembered the conversation she had begun earlier. "That was how I learned how you used to sneak out to the villages to go among the people, to share their revels. But I think Father misunderstood you."

"Oh?"

"He tried to tell Edward that it was only in anonymity that anyone could shed the expectations that people had of them. But you told me once that you did this to learn your people's real feelings, to hear them speak with honesty about the things that concerned them. In truth, you were looking for more responsibility, not less."

Just then the sky seemed to darken. The King stood, mesmerized, and took a step toward the horizon. Suddenly he winced.

"Sire?"

"My shoulder. I pulled it in archery the other day and it pains me still."

"If we were inside, I would knead it. I am said to be quite accomplished."

He raised an eyebrow.

"No, really. I used to rub my parents' shoulders. It was the only thing I ever did that my father completely approved of."

The King still looked skeptical, so she continued. "And I do it for your wife all the time – I think it is why she has kept me as one of her maids all these years."

She felt him tense at the mention of his wife. Good. That would keep him in check. And she would be careful to keep the massages therapeutic rather than erotic. Jane knew her place, her strengths. Edward and Carew would love this latest twist. An opportunity to use her innocence to strain his desire all the further. It was a bit early in the game, but by this time he was already kissing Anne Boleyn's dukkys. This was a good move.

CHAPTER FIVE – 1536

JANUARY / FEBRUARY

January 1, 1536 … 1 p.m.

*C*romwell stood as the Spanish Ambassador lumbered into the room. At 44, Eustace Chapuys was a man plagued by pain in his joints, and it showed in the stiff way he walked and stood.

"Thank you for seeing me, Master Cromwell, and on this holiday." He bowed. "I am grateful to you and wish you all the joy of the season."

"I wish the same to you. You are welcome. Please sit."

Gratitude swamped Chapuys' face as he sank into the chair in front of Cromwell's desk. Cromwell smiled. The King would have made the Ambassador stand, deliberate punishment for representing the interests of Spain as well as he did. Cromwell was not so cruel. Not without reason, anyway. And especially not with friends.

"I hope you are enjoying our holiday celebrations, Señor Chapuys." Cromwell hesitated, then twisted his face into a playful grin. "Though I daresay I wish we could get you dancing a bit."

Chapuys chuckled. "Ah, I was never a dancer, even before my dancing days ended." He paused, then continued with an archness to his tone. "Though now I understand your master has reason to dance. I hear he is sending gifts to one Jane Seymour – to the great consternation of the Boleyn family."

"Ah?" Thomas Cromwell kept his tone deliberately vague. If Chapuys sought confirmation of his gossip, he wouldn't get it from Cromwell.

Chapuys raised a single disdainful eyebrow and tried again. "I understand he is quite smitten with Mistress Jane, and tired to satiety of…the Lady."

In the almost three years since Anne Boleyn had been crowned Queen of England, Chapuys had avoided any statement that even suggested acceptance of the situation. In conversation he referred to her as "The Concubine" (or worse), though he was careful to use the kinder "the Lady" with the King. But since the King was not present, Chapuys' discretion indicated he wanted something. Badly.

"Someday you will have to call her Queen, Chapuys," Cromwell replied jovially. "It is the law of the land."

"Your land, not mine."

"Thank the heavens," Cromwell said with a mischievous smile.

"You sadden me, Master Cromwell. I come to you with great joy in this evidence of the King's changing affections, and you mock me."

Cromwell laughed. "The King's lawful wife is with child. The King's affections are fixed on his coming son and heir and there is no room for anything else. You of all people should know this."

"I well understand he is committed to this marriage right now, but I have to say this new interest seems different. I mean no ill, but I live for such rumors. You understand, don't you?"

Cromwell smiled and shrugged in a gesture of agreement that verged on the conspiratorial. Not that his understanding changed anything. While the two men genuinely liked each other and managed to be friends when circumstances permitted, they were locked into their respective positions by the nature of their offices. Both men knew Chapuys would champion Catherine of Aragon until the day she died...a day that was imminent, according to Cromwell's spies. Which was probably why Chapuys was here right now.

"So how can I be of service?" Cromwell asked.

"I need permission to visit the Queen."

"The Princess Dowager," Cromwell corrected.

"My former mistress. I heard several weeks ago that she had recovered from her latest illness, but Dr. Ortiz informs me as a matter of urgency that she has had a serious relapse. I would be with her in her time of need."

"Is it that soon?" Cromwell's voice was level, as if he had no idea.

"Soon enough that I ask that her daughter be allowed to accompany me to say farewell."

Chapuys' voice trembled with passion, and his throat caught on the words. The man was skilled at the art of persuasion, but Cromwell had learned long ago to resist emotional tricks. He kept his countenance neutral. "Señor Chapuys, for the past two years and more, mother and daughter could have been constantly together. All they had to do was accept the King's position as Head of the Church and swear the Oath of Succession."

"How can the King keep his grieving daughter from her dying mother?"

"How grieving is the daughter if she cannot acknowledge the change in her status? How near to death is the mother if she will not admit the truth?"

Chapuys tried again, frustration raising his voice by an octave. "So the Princess Mary may see her mother if she will proclaim her a whore who lay with a man outside of marriage, and the Queen may see her daughter if she names her the bastard product of a sinful union? Is this reasonable?"

The Spanish Ambassador was not the only one who knew how to infuse passion into his voice and manner. Cromwell's face darkened. He thumped his hands on the table and leaned forward, noticing with some satisfaction Chapuys' wide eyes and intake of breath.

"You have repeatedly threatened that the Emperor is a single step away from invasion," Cromwell snarled. "We are not such fools as to do anything that might increase his chance of success."

"I don't understand."

Cromwell snorted and he sat back in his chair. "My dear Chapuys, Catherine of Aragon and her daughter together in the same place – what a temptation for your master to spirit them away and make them symbols to his armies. Do you think we would risk this danger? Let the girl sign the Oath, renounce her right to the English throne. Then we would know her intentions are true."

Cromwell watched as Chapuys hung his head. Good. He understood that Mary would never be allowed to comfort her mother in her final days, and he understood why. Catherine had fought to protect Mary's rights, but now they both must accept the cost.

"I will set aside the issue of Mary," Chapuys said in a thin voice. "Right now, I ask you for me. May I go?"

"Yes."

Chapuys bowed his head again and sighed deeply. "I thank you," he said, and rose to leave.

Cromwell handed him a sheet of vellum with the royal seal already affixed.

"What is this?"

"Your guarantee of safe conduct. Signed by the King's own hand."

Chapuys narrowed his eyes. "So this news comes as no surprise to you."

Cromwell smiled. As if he could be caught out so easily. "We have expected this day for a long time, Señor Chapuys. The permit is undated."

"Ah." Chapuys rose stiffly, grimacing. "I thank you, and I thank your master for your kindness." He bowed to take his leave.

Cromwell nodded and watched Chapuys limp off slowly. Not a bad conversation, after all. Cromwell looked forward to reporting it. Henry would be satisfied their position had been heard, and he would enjoy the self-righteousness of having extended a final visit to his former wife's countryman. Of course Cromwell would not repeat the gossip about Jane Seymour. Not without a need to do so anyway. Not when he wasn't sure of his master's mind.

January 8, 1536 ... 2 p.m.

Jane shielded her eyes and squinted against the sun that brightened the quickly-constructed archery field on a lawn at Greenwich Palace. The King adored the sport, so much so that, in his youth, he had issued a royal decree requiring every Englishman to keep a longbow in his home and teach his sons to shoot properly. (A subsequent decree promised a pardon to any man who accidentally shot a passer-by while fulfilling his obligations under the first decree.) Today, the King defended his long-standing title in a special tournament arranged the night before.

Jane had eschewed the Queen's tent, instead sitting in the stands that ringed the back of the field, safely out of the path of the arrows. She watched as the King prepared to shoot. He was magnificent. Her eyes drank in the sight of him, making her pulse race. He wore yellow from head to toe, except for one white feather in his cap. All to celebrate that Catherine of Aragon had died at dawn the day before, in her lonely exile at Kimbolton Castle.

Jane closed her eyes. Poor sad woman. Even sadder that so few mourned her – and that the ones who did were forced to hide it. When the King received the news, he immediately shared it with the court, exclaiming, "God be praised that we are free from all threat of war." The Queen was with him, and she made a great show of giving the messenger a rich gift to reward him for such glad tidings. There were toasts and hugs and general merriment. Over the death of a good woman who had loved her husband.

Catherine of Aragon had indeed loved her husband. She reminded him so in a final letter, dictated with her eyes closed as life ebbed from her. She ignored all the rancor of the last ten years, forgave him everything, and asked him to be a good father to their daughter. Her last words were the most touching. "Lastly, I make this vow, that my eyes desire you above all things."

Still, that great love had not prevented one final rebuke. She signed the letter not Catherine, but Catherine the Quene. That last claim to her title, read aloud by the secretary, had narrowed the King's eyes to slits, hardening the soft tears that some thought her words had brought to his eyes. It was a stark reminder of how her stubborn insistence on her rights had almost plunged the country into war.

And now the court celebrated. The King and Queen wore yellow, and trumpets heralded their every move, including their procession to Mass that morning. This archery tournament would dominate the day, to be followed by dancing at night. Orders had also been given for a jousting tournament later in the month – it was to be a tourney open to tilters from around the country and would last a full week, so it needed more preparation than could be accomplished in a single night.

Jane sighed. Such a display when so little had changed. Despite the Boleyn's excited claim, "Now I am truly a queen," those who didn't believe in her legitimacy before would not change their minds now. Jane's heart excused the King. He needed an heir, he'd had no choice but to set aside his aged wife. The fault lay with his this new one .

Jane gave a start as her sister-in-law Anne suddenly took the place next to her and began talking in her usual self-important rush. "The Queen has given us all yellow ribbons to wear tonight on our arms. Here is yours."

"You can keep it; I don't want it."

"You must. How angry will the King be if you of all people do not wear it? Edward will not be pleased with this."

Jane took a deep breath before responding, the better to marshal her thoughts. She needed to be guided by her own internal compass, but she needed to understand its direction. A large part of her wanted to do the opposite of what Edward had counseled, if only to teach him to stop trying to control her actions. Lately his advice had been a mess of contradictions, his frustration over the uncertainty of Jane's position leading him to question everything she did. Meanwhile inside her head a soft voice worried that Edward might be right, that the King might be angry at her for flouting his example. She firmly ignored both of those notions, and focused instead on the feeling in her stomach.

"I cannot celebrate such an event," Jane declared firmly. "If Edward thinks the King will be angry with me, then I will claim illness to avoid the situation."

Anne opened her mouth as if to respond, but closed it immediately and pressed her lips together. "I will talk to your brother and let you know what he advises."

Jane shrugged her shoulders, and went back to staring at the King. What a handsome man he was.

January 24, 1536 ... 1 p.m.

It was a flawless winter day. The sun shone, the air was clear and crisp, and the wind was just enough to waggle the banners that flew from every pole. It was the perfect day for a joust.

The lists, the runs where the jousts actually took place, were fenced off in the center of the field. Wooden bench seats had been erected down the sides for the general public, separated from the round tents in galleries that had been constructed at the end of the field for more important guests. Anyone with apartments at court, usually barons and above, had a tent in the first or second row. More tents, adding third and fourth rows to the small village, were offered to mayors, aldermen, and sheriffs who had come with contestants from around the land, representatives of the different craft guilds, even clergymen – at least those who supported the reform cause. Everyone loved a joust.

The Queen had skipped the morning's festivities, preferring to rest quietly in her bedchamber. But she had excused her ladies to allow them to attend and use the well-appointed tent that had been prepared for her in the front row of the pavilion, across from the King's. And so Jane was among the spectators, happy she was there and even happier the Queen was not. While this pregnancy had temporarily and perhaps permanently dashed Jane's hopes of an honest future with the King, it did have its occasional advantages.

Madge stuck her head in the tent and called out to them, "The King is about to tilt."

The women hurried outside, craning to see the course. The King would start from their side of the field, his adversary from the other. He happily acknowledged the well-wishes from the crowd around him, all the while gentling his horse to keep it settled and focused before the contest began. He wore Anne's favor, not Jane's, a handkerchief attached to his arm. That rankled a bit – he could at least have asked Jane for a ribbon he could wear discreetly, something no one else could see – but truly it was better this way. Jane remembered how mortified the young Anne had been when the King had used a joust to declare his love for her. He had tied a banner around his lance that read, "Declare je n'ose" ("Declare I dare not"). As though no one would understand the allusion.

The run began like any other, the riders on each side saluting with great circumstance, then ritually snapping their visors closed and lowering their lances. There was a sudden shout, then a burst of hooves and a continuing thunder as the horses approached each other, separated only by a skinny fence. Each lance was leveled above the fence, aimed directly at its rider's opponent in the hope of unseating him. Suddenly one lance caught and the King was thrown hard from his horse. He landed on his head. His reins, wrapped around his arms, dragged his horse down and it fell on its rider with a metallic thud.

The horse squirmed in a frantic effort to right itself against the hundreds of pounds of metal that pinned him down. Men surrounded it immediately, trying to get close enough to move it off the King crushed below. The King who seemed totally still.

When they finally raised the horse off the King, they ripped off his helmet. He was clearly unconscious, deathly white. Jane tried to run over, but too many others were faster. A solid wall of people rose between her and the King, with more people pressing in every second. She found herself pinned and buffeted, and panic rose in her throat. Cries rang out, information passing from the center of the crowd to onlookers farther away.

"He's not moving."

"He's unconscious."

"He's not breathing."

"He's dead."

Then the group swarmed toward the King's tent, where attendants must be carrying him. Were they worried that he might die right there, in front of a crowd, or did they just want to give him more calm to revive? Please God, let it be the latter.

"Give him room."

"Give him air."

More shoving ensued as the crowd was turned away from accompanying the King's limp body into his tent. Jane stepped back, daunted but still hoping for news. After a few minutes, Edward emerged, tight-lipped and grim faced, and pointed her toward the Queen's tent. Jane held her question until the two were inside. "Is he dead?" she asked.

"I saw his chest move, though it was very faint. He's not dead, but it's not certain yet that he will survive," Edward said with blank eyes. "We need to pray that the Lord will succor His champion."

Madge screamed and ran off, and the other ladies who had been waiting in there followed her. Jane looked around, and seeing no one left, walked over to pour herself a cup of wine. Edward came up behind her and poured himself one as well. The two slumped into nearby chairs.

A giant void enveloped Jane. Why would God do something like this to the King, His faithful servant? Or, more aptly, why would God do something like this to her? All her life, happiness had been snatched from her just as she had begun to believe in it. And now the man she loved might be gone. Yes, she loved him. There, she had said it. Yes, she wanted more than anything to be with him, his wife if she could but his mistress if that were her only option. Now that dream might be shattered. "What happens if he dies?" she asked in a small voice.

Edward took a ragged breath but his voice was matter-of-fact, detailing the possibilities with mathematical precision. "There are three choices, Elizabeth, Mary, and FitzRoy. FitzRoy is the best candidate – a boy, and sixteen – but he is also a bastard with the lowest claim. Normally Elizabeth would not have strong backing, as she is only three. But Parliament and the country have sworn to recognize her as heir. More important, her mother is pregnant with the son that would supplant her."

"What then of Mary?"

"Actually, Mary might be the most likely choice. Especially since Spain will surely invade to support her. But this is all conjecture. It is death to support the wrong candidate. We say nothing until the future is decided."

Jane had to struggle to maintain her composure. It was too terrifying to think what would become of the country without the King. Great Harry, England's beloved leader. She closed her eyes and said three fervent Hail Marys in quick succession, a plea for grace. When she opened her eyes again, Edward was leaning forward in his chair, his elbows propped on his knees, staring at the floor. His face was ashen.

"What happens to me?" she asked quietly.

"You?" Edward asked, as if her question were foolish. "You would probably do best to leave court for a time. We all would, until things are resolved. If Mary wins, we will return – Chapuys knows you love her well. She will accept you happily."

"And if Mary loses?"

"You might well have a place in FitzRoy's court." Edward paused. "Of course, you will not be able to show your face if the Boleyn becomes regent for her daughter."

Jane considered his words, and found that she didn't really care. She felt hollow, as though she had been kicked in the stomach. If the King died, she would spend the rest of her life grieving for a man who had never quite been hers to mourn, lamenting the potential that had existed for a short and blessed time.

A commotion arose outside as people began running back toward the palace. Jane's throat tightened. "Oh my God," she croaked. "Is he dead?"

"I will find out," Edward said, and ran out.

Jane rose to follow him but her knees buckled and she sank to them, praying harder than she ever had in her life.

"He's alive."

Her head jerked up at the shout, and for a moment it meant nothing. Then hot relief flooded her. "Alive?"

"Alive, praise God," Edward confirmed and ran back out. This time Jane followed him in time to see the King walk slowly toward the palace, supported on both sides but still carrying himself. Her first instinct was to run to him, but she checked herself. It was not her right. It was not her place.

Cheers broke out around him; calls of "God save Your Majesty" were everywhere. The celebrations of the masses made her feel a little forlorn. She was no closer to the King than they were, for all his gifts and attention.

Jane stepped back into the tent. She went over to the flagon and poured herself another glass of wine before sinking into her chair and letting giant sobs rack her body.

January 29, 1536 ... 1 p.m.

Jane paused at the entrance to the King's library at Greenwich. It was a glorious room that never failed to take her breath away. Gilt shelves stretched up to a second floor, while windows acted as columns between them to welcome the streaming sun that warmed the room's golden hue. The page rapped his stave to signal Jane's arrival. He had stopped calling her name weeks ago, clearly on the King's orders and even more clearly because of her certain welcome. Jane closed her eyes for a moment in a wave of gratitude and stepped into the room.

For some reason the sight of the King, standing tall and glowing with health, brought to her mind the terror of the other day. It didn't make sense – she had seen him since then, she had been fine those other times. But this time her knees buckled and she sank to them. The King rushed over to raise her up, a look of worry on his face.

"I am sorry, Sire." Jane kept her voice soft, but there was intense emotion behind it. "I am just so glad to see you well."

He brought her hand to his lips. Jane swallowed and continued. "To see you that day, pale and lifeless...it was the most terrible moment of my life."

"I would say mine too, but I missed it."

Jane looked up at him, a little puzzled until she caught up to the joke. His smile was twisted, and she giggled in spite of herself. "You were indeed better placed than the rest of us. Though you missed some of the most intense prayer I have ever known."

"I prayed too, Mistress. I still do. I pray every day that God will give me a son and enough life to see him through his youth.

I pray so much that my knees are raw and aching despite my fine cushions."

He sank into a chair and lowered his head. His anguish stirred Jane and she raced over to kneel before him. "He is protecting you, guiding you. Your wife is with child and you are young enough to..."

As if to stop her babbling, he took her by the arms and raised her up. He turned her around and sat her on his lap, gripping harder as she tried to twist away. "Nay, Jane, stay. I just need to hold you. Your confidence gives me strength. Just stay like this."

The embrace overwhelmed her. A wave of emotion rose up in her and she began to cry, gripped by the intensity of her recent fears and present relief. He held her tighter, stroked her back, and murmured soothing sounds. She felt safe and protected, and she instinctively relaxed. For the first time in a long time, she felt that everything would be just fine.

"You whore!"

Jane startled at the vicious invective and looked up. Anne Boleyn stood in the doorway, her hands clasping her pregnant stomach. The King stood, toppling Jane to the ground as he rushed over to soothe his wife. Anne ignored him: her eyes were only for Jane, who slowly rose to her feet. Anne pushed her husband away in her quest to shove Jane back down to the floor. Her arms flailed, as if to slap Jane, to yank off her hood, to inflict physical harm. The King worked to hold her back. Jane was just trying to leave the room. Finally she raced to the door before turning for the quick bow that even a situation like this required. She saw the King's arms around his wife, Anne's bulging eyes and swinging arms. Jane heard, "Peace, sweetheart, calm yourself," as well as "I want her gone."

She fled.

~

THOMAS CROMWELL SAT AT HIS DESK, SIFTING THROUGH HIS mountain of papers. His office was his favorite room in his rich suite of apartments, rooms that had been given to him largely for the King's convenience. They were right next to the King's, which demonstrated Cromwell's favor. More importantly, they were connected to the King's through a secret hallway. This ability to confer without anyone knowing had proved invaluable during the breach with Rome, shielding their plans completely. It was even more so now while they planned the dissolution of the monasteries. The combination of the Queen's pregnancy and Jane Seymour's virtue meant the King had little to do at night but read and work. And so it had become a regular habit to call for his minister quite late. Far from being annoyed, Cromwell was grateful for the opportunity. He kept his side of the connecting doors constantly open, except during the few short hours when he actually slept.

Right now, though, it was afternoon. A quiet afternoon, save for a commotion earlier when the Queen found Jane Seymour seated on the King's lap. It was not clear how many other people knew of the incident; it was unlikely that even a handful were close enough to hear the Queen's screams. Cromwell was, of course. He had immediately run out into the hallway, but had seen only Lady Rochford ushering the Queen down the hall, her face ashen and her hands clawing at her belly. Not a good sign.

Cromwell had given orders to his most trusted assistant, Ralph Sadler, to station himself outside the Queen's chamber and notify Cromwell the second there was any news. Sadler's looks, good enough to somehow make people open up to him, also often helped him achieve his tasks. Handsome, but not so much as to intimidate. Intelligent brown eyes in a rounded face, with a beard to match the King's.

Now Sadler was at the door, his face grim. "The Queen has miscarried."

Miscarried. And today of all days, the very day that the dead

Princess Dowager was committed to the ground. Poetic revenge, perhaps. "Are you sure? How do you know?"

"Lady Rochford told me. She was on her way to notify the King, and I asked her."

"She told you?"

"She snorted when she saw me. She said 'I should have known' or something like that. And then, 'You can tell your master that the King will be in a foul mood from the news I bear.' It was a boy, by the way."

Cromwell closed his eyes. "Foul mood" was an understatement. Lady Rochford would be lucky to keep her head for such tidings.

"I should go and see if anything is needed," Cromwell said with a sigh.

The King's men were in the hallway, along with some of the Queen's women, whispering together in small groups. Lady Rochford was there, and Cromwell went right over to her. "It was a boy?"

"It was," she answered.

"Why are you out here and not comforting the Queen?"

"The King is with her. I…he may have misunderstood what I told him."

"Why do you say that? What did you say?"

Lady Rochford put her face in her hands. Cromwell had to strain to hear her whispered response. "I…I told him the Queen had delivered of her son. I was about to tell him that he was born dead, that it was before her time, but he raced out of the room too quickly."

Cromwell looked over at the door. "How long has he been in there?"

"You arrived just after him."

Suddenly they heard an angry roar through the closed door. "You killed him."

The response was anguished. "No."

Unintelligible words followed, a combination of the King's

accusations and the Queen's whimpers. Then suddenly the door was open and the King was in the entry, still turned toward his wife. "You will have no more sons by me," he snarled and stomped away.

The King's wild eyes fell on Cromwell. "Attend me," he ordered as he hurried off.

Cromwell had to take two steps to each of the King's to keep up. Henry threw open the door to his apartments, and the wood hit the stone wall with a loud smack that made the minister jump. The door bounced off the wall back to Henry, and he kicked it closed with a growl.

"He is dead," Henry spat. "The Great Whore had him dead." He began pacing in a frenzy of self-absorbed fury, snarling like the lion that was caged in the Tower, the animal a gift from Suleiman the Magnificent, Sultan of the Ottoman Empire, to celebrate their joint hatred of Charles V. Henry's eyes bulged, as if he wrestled internal demons.

Cromwell calmly poured a goblet of wine and handed it to the King, who drained it in two gulps, grabbed the flagon and poured himself another drought. This one was to hold, to sip. He took a deep breath. He was calmer now, but his anger was more menacing. "I see God will not give me male heirs."

Cromwell closed his eyes and bowed his head in a show of silent commiseration.

"It was a son, barely formed and cursed."

Again Cromwell offered a closed-eye bow. There was no comfort he could offer his King, other than to share his grief and horror.

"How could such a thing be? What did she do to it?"

Ah, the blaming had begun. Cromwell kept his eyes lowered, it wouldn't be much longer.

"It had to have been her. I have followed God's word in everything. The evil is in her, not me. I was bewitched into this marriage, and this is my punishment."

Suddenly Henry stopped pacing. He took a deep but ragged

breath and sank to the floor as if in agony. The King knelt, his arms outstretched toward the ornate ceiling. Workers had spent months carving Henry and Anne's initials into every intersection of the decorative rafters, and now those inscriptions formed a thousand raucous testaments to his tragedy. "HA, HA, HA," they mocked, over and over. "Tell me what to do," Henry cried, and the tears streamed from his eyes. Such deep emotion prompted Cromwell to sink to his own knees in respectful solidarity.

Just in time, too, since when Henry received no immediate answer from the ceiling, he looked around for Cromwell. Seeing his minister sharing his pain, the King nodded and sat back, then let his gaze drift away. Cromwell waited patiently, imagining the inner struggle. Over the past year, when Henry had asked Cromwell whether it might be possible to leave this wife, the living Princess of Aragon had stood in his way. Now that all impediments were gone, the King was free to decide whether he truly wanted to proceed down that path. Certainly the seven years he had spent consumed with love for the woman urged caution. Though now that his passion was sated, the deformed fetus and this new interest in Mistress Jane would likely sway him to action.

With a deep sigh, the King turned to his minister. "Will you send Cranmer to me? I need to pray."

"Right away." Cromwell pushed himself to standing and bowed out of the room. *The Boleyn's days were numbered,* he said to himself.

February 15, 1536 ... 3 p.m.

Jane looked around at the circle of ladies tightly surrounding the Queen. Sewing. That's all they seemed to do lately. The Queen was in no mood for dancing or merriment; that left little else. The ladies, as always, sewed clothes for the poor; the Queen embroidered a shirt for the King. Jane stifled a sneer. Catherine of Aragon had continued to complete that wifely duty for years after the King initiated annulment proceedings. Anne Boleyn nagged incessantly for him to stop accepting any more shirts from Catherine, and when Anne was finally allowed to take over that task she trumpeted the change as a grand victory. Jane wondered whether Anne had ever realized that the shirts didn't matter.

Jane was well outside that circle. Since physical proximity to the Queen signaled a lady's relative favor, it was not surprising that Jane was the farthest away. That she was still at court was due to the fact that the King had ultimate control over his wife's ladies. Two years ago, the Queen had tried to dismiss a maid the King had taken as a mistress; the King had intervened, publicly embarrassing Anne and forcing the girl's reinstatement. Anne would not make that mistake again, so Jane was safe. Safe but paired with Jane Rochford, even farther away than the musicians playing quiet, soothing tunes.

Elizabeth and Anne were solidly in the middle – the Queen liked them well enough but punished them for their relationship to Jane. Still, they remained close enough to hear all the bawdy talk. It was the day after the feast of St. Valentine, so loose women told stories of the men who were in love with them and how they had shown it. And exchanged mean advice on how to test their knights' devotion, as if such trickery deserved a place in courtship.

Jane was smug. Her fortunes were on the ascendancy right now; it looked like her dreams might very well come true. If she played her cards well, she might end up married to the man of her dreams. She, Jane Seymour, might end up as Queen of England. The thought made her straighten her back and take a deep breath. She could do this. She would do this.

Yes, the King had sat through a brief dinner with his wife yesterday, but he had left quickly to enjoy a more leisurely meal with Jane. Anne had not been churched yet after the miscarriage; she hadn't been purified from the blood of the child so the King couldn't touch her. Between Anne's pregnancy and her miscarriage, it had been a long time since the King had taken his pleasure with her. It would be a while still, but Jane already knew how she would handle it. Edward, Carew, and Tom had dictated her response.

"You have to make sure you are with the Queen when he visits her. He has to see you there, like he saw you that last time," Tom had said.

"She will make sure of that. She will want me to 'brush her hair so that it gleams,'" Jane replied.

"I don't think she will," Edward said. "It goes against her own game. She always benefitted from being there when the King visited Aragon. Why should she let you play her the same way?"

"You might be right about that," Carew said. "But whether you are there or not matters little. It is just that it is the right timing for you to have the conversation the next day."

"What conversation?"

Carew drew his hands to his chest as if in prayer, and feigned a falsetto. "Your Majesty, you are married and there is no hope for me. I should not come between you and your wife. I am going back to Wolf Hall for a time."

"She can't leave. She'll give up the game if she does," Edward snapped.

"We need to push him to begin thinking about the possibility of change," said Carew. "Fear of her leaving will make him search for ways to keep her."

"You really think this will put this thought in his mind? Surely you can't believe it hasn't already occurred to him?" said Edward.

"It's time to raise the stakes," said Carew. "She needs to force the issue. This is the time to strike – Lent begins a few days after the Queen's churching so that's another forty days of enforced restraint."

Jane was about to add her own objection when the genius of

the plan exploded like a perfect section of orange in her mouth. "He's right," she said.

Edward and Tom look unsure. Carew explained. "You were not yet in the King's household during his earliest days of courting Anne Boleyn. You never saw the many times that Anne Boleyn made a strategic retreat to Hever Castle – or how her absence fueled his desire."

Edward and Tom hadn't, but Jane had. Anne would disappear for months at a time, and return sporting a new piece of jewelry. Or finally a marriage proposal.

Jane thought about that example while the three men debated whether the trick would work again, which depended on whether the King's desire for Jane was as great as it had been for Anne Boleyn. Yet another insulting conversation that Jane threatened to leave. But in the end they had all agreed that retreat to Wolf Hall was an arrow in her quiver that she would use when the King next bedded his wife. Anne would be churched on March ninth, the fortieth day. The next move in the game would be played then. And Jane was ready for it.

"Your stitches are huge, you'll have to do that whole piece again," jeered Madge Shelton, too loudly. Jane jumped. Her cheeks flamed as she realized that all attention was on her. The heat intensified when she looked down at her work and realized that Madge was right. One big disadvantage of the King's attentions was the constant carping Jane had to endure from those who called themselves friends of the Queen.

"What?" It was a single word, but it struck dread into Jane's heart. The Queen had heard the exchange. Worse, the Queen had decided to use the opportunity to confront. She stomped over to tower over Jane. "Show me."

Jane held up the shirt, head bowed.

"Look at me," Anne Boleyn snarled. The vicious slap came as soon as Jane did so. Followed by a pinch on her neck, just below her jaw. "You idiot," the Queen added as she swept back to her chair.

Tears welled up in Jane's eyes. It was so hard to continue this way. Her hands went to the jeweled locket she wore on a chain around her neck, an ornament that had already become a talisman. The strength she derived from touching it was not enough. She had to open it, to smile back at the miniature portrait of the King it contained. He had given it to her the day before, a thoughtful Valentine's Day gift. She snapped it closed but then had to open it again immediately: his gaze brought her comfort and made it easier to bear her lot with the Queen. Jane stared at it, knowing she should get back to work but wanting to enjoy herself just a little while longer.

Suddenly a shadow loomed over her. "Give me that." Before Jane could look up, she felt the locket snatched out of her hands and a sharp pain in her neck where the chain was ripped away. Then a rustle of skirts as the Queen turned and stormed off without another word.

Jane raised her eyes. All the women stared at her, clearly mesmerized by the spectacle, their mouths agape and their faces twisted in disgusted fascination. Jane stood and left the room. Elizabeth followed her.

The hallway was empty. Elizabeth motioned toward a quiet seat at the end. They walked over and installed themselves there.

"Sweet sister, thank you," Jane breathed as soon as they were settled.

But instead of responding in kind, Elizabeth whirled around at her. "How could you do that?" Elizabeth asked.

Jane froze. Elizabeth seemed angry, but that made no sense. "How could I do what?"

"I saw you. Everyone saw you. You deliberately made a great show of opening and closing the locket. You challenged her to notice. You baited her."

Jane felt bewildered. "I did no such thing," she said. But a small voice inside her wondered, *Are you sure?*

"You make things very difficult for me," Elizabeth said in a tight voice. "You know that I owe a great deal to the Queen. I know she can be sharp with you, but she was quite generous with my poor dead husband and me. She persuaded the King to appoint him Governor of Jersey. She granted us a lifetime interest in a manor house, for goodness' sake. And now…"

The cords in Jane's neck tightened. What was her sister thinking? How dare she? "I didn't mean to bait her," she grumbled. "But if I had, would it have been such a terrible thing? She deserves it, and more."

"There is no need to be cruel. You shouldn't—"

"Cruel? Did you not see her attack me? She is the one who is cruel." Jane shook her head. "I am doing no more to her than what she did to good Queen Catherine. Indeed, I am doing considerably less."

Elizabeth rolled her eyes and looked away. The gesture hurt Jane far more than the Queen's slap from earlier. How could her own sister see her as the villain? "I am proud of my actions. My confessor is proud of them too," Jane said. "He agrees I am doing nothing wrong. The decision and action is all with the King, nothing with me."

"Stop it," Elizabeth snapped. "It is all with you. I have heard you plot with Edward and Sir Nicholas. And Anne delights in repeating stories to me as well. This is entirely you and it is wrong. And it is not a game that you will win."

Jane was stunned. How could Elizabeth misconstrue the most important fact in the situation? "You cannot condemn me and defend her. I am God's instrument in Catherine's revenge."

"God's instrument, is that what Edward is telling you? That this work is holy?"

"Elizabeth, I have been chosen for this task. Don't you see the hand of God in this?"

"So you admit that you are actively working to unseat the Queen."

Jane shook her head. How could her sister not understand?

"Mary needs a champion, a savior. The Queen would see her dead, but I would see her restored. And Catherine vindicated."

Elizabeth closed her eyes. "The Princess Dowager was never so kind to me as the Queen. When you fail, she will punish you. And me."

When you fail. Elizabeth didn't think Jane had a chance. That's what this was all about. Jane felt a weight in the pit of her stomach. And then the shame hardened to anger. "You have no part in this. You never had a part in it, just the opposite," she said. "You think I will fail because I am plain and boring. This has been my problem all my life: my own family believe I am too lacking to ever find an admirer. Now I have one. The King finds me attractive. He has honored me above all other women at court, but still that is not enough for you. Well, it is for me."

Elizabeth stayed silent.

Jane continued. "I do not intend to stop. I leave the outcome to God, but I will fulfill my part with whatever I need to do to live my dream. I have done nothing wrong. I will do nothing wrong. My conscience is clear."

Elizabeth shook her head but still said nothing.

Jane opened her mouth to continue to defend herself, but stopped. This was not a time for words, this was a time for deeds. Elizabeth did not believe in her. Most people didn't. Jane could not argue with them; all she could do was wait and hope the outcome would speak for her. She was determined. Hopefully she would succeed.

For the second time that day, Jane Seymour rose to her feet with all the dignity of a queen and swept out of the room.

March 11, 1536 ... 10 a.m.

The King turned to look out the window. Thomas Cromwell took advantage of the moment to shift his weight from one foot to the other. The King was in the middle of an angry tirade, and

Cromwell knew not to call any attention to himself. Life was safer that way.

"I never want to touch her again. You need to get me out of this marriage, Crum. It is robbing me of a real union. Undo this travesty for me."

It was two days after Anne Boleyn's churching. The Queen had been sprinkled with holy water and allowed to return to the King's bed for the first time since her miscarriage. It had been forty days since their last encounter, and because Lent was about to begin, it would be forty more before their next. She must have been overjoyed to have this brief time in which to reconnect with her husband. What a bitter pill to swallow, to find him unresponsive. To say nothing of having to endure the church ritual without a child bouncing on her knee.

"He spoke long ago, but I did not understand. I thought He was testing me, but it was so much more than that." Henry's voice was quiet. "My friends hate her, my country hates her, the world hates her. And now I hate her."

Cromwell narrowed his eyes. This definitely sounded like a firm decision, not a passionate reaction that might be forgotten the next day. Admittedly, the King had leaned in this direction for some time, all the more so since the lingering pain from his near-death experience in January had eroded his patience for any kind of frustration. But until now, there had been a much greater chance that the King might change his mind. Cromwell had seen Anne Boleyn worm her way back into the King's affections many times, usually in bed. Not this time. She had purchased Venetian fringes and tassels of Florentine gold to adorn her great bed. She had commissioned a new tawny orange *robe de chambre* of the finest silk, with lengths of fine ribbon to match. From what Cromwell heard, she had even set out incense all around to remind the King of the Church's blessing. To no avail.

"It can and will be done, Your Majesty."

"When you leave here, go straight to Eustace Chapuys. Tell him I desire peace with the Emperor. Tell him I was bewitched into this marriage by means of sortileges and charms, and that the thorn that bothers them most is about to be removed. Tell them whatever they want to hear to remove all threat of war."

"I understand, Your Majesty."

Henry clapped Cromwell on the back in a gesture that constituted both gratitude and a dismissal. Cromwell bowed out, but paused before he left the protection of the antechamber. He was transported back to the beginning of his career, his days as clerk to Cardinal Thomas Wolsey. Back when the King had decided that God wanted him to annul his marriage to Catherine of Aragon and he had come to Wolsey with the same request – "Get me divorced, whatever you need to do" – and Wolsey had focused on the politics. He had made an arrangement with France to shift the balance of power and force the Pope to rule in the King's favor. It would have been the perfect move, except that Henry refused to marry the French princess who was needed to complete this brilliant political coup. He wanted to marry Anne Boleyn, a woman who hated Wolsey and had vowed his destruction. Both those facts had caught Wolsey by surprise – he had never expected the King to marry his mistress, and he never understood the depth of the grudges people held toward him. Such a smart man to make such stupid mistakes.

Cromwell knew not to be so naive. If the King wanted to marry his mistress again, Cromwell would see to it. It helped that the European political landscape was not at all tempting: France was not a real option right now for a king tired of French manners, and Spain would be reluctant to entrust another of its princesses to the fickle English monarch. A good English bride would fix things nicely.

All Cromwell had to do was wait for the King to decide, though Cromwell was smart enough to have already begun to court the Seymour family. Only two weeks ago, he had maneuvered to have Edward Seymour made a Knight of the King's Privy Chamber – a brilliant move in light of the current circumstances, since it had not only earned Seymour's deep gratitude but also further marginalized the Boleyn faction. Whatever happened to Jane, Cromwell had another firm ally.

Now the question was just about how to procure the annulment. The King had used the word "bewitched." Was that just a product of his irritation or was it more sinister?

CHAPTER SIX – 1536
SPRING

March 21, 1536 ... 11 a.m.

*J*ane sat in the upstairs library at Wolf Hall, sewing to pass the time and distract her from the increasing nervousness she felt. It had been a week since she had left court. The Queen had been churched, and the King had bedded her. She had been smart enough to keep Jane away during his visit, but Jane had still followed through on her plan the next morning.

But instead of protesting, the King had remained quiet, uncommunicative. As if he did not believe Jane would really leave, or did not care. She had never seen him that detached, not since their day in the garden.

She went to find Edward and Carew to tell them about the King's astonishing lack of reaction, and they were as surprised as she was. They tried to reassure her, suggesting that he might just have been tired, or that she may have misunderstood. But no explanation excused the lack of any plea to stay. They had little other advice after that, except for parting words reminding Jane to be patient and strong – which sank her heart even further.

She spent the two days of the journey home staring off without seeing anything. How could he? How could he let her go without a fight, without a word? No attempted reassurance, nothing. Was this just another in the endless string of instances in her life where joy was snatched from her?

By the time she reached home and greeted her parents and Elizabeth, they knew the story already. Tom had ridden ahead to share the situation and explain the strategy, but they had her tell it again over savory pies and cheeses.

"And you thought this would make him want to marry you?" said her father.

"Sir Nicholas thought it would advance the situation and Edward agreed."

Every day, every meal, they made her recount the same story and asked the same questions. Their reactions steadily deteriorated from cautious understanding to utter scorn.

This morning when they broke their fast together, Father sneered after the telling, pronouncing Jane an idiot for her miscalculation. Mother avoided open censure but conveyed her disdain through her curled lip. Elizabeth made Jane feel worst of all. "At least this will stop your declaring yourself God's anointed," she drawled.

Jane opened her mouth to respond, but quickly shut it. What was the use?

Elizabeth continued. "I was right to leave when I did. I would never be allowed back to court if I'd stayed." She paused. "I would be stuck here with you."

Jane looked away. "You never believed the King could love me," she said to the wall.

"I believed the King wanted you, and that you were alienating the Queen by the way you managed him," Elizabeth said. "Be reasonable, Jane. You are a worker, not a beauty or a wit. You value yourself far too highly."

The words of a sister who had always been so supportive were far more painful than the Boleyn's slaps and pinches. Jane's heart plunged, but then the anger she found in the abyss of her despair gave her the clarity that had eluded her. "So this is your judgment of me?" she said, looking her sister in the eye.

"It is time that someone pointed out the truth."

"Mother and Father were doing a fine job." Jane turned away and left. It wasn't worth speaking any more. She valued herself too highly to try. She was right to do so. And she would continue to do so. Her whole life had turned around after she stopped discounting her every attribute, and she refused to stop. She needed to trust herself.

It had only been a week since she'd left court. It was not yet time to worry. The strategy was sound. Anne Boleyn used to spend months at a time at Hever. Jane would win the game only if she dared to play it. She had to be patient.

Agnes's voice broke out from downstairs. "Mistress Jane! Mistress Jane!" she called.

"Jane! Jane!" came Tom's voice through the open window.

Jane looked up and out the glass. She could see a rider at a great distance. His telltale green and white livery was unmistakable. A royal messenger.

Her heart soared. The King missed her. He wanted her back. He cared for her.

A rare feeling of gloating bubbled in her breast, then just as quickly dissipated.

He hadn't come himself.

Did that matter, that he had waited so long to reach out to her, then sent a messenger? Was it reasonable to hope he might come himself? True, he had often ridden to Anne personally, but not always. And Wolf Hall was not Hever Castle, it was not the trip of a morning.

She crossed herself and raced out just as Agnes reached the room. They almost collided in the doorway.

"Mistress, it's a messenger," the woman almost screeched.

"Praise the Lord." The servants all knew what was going on. Servants always knew everything.

"Thank you," Jane said. "Have him come wait on me in the garden. The kitchen garden, by the bee balm."

That was the exact spot where the King came upon her last October. The setting would give her strength and send a statement. The messenger would begin his report to the King, "Mistress Jane received me in the garden." She wanted the King to remember this spot, conjure that day, when he heard her reply.

Tom came upon her downstairs, on her way to go out through the kitchen. "Agnes tells me you will receive the messenger in the garden. Edward and Sir Nicholas would approve."

She smiled and hugged him and hurried on.

When she reached the spot, she turned and arranged her skirts. She folded her hands in front of her and took long, deep breaths to calm herself.

When the King was last there, the garden was coming to its end. Now it was springing back to life. The early cherry trees were pink clouds dotting the somber March sky, and blue and purple lungwort plants splashed sprays of color against the moist earth. She was sorry he was missing this, but she looked forward to telling him about it when she returned to him, as she surely soon would.

Not like she had long to wait. The page practically ran toward her. When he was five feet away, he stopped and bowed.

She lowered her head. "Yes?"

"I bring a present from the King," he said. "And a letter."

She ignored his pompous tone and looked down at his outstretched hands. He proffered a velvet bag in one and extended a sealed letter in the other. She took the bag. It was heavy. She felt the outlines of the gold coins through the fabric, heard their muffled clinking sound. It was an entire purse of sovereigns. There were at least twenty of them in there, more. She could buy Wolf Hall for what was in this bag.

What did it mean? This was fortune enough to provide a

dowry for a fallen woman. Was that what he offered? Was that all she meant to him?

Or was he just trying to express the depth of his remorse? Rich gifts were how the King showed love. Anne Boleyn had been showered with jewels from the earliest days of their relationship: emeralds, rubies, and diamonds, which she then mounted in necklaces, brooches, and tiaras, and even in decorations for her hoods and dresses. The King had supplied her with linen, clothing, and rich furs. He had given her spending money. Far more than this. Yet those gifts all followed Anne's refusal of his advances. He had not as yet made any to Jane.

Was that what was in the letter?

The page shifted from foot to foot, waiting for her answer, but Jane would not be rushed. There was a part of her that wanted more than anything to read his explanation for the delay and his absence, to hear his reassuring words of love. There was a part of her that was terrified at the reality he might be suggesting with his present of money. But there was also a part of her that recognized the opportunity he had, wittingly or unwittingly, presented her.

The perfect verses formed in her mind – *Whoever said I had no talent for poetry?* – and she quickly committed herself to the course of action. She took a deep breath and gave the purse back to the bewildered messenger. Then she took the letter in both hands. Making sure she had his rapt attention, she kissed the seal and then returned that as well. She let the poor man puzzle over the packages in his hands, then threw herself to her knees. "Please, Sir, give the King thanks for the attention he shows me. But also tell him that I have my honor, and I would not harm it for a thousand golden guineas. If the King should like to give me a present of money, I hope he would do so when God sends me a husband to marry."

She rose, curtsied, and returned to the house before he could react, since she didn't know what she would say. All she knew was that no good could come from reading the letter. Far better to play her own game. As long as she didn't know the question, she was not limited by it. She could choose her own message, and she had. She had reminded him of their roles, hers as an honest woman and his as the chivalrous knight who would never dream of dishonoring her. And she had finally refused him. Carew and Edward wanted her to raise the stakes. Well, she had exceeded their wildest hopes.

Her knees were weak as she walked. Yes, she valued herself.

April 5, 1536 ... 1 p.m.

Cromwell's mind was lost in thought, wondering how he would untangle this Gordian knot before him.

He had to do it, and he had to do it quickly. The Queen had become dangerous, she had to be silenced. Three days ago, on Passion Sunday, she had her almoner, John Skip, deliver a sermon on the story of Queen Esther. Skip likened King Henry to King Ahasuerus, deceived by his adviser Haman (Cromwell) into ordering the killing of the Jews (the English clergy). The Jews were saved when the King's mind was changed by his wife, the good Queen Esther – and that was precisely the Boleyn's goal. She wanted to halt all further reform. Skip actually urged the King's councilors to take heed what advice they gave in altering ancient things, warning that people wanted to keep the sacred symbols of the Church.

How dare she take such a position. She had been the flagship of the movement, had pushed the King down the path of reform for her own ends. And now she wanted to retreat from that position? Worse, she intended to destroy Cromwell in the process. Not for the first time, she threatened that she would see his head off his shoulders.

Praise God Cromwell's own interests were aligned with his monarch's here. The King wanted her silenced as well, since her principal complaint was that the monastery gold was not being used to help the poor or further education. She did not understand that her husband wanted the gold for himself – or that he had decided to leave her even before this latest miscalculation.

The King wanted to marry Jane Seymour. The girl had delivered a massive reminder to him of her innocence. The King had sent her a purse of gold, and she had refused it "for her honor." Cromwell had been with the King when the messenger delivered the report of the exchange. Carew and Edward Seymour had been there too. They had each turned deathly pale during the telling, at least until the King reacted. "I like her modesty," the King said. "She reproves us, but gently so."

He made no mention of her use of the words "husband" or "marriage" but instead turned to Edward Seymour. "Sir Edward, tell your sister that I value her honor as much as she does, and to prove it to her I will henceforth speak to her only in your presence – or that of other relatives. Please have her return to court. She belongs here."

The King then announced that he wanted Seymour and Carew to go hawking with him, but pulled Cromwell aside first to inform him that nothing was more important than the speedy annulment of his second marriage. And so it was that for the last three days Cromwell had toiled over the process of replacing Anne Boleyn.

Spain was the first issue on the list, though Cromwell had already dealt with them in part, holding careful conversations with Eustace Chapuys in which they had admitted nothing but agreed on everything. In one of those discussions, Chapuys had casually hinted at the rumors that the King planned to take a new wife, and suggested such news would be more than welcome. "Under the circumstances, I would not but wish him a more gracious mistress."

Because they had been in a public place, Cromwell responded first with words intended to be overheard: "The marriage has turned out to be a solid one, and I believe the King will henceforth live honorably and chastely, continuing in this present marriage..." But then Cromwell covered an obvious smile with his hand and dropped his voice to deliver quiet reassurance: "Though if the King did take another wife, it would certainly not be a French princess."

Chapuys departed with a clear understanding that the cause of enmity between Spain and England was about to be removed without England making a special alliance with France. The letters he wrote to Charles, which Cromwell intercepted and read before sending them on their way, crowed with pleasure over the opportunities this new friendship afforded. Good. That would make Spain more likely to agree to the one requirement that would never be dropped: the acknowledgement of the King's right to govern England as he chose. That would be its own difficult task, but at least the path was eased.

The English people were the next issue on the list. Few of them supported Queen Anne, at least not genuinely. She did have a faction at court that would have to be neutralized somehow. The magnitude of this problem would depend entirely on exactly how the Queen was deposed.

This was the real issue. How to remove her from the throne? Anne Boleyn had to die, that was clear. And this was not just Cromwell killing her before she could kill him. No, this order came from the King. Witchcraft was punishable by death, and that was the charge the King had instructed Cromwell to use. Henry wanted the Boleyn permanently removed to make sure the legitimacy of his next marriage – and therefore the succession – would never be in doubt. He didn't want another instance of an anointed queen fomenting opposition from her exile. Divorced, she would remain Marchioness of Pembroke, a quasi-royal peerage with a rich revenue and an important platform. She had to be silenced. She had to die.

What the King hadn't said, but what Cromwell understood, was that her reputation had to be destroyed in the process. This was a pattern of Henry's that had become part and parcel of how he treated those who chose to defy him – but the pattern began when he first acceded to the throne. A new king, not yet eighteen, he had quickly executed Edmund Dudley and Richard Empson, his father's most hated ministers. Henry VII had been a miserly king who taxed his people severely to solidify his hold on the throne, and Dudley and Empson were the powerful forces behind the harshest measures. By feeding Dudley and Empson to the people, Henry VIII had made himself immensely popular and established his power. No one cared that the charges were not actually treason but only "constructive treason," or that the conduct in question was widely believed to have been made up. No one even cared that their taxes remained unchanged after the executions. All the country's anger had died with the two men, and so it would be with Anne: she would be another goat of Azazel sent out to the wilderness to carry with her the blame for everything from the King's poor choices to the meager harvests and bad rains. Her death would be a grand gesture that would right all wrongs.

In fact, this construct was a relief, since the arguments substantiating annulment were impossibly flawed. Oh, they would be used in the religious proceedings, but only after her impending death was clear. At that point, they would be accepted with minimal scrutiny.

Leviticus prohibited uncovering a brother's nakedness. It was a linguistic stretch to include a sister – and it was the same argument used with Catherine of Aragon. Worst of all, the King had been well aware of the issue before the marriage. If the head of the Church of England were to be considered as infallible as the Pope on matters of religion, he could not admit to such an error in judgment.

The precontract argument was no better. When she had first returned to England from France, Anne Boleyn had a dalliance with Henry Percy, back when he was the son of the Earl of Northumberland. But when the King thought to marry her, it was important to make sure their union would be valid. The young lovers had each sworn before the Archbishops of Canterbury and York, before the King, the King's cannon lawyers, and the Duke of Norfolk, that there had been neither promise to marry nor sexual contact. It would not be easy to reverse those oaths now. Though of course Cromwell had written to Percy to try.

Yes, Cromwell was glad to have a different approach. Except for the sheer difficulty of trying to prove the charge of witch-craft. He couldn't just rely on rumors – even though there had been grumblings of witchcraft since the day the Boleyn had arrived at court, gossip fueled by her black hair, the mole on her throat, and the beginnings of a sixth nail on her left hand. No, he needed to find evidence of some action on her part. He couldn't imagine how he would get it. He needed to question the Queen's ladies – but he had to do it in such a way that didn't alert anyone to his plans. He had to have the facts before he presented the charges, otherwise people would doubt the accusation when it was made and that would be fatal to the outcome. But he was at a loss as to how to draw out those all-important facts without a good pretext…

He felt more than heard the strike of the page's metal staff on the stone floor. "Edward Seymour."

"Ah, Sir Edward," Cromwell smiled.

"Master Cromwell," Edward inclined his head. "I bring you greetings from the King. He sends me to ask if you could attend him no later than three, to prepare him for the audience he has granted the Spanish Ambassador."

"Ah, thank you for the message. I am happy to come now."

"Actually, when I left him he was preparing to show Jane and my wife the latest flowers in the garden."

"All the better," Cromwell reassured. "I will wait on him immediately when Mistress Jane returns to serve the Queen." His voice changed slightly, a teasing note added. "Though I am surprised the Queen let the girl out of her sight."

Edward chuckled. "The Queen does indeed try to keep my sister busy with many tasks. But the Queen has been shut away with Lord Rochford after the fight between the Countess of Worcester and her brother. Hadn't you heard?"

"No, what happened?"

"Well, you know how Lady Elizabeth can get overly flirtatious at times. Sir William chose today to chastise her for her immorality and Lady Elizabeth fired back."

"Fired back?"

"She began to describe all the behavior of other ladies that was worse than hers."

Cromwell snickered. "That must have been quite a list."

"She even argued that it was light of the Queen to admit some of her court to come to her chamber at undue hours. She told her brother he should first cast out the beam from the Queen's eye before examining the mote in hers. By this time she was screaming, and Sir Anthony was pleading with her, terrified that her insults would get back to the King or Queen."

Cromwell waved a dismissive hand. "The Lady Elizabeth is one of the Queen's closest friends, she will be forgiven. And the King would not get angry over this as he had in the past. He—"

Cromwell stopped mid-sentence from the blinding idea that suddenly hit him. He felt a mix of excitement at the solution and annoyance that it hadn't occurred to him already. Adultery. The Queen was a notorious flirt; perhaps she had crossed the line? Regardless, he now had a character witness – and there might be more such gossip he could mine.

Next he needed a paramour. Another thunderbolt: she was shut away with Rochford this very afternoon; she was often shut away with Rochford for hours at a time. Alone. He could charge her not just with adultery but with incest. This neutralized Rochford – the Queen's strongest ally.

Cromwell reeled again as the final pieces of the puzzle fell into place. Deformed fetuses resulted from deviant sexual acts. Now it wouldn't matter if word ever leaked that Anne's dead child had not been fully formed, since this would prove it was entirely her fault. And if word ever spread about the King's occasional impotence, they could point to Anne's crimes. *God's Death.* This was perfect in every way.

"Master Cromwell?" Edward looked a little worried, and that brought Cromwell back to himself.

"My apologies," he boomed, with more happiness in his voice than he had experienced in some time. "I distracted myself, it happens from time to time. May I offer you wine?" It was time for a celebration.

April 18, 1536...1 p.m.

Easter Sunday. The court was at Greenwich Palace, the favorite choice for important holy days because of the magnificence of its Chapel Royal, larger than many churches, with pompous marble and gilt softened by light filtered through massive stained glass windows. The King and Queen proceeded down the corridor, their gentlemen and ladies following behind. They walked slowly and formally, her hand on top of his. He had chosen cloth of gold for his coat; she had selected the same fabric for her pleated gown. It was clear that they had planned their outfits together. Indeed, when the King arrived in the Queen's apartments that morning to fetch her for the parade to the chapel, he whispered a quiet "perfect" before kissing her hand. He hadn't even noticed Jane, at least he hadn't paid her any notice. Several ladies stole glances at her, but Jane ignored them. She understood.

The King and Queen entered the vestry, then paused. Lady Rochford was waiting for them. She curtsied, then nodded. The King looked at his wife and took a deep breath before nodding back. Lady Rochford opened the door to the chapel and the royal couple entered. The ladies began to follow, but the Queen stopped suddenly and turned around. She curtsied. All eyes went to the recipient of the reverence, Eustace Chapuys.

This was the carefully planned moment. The King had explained its significance to Jane the other day, the day Jane had returned to court. Flanked by Edward, she had gone to greet the King in his library. He got down briefly on one knee and kissed her hand, to apologize for the unintended insult of his gift of money and to thank her for returning. The gesture stunned her and she could not respond.

He rose to his feet to put her at ease and called for wine for all of them. When each had a glass, he raised his, and they did likewise. "To new beginnings."

They engaged in innocuous conversation for a short time, then Cromwell arrived. "Ah, Sir Edward," he said after the initial greetings. "You will be interested in this. Thomas Cranmer recently gifted the King a magnificent volume. The illustrations are inspiring."

"Ah? Thank you."

Cromwell turned briefly to the King. "Will you excuse us for a moment?" Cromwell asked. Without waiting for an answer, he took hold of Edward's elbow and guided him over to the other side of the room.

The King in turn guided Jane over to the window seat and they made themselves comfortable. He began talking almost immediately, telling her about the court gossip she had missed, about the latest blooms that graced the gardens. He announced his desire to create a new rockery at Windsor, and the two of them spent almost an hour planning it before the King called to Cromwell and Edward to return from their corner. The conversation quickly became serious.

"Earlier I toasted to new beginnings. This Sunday will be an important new beginning for England."

Jane managed to keep her gaze on the King, but felt Edward steal a glance at her.

"It is the day that Chapuys will bow to my wife or cause a war with England. Cromwell has worked out a scheme."

Jane's insides churned. What sort of new beginning was this? First he told Edward that he valued her virtue, now he was working to advance his wife? Did this mean that he accepted Jane's resolve and respected it? That henceforth he would be happy with his wife? New beginnings. Jane had overplayed her hand and she had lost everything…

"And then I can leave her."

Jane's stomach flipped again. "Your pardon, Sire? I do not understand."

The King looked her deep in the eyes. "I have come to understand that my marriage contravenes God's rules. It should be as if it never was. When that is done, I shall sue for your hand, Mistress."

Jane was stunned. She still didn't understand why Chapuys needed to bow for this to happen, but she pushed that thought aside. Henry had said it. He wanted to marry her. He intended to marry her.

The King turned to Edward. "With your permission, of course. And your father's."

Edward opened his mouth but no sound came out. He just nodded his head while he looked for words to speak.

The King gestured for wine. Cromwell brought the flagon, refilling all their glasses with a small smile on his face.

"All of England will celebrate on our wedding day, all the world too. But before that happens, I must have Spain accept the choice I made and my right to make it, however ill-advised it may have been."

Another flip. "You wish them to deny the Pope and accept you as Supreme Head of the Church?" Jane tried to keep her dismay off her face. They would never do that.

Cromwell broke in. "We do not ask them to deny the Bishop of Rome, only to accept the King's authority in England. That is an important distinction. All Chapuys needs to do is bow to the Queen."

Edward found his voice. "Chapuys has refused to do so for nigh on three years. Surely he will not do so now."

Cromwell smiled. "Ah, but Chapuys has managed to avoid the Queen thus far. If we arrange a confrontation, he will have no choice."

"Pardon me, Master Cromwell, but he could still refuse," Jane said.

"That would be an inexcusable breach of protocol, Mistress Jane," Cromwell said. "It would escalate the situation, even require an apology from Charles to avoid war. Chapuys is too cautious and smart to force his master into such a position."

"By God, I hope you are right," said Edward.

"We shall find out on Sunday. They will come face to face at Easter Mass."

AND NOW THEY HAD.

The Spanish Ambassador let show a stunned look, his face slack jawed. He had carefully averted such a moment, but finally he was caught. Looking slightly dazed, he bowed back.

He had acknowledged the Queen.

The King waved his wife on and went right over to Chapuys. He clapped him on the shoulder and engaged him in friendly conversation as the Queen led the rest of the ladies and gentlemen down the aisle to their seats at the front. The Queen's bearing exuded her triumph, an exaggerated flounce that would have been called a swagger in a man. The entire chapel buzzed, but Jane kept her face impassive. Let the Queen have her moment; it was not the success she thought.

The irony sustained Jane for the rest of the Mass. She kept her eyes downcast to avoid watching how the Queen kept affectionately brushing her husband's shoulder with her own. After the ceremony, Jane showed restrained patience when the Queen looked at her with a smug sneer. "You are excused for the afternoon, Mistress. I shall not have need of you." The fool. Jane ambled off with Edward and Anne to celebrate in Cromwell's apartments.

And what apartments they were. As they entered the Presence Chamber, the anteroom that led to the rest of his suite, Jane was struck by how the arrangement was almost as royal as the

King's own. The room itself was ample, with open doors leading to a sunlit office, as well as two bedchambers. Everything was immaculate, with no personal touches beyond vases of fresh-cut flowers, magnificent silver candelabras and plate, and crystal. That kind of restraint seemed so out of character for Thomas Cromwell. The man had lived everywhere, he knew about everything, he should have collected mementos somehow. Even the man's desk, which Jane could see through the doorway, was pristine. Not a paper in sight, certainly not the pile of documents that she expected from a man with an indelible ink smudge on his middle finger. It almost looked as if he didn't actually live here.

They sat only long enough to pour wine and clink glasses when all of a sudden a section of the wall opened somehow and the King appeared. Jane could see from the open mouths on Edward and Anne that they were as shocked as she was. Cromwell did not act at all surprised. "Ah, Your Majesty, welcome," he said. "I did not expect you to be able to join us."

"I cannot stay long," the King replied, "but I wanted to make sure to thank you. I have long waited for Spain to bow to my sovereignty. Though Chapuys refused my invitation to dine with me in the Queen's apartments."

"One step at a time, Your Majesty. That will be for another day. If you still desire it."

At Cromwell's words, the King turned to Jane. "Has Cromwell spoken to you?" he asked her.

"Beg pardon?" She didn't understand.

"I told you the other day, I have plans for you. I believe my marriage is invalid, and now I am at liberty to begin to establish my case. The Levitical prohibition is clear, and there was also a precontract. The process should not take long."

Jane's insides gripped. Anticipation and excitement rose in her like a river flooding an underground cave.

"I think it is time that you stop serving that woman. It is unseemly. You must have your own apartments."

Jane smiled. She wanted to thank him, but couldn't find the words.

"These apartments."

The words didn't make sense, turn them over though she may.

Cromwell explained. "I have a house at Austin Friars. I stay here only rarely. It would be my pleasure to cede them to your brother and his wife. In this way, the King can visit you without advertising his change of heart. And, more importantly, without damage to your reputation. Of course your family will be ever present during those visits." Cromwell turned to Edward. "Sir Edward, do you accept?"

"With...with pleasure," Edward stammered. "That is, if you're sure. I wouldn't want..."

"I am more than sure, I insist," Cromwell replied. "Indeed, I have already removed my personal effects. The suite has been fully prepared for you."

The King's voice broke in. "Do you accept, Mistress?" His eyes were piercing as he looked deep into hers.

Jane took a deep breath to quell the sudden and curious panic that gripped her over such a quick and dramatic change in her fortunes. "I do," she whispered.

"Excellent," replied the King. "I shall return after dinner."

As suddenly as he had appeared, he was gone and the wall closed up again. Jane looked at Cromwell. "Does the King always arrive so quickly, without warning?"

Cromwell smiled indulgently. "You will learn to hear him coming."

"I actually heard a noise in the hall before he entered," said Anne. "I just had no idea what the noise meant."

Jane turned this information over in her mind. Anne continued. "I will go and fetch our things from the Queen's apartments."

"No need, Mistress Jane," Cromwell said. "I already gave orders to have them brought here. Yours too, Sir Edward. It was done while the court was at Mass. I did not want any attention called to the event. And everything else that you might need or desire has been prepared for you. Allow me to give you a tour now."

Cromwell took them through the rooms, first to the office which opened up much more than could be seen from the doorway. It was a library and study, classic and comfortable like Jane herself, a space that she never wanted to leave. Next was Edward and Anne's bedchamber, with a small garderobe in the back already hung with Anne's gowns.

Right before he led them into Jane's room, Cromwell turned to her. "We thought your sister Elizabeth would share your room when she returned to court. Until your marriage, of course."

"My sister is not planning to return to court," Jane replied. No need to explain that Elizabeth would not return unless and until Jane actually married the King. And even then, Elizabeth might tarry for a time. That decision still rankled and Jane walked in, annoyed.

What she saw made her gasp. A magnificent bed dominated the room. A queen's bed. Below its canopy streamed valances and bases of crimson velvet, works paned with white cloth that looked like silver. The bases were fringed with a narrow border of Venetian gold and silver, and the valances were edged with a double deep trim, one side of red and white silk, the other of Venetian gold and silver. The bed had a counterpane of crimson and white damask bordered in gold, and five curtains to match. It struck Jane immediately that there were no badges featured anywhere, none of the pieces had yet been embroidered. This was the perfect blank canvas for her skills. Her heart softened and a smile curled her lips at the thoughtfulness of this gift.

"Well, then," said Cromwell. "I will take my leave of you and allow you to settle in to your new home. I've taken the liberty of ordering supper to be brought here for you; it will be set up in the Presence Chamber at five. Oh, and your needlework is in the study. I know you'll be looking for that."

After he bowed and left, the three Seymours spent several moments just looking at each other with wide eyes. Anne broke the spell. She dashed over to the rich tapestry that dominated the main wall and ran her hand over it. "This is magnificent," she said.

"These are truly lovely apartments," Jane agreed.

"Aye, but you'll have better ones still, my dear," purred Anne. "Now that the King has declared himself."

"I need to sit down," Edward said, carding a hand through his hair. "I am a little dizzy from all this."

Anne put a solicitous hand on his shoulder. Jane just waited. She was lightheaded herself and she didn't want to move until it passed.

"I like that this arrangement allows the King to visit discreetly," said Edward. "It is best that no one know the extent of your involvement while this necessary business proceeds."

Jane shrugged and walked over to the chest that Cromwell had identified as containing her needlework. It was all there, hers and Anne's, arranged more neatly than Jane could have done herself, along with hoops, frames, and an entire rainbow assortment of yarns. She picked one of the pieces and settled into the window seat. "I suppose that if he can come any time then I must always be ready," Jane said. "Very well. I would be happy to have him find me like this."

Anne walked over to join her. Edward shrugged. He walked over to a nearby table set up for cards and dealt himself a hand. They sat silently for a time in the careful tableau they had created.

"You'll need a motto," Anne remarked suddenly. "You will be Queen of England, part of history. People will tell stories of you as we now tell of Eleanor of Aquitaine and the Empress Matilda."

Edward leaned forward, intrigued. "She needs a motto that will distance her from her predecessor and confirm her place on the right side of legend."

Anne snorted. "Anne Boleyn is universally hated as the witch who seduced the King away from Good Queen Catherine. They call her a whore, the Great Whore, actually. It would be very difficult for Jane to find herself on the wrong side of that legend."

"You are right that she could not choose worse than the Boleyn's," Edward smirked. "It is hard to lose posterity's judgment to the maxim 'Me and Mine.'"

"Well, it did reflect what was going on at the time," Jane chimed in soberly. Jane had spent an enormous amount of time analyzing Anne Boleyn's every action, and Jane actually respected that move for what it was – typical Anne, sarcastic and brash. While Jane carefully shied away from sarcasm, she did need to conjure some of that confidence. Like she did when she refused the purse of gold. "The need to choose it arose very early on in their relationship, when the King's elevated her father to the Earldom of Wiltshire. She was so young then…she did much better with her official motto, 'The Most Happy' – it's what was struck on the commemorative coins issued when she was pregnant."

The three were quiet at this. Edward turned over a card, then continued. "Don't forget about 'Ainsi sera, grogne qui grogne,' which was her favorite until its Spanish origins were explained to her."

"'Let them grumble, this is how it's going to be,'" Anne said absentmindedly.

Jane wondered briefly why Anne had translated from the French, whether she was merely turning it over in her own mind or whether she thought that Jane might not understand the words. Jane carefully suppressed the resentment that her sister-in-law so easily elicited. With Elizabeth gone, Jane was lucky to have any ally and she needed to act accordingly. She responded directly to Edward.

"She knew it was Spanish," Jane said flatly. "That was part of the twisted humor of the choice. Not something I intend to

emulate, though the motto was a fine one for its circumstances."
Indeed. It was the one the Queen had adopted when the King
titled her Marquess of Pembroke. The title made her the highest-
ranking noblewoman in the land, forcing everyone to bow to her
even before she was crowned.

"You should ask him to do something like that for you,"
Anne threw in. "Why not?"

"The real title will come soon enough," Edward snapped. "It
took the Boleyn seven years to reach the point in their relationship that Jane has reached in only seven months. She shouldn't
chance things now."

"Chance?"

Edward rolled his eyes at Anne. "Were you not aware that
the title bought the Boleyn's maidenhead?"

Jane's stomach tightened. She hated thinking about that; it
made her more jealous than she thought she could ever be. The
King had been so...passionate...with the Boleyn. He wasn't like
that with Jane. This incident especially. Edward was making it
out to be just another of the calculated moves on the Boleyn's
part – but it was so more than that. She was elevated right before
they went to visit France together to greet its king and sign a new
treaty. Her triumphant meeting with Francis I, the way she
secured his personal support for their marriage...it transformed
her into the queen she became. Paradoxically, it was the one time
Jane really believed the Queen loved Henry the man more than
Henry the King. And it pushed her to give herself to him in that
romantic castle in Calais, where they stayed closeted in their
rooms for an entire week.

Jane stood quickly, both to banish the memory and to look
down at her brother and his wife. "The King has never pressured
me to cede to him and it would be a mistake to ask him anything
now," she said through tight lips. "It would jar with the careful
course I have charted. I don't need a title before marriage."

Edward began to chime in, but Jane shot him a sharp glance
that stopped him immediately. "Even if he changes his mind

about marrying me, our history would lead him to see me much better placed than I am now."

"You can't expect... "

"I don't expect. That is my strategy. Instead, I see and love the good in him, which encourages him to live up to that higher self. I declare no goals, I only obey and serve."

"There's your motto! 'Bound to Obey and Serve,'" Anne said excitedly.

Edward's eyes glittered. "That is perfect."

Jane stared hard at them, then nodded slowly. "I like it."

"You've already shown yourself to be easygoing in much of your heraldry," Anne said. "It will take little effort for the craftsmen to transform the Boleyn leopard into the Seymour panther." Her point was well taken. A queen's initials, badge and heraldic arms were featured prominently in all aspects of decoration – from wooden carvings in the ceilings to paintings on windows. Dozens of workers had spent the last three years combing the royal residences and replacing the pomegranates of Aragon with the leopards of the Boleyns. Meanwhile, the Queen had spent the last three years berating the craftsmen for the stray places they had missed. Nothing angered her more than being confronted with her predecessor's presence.

Edward nodded. "That will make for a faster transition and much less awkwardness, praise God. But there is still the matter of your badge. You should do something with a Tudor rose – to stress your noble blood. We are descended from Edward III, after all."

"No," Jane broke in firmly. "I had a dream last night that got me thinking about this. I am the love rising from the shambles of his failed marriage to the Boleyn. I am a phoenix and that will be my badge."

Silence greeted the announcement as Edward and Anne tried on the idea. Edward spoke first. "You know the phoenix is also a symbol of self-sacrifice."

"I do know," Jane declared. "All the better."

Anne burst into a broad smile. "I love it. I see it rising from a castle, as you rise from the King and bring the country to safety."

"Well, can we add some roses around its feet?"

Anne laughed at Edward. "You and your roses."

Jane waved her hand. "Actually, I like that idea. But not because I want to stress my royal background – rather, because they are a symbol of fertility, of hope for the future. That is the better message to send."

She lowered her eyes, humbled once again at her great good fortune.

April 23, 1536 ... 3 p.m.

The sun was still high in the sky on a glorious spring day, the air heady with the moist peat that blanketed the ground. Jane tightened the reins on the chestnut palfrey she rode to get him to lift his legs more and adopt a slow *piaffe*. The King, whose own horse already demonstrated the gait, nodded approvingly at her skill.

They were hunting in Greenwich Park, an outing arranged on a whim that – besides Jane and the King – involved Edward, Nicholas Carew, and Will Somers. Thomas Cromwell had promised to join them provided he finished some business.

They had chosen a deer stalk rather than a hunt *par force*, since there were so few of them. The King of course led the small pack, and Jane rode next to him. The Queen's position. She could take that place with honor because she was the only woman there, and was therefore properly paired with the highest-ranking man. But the situation was still awkward, at least until Carew began joking.

"Ah, Your Majesty, you have no more loyal servant than me, but I wish for just one moment that our positions were reversed, so that I could ride with such a pearl of womanhood instead of her brother. Sir Edward is nowhere near as fine."

"I can well understand your envy," laughed the King. "It is a blessing to have Mistress Jane beside me."

"Be thankful you have me, Sir Nicholas," chided Edward. "Otherwise you would be riding with Will Somers, and he tends to wind this time of day."

After that, there was no question where Jane should ride. And of course once Cromwell finished working out the details of the Boleyn annulment, the issue would never arise again.

After a silent but hopeful hour spent stalking deer, the King stopped his horse and looked around. They had slowly wandered the edges of the clearing, taking advantage of the visibility afforded by the bare branches to scan for possible movement. Nothing.

"We'll not eat tonight at this rate," Will whispered and they all laughed.

"Well, I had a splendid day yesterday," said the King. "It must be you, Will, who brought us this ill luck."

"Ah, Sire, you forget I was with you then too. Perhaps we could blame Mistress Jane. Her beauty might be too intimidating to the does."

Jane smiled but said nothing. She had learned that she didn't need to respond to banter, just acknowledge it gracefully. This insight made life so much easier.

I will make a good queen.

She felt a twinge at the unbidden thought. On the one hand, she needed to believe that. It was important that she act as though she already was, to reinforce the decision the King had made. But on the other, she didn't want to be overconfident. There was still nothing that stopped the King from changing his mind. What if the Boleyn seduced him? He had avoided her bed since the night that drove Jane from court, but now the religious injunction was gone. What if he succumbed – and fell back in love with his wife?

Carew swore that the King's heart would not let him abandon the chase before it was over. Edward swore that the politics wouldn't let him. But Jane was not sure. She had never had a man in love with her. Certainly never one who had stayed in love with her through adversity.

Oh, God, please don't take this away.

The sound of approaching horses' hooves interrupted her thoughts. Through the sparse leaves on the trees, they could see a black-robed rider slowly approaching.

"That must be Cromwell," said the King, and blew his horn.

As Cromwell rode up, Carew called out to him. "I say our poor luck is your fault."

"Your words make me think I have not missed much for my diligence," Cromwell laughed.

"You have not," agreed the King.

"Well then, my happiness for my gain is tempered by sadness at your own loss."

The gallantry was typical for Cromwell, but there was a distinctively plaintive note in his voice that struck Jane and made her look at him closely. He looked tired, or rather, hurt and upset.

Apparently she was not the only one to notice. The King remarked as well. "There seems to be a heavy burden on your shoulders, Crum. What is wrong?"

Cromwell closed his eyes briefly and gave a small, rueful smile. "Ah, Sire, I thought to wait until after the hunt to tell you, but there is no hiding from your discernment."

"Go on."

"And, in truth, away from court, surrounded by real friends…this is the best way for you to hear my news."

Jane and Edward exchanged worried glances. She noticed Carew and Somers doing likewise. Only Henry held Cromwell's gaze. The King lifted his chin to signal Cromwell to continue.

"Several days ago I mentioned that I was examining abnormalities. I did not mention that those abnormalities involved your wife."

"Is it a problem with the annulment?"

"It began with the annulment, but reasons quickly arose to expand the inquiry."

Jane had never seen Cromwell act so distressed. It was unlike him enough that she wondered whether he might be manipulating the King. Or even her. Was this a ruse? Was he about to announce that an annulment was not possible? Were her worst fears coming true?

Cromwell sighed. "And now I must go even further, Sire. Tomorrow morning, I will appear before your Council to have it authorize an investigation into unspecified acts of treason."

She inhaled sharply. *Treason?*

"Treason," Cromwell repeated. He turned to Carew. "Sir, you sit on the Council and I ask your discretion until the morrow."

"You have my discretion forever."

"Good." Cromwell turned back to the King. "We have reason to believe your wife has committed adultery. Do you remember Lady Wingfield, one of her ladies a year or so ago?"

Jane remembered her. An older woman, a little lazy. Too haughty to be nice to Jane, though never close with anyone.

"Of course," said Henry.

"Shortly before she passed on, God rest her soul, she cleared her conscience by imparting a distressing tale to one of her own, who shared it with me. I looked into it, and uncovered more allegations. While the formal inquiries have not yet been conducted, I have no doubt of the Queen's guilt."

Adultery. Treason. Jane's fingers tightened on the already taut reins. Anne Boleyn would die for such a crime. How could she think she would get away with something like that?

The King drew back his lips in a snarl. "I married a witch. An evil monster who has spread her wickedness to the world around me."

They all flinched, intimidated by the contempt. Contempt that was quickly replaced by self-righteousness. "James 3:16 tells us that bitter jealousy and selfish ambition is not the wisdom that comes down from above, but is earthly and demonic, and carries with it disorder and every vile practice. And it is true. Look at how she tried to poison my daughter Mary, how she may have poisoned Catherine." He paused a moment, like a preacher letting his words sink in. "Her despicable practices have ruined my life. She has cost me the respect of the world, the love of my subjects. All I ever wanted to do was to follow the Lord's word, and look at how far I have come from that."

"You cannot be blamed for this, Sire," said Cromwell. "You were seduced into this union."

Henry concentrated the full force of his personality on Jane. "She led me astray."

Jane was struck by his intensity. She had become used to his general demeanor, but she had forgotten how persuasive he was. He commanded the very air in a room, and created a physical need to agree with him. He was in pain now, over a heart-breaking betrayal by the woman he had once loved and trusted. Jane's heart flew out to him. "Your Majesty," she said, reaching out to touch his knee.

He grabbed her hand and held it tight against his chest. "I know she was cruel to you. And now this. I am angry, deeply angry."

"I am so sorry you have to endure this," Jane said.

He sniffed. That broke the spell a little – it seemed self-pitying – though goodness knew he had every right to be so.

"This is what it is to be a king," he said. "To be forced to do what most men could not. To use your power for the good of the country."

Immediately she felt guilty over her lack of support. "It is a hard duty," she said, and meant it.

"It is one you will soon share," the King said. "Though I can and will spare you this part now." His eyes flickered at Cromwell, but only for a second. "I don't want you here during this time, close to her evil. It pains me to tell you this, but you must leave court."

Leave court? Why?

The answer burst into her brain. *So people don't blame you for these doings.* Jane's stomach turned over but she made the gesture seem prompted by movement from the horse.

Cromwell broke in. "That is a wise suggestion, Sire, very wise. This is not the place for an honest woman right now. To say nothing of the fact that we would not want Mistress Jane associated with this in any way."

"God, no," said Carew. "She should be far away while such charges are investigated."

Jane couldn't agree more. "I will return to Wolf Hall."

"Nay, you should stay at one of my manors closer by. I want you to be able to return quickly when matters are settled. And I want to be close enough to perhaps even visit from time to time."

"Your Majesty…," Jane began.

"Discreetly, of course," the King said. "You are purity and light in my life. I cannot be away from you for too long."

"Perhaps she could stay at Beddington Park," said Carew. "We used to reach it in half a day. And it is far enough for complete discretion."

Out of the corner of her eye, Jane could see Somers' eyebrows lift. "I know your house well, Sir Nicholas, I've enjoyed its pleasures. Mistress Jane will be most comfortable there."

"I take that as a great kindness, Carew," said the King.

Carew nodded and turned to Edward. "Your wife should of course accompany Mistress Jane. Mine will be there to receive them both. I can vouch for her loyalty and discretion as well as my own."

"Thank you, Sir Nicholas," said Edward.

"I am grateful for your generosity, Sir Nicholas," said Jane. "It will be a pleasure to stay in your home."

The crack of a branch about twenty yards away drew their attention. There was a faint rustle and then a stag stepped out from the woods. With fully twelve points on its antlers, it was regal, majestic.

Henry was the closest to it, and he had a clear shot. He lifted his head, then held up a finger to halt them all. Not that any of them would ever have robbed him of this prize.

Without taking his eye from his quarry, Henry silently reached a hand up and behind himself to draw an arrow from his quiver, his movements achingly slow and graceful to avoid spooking the buck. The other hand raised his bow, equally gradually. The animal's ear twitched, suggesting that it might have discerned movement, but the King froze and waited for his prey to reassure itself that no, it must be mistaken. Only then did he continue his imperceptible but inevitable creep.

Every muscle in Jane's body was clenched. She did not want to move, she barely wanted to breathe. Anything might spook the apprehensive animal.

Somers' horse whinnied, or perhaps it was the pack horse he was guiding, and the hart lifted its head. But Henry was too quick for it. Before it could bolt he had already loosed his arrow, which hit the stag in the neck and dropped it.

They all rode over and circled the still-twitching deer. Carew handed his spear to the King. "Your right, Sire. Both by rank and by deed."

The King let out a proud bellow and stabbed the body with a savage blow. He pulled out the lance, and watched the blood drip from the tip. Instinctively, Jane crossed herself.

"That was perfectly done, Sire," said Edward.

"And it will make for wonderful dishes at tomorrow's supper," said Cromwell. "I shall see to it that the chef prepares accompaniments for it that is worthy of such skill."

"Thank you," said Henry, a self-satisfied smile on his face. "Carew, will you see to the unmaking?"

"I would be honored," Carew answered, bowing.

Carew removed his doublet and threw it over his saddle to begin the ritual, the process by which the deer would be stripped of all humanity in the establishment of their rightful dominion. He laid the deer on its back and crouched in preparation for the first cut, the one that tested the quality of its flesh.

No one sang. Jane flashed back on those early years of the King's courtship of Anne Boleyn, when Anne would sing and Henry would harmonize with her and the company would be moved to tears. Did they expect Jane to perform those honors? Never. At her best, she had a mediocre voice. This was not a contrast with her predecessor that would help her cause. Jane would not sing. But the silence was awkward.

Edward began to croon an old Welsh ballad. It was the perfect choice, appealing to the King's dynastic pride, and making the Boleyn's preferred French or Italian tunes seem patronizing. One by one, they all joined in, and Jane was confident that she was not the only one moved to tears. She shot Edward a grateful smile, and was happy to see the King do the same.

Carew carefully drew his knife along the stag's brisket toward its belly and spread the slashed flesh to be examined by the company.

The King bent down to look closely. "Healthy," he said. "Admirable."

"Perfect," the others chimed in agreement, leaving Carew to dissect the animal.

First he carefully removed the entrails and set them aside. These would be brought to the hunt master's dogs to help their training.

Next came the organs: the liver, the kidney, and the heart. The first two were carefully displayed, approved and packed away, but the heart was cut into six pieces. Carew went in rough order of precedence to offer the morsels, first to the King, next to Jane, then Cromwell, Edward, and Somers. When they all had been served, Carew enjoyed his own piece, licking his fingers with relish.

With that, he set to skinning the animal. Although he was

skillful and worked quickly, Jane's mind wandered, back to the momentous topic that the buck's arrival had interrupted. She turned over in her mind the enormous unanswered question: Who was the Queen's partner in this horrible crime? Jane could not think of a single gentleman to accuse. No man had been with the Queen unchaperoned, except for her brother George. No one had been inappropriate or had been shown special favor. Above all, there had been no catty gossip or raised eyebrows. How astounding that the Queen could have committed such a heinous crime with so little trace.

Assuming the charges were real.

The thought jumped into her mind, but Jane quickly swallowed her concerns. The charges must be real. Cromwell would not indict the anointed Queen of England for a crime she had not committed. That was impossible.

Besides, even if Cromwell would consider such an act, the man she loved would not allow such a travesty. He was a good and honest man. He would never do such a thing.

"And that's it," she heard. Carew had finished.

Somers jumped down to help Carew carefully hoist the carcass over the pack horse, positioning the sharp antlers outwards to avoid hurting the mount.

The congratulations continued as the group rode off back to the palace, though the conversation quickly fell off.

A sneeze behind Jane made her turn around to offer her blessing. She caught sight of the eviscerated stag astride the horse. Its large black eyes stared vacantly and lifelessly. They were Anne's eyes.

Jane shuddered and turned back.

April 30, 1536 … 10 a.m.

Thomas Cromwell looked at Mark Smeaton. It took considerable effort to let nothing show on his face, neither disgust at the man's stupidity nor excitement that Cromwell had landed his fish.

Smeaton was a handsome young musician in the Queen's household who played the lute, the viols, the virginals, and the organ masterfully. The Queen favored him, enough to give him gold for his playing. The inappropriate gift was precisely the opening Cromwell needed. A week ago he had shared certain unspecified "doubts" with the King's Privy Council to get their official approval for his investigations into "treasonous activities," the first necessary step in this tragic comedy. Of course, he had obscured the extent to which the investigation surrounded the Queen – after all, Thomas Boleyn sat on the board, and if he knew he would surely warn his daughter that she was in danger. Not that it mattered anymore. Involving the Council had given Cromwell the pretext he needed to conduct the conversations he wanted to have. He had begun with the Countess of Worcester and Viscountess Rochford – he knew they could provide the evidence he needed to support his claim that the Queen had committed adultery. He had also spoken to every single one of the Queen's ladies, as well as the servants who attended them, looking for other gems. Now Smeaton would provide the incontrovertible proof. This interrogation would nail the coffin shut.

The last hour had been a deliberate jumble of dates and places, and Cromwell could tell that Smeaton was not following it completely. He was an artist, not a lawyer; he wasn't used to such details. Which was helpful because much of the information was invented. As was the excuse for this meeting itself: a maid's complaint that Smeaton did not render honest hours of work for his pay. Cromwell claimed that of course he was prepared to believe his talented friend rather than a common shrew – the Queen wanted it thus – but he needed to document Smeaton's activities. That had loosened the man's tongue and made him work to be helpful. Smeaton had easily agreed with the parts that sounded right – that he was at such and such palace with the court, that so and so was or was not in attendance as he played music for the Queen or taught her a song. And that most of these engagements took place in her Privy Chamber.

Smeaton was less certain of the exact dates but Cromwell was encouraging enough that Smeaton had not quarreled. "Might it help to think harder," Cromwell asked with a furrowed brow when Smeaton questioned one of Cromwell's premises. "I could take you through the timeline again." Most times, that was enough to get Smeaton to concede. Until finally it was all agreed.

"Just a moment, Master Smeaton, I am done with the dates. I just need to organize my notes so you can sign them."

Smeaton waved his hand in invitation. Out of the corner of his eye Cromwell could see him looking around the office, at the bookshelves lining every wall and the tables in front of them stacked with papers. He looked vaguely fascinated and hopeful. Cromwell felt a twinge of pity. The men were, after all, from similar backgrounds: Smeaton was the son of a carpenter, Cromwell the son of a blacksmith. *There but for the grace of God...*

"Are you almost done?"

The words were spoken with a touch of arrogance, and Cromwell's token sympathy quickly turned to contempt. Smeaton was one of those who believed that artists had special rights in this world. He had never shown Cromwell the respect he had earned. "Just one moment," he said, hoping he didn't sound smarmy. "Please help yourself to ale."

In less than five minutes, Cromwell was done. All his papers were in order. The preliminary ones, that is. "Here we are. Now you may sign."

The boy signed with a firm hand. Cromwell took the paper, looked it over, then calmly put it down. Now for the rest of it. "So, Master Smeaton. This past Saturday, you played the virginals for the Queen in her chamber."

Annoyed, Smeaton responded. "I thought we were done."

"Not quite. You played for the Queen this past Saturday?"

"Yes."

"Apparently you had a sad look on your face that attracted

attention. The Queen knew right away that it was for love of her. She cut you down. Reminded you of your low birth, let you know not to expect her to talk to you."

Smeaton cocked his head and sneered. "I would have thought you would be the last person to disparage my parentage."

"You answered 'a look sufficeth, thus fare you well.' Tell me more about why you said that."

Smeaton looked puzzled. "What?"

Cromwell leaned forward, trying to keep the ferocity he felt from showing in his eyes. "It is said that you were in love with the Queen. That she paid you to bed with her to conceive an heir to the throne because the King was unable to."

Smeaton looked at him, his entire being a combination of outrage – and sudden terror. "I never thought to touch her, I barely ever spoke to her. I worship her as any subject worships his queen – but I never was alone with her, I never touched her, I never…anything."

Cromwell looked down at his notes again. The notes Smeaton had signed. "But I have it right here. You are accused of bedding her at Greenwich on June 28, 1534. You were there by your own admission, alone in her Privy Chamber. And here, on—"

"I may have been at Greenwich on that day, but that doesn't mean I ever touched the Queen."

Cromwell spoke, keeping his voice as gentle as a cat's purring. "I have witnesses that suggest you did. I have your own admission as to the dates and the opportunity. I have everything I need, according to the law, to condemn the both of you."

Understanding spread over the musician's face. Cromwell decided to draw out the moment to stress his advantage. He stood and moved to the side table. He picked up the bottle of ale and looked at his guest, deliberately pouring only himself a glass.

"Do you know what the penalty is for adultery with the Queen, Master Smeaton? This is a charge of high treason, no less

– and the penalty reflects the crime. A nobleman would have his head smitten off. He would commit his soul to God, he would kneel, and it would all be over. Such a simple thing."

"But I swear to you, I never…" Smeaton pleaded.

Cromwell simply spoke louder. "But as a commoner, ah, as a commoner the story is quite different. A traitor's death will not be so gentle for you. First you will be hanged for a time, just until your breath comes hard to your body. Then you will be cut down, and your limbs tied to four horses. Grooms will hold the horses in place while your bowels are opened, then the horses will bolt and tear you apart…limb by limb."

"But I didn't…" Smeaton argued weakly, close to fainting.

"I will help you if you help me," Cromwell said harshly. "I want a full confession in this matter. If you give it to me, I will secure the King's mercy for you. You will die the easy death. You have my word on that."

"But I am innocent!" Smeaton claimed.

"If you continue in your obstinacy, I cannot help you." Cromwell paused for a moment, to give the man time to reconsider. When Smeaton remained silent, Cromwell loudly ordered him removed to the Tower. Guards surrounded the youth immediately, twisting his arms behind his back and lifting him until his feet were almost off the ground. Right before they took him away, Cromwell leaned in close. "Remember my word. You can choose at any time to have the easy death."

Then Smeaton was gone, Tower bound. There he would be racked until he confessed. And if it turned out he possessed unexpected fortitude, well, they had the papers he had already signed. There would be no escape from this trap.

CHAPTER SEVEN – 1536
MAY

May 7, 1536 ... 6 p.m.

*J*ane watched the storm approach from the other side of the lake. Fog obscured everything beyond the bank and gradually moved toward her. White foam dotted the churning waves. A bolt of lightning startled her, followed by thunder only seconds later. Part of her wondered whether she should be superstitiously scared by such a display, but the sky hadn't darkened, only grayed. The scene before her glowed with a comforting whitish light. It seemed a kind caution that times might be difficult, but God was with her.

Jane was in the garden that opened out from the master set of apartments at Beddington Park. From London, she and Anne had reached Sir Nicholas Carew's country home in only three hours, and found it as magnificent as promised. Lady Carew had received them warmly, to show that she supported Jane as much as Sir Nicholas did. Of course, the three women had served Catherine of Aragon together, and had always been friendly.

Now the good company made the days pass quickly. The three women rode together in the mornings, across the vast grounds that contained gardens, an orangery, a rockery, a dove-cote, and a giant lake whose size was rivaled only by an enormous deer park. The configuration had been created some one hundred and fifty years before, when Carew's grandfather united two estates. The moated medieval castle had been expanded and modernized, creating a truly regal house with an impressive red brick exterior, and a full banqueting hall topped by a fine hammerbeam roof. The King had stayed here often with Carew back when they were young rakes together, and Jane had been given the King's old quarters. Part of her new royal treatment.

As advertised, it was far enough away that Jane was fully shielded from the goings-on at court, but close enough that Edward could bring them news almost every other day. And what news! Mark Smeaton's shameful confession. The arrests of George Boleyn and Henry Norris. The Queen's hysterical babbling following her arrest and how it had led to the indictments of Francis Weston and William Brereton. A mountain of evidence to seal the fate of a wanton woman.

Yet Jane was troubled. Oh yes, Lady Rochford had often complained that her husband preferred his sister to all other women, and yes, the siblings were often alone in the Queen's bedchamber, but that did not prove incest. And none of the testimony – beyond Smeaton's confession – proved adultery. Even the dates they used were wrong, Jane was sure of it.

"When did these incidents take place?" she had asked.

"The Queen lay with Norris three Octobers ago, and with Weston and Smeaton two Junes ago," Edward replied. "As for Weston and—"

"Wait. That can't be right. Three Octobers ago was 1533, right after she gave birth to the Princess Elizabeth. She was still suffering from white leg – her thigh was swollen to twice its size, and she was making all us ladies miserable with her moaning and complaining. Also, she wasn't churched until late that month."

"Perhaps it was—"

"And two Junes ago – she was big with child then. I remember that, she was only weeks away from taking to her chamber. We were all going to go to France with her after the birth of the son she expected, until she lost it. That is impossible. It..."

"You think the woman would worry about church rules when she is betraying her sacred marriage vows?" Edward had snapped. "Or perhaps I am wrong about the dates. Do you really expect me to be able to repeat every tiny detail? Cromwell is careful; I am sure he has it right."

And now Sir Thomas Wyatt and Richard Page had been arrested as well. Why was Wyatt brought into this? Wyatt, a poet, had adored the Queen long ago when they were still youth in the countryside, before the King had his own interest piqued. Wyatt had even tried to challenge the King as to which of them should be her chief suitor. Jane did not believe the Queen had ever ceded to Wyatt, either before or after the King had declared himself. And Richard Page, a mere hanger-on, was even more unlikely. He and the Queen had long been friends, but he was rarely at court, and truly Jane could never remember him presenting himself in any of the Queen's rooms, not even her quasi-public Presence Chambers.

"Neither of those men seems to have had the level of access to the Queen that the others did," Jane argued. "Their assignations would have to have occurred during a hunt."

"Page made a horrible nuisance of himself when news of the Queen's arrest was about," Edward said. "He called on Cromwell constantly, to dispute him about the details. Of course such behavior aroused suspicion. Why should he so defend the Queen unless he loved her overmuch?"

Perhaps he just believed her innocence, Jane wanted to yell at him. But she could never say that out loud. Instead, she felt her blood chill to ice with fear. This was so different from the plan. Jane was only supposed to unseat the Boleyn the way she had unseated Catherine, and so right that wrong. Jane was

Catherine's God-appointed scourge, the instrument to inflict on Anne the indignities she had herself meted out.

But now the Boleyn was to die and as much as there was a man confessed, some of the evidence seemed wrong. What could Jane do? The voices rose in her head, arguing loudly and vehemently for and against each other. Which one represented the real Jane she could not say.

I prayed for this, but not like this.

She tried to kill Catherine. And Mary. This is fair punishment for that.

But now it lacks the symmetry.

Now it gains the symmetry – Henry leaving Catherine had brought him close to war with Spain and rebellion in his country, and his leaving Anne will restore peace with Spain and calm in the realm.

But death? Surely a lesser penalty would suffice.

The Crown must prevail.

She always ended there, remembering Sir Thomas More, Bishop John Fisher, and the hundreds of men who had died because they refused to recognize the King as head of the Church of England. The dozens executed over the years for other actions that diminished the King's authority. All treason, as this was. To betray God's anointed, however it was done, was punished by death. The whole world knew that. Anne Boleyn certainly did.

The King had turned from her, as he did from all traitors. He spent every night on his barge surrounded by beautiful women who threw themselves at him in the hope of becoming his next wife. Edward said the groups were loud and festive, musicians played gay tunes, and the King tarried until well after midnight every night.

The news troubled Jane. The King had not visited her since she had left court, had not sent her any letters. Only casual greetings through Edward. He might already have tired of her. Oh, God, what would she do if he had?

And with that, as it did every day – nay, every hour – since Jane had heard the news, her turmoil gave way to desperate fear, terror that this all would be taken away from her. She didn't want to go back to her old existence, didn't want to be the sad thing she was in the days before the King. For the first time in her life, Jane felt happy, beautiful, loved. Oh, God, what if that all disappeared?

"Jane?" Anne asked, startling her.

Jane looked around, and realized they were at the other end of the garden already. They had somehow walked more than a furlong. "What?"

"You haven't heard a word we've said."

"I suppose not," Jane admitted.

"I said she would not be burned," Edward repeated.

Jane froze. Of course, that was the choice the King always had. A traitor was burned or beheaded, whichever the King's pleasure decreed. She hadn't considered that Anne Boleyn might be burned. That was too frightening a thought. "No?"

"Cromwell tells me she will even be spared the axe. The King intends to order a swordsman – the Executioner of Calais. He is said to be the most skillful at these things."

Jane lowered her eyes. The Queen had not yet been tried, but her end was already arranged. Jane kept her voice steady. "That is certainly a kinder end than the axe or fire."

"Cromwell must trust you a great deal, to share all this news," Anne simpered. "More important, he must be confident that you will soon be closer to the throne than he himself."

"I was thinking the same thing," Edward said. "He also said something else encouraging. He told me again how much the King missed Jane and hinted that she could come closer to court next week, once the trials are over. The King is in residence at Whitehall now. He would settle her in Chelsea and visit by barge."

"He seems to spend a lot of time on that barge." Anne's tone was arch.

"It is private. Do you understand what his life is right now? He is in hiding. He gives no audiences, attends to no business. He no longer hunts or rides out among his people. He does not come out of his rooms at all during the day, only at night. And even then he will only go to his garden alone or out on his barge. It is his only respite."

"It is not a good thing that all those women are about," said Anne. "That can only be trouble for Jane."

"I disagree," said Edward. "What better way of making sure his love for Jane will go unnoticed but to entertain other women? As for those women, he sees what they are about. He sees they are all trying to capture his attention, and he thinks less of them for that. They reinforce the King's pure love for Jane."

Hearing them address her fears was comforting – but devastating. Even worse, they were talking about her as if she weren't even here. The way they always used to, the way everyone always used to, before the King found her interesting. Oh, God, it was already happening.

"I will be in my rooms," she burst out, then ran off. Anne and Edward called after her, but she ignored both of them. She didn't stop running until she reached her rooms, where she locked herself in before slumping onto the floor and sobbing wildly. She had no idea how long she spent there, but finally her emotions were spent and she felt a little silly. She stood and picked up her needlework, desperate to distract herself. *Thy will, not mine, be done*, she repeated to herself over and over with every stitch she took. She needed to get back to the King or she would go mad.

May 19, 1536 ... 9 a.m.

The Tower of London was an imposing fortress that had served as both royal residence and royal prison since the eleventh century. Every monarch's coronation commenced there and proceeded to Westminster Abbey, to be witnessed by thousands of reverential onlookers shouting praises and blessings. And most criminals' executions began there and proceeded to Tower Hill, to be witnessed by thousands of bloodthirsty spectators shouting unruly curses. Anne Boleyn would be one of the few to experience both those extremes: almost three years earlier she had come to the Tower in triumph for her coronation, and now she was lodged in those same rooms, awaiting her execution.

But she would not be killed on Tower Hill. No, for her they had chosen Tower Green, a private space within the Tower grounds. This choice of venue limited the audience, to spare the Boleyn any jeering insults – and shield the King from harsh judgment for killing his wife. Even so, there were close to a thousand people – lords, aldermen, sheriffs, and representatives of the different crafts guilds – all come to witness the royal justice. Not the King, of course. The King was both the object and the source of justice; other people witnessed it for him. He was represented by his Council, by Thomas Cromwell, the Dukes of Suffolk and Richmond, and the Lord Chancellor Audley. They were in the first row of chairs ringing the scaffold.

The scaffold was arrayed differently than it usually was, since the first English queen ever executed would die by a French sword. That had been the King's idea, and Cromwell still felt nausea from the panic that gripped him when he'd heard. They were discussing her trial when the King blurted, "She shall not be burned. I'll even spare her the axe." Cromwell experienced a period of near-blackness when he thought that the witch had escaped the trap. She would have destroyed him, no doubt of that. Instead, Henry took a deep breath and looked down before he continued, but whether in disgust or regret Cromwell couldn't tell. "She always thought the English so coarse and the French so refined. Let her die as a Frenchwoman. By a sword. See to it."

Whatever his intention, it was mercy, even true chivalry. Too often the English axe was blunt or the executioner inexperienced. It was a fearful spectacle when it took several strokes to sever a head. And fire, well, that was true torment.

Cromwell felt the murmur rise from the crowd, and he turned

to see Anne Boleyn step through the shadows of the arched stone doorway into the sunlight. She was magnificent. Her countenance was untroubled, as if she were preparing to greet an honored guest. For the first time in a long while she looked younger than her 36 years. The dark gray of her damask cloak enhanced her coloring while letting peek a kirtle of deep crimson, the color of martyrdom.

It was a theme she had also invoked the night before. Cromwell had been with the King when William Kingston, Constable of the Tower, had come to inform them the ceremony had been scheduled for the morning – in case there were any final, perhaps countermanding, orders. "Your Majesty, I also have a final message from…the lady." He could not call her Queen, since that title had been removed from her already.

"Go on." The King's teeth were clenched, but he could not avoid this formality.

Kingston shifted his weight from foot to foot. "She didn't give me the message until after I'd promised to repeat her words exactly as she'd spoken them. I had no opportunity to remonstrate with her. She even—"

"Go on," the King repeated, and he sat back as if to brace himself.

"Your Majesty…" Kingston faltered a moment, then continued in a rush. "She said, 'Tell my husband this. That I thank him for ever having been diligent in his career of advancing me. From a private gentlewoman he made me a marchioness. From a marchioness he made me a queen. And now that he has no greater title left to give me, he gives my innocence the crown of martyrdom.'"

When he finished, Kingston immediately bowed low. Cromwell would have loved to join him, but that would have given even greater weight to an already successful barb. Instead, he glared at Kingston just as the King was doing. Out of the corner of his eye, Cromwell could see the vein throbbing in the side of the King's forehead – a sure sign of impending explosion.

"Are you finished?" was all the King said.

Kingston nodded, his cap clasped close to his chest. "Yes, Your Majesty."

"Good. You may go."

After Kingston left, the King called immediately for the barge that would bring him to Jane Seymour. He was done with this wife. He was ready for the next.

Although one last detail remained. Cromwell would see to it.

The Queen – her demeanor entitled her to this name at the last – walked slowly down the aisle, eyes locked in front of her as if to avoid seeing that the blade of every guard's axe was turned toward her. Head held high, she mounted the three steps to the black-draped scaffold. She turned slowly to look out at the crowd, eyes flashing.

Cromwell held his breath over what she would say. Convention required that she speak nothing against the King or the justice that had condemned her. Surely she would not do anything to disadvantage her daughter more than she already was.

Anne Boleyn licked dry lips and took a deep breath. "Good Christian people, I have come hither to die." Her voice was soft yet it rang across the whole of Tower Green as the onlookers stood in utter silence. Gone was the hysteria that had gripped her during the early days after her arrest, the fear that prompted her to unwittingly supply incriminating details that bolstered the case against her. "Norris is accused with me?" she had babbled. "I told him he should not look to have me, that he looked to dead men's shoes." That brought the charge of conspiring to contemplate the death of the King; that was treason by both of them. Or when she had tried to guess the names of the others accused with her, information that had been carefully withheld from her on Cromwell's orders. Her suspicion that it might be Weston and Brereton was enough to condemn those two men.

"I come here only to die, and thus to yield myself humbly to the will of the King, my lord. And if, in my life, I did ever offend the King's grace, surely with my death I do now atone."

Well done.

"I come here to accuse no man, nor to speak anything whereof I am accused, as I know full well that anything I say in my defense does not appertain to you."

As she spoke, Cromwell noticed a slight French accent lilting at the corner of her words, as it hadn't in years. When had she lost the accent she had brought back with her? Catherine of Aragon had kept Spain in her voice forever, but Anne Boleyn had reverted to the rough notes of the Germanic English as the fight to power had toughened her. Over the years, adversity had stiffened her chin and thinned her lips, turning her voice whiny and shrewish. Now she was young again, graceful again, charming again. The flame lucky to flare a last time before burning out.

"I pray and beseech you all, good friends, to pray for the life of the King, my sovereign lord and yours, who is one of the best princes on the face of the earth, who has always treated me so well that better could not be." Her voice quavered a little over this sneer disguised as a compliment, but she recovered quickly and continued.

"I submit to death with good will, humbly asking pardon of all the world. If any person will meddle with my cause, I require him to judge the best. Thus I take my leave of the world, and of you, and I heartily desire you all to pray for me…"

The executioner stepped forward, sword in hand, as her voice trailed off.

She knelt and allowed herself to be blindfolded, then crossed herself slowly. With a last "Jesu have mercy on my soul" she clasped her hands, still upright, and waited for the blow. The executioner slipped off his shoes and called loudly for the sword that was already in his hands. That caused the Boleyn to turn her head slightly to the source of the sound. While she did that, he leaped silently to the other side of her, sword raised behind him.

The patterned steel paused for a moment, glinting in the sun, then swung suddenly in a delicate balance of grace and savagery. Her head was separated so quickly from her body that her lips continued to move in their prayers as it fell to the floor. One of her women quickly threw a handkerchief on top of it to shield it. And so it was over. The crowd had been absolutely silent the entire time, and even now only fervent murmurs could be heard.

"So perish all the King's enemies," came the call.

"Good riddance," Cromwell heard the Duke of Suffolk mumble, and it irked Cromwell immeasurably. That wasn't necessary. The deed was done; there was no reason to gloat. That was hubris. And childish.

For Cromwell, this was not personal. It was practical. It was a question of her or him, her or the safety of the Church, her or the surety of the realm. The choice was clear. Too many people hated her violently, and were beginning to hate the King because of her. Had she borne a son, it would have been different. But God's harsh judgment could not be ignored, and had to be directed at her. This was the best way to do it.

Cromwell felt a slight quiver, a lingering guilt over the men who died with her. But they were needed for the case. And guilty in their own ways. Cromwell had saved Wyatt and Page; he could do no more without endangering himself. And that would serve no one. The woman had to die, and Thomas Cromwell had to make it happen. Moses could stand up to Pharaoh because Moses had been brought up in the palace; Cromwell could fight dirty because he'd been raised on London's streets. Streets he'd never return to.

The King hadn't said anything but Cromwell knew a reward was nigh. Finally, he would have his barony, and probably old monastery spoils as well. He would be a rich peer, he would be safe. Even if he lost the King's favor, Cromwell would live in genteel tranquility. But why should he lose his place? This new queen would not come against him as the Boleyn had. And her brother was a good friend too, not like George Boleyn. Edward

Seymour was a real reformist, and a quick learner. They would do great things together, once Cromwell taught him how.

JANE BENT HER HEAD OVER HER SEWING, FINGERS FLYING AS SHE added pearls to the bodice of a magnificent dress for her trousseau. Half a dozen seamstresses had been hired to make her a series of new gowns and caps of the richest materials, all finer than the last. Silks of reds and purples, cloth woven with silver and gold. The splendor of the fabrics – and the jewels that the King lavished upon her to complement them – made her skin glow and enhanced her appearance. She had never looked so beautiful, and she knew and loved it.

Her terror had given way to subdued excitement. She had surrendered to destiny. She had tried to do it earlier, but it had all been lip service until she resurrected the special trick she learned when she was eight years old. An enormous snowfall that year had blanketed Wolf Hall's countryside with a layer of white that reached to their waists, and the Seymour children had run out to the hill with sleds from the second barn. Jane was jealous of how the others all threw themselves screaming and laughing down the hill, over and over. She had tried to do the same a few times, but her fear always made her put a foot down or turn the handle to slow herself, movements that quickly catapulted her to the ground. But finally she had just surrendered. She stopped trying to control the ride, stopped trying to protect herself. She accepted her precarious balance on the crazy contraption and let the experience unfold. And the strangest thing happened: when she didn't resist, she didn't fall; she enjoyed it. Like now. She was careening down the hill of politics, freed by her acceptance of her complete lack of control. *Thy will, not mine, be done.* Now she meant it. Of course, now there was much less that could go wrong.

As Edward had surmised, the distance afforded by Sir

Nicholas Carew's house was not needed once most of the pieces were in place. Right after the convictions of the Boleyn's paramours, which had sealed the woman's fate, Jane was moved to this new house in Chelsea, only a single mile away from the King at Whitehall. Chelsea Manor was the newest of the royal residences, just acquired from Sir William Sandys. Henry planned to renovate it for his daughter Elizabeth, but it really didn't need anything. It was more than grand enough for immediate use, especially since a contingent of the court's servants had been tasked with outfitting it properly. It was the perfect temporary home for Jane right now, and her moving in there changed everything. The King stopped flirting with other women and began visiting Jane every night. He even began small assaults on her virtue, though she could tell that he was relieved when she stopped him. He loved her modesty; it was part of her charm. They were happy together, blissful together, and all Jane's worries receded. God was smiling on Jane Seymour.

And Jane kept her promise. She spoke to the King about Mary, to right that terrible wrong. The perfect opportunity arose when he announced to her that his marriage had been annulled, observing wistfully that he had no legitimate heirs left.

"Actually, I would hope to see Mary reinstated as heir apparent," Jane said. "You did not know when you begat her that your marriage was invalid, so she was born in legitimacy. Let her be so again."

"You are a fool, sweetheart," he said gently and stroked her cheek. "You should be thinking of the advancement of the children we will have together."

Jane felt a slight twinge at his words but let it pass. That was Anne Boleyn's approach, to insist that Elizabeth unseat Mary. Jane wouldn't need to do that, because God would not deny her sons. "I do think of them, but also of your own piece of mind, for unless you show justice to Mary, your people will never be content."

Henry had said nothing further, but he seized her hand and

brought it to his lips. To her, that was a yes. If not yet, then sometime. He would let her lead him back to righteousness. That was her role, and she would happily fill it. As Queen of England.

SUDDENLY JANE'S BODY WAS SHAKEN BY THE CANNON FIRE OF the Tower's great guns. That was the signal. So perish all the King's enemies. The King's wife – or rather the woman he had worked so long and so hard to make his wife, the woman who had brought him and his realm so much strife, the evil witch – was dead. Jane felt her entire body relax, as if she'd been holding her breath up to this moment. It was done.

She took a deep breath, ignoring the glances from Anne and Edward, and hoisted herself out of her chair to go to the window. Drawing the curtain, she looked out on the glorious May day and opened the casement. The sun shone on the world, and a gentle breeze tickled her face. The water of the Thames stretched out before her, and behind it loomed the spires, turrets, parapets, and merlons of the castles in the distance. The message was clear: there was nothing standing between her and her dreams.

A hint of a shadow crossed the horizon, then quickly disappeared. *Good riddance,* she thought, and crossed herself.

It was a sign, and Jane knew it. There had been others. Like last week, the day after the woman's trial, when the wax tapers around Catherine of Aragon's tomb in Peterborough Cathedral had kindled themselves at the start of the first morning Mass – then quenched themselves without human aid at the singing of the Deo Gratias. The Boleyn's death had restored order and grace to the world. Praise God.

Jane crossed herself again then pushed away from the window. The King would have ridden off at the signal. He would arrive within the hour. She should prepare to receive him.

PART THREE: QUEEN

CHAPTER EIGHT – 1536
SUMMER

May 30, 1536 ... 7 a.m.

*S*ilence surrounded Jane as she walked to the Chelsea Manor dock. Gray clouds crouched low in the sky, indistinguishable from the thick mist that rose from the water. For the second early morning in ten days, Jane Seymour gave her hand to the captain and stepped onto the royal barge.

On May 20, Jane had been rowed the short distance to Hampton Court Palace to be formally betrothed to the King. Edward and Anne had been with her, to witness the signing of the contract, then the three of them had been whisked back to Chelsea to prepare for the wedding. The King was still keeping things secret – remarriage so quickly after a tragedy looked wrong – but the Lord Chamberlain and the Lord Steward had come to confer with her, bearing bolts of gold, silver and purple cloth and another team of seamstresses to prepare still more of the rich gowns that were needed for Jane's new life. They had interviewed Jane in depth and made extensive notes of her habits, favorite dishes, preferred amusements, choices in music, and anything else they deemed important for the chefs, musicians, and servants to know.

Today, Jane was being brought to Whitehall Palace to marry the King, accompanied by Edward, Anne, and Tom. Jane wore a white gown over a light green underskirt, both of which were heavily embroidered with golden designs and adorned with diamonds and pearls. She boarded the barge first, based on the precedence of rank that would soon be hers by right. Her family followed and settled in beside her on the cushioned seats under the canopy that hid them from public view. A quick nod from Edward brought a bellow from the captain. Nine pairs of oars pulled together in unison.

The ride was silent. No musicians played this morning, none were on the boat. Jane gave a start when she felt Anne's hand touch hers to gently point out that she was twiddling the ruby ring the King had placed on her finger the week before. Jane gave a guilty smile in thanks and slipped her treasure back onto her finger, once again completely enchanted with his choice. Rubies were said to be the most powerful gem in the universe, symbols of friendship and love, vitality and royalty. It was the perfect symbol of the promise he had made.

As the white stone spires of Whitehall came into view, Jane shuddered. She was so close to her goal, so very close. It still didn't feel real. She actually felt numb. While she had decided to surrender to her fate, she still had to make that choice over and over. She could not help but be painfully aware that something could easily happen to interfere with her happiness. Just as it always had in the past. Even now. Especially now.

Edward and Anne were equally apprehensive. They both wore dour, determined looks on their faces. Only Tom smiled. Of course. He had been at Wolf Hall for a time, and had missed almost all the drama. And it was in his nature to worry less.

The mile-long trip went by in an instant eternity. As they approached the quay, Jane could see the King's almoner, along with the Lord Chamberlain and Lord Steward and several men at arms. She closed her eyes and breathed deeply to calm herself until they finished docking. Then she gave her hand to the captain to lead her off the barge. When she was on solid ground, the men bowed, holding the pose until Jane's entire family was ashore. She curtsied back.

"Welcome, my lady," said the Lord Chamberlain, holding his hand out for her. "Please come with us."

They took her directly to the Queen's Closet, a private wood-paneled oratory adjoining the imposing Chapel Royal. The King awaited her there, at the altar next to Archbishop Cranmer. They both smiled when they saw her, and she smiled back before dropping her eyes demurely. The almoner took his place at the altar table and it began.

She tried to savor every moment, but the ceremonial Mass flew by until it was time for the vows. Her eyes misted as the King promised to love, comfort, honor, and keep her, and her fingers trembled as he slipped the plain gold band onto her finger. Then he kissed her and she shivered all the way down to her toes.

She was married.

To the King.

As she was still digesting this reality, they turned to receive the congratulations of the people in the room: Jane's family, Thomas Cromwell, and Will Somers. Again, time went by in a blur, until the King stopped and looked at her. "Ready?" he asked.

She nodded, too afraid to speak. He put out his hand for hers, and thus they proceeded to the Great Hall, the others falling in behind them. As they entered the room, Jane noticed that the ceiling had already been reworked to intertwine her initials with the King's, and to display her phoenix in place of the Boleyn's falcon. The walls were festooned with garlands of rosemary and roses, the giant feast table was strewn with flowers. The King's men waited there for them, along with the women who would be her ladies – every one of whom had previously served Anne

Boleyn. They cheered when the couple walked in, yelling "God save Your Majesties" and "God bless you" as they curtsied and bowed happily.

The King led Jane over to the two great chairs of estate that had been prepared for them on a dais, and they sat down. Jane found herself the absolute center of the room's attention. That every single person smiled broadly didn't make it any less terrifying. Thank heaven that it was such a small number of people, only about thirty in all, plus servants. She arched her back, worried about her posture. Would she always be stared at like this? She hadn't thought about that before. It would take some getting used to, even though she had been practicing almost her entire life. Since the age of eight she always pretended that she was being watched, that her confessor was hidden behind a curtain waiting to catch her in sin – or in virtue. The practice stemmed from her parents issuing orders, leaving her, then bursting in without warning to see how well she had obeyed. She had quickly learned to order her life in a way that could bear sudden scrutiny; hiding a pretend witness became a way to get more of the approval she craved. Though now that attention was a bit stifling. And it would only get worse.

The guests approached and began commenting and asking questions, which were thankfully about the future rather than the past. People wanted to hear about the festivities that had been planned to celebrate the wedding, about her upcoming coronation – all topics for the King, not for her. Jane relaxed momentarily, happy to simply smile and nod and add a "Yes, very" or "Yes, thank you" to her new husband's answers. This was another thing she needed to learn, the art of speaking, engaging, conversing. But thankfully not now. Right now she was blessed that her naturally quiet approach sufficed. More divine grace.

"Let us feast!" the King called out, and pages immediately streamed in. First, two burly young men brought a table to the dais and placed it before the King and his new queen. A slimmer man followed them with a cloth to cover it, and two more added the plate – candlesticks and utensils, even a small vase with the red and white roses for which Wolf Hall was famous. Jane was touched by the gesture. She wondered for a moment whether the Lord Chamberlain had sent for the roses specially or whether he'd had new bushes planted in the royal gardens, but her attention quickly returned to a dozen pages in a line, each bearing a salver with a new dish on it. After Jane and Henry had selected their choice morsels, the trays were brought over to the main table at which the rest of the attendants had taken their seats. Jane was in awe. She had seen this happen in the past, but only from that other table. Now it was all happening around her.

Thomas Cranmer, Archbishop of Canterbury, walked over to the dais. In a loud voice he blessed the King and Queen, their union and progeny-to-be, the guests in the room, absent friends, and the entire population of England. His kindness was sweet, welcoming. It was comforting too, given how close an ally he had once been to the Boleyns.

Next Edward stood, his glass raised in his hand. "Forgive me my boldness, Sire, but I must add my own prayers for my King and his queen, my sister. I wish you all the best, and I pray the Lord will bless you above all others."

With that, the crowd turned to the drinking and eating that the occasion heralded. Because of the importance of the occasion, the chefs had been careful to outdo themselves. The main dishes, like *filetes en galentyne*, a pork offering in gravy, were rich and yet still nothing compared to the desserts. Apple fritters and gooseberry tarts with saffron pastry, which would have been enough for the most discerning palate, bowed to the marzipan cakes with gold-leaf cutouts. Jane enjoyed every morsel until, replete, she put a hand on her belly and took a deep breath.

Her new husband reached for her hand to kiss it. "Soon, my dear," he said.

Abrupt understanding shook her newfound confidence and she flushed. The moment she had craved and dreaded for an eternity loomed.

She was proud to belong to that superior species of women able to dominate the base cravings that had caused Eve's – and mankind's – fall. The King loved that about her, and had restrained himself equally to honor her during these past few months. And yet a small voice wondered whether she was just unnatural, whether she would always lack the full passion that other women talked about. Or whether he did.

Jane had come to understand desire from the limited kisses and caresses she had permitted. But Henry always withdrew from his halfhearted assaults on her virtue if she so much as shifted in her chair. Yes, she had worked hard to cultivate this reaction, yes, she appreciated that he loved her virtue, but it meant that this new phase in her life was still shrouded in mystery. The new phase that would begin soon, as he had just reminded her.

But it was still morning. How soon did he intend? Her eyes widened and she cast them down to hide her reaction. Needing something to do, she pushed the leavings around her plate as if neat rows would save her. This first time would set the tone for the rest of their life together. Should it really happen in the light of day?

What if she disappointed him after his experience with the wanton Boleyn, or the exotic Catherine? Or even... Her predecessor's words swirled around her mind, like bats in a cave near sunset. *Ni vertu ni puissance.* What if that was true? What if that was behind his respectful reticence?

Henry leaned over to whisper. "Go ahead and retire now if you wish. I will join you within the hour."

She looked into his eyes and was reassured. She saw love behind them – and a look that melted her fears. There was no reserve in his gaze now. She looked up at him timidly and nodded. She began to stand, but quickly sat back down.

"Do I announce that I am leaving?" she asked. "What do I say?"

A smile spread across his face. It looked proud somehow.

"Lady Seymour," he called out to Anne, "please bring your sister-in-law to her chamber."

A hush came over the room, then a roar and applause.

"To your pleasure," called one of the men.

"And the Queen's," called one of the ladies.

For the first time, it struck Jane just how public this most private of topics would henceforth be. She stood and left the room with as much decorum as was possible under the circumstances.

Once in the Queen's rooms, Anne quickly untied Jane's kirtle. "Let him do with you what he will," she said. "You promised to be *bonnair* and buxom, in bed and at board. Remember, you must emit seed to create a child." The intensity in her eyes was jarring and Jane had to shut her own. Which was helpful, actually. It was easier to bear the pressure of such words if she didn't have to look at Anne as well.

Within minutes Jane stood in her chemise, carefully selected for this very moment. Well, for the moment she had thought would occur twelve hours from now. Jane looked down. The sight calmed her, reminding her how well she'd chosen. The filmy white silk with full sleeves was capped by a neckline wider and deeper than Jane usually wore, and artfully decorated with white thread and seed pearls. The effect matched the paradox of sensual modesty that Jane herself worked so hard to present.

"Here, let me see to your hair," Anne said. She grabbed a brush and added three drops of scented oil to make Jane's hair shine.

Jane drew back, a sudden panicked thought in her mind. Ambergris oil was one of the Boleyn's rituals before a royal coupling. The last thing she wanted to do was conjure such a memory – for either of them. "What scent is that?" she asked.

"Damask rose," Anne quickly answered, understanding.

Jane nodded, relieved. Damask rose was the perfect choice. It was the one Jane used in her pomander, the one Henry loved to grab and hold to his nose himself.

"Take off your hose and get in bed now," Anne said. "I will close the curtains."

Jane watched Anne walk over to the windows, and noticed that the Lord Chamberlain had switched to the lighter-weight summer curtains early, or maybe he had just had new ones hung to reflect the room's new occupant. Either way, she appreciated the gesture, especially when the room darkened enough to lend it an atmosphere much more conducive to what they were about to do. Jane walked over to the great bed, a little unsteady on her feet, and sat down gratefully to remove her stockings. When she didn't move after that, Anne brashly picked up Jane's legs to push them under the covers. That did it. Jane settled in while Anne busied herself, first with positioning the pillows, then grabbing the brush again to arrange Jane's hair carefully over her shoulders. And then, somehow, Anne strew rose petals over the sheets.

"What is this?" Jane asked.

"A magical touch. You are the Queen of England after all, and this is your wedding night."

As Jane digested the thought, the quiet knock came at the inner door. She swallowed before answering. "Come."

Her husband stood there, in a black and tan robe left open to reveal his own white nightshirt. His face was solemn. He stepped into the doorway to let another person in. Archbishop Cranmer.

Jane reflexively pulled the covers up closer around her neck, though she was happy that no one noticed her discomfort or acted like they had.

Cranmer carried a vessel of holy water. He dipped the aspergillum into the aspersorium and cast droplets over the bed then onto the King and Jane. Jane shut her eyes to take a deep breath, comforted and succored by the special blessing. She crossed herself as Cranmer made the sign of the cross over them, and exchanged a small smile with Henry as she saw him do the same. *This would not be so difficult.*

It was back to serious business as Cranmer began to pray, the four of them bowing their heads to strengthen their pleas and the resulting grace. After his amen, they all crossed themselves again, and he smiled and spoke. "May the Lord bless you and your union, and so bless England and your people," he said simply. Then he bowed and walked out, Anne on his heels.

They were alone.

Henry walked over to her slowly, eyes locked with hers. He only looked away when he climbed onto the bed, and then only to draw the bed curtains around them. The room darkened still further when he did, and the small space was as intimate as she could have wished.

He cupped her chin in his hand and leaned in slowly to kiss her. Her heart thumped against her chest and she thought she would scream until his lips touched hers. Soft and full, with a hint of a scratch from his beard. Purposeful and insistent in a way he hadn't been before.

All her fears fell away.

"I love you," she said, and kissed him back.

May 31, 1536 ... 4 a.m.

Jane opened her eyes. It took her a few seconds to realize where she was. In bed. The morning after her wedding night. Awe came over her again. It was all as wonderful as she had ever hoped or dreamed. She giggled in proud embarrassment. It was almost scary how perfect things were. *This too shall pass,* she had always reassured herself in the past when an event brought strong emotion. But in the past the things that passed were disappointments or ills. This was wonder, and she could not bear the idea of losing it. *Stop it,* she thought. *There is no reason to think of loss at such a time.*

The bed curtains were ajar and she could see her new husband in the doorway. He had thrown on the white sleeping tunic that ended just above his knees and bared the fine calves of which he had always been justifiably proud. Their strong shape was familiar to her because of the hose he wore to show them off, but she was mesmerized by the soft reddish fuzz that covered them, and found herself blushing at the intimate sight.

He was whispering instructions to someone on the other side. Probably to have more food sent in, hopefully to have more food sent in. She was starving, even though they had enjoyed almost two full meals in their bed, including some of that Blanquette de Limoux produced by Benedictine monks. A point in favor of preserving the abbeys, she had told him, and he had laughed easily.

Suddenly her wonderful husband was upon her, lying on top of her, his face an inch away from hers, smiling. "You need to wake up, it is time for Mass. Can't miss Lauds on such a blessed day as this."

Lauds. Of course. The gentle ringing of the chapel bells flowed into her awareness. How had she not heard them? She shifted to sit up but Henry didn't move. She giggled nervously, realizing that he was about to love her again, right then. "What about our worship?"

"I told them we were coming. They can wait for us."

His eyes were intense, and almost silenced her until fear made her speak. "But we are to take communion," she whispered.

"We'll not drink or eat anything."

His kiss quashed any response from her, and caused her mind to quickly relent and surrender to the pleasure. All guilt was gone, only joy and triumph remained. *Let them wait,* she thought as sweet languorousness took over. After all, they were the king and queen and this was a holy obligation…

After a short eternity, he rolled off her and kissed the tip of her nose. "Now we can praise the Lord. Again," he said with a mischievous grin that made her smile too.

"It is only proper, after having glorified Him in our body," she said, equally playful.

He nodded approvingly at her allusion to Corinthians, then

rose and grabbed for his robe on the nearby chair. "I will go dress in my rooms and come back for you," he said but then turned and leaned over to kiss her again before he left.

Jane smiled and pulled the covers up to her chin for a moment to hug herself. She would have tarried like that for longer, but too quickly Anne entered the room with a dress over her arm and worried smile on her face. "You are leaving your bed on such a morning?" she asked.

Jane laughed. "We can think of nothing more fitting than to give thanks right now for such a perfect time."

Anne crossed herself. "Praise God. I was so worried when I heard. It was so different from...he never..." Anne took a deep breath before continuing. "I attended Anne Boleyn right after her marriage. They didn't leave her rooms for three days."

Jane's face darkened at her sister-in-law's presumption. *How could she?* "We were quite happy in our bed," Jane said firmly. "There were no ghosts. And I don't appreciate you putting one there." She blushed and grabbed at the gown Anne held, wanting to cover herself.

Anne began to tie the laces of Jane's kirtle and babble apologies that went nowhere. "I didn't mean to suggest...I just thought..."

"We are not lust-driven teenagers, for sweet Jesu's sake. We are the King and Queen of England," Jane said with as much ice in her tone as she could inject.

"No, of course not...it was foolish of me...I should never..."

The abject contrition did its job and Jane's anger passed. There was no reason for it. Jane herself had been secretly worried about her wedding night; she couldn't fault Anne for the same fears. Jane had gotten her reassurance; Anne deserved some too.

Jane took a deep breath and explained. "Our souls touched last night. I cannot begrudge the pleasure my husband once derived from any of his mistresses. I can only thank God for the blessing He has given me now. I ask for no more than that. Can you understand?"

Anne nodded, clearly relieved. "Absolutely," she said, and hummed through the rest of her task.

They were just finishing up when Henry burst back into the room. "Ready, sweetheart?" he asked as he approached to kiss her hand.

Jane felt a slight twinge. The endearment was one he had used with the Boleyn, and she wondered whether Anne noticed this as well. *To hell with Anne,* Jane thought, shocking herself with her reaction. "Ready," she answered.

"We'll not be gone long," he said softly, a conspiratorial grin on his face.

All of a sudden, Anne's fears didn't matter anymore. It was just another incarnation of her old high-handedness – something Jane hadn't accepted for a while. Something she didn't have to accept ever again.

"We'll need food to sustain us," she answered with an equally sly smile. Then, to Anne, "See to it."

June 4, 1536 … 9 a.m.

The morning sun streamed through the stained glass windows of the Chapel Royal at Greenwich, lending the sanctuary a magical glow. Jane glanced over and saw her husband's eyes glued on the priest. She smiled and looked down, gratified at the attention the King was paying to this moment. On most other mornings, he used Mass as an occasion to discuss business – it was actually his favorite time to do so, he said it reminded him that God guided his work. Of course, most other mornings he heard Mass in the oratory in his Privy Chamber, so people weren't generally aware of this habit. Still, Jane was glad that he was fully present to share the importance of this day.

Today was the day that their private honeymoon would come

to an end. Today was the day the entire country would learn that the King had taken a new wife.

For the last three years, during the Eucharistic prayers, every man, woman and child in the country had prayed for the health and well-being of King Henry and Queen Anne. For the last two weeks, they had prayed for King Henry alone; it was how they had learned of the Boleyn's death. Today, they would pray for King Henry and Queen Jane. Would anyone walk out, as they had when Queen Anne had supplanted Queen Catherine in the prayers? Or would they be satisfied that justice had been done?

This was the ultimate test.

"Lord, protect your Church, save it from those that would try to destroy it," intoned the priest.

Jane's mouth went dry. It was beginning.

"Pray, Lord, that King Henry and Queen Jane shall so use their power that your people may lead a quiet and peaceable life in all godliness and honesty."

She closed her eyes, bowed her head, and said the response with all the strength of her heart. "Amen."

The responsatory prayers went on, but Jane had trouble focusing on anything but the noises from the crowd. She kept listening for grumblings, or even whispers, but heard none. Of course, the people hearing Mass with them in the Chapel Royal already knew of the marriage. They would not react badly. No, she would have to wait until they heard the reports from the dioceses across the land.

In the meantime, a series of celebrations had been scheduled to cement her role. Her husband and Cromwell had carefully designed them to give her measured steps on her path out of obscurity. On the morrow, Jane would preside with the King to elevate Edward to Viscount Beauchamp of Hache (Thomas was not altogether left out: he would be made a gentleman of the Privy Chamber). On Tuesday, Jane would be presented to court at a dinner that, while technically public, still only assembled one hundred fifty people. For several days after that, she would preside over pageants and masques from a safe vantage point on a raised dais. Next weekend, the spectacles would move to the river and culminate in a full procession from Greenwich to Westminster so that she could be formally presented to the country and the world. Cheering Londoners would line the banks and litter the Thames, and then more than a thousand courtiers and foreign dignitaries would crowd Westminster's Great Hall.

Jane took a deep breath. For now, things were still relatively private and her husband was patient with her nervousness. He even seemed to enjoy her anxiety; it brought out all his gallantry as he praised every improvement in her skill.

He also delighted in sharing with her Cromwell's daily reports of people's reactions to her – and she loved to hear them, though modesty made her hate to admit it. She especially loved the comments that people made privately, though it had taken her a bit to come to terms with the extent and efficiency of Cromwell's spy network. He had actually managed to collect copies of every letter that had been sent abroad to report on the change in queens. So Jane had been able to hear that Sir John Russell had told Lord Lisle, "The King hath come out of hell into heaven for the gentleness in this and the cursedness and the unhappiness in the other." Other reports had been equally kind – and Jane so desperately wanted the approval to continue. She had been so confident that she could handle this; it surprised her that she was so gripped by fear in this moment. It was as if the hum of the invisible crowd had reawakened all Jane's shyness and reticence.

The pox on any naysayers, she thought to herself. Her brother's advice echoed in her mind: the world wanted Jane to succeed, so they would be gentle to her in this journey. So far, he was right. Jane looked over at her husband and rested her hand lightly on his knee. Her wedding ring glinted in the light, the thick gold band a reassuring reminder of sincere love. He smiled warmly at her.

When Mass was finally over, they walked down the center aisle together, smiling as they went.

"You should return to your apartments. I will fetch Chapuys and meet you there," Henry said to her right before he kissed her hand. Jane nodded and led off her ladies as instructed.

Back in her apartments, she went straight to her chair of estate to await this audience. She was glad she could sit for a bit, even though she had been sitting for the last hour. Nervousness made her unsteady on her feet, and this would be, after all, her first audience. What a relief to be able to compose herself first and cool the furnace in her chest beforehand.

"May I bring your needlework, Your Majesty?" asked Lady Zouche.

"Thank you, yes," Jane answered. Small mercies. Sewing always did calm her down. Industriousness reassured her, made her feel worthy. And it fit the impression she wanted to convey. "The altar cloth."

She and her ladies were working altar cloths for the Chapel Royal. Anne Boleyn had focused on shirts for the poor...but Anne Boleyn's needle skills were not as strong as Jane's. Jane would give coins to the poor and focus her skills on the Lord. That had been an easy decision.

"Mistress Coffin, will you read devotions for us?" Jane asked. That was another part of the tableau – and a good way to quash the loose gossip that had so often accompanied the sewing in the Boleyn's day. That and requiring her ladies to dress more modestly. No more French hoods, for one.

Suddenly she heard a slight commotion at the entrance to her apartments. Her husband had arrived, and was leading the Ambassador to her. She looked up with the smile she had carefully practiced with Anne and Edward, a close-lipped welcome that accompanied an incline of her head. "Señor Chapuys, I am honored," she said.

"It is I who am honored, Your Majesty," he replied with a low bow.

Jane could feel the entire audience exhale as one. She understood the enormous political implications of this reverence, and she cherished the contrast with his grudging nod to her predecessor. Henry clapped the Ambassador on the shoulder and the two men approached. Henry rested his foot on the first step to the dais, while Jane stood and descended one step. That put Jane at eye level with her husband, and both of them above the shorter Spaniard. Henry had worked that out with her beforehand.

Chapuys bowed again, and unleashed a flow of extravagant compliments. "Although the device of the lady who preceded you on the throne was 'The Happiest of Women,' I have no doubt that you yourself will fully realize that motto."

"Thank you," Jane replied.

"And I am certain that the Emperor will rejoice – as indeed your husband has done – that such a virtuous and amiable queen now sits upon the throne."

"Thank you," Jane repeated, hoping her response was enough but unable to think of anything else to say. She looked over at her husband in the hopes that he would step in and save her, but the other courtiers had gathered around and distracted him so that he was twisted with his back to Jane and deep in conversation with giggling ladies. Jane found herself thus locked in her one-sided conversation with Chapuys.

"I daresay you deserve the honorable name of Pacifica."

"Oh?" *What was he talking about?*

"Since you are after all the author and conservator of peace between England and Spain."

"Ah?" she asked uncertainly, then suddenly she understood, or thought she did. "Thank you."

How was she supposed to react to overly extravagant praise? She sent telepathic screams to her husband. *Help,* she pleaded in an internal screech, supplemented by a firm hand on his sleeve, which he ignored. She was still on her own. She ran through her options. Should she respond in kind? Should she speak of the Ambassador's kindness or the Emperor's friendship? Best just to downplay her role. "England and Spain have long been friends. It is a joy that we can be so again."

Chapuys smiled and bowed. Did that mean she said the right thing? How was her husband not coming to help her? What were those silly girls saying to so divert him from his duty? She gripped his sleeve harder as if to force him to turn around.

As Chapuys rose, he continued. "It is also a joy to see the pleasure which Englishmen of all ranks have felt at hearing of your marriage, especially as it is said you are constantly trying to persuade the King to restore Mary to favor."

There was a clue. Mary. Jane could do this. "I have promised myself to show favor to Mary, and will do my best to deserve the title of Peacemaker with which you so gallantly address me. I will do all I can to make peace between the King and his daughter."

The Ambassador's broad smile was all the reward she needed, and the ice in her veins began to thaw. Just then, with a sheepish smile, her apologetic husband finally turned around and broke in to save her. "Do not overtax my wife in her new duties, Sir Spaniard," he boomed, wagging his finger in a way that was both jovial and warning. "You are the first ambassador she has greeted, and she is not used to it."

"She is clearly born to the task, Your Majesty," Chapuys said with a smile. "See how she has not only created the peace but now she keeps it with friendship and courtesy."

Jane smiled and inclined her head. She was beginning to get the hang of it. It was not so hard, as long as Henry helped.

"There I agree with you," he said, taking her hand and kissing it. "Her nature is gentle and inclined to peace, and I daresay that she would not for the world wish to see me engage in war. She would never want us so separated."

"Your Majesties," Chapuys said as he bowed to them both.

Henry bowed back to him, then turned back to Jane and winked at her as Chapuys backed off. Jane wondered to herself how exactly it had been signaled that the interview was over. She would ask Henry later. Though he seemed so pleased with her. Maybe she would just confer with Edward instead of possibly disappointing the King by seeming slow.

She took a deep breath and realized she had done it. Her first audience. The first of many. Her exhale drew her husband's attention and he looked at her quizzically. She shot him a small smile and rolled her eyes slightly to signal her great relief. Henry grinned back and clasped her hand tightly as he turned to face the court with her. Their court.

June 14, 1536 ... 3 p.m.

Thomas Cromwell was seated at his desk, glad to be back in his old office at Greenwich Palace. Although he had given up the lodgings to Jane Seymour – *was it really only two months ago?* – in the name of discretion, now she was the Queen and had even richer ones. And Edward Seymour, the new Viscount Beauchamp, had been more than happy to cede these apartments for ones that were a little farther away but still just as rich.

The jangle of a sword on a belt caught his attention. He looked up to see Ralph Sadler stride through the door.

"The King has asked me to come retrieve you. The Duke of Norfolk and the Earl of Sussex have just returned from their visit to the Lady Mary."

Norfolk and Sussex had gone to have the girl finally swear the Oath of Succession like the rest of the country had already done. She had sent a letter as soon as she heard of the marriage, to congratulate the King and "his wife, Queen Jane" and wish them issue. While that was more honor than she had ever given the Boleyn, it was not enough – the King wanted Mary to acknowledge him as head of the Church and herself as a bastard.

"Well? How did they look?" Cromwell asked.

"Grim. Their Lords spoke to the King privately for five minutes or so before he called for you. I'd guess their news was bad."

They must not have succeeded. Christ's blood, how could those idiots have failed? The letter was inadequate, but the girl had taken that step on her own, unguided. Chapuys had written to her since then, so had Cromwell and many others. The Countess of Worcester had gone to visit her. By all rights, Mary should have submitted. How had Norfolk and Sussex bungled this?

"We'd best hurry then," Cromwell said.

The two men quickly took off down the hallway. Any delay was dangerous. Norfolk would say anything to shift the blame away from himself. The King's temper could escalate quickly.

Cromwell sighed. He had hoped for a longer honeymoon period, and a more transformative one. With so many problems solved by the death of the old queen, the King should have softened more. Instead, he proved to be even more incensed that any issues remained. Like Mary's disobedience. As if it were really true that Anne Boleyn had been the cause of all the evils in the world rather than just a convenient scapegoat.

Cromwell's fears were confirmed when he entered the study. The King was scowling. "Sire," Cromwell said as he bowed.

"Mary has refused my councilors," Henry growled.

Cromwell turned to the Earl. "What happened? What did you say to her? Were you not firm?"

Sussex blustered. "We arrested all her servants to show her how serious we are."

"And I told her that if she were my daughter, I would beat her and knock her head so violently against the wall that it would soften like baked apples," Norfolk added. "Was that not firm enough?"

Cromwell kept his face impassive. Did they really not understand the difference between resolute persuasion and bullying? Did they really believe their tactics would serve to persuade the King's daughter? If so, they understood nothing of people.

"She is a traitor, and Your Majesty should not hesitate to punish her," Norfolk said.

The shortsighted idiot, always spoiling for a fight since in his experience men always backed down. In this case, it was not worth the risk.

"By God you are right. I have pardoned her for too long on this issue," the King snarled, and rubbed his leg.

His leg pained him? What poor timing. Cromwell turned quickly to Norfolk. "When did this conversation take place?"

"I was with her four days ago. It happened then."

Four days. An eternity. That would have been before the Countess of Worcester's visit. And Chapuys' letter had only just left Cromwell's offices after being intercepted and copied, so she wouldn't have received it yet either. Mary would not have understood at that meeting how serious her situation was. Of course she stood up to Norfolk's ridiculous browbeating. Cromwell turned back to the King. "I implore you to be patient just a short time more. Give her one chance more. Chapuys assures me she will bend."

"Are you sure he is not lying to you?" the King said. "Or that he is not referring to her simplistic allusion to my wife as queen? You persuaded me to tolerate that from Spain, I will not accept that from my own daughter."

"Nor should you, Sire. But, again, my conversations with Chapuys suggest that there may be a misunderstanding. I will write to the girl to make sure she realizes what is expected of her. I have no doubt she will do everything you require."

"Why do you think you will be successful where Norfolk was not?"

Because Norfolk is an idiot, Cromwell wanted to say, but stopped himself. "My Lord Norfolk was perhaps a bit too harsh. I will be more reasonable."

"Seven years we've been reasonable," barked Norfolk. "It's no more time for that."

"By God, you're right," Henry yelled. "We have tolerated her treachery for too long." His eyes grew and he raised his index finger to point it at Cromwell. "She is a traitor, and you are a traitor for counseling leniency for her."

The blood froze in Cromwell's veins. *Oh, Lord.* He was being blamed somehow for this situation. How in the world had that happened? His blacksmith father's constant warning sprang to mind: *You're only as good as your last weld.* The King was ready to make this one problem lethal to the man who was his greatest servant. Not three years ago, Cromwell had freed the King from an impossible marriage by creating the Church of England. Not three months ago, Cromwell had passed legislation that would place all the English holdings of the Catholic Church into the royal treasury. Not three weeks ago, Cromwell had freed the King from another bad marriage in a context that served all his needs. But today Cromwell was called a traitor because he hadn't procured Mary's immediate submission.

Cromwell swallowed his resentment. This was neither the time nor the place. Right now he had to chart his course. Should he retreat? No, that would be stupid. Mary would submit. He knew she would. He could get her to do it.

"Sire, forgive me. I agree that you must completely withdraw your affection if she does not renounce her rights, but I believe she will do so. I swear I do," Cromwell said.

The King snorted and motioned for wine. Cromwell waited to continue until the King had taken a deep swallow. "The Queen actually said the very same thing to me this afternoon, before we heard this news. She told me she believes the Lady Mary will do the right thing and begged me to be patient with her." Cromwell kept his voice smooth at the careful reference to the Queen, who sided with him on this issue. Jane Seymour loved Mary, and she too was working to placate the King. Cromwell would talk to her later today, and ask her to redouble her efforts.

Henry harrumphed.

"I will write to the Lady Mary tonight to clear this up," Cromwell continued. "I am confident she will submit as you require."

"Fine. But you will answer for her obstinacy if you are wrong."

It was a dismissal. Cromwell bowed and left, praying that Norfolk would not reignite the defused situation. Cromwell needed time. As he walked through the King's Presence Chamber, Ralph Sadler jumped up to join him.

"Ralph, thank goodness," Cromwell said. "Walk with me to my office."

Concern flooded his friend's eyes. "What's wrong? How can I help?"

"I need to write to the Lady Mary as a matter of urgency. Whom do you know who can deliver the letter and bring me her reply? Hopefully by tomorrow? I would go myself but I dare not leave Norfolk alone with the King for too long. Lord only knows what he'd counsel."

"I can do it. Tomorrow is my free day," Sadler said. "But what has changed to make this so pressing? I thought Queen Jane was…that she…"

"Queen Jane is a wonderful influence, but she is not enough. The King has lost his patience with Mary. She must submit immediately – and if I can't make that happen, she and I will both die."

"He wouldn't really…"

Cromwell shot him a withering look. Ralph Sadler had been at the English court for ten years, first as Cromwell's secretary and now as the King's man – how could Ralph be so naive? They had all just seen what the King was capable of.

Ralph gulped. "I will go make my preparations now."

Cromwell nodded. "Thank you. I will be ready when you return."

Cromwell entered his office and sat down at his desk. He took out two sheets of paper and laid them side by side. One would be a letter to Mary explaining again what was required of her. But because this might not be clear enough, he would also write a submission for her, a template to make sure she said everything she needed to say to remove the danger she was in.

Again, he blessed his forethought for pressing so hard with this. Chapuys' letter had been a masterful appeal that included the Pope's promise to absolve Mary of any vow made under duress; and the Countess of Worcester, whom Mary loved and trusted, was the most persuasive woman he knew. She would have calmed Mary down after that sluggard Norfolk's ridiculous posturing, helped her understand she had no choice but to bend. No, there was no reason for Mary to continue rebelling, thank goodness.

And again, Cromwell bent his knee to God. This was needed for His fledgling English Church. A Church that was built upon the word of God and rejected the fiction that corrupt priests or dead saints could secure a man's salvation. A Church that spoke to Cromwell's soul. If Mary were arrested, Spain might well invade to save her – and if they were victorious, they would lead England back to Rome's superstition and trickery. That had to be avoided at all costs. Cromwell had brought England so very far, he was sure he could push the King further still. It was merely a matter of identifying the various ways that reform could further the King's desires or answer his complaints. There would be many such opportunities; Cromwell just had to be patient. And of course avoid the current trap he was in.

Cromwell took a deep breath and began to write Mary's submission. He was distressed right now, and he would channel that into creating the abject contrition that must shine from every word. Once he had that emotional piece down, he would feel better and could more calmly explain the situation. That would be the way to persuade Mary to do the right thing. And quickly, before the King's ebbing patience was completely gone.

July 6, 1536 ... 2 p.m.

Jane Seymour took the chair of estate that had been prepared for her next to her husband's. They were in the Great Hall of a house in Hackney, about to see the Lady Mary. Jane looked around, and stifled a smile at the careful arrangement of the room, thinking of how she had conducted a similar analysis only a year ago.

Two large banners were in place, featuring the arms of the King and Queen Jane. The furniture had been removed, except for one small trestle table against the side wall and two stools in front of one of the window bays. Mary had placed the thrones diagonally across from the entrance, to maximize the ceremony and allow her to approach without having to navigate a turn in the path. Smart girl. But of course she was. Look at her parents.

Jane took a deep breath to calm her nerves and noticed that Henry was tapping his foot almost violently. She put a hand on his knee. "It won't be long now," she said.

"Even that is too much."

It was so gratifying to hear him say that. Jane was so relieved that all had worked out as she knew it would. The girl loved and respected her father, she just hated the evil that was once Anne Boleyn.

That witch had kept Mary far away for more than six years to harden Henry's heart. The last time Jane had seen her, Mary had stood happily at her royal mother's side, an engaging ten-year-old girl with streaming red hair and kind eyes that were wide and curious about everything.

Henry had seen her more recently. A little less than three years ago, to be exact, though only from afar. It was right after the witch had birthed Elizabeth and decided to slap Mary in the face with her bastard status by forcing her to serve as a maid of honor to the princess who had supplanted her. Although Mary was prevented by guards from seeing the King when he visited his infant daughter, the confusion posed by a royal visit allowed her to sneak out of her rooms and climb up to the roof just as her father was leaving one day. She called out to him – a plaintive, breathy "Your Majesty" – and sank to her knees when he turned toward her. Henry took off his cap in greeting and bowed back, prompting the rest of the people in his party to do the same. He paid dearly for that kind gesture when his then-wife heard of it.

Now he and Mary would actually speak.

Jane bit her lip in nervousness. It was good that this reunion was private. There had been talk of having the meeting at court, as part of the girl's formal return to favor now that she had submitted to her father's authority, but Mary had fallen ill right after sending her letter, and so Henry and Jane had come here. They would spend the day with her, then leave after Vespers. It was better this way, this unpressured privacy. It removed any need on the King's part to send a warning to any onlookers. Instead, it offered an intimacy that would help rebuild their relationship.

Jane pulled her shawl tighter across her shoulders and looked down at the large diamond ring that garnished her index finger. It would be her present to Mary. The King planned to give Mary a thousand gold crowns, "for her little pleasures," as he put it. Gifts fit for a princess, even though she was still a bastard. That would change with time, as all the damage of the past years was slowly reversed. The King loved his daughter, Jane knew he did. It was one of the reasons he had been so hurt by Mary's rebellion. After he had shared her letter with Jane in the privacy of their rooms, he had cried over how angry he had been and what he had almost been forced to do. He was a king, after all, and his own feelings had to take second place to the realm. Hopefully Mary's expressed obedience and obvious contrition had permanently dispelled all his doubts. They'd soon see.

A page entered and rapped his staff on the floor. "The Lady Mary," he announced.

She paused in the doorway, slight and somewhat frail, and Jane was struck by how different she looked.

Much of that was of course age: she was twenty now, fully a

woman. But it was also her bearing: she looked timid despite a back that was straight as ever.

Jane searched the girl's drawn face as she approached. Her beautiful tresses were hidden under her gable hood, which highlighted the deep crease between her wide eyes and made her look more frightened than interested. Of course, the crease might well have been caused by repeated squinting: Mary was known to have vision problems, even at this age. And headaches.

Jane's heart went out to the girl. Happiness had certainly been snatched from Mary the same way it had long been from Jane. The girl had gone from Princess with a revered mother to bastard stepdaughter of the great whore of Christendom. But no more. Just as Jane had been exalted, so would Mary be. Jane would make sure of that. Praise God.

Mary took a step into the room, then offered a low reverence. She rose slowly, her eyes wide and intent on her father's face. She took seven more steps, then another reverence. Seven more, and another. Finally Henry leaped up from his chair and went down to raise her himself. "Greetings, my child," he said in a husky voice, and they hugged tightly.

Jane was moved beyond words at the wonderful reunion, as tender as she had hoped. She rose to her own feet and went to join them to offer her own salutation.

Mary immediately dropped to her knees again. "Thank you, Your Majesty, for all of your kindness," she said.

Jane's throat was too tight to speak. "Mary," was all she could say in response before she raised the girl to hug her as well.

They separated, and Henry hugged his daughter again for a long moment. "You are safe from the harridan. Thank God you are safe from her evil and witchcraft," he said with tears in his eyes.

"I thank God every day for sending you good Queen Jane," she replied. "I pray He sends you issue so that I may bow to my younger brother."

"We all pray for that day," Henry replied.

The conversation turned to the plans for her return. "You will rank as the second lady at court, right after the Queen," said the King.

Mary curtsied, clearly moved. She opened her mouth to thank him, but the King went on. "I am sorry to have kept you so long from me. I will not make that mistake again."

"I am sorry for my obstinacy," she answered in a small voice. "I thank God for your forgiveness."

The two embraced again. When Henry pulled apart, he wiped an eye and composed himself slightly before moving on to a happier subject. "I already know the apartments you will have at Hampton Court and Greenwich. And we will build new lodgings for you at Whitehall," he said excitedly. Jane smiled. He did love to build, and he hadn't in quite some time. It would be nice to share such a project.

Praise God, her husband was as loving and wonderful as she had hoped, had even discussed Mary's disobedience without anger. Jane had done her duty. Mary was safe. Her long ordeal was truly over. She was reunited with her father, and nothing would threaten her again. And if Jane birthed a son, Mary would surely be restored to the succession, to her rightful place in the world. Jane felt a twinge of impatience, then stopped herself. It would happen soon enough now. Now that they had completed His will, their reward was inevitable.

July 8, 1536 ... 2 p.m.

Thomas Cromwell walked faster than most people; he saw it as a reflection of the pace of his mind. Edward Seymour, or rather, Viscount Beauchamp, was also a fast walker; it was another bond. Though now they walked slowly, just pacing up and down the Long Gallery at Hampton Court. It was pouring outside, so they had nowhere to go. The castle was filled with courtiers lolling around, sitting in groups in each window seat area with people they thought were likely to help them advance. Standard fare. Everyone always sought advantage in one way or another, and real friendship was rare. This link with Beauchamp was close to that, though of course it too provided benefits to both sides: in exchange for mentorship, Cromwell gained another mouthpiece in the many conversations the King had with his courtiers. You always wanted as many people as possible around the King to sing with the same voice.

Right now, Cromwell was trying to soften Beauchamp's natural stance on a bit of a thorny issue. There was plague about, several confirmed cases farther north. Which meant that the pestilence was likely to reach London in September or October, right when Queen Jane's coronation was scheduled. Should they continue their plans, or postpone them? Cromwell was one of the voices that urged postponement. Coronations were expensive undertakings, and the sale of monastery properties and wealth had not yet replenished the coffers adequately. There were other priorities, like the country's defenses, that should take precedence. But of course this was not something he could say directly.

"To announce a delay, in advance of an actual outbreak, would send the wrong signal. It would spread unnecessary fear," said Beauchamp. "The pageantry is important to the people."

He had a point. A self-interested point, since he clearly wanted his sister crowned, but a point. Seeing the King in extravagant splendor lent credence to his claim of semi-divinity. It cemented his majesty enough to get people to overlook, or at least forgive, his foibles. And it would be good for the populace to celebrate a wife that didn't remind them of the King's lust, and therefore humanity, as Anne Boleyn always had.

"I agree," said Cromwell. "Though spectacle did not make them love or honor the Boleyn."

Not that the King hadn't tried. Four days of pageants and celebrations in which no expense was spared in the effort to impress and amaze. Just for the water procession, royal craftsmen had constructed a mechanical dragon that belched out flames and smoke. Gold leaf was slathered on every surface, trumpets blew, minstrels played, wine flowed freely from every fountain – but very few cheers rose from the crowd. Some people even hissed. In all, about seventy thousand pounds was spent for nothing. There hadn't been such wasteful stupidity since the Field of the Cloth of Gold. Both of which had turned into sources of deep embarrassment.

"I would not announce a delay now, you understand," said Cromwell. "I would continue with all the plans so that we are ready. I just don't want to chance sickness if it comes."

"I am glad to hear you say that. We would never set a date if we waited for the perfect time."

Suddenly, low but distinct voices came to them from just on the other side of one of the hall's doorways. "Baron Cromwell, a peer of the land?" Cromwell and Beauchamp instinctively froze. "From ruffian to lawyer to this?"

He couldn't place the mocking voice, but it was tantalizingly familiar. Who was speaking of him so dismissively? Was it a servant or a courtier?

Another almost-familiar voice answered. "Don't forget he was made Lord Privy Seal just last week."

Neither of the men had accents. That meant they were neither ambassadors nor servants. But who were they? Low or high? Most likely low, but what if they were high?

"At least being stripped of that honor let old Thomas Boleyn leave court. Though I'm surprised he kept the post a second after his daughter's conviction."

Cromwell felt Beauchamp look over at him but kept his own wide eyes fixed on the door.

"Ah, but you forget that his was one of the votes for that conviction. I'd consider that he earned a longer extension than that."

"Well, his vote to kill her was just one among many. It was

Cromwell who put her head on the block, so his payback is the richest."

How could these idiots not know to hold such conversations only in the window seats, never in the doorway? They had to be newcomers. Cromwell let his mind roam over the possibilities but no two people came to mind.

"He deserves value for his work. Edward Seymour was made Viscount Beauchamp simply for being born brother to the new Queen – surely a title was owed to the man who put her there."

Now they were talking about Beauchamp. Cromwell briefly wondered whether the insults might be deliberate, whether the men knew they could hear them.

"It's not like the new Beauchamp is a fool. He helped advise—"

"He did little more than fan the King's flame and guard his sister's innocence. A woman's role, no more."

There was no response to that statement, and the silence stretched for longer than it should. Cromwell and Beauchamp exchanged glances and approached the doorway. Cromwell could make out rustling, maybe footsteps. They must be walking away. Cromwell had a burning need to know who they were, and Beauchamp's wide eyes surely meant he felt the same way. By silent agreement they both jumped through the door but all they saw were two black coats disappearing around the hall's next corner…and Suffolk on the other side walking toward him.

"Ah, Lord Cromwell," the Duke boomed. "And Viscount Beauchamp," he added, bowing. "Congratulations to you both. I have been looking for you. I need to—"

"Ah, my Lord Suffolk," Beauchamp said quickly. "We were curious about those men you just passed in the hall."

"Did I? Well, I'll be no help to you. What did they do?"

"We thought they might have dropped a purse and wanted to return it to them," answered Beauchamp, somewhat lamely.

"My good Duke," Cromwell broke in. "I regret that we are on our way to the King right now. May I wait on you later this afternoon, once His Majesty has dismissed us?" Cromwell felt no guilt at the lie, only hope that it would not be detected. And urgency as the men got farther away. But this was after all the Duke of Suffolk. Rudeness would not be tolerated – or forgiven.

"By all means. I shall be in my apartments," he agreed.

"Thank you for your patience. I will be there as soon as I am able."

Cromwell grabbed Beauchamp's sleeve and pulled him along. The two men rushed down the hall but the black coats were gone. Damn.

"Did you recognize either of the voices?" he asked Beauchamp.

"No. They didn't even sound familiar."

That supported the low-born theory, but Cromwell still worried. "How about their clothes? Did you see any decoration at all on their cloaks? Any embroidery? Silver or gold thread? Any hint of a scarlet or velvet lining?" The sumptuary laws prescribed what colors and decorations people could use in their attire. Silver or gold thread, or scarlet or velvet cloth, would have meant the speakers were of high rank.

Beauchamp shook his head. "Nothing but a flash of fur around their collars. Maybe rabbit."

Rabbit, thank God. That ruled out anyone who mattered. "Good detail," Cromwell began. He tried to continue, but noticed that Beauchamp looked nauseous. "What is it?"

Beauchamp's lips trembled before he blurted his complaint. "It is horrible to be spoken of thus. All my life spent working hard to rise by my strength, and now I am seen as nothing more than the Queen's bumbling brother."

Better the Queen's bumbling brother than the King's murderous henchman, Cromwell thought. His annoyance quickly abated. The unknown voices had not accused him of treachery, they had merely noted his effectiveness. Given that, Beauchamp was right to be more offended. Though what did he expect?

"You're not used to people disdaining you," Cromwell said. It was a statement, not a question.

Beauchamp smiled ruefully. "No."

"You are a capable and honest man," Cromwell said. "It is jealousy that caused them to say what they did. You cannot let it bother you. It matters not."

"My career will stall if I am seen as a fool by my peers."

"The King has the only opinion that matters, and he will be patient. Just continue to act as you have, give your counsel, and do your job well."

"They would never speak that way of my brother Tom."

Cromwell kept his face impassive. Beauchamp was unnecessarily self-pitying. It was not wise to let people – even friends – see your weaknesses. It put you in their power. Still, the truth was that this changed nothing: Beauchamp was already in his power. As was his brother, who with Beauchamp's elevation had gained title to the Seymour moniker. But it was a good reminder.

"Your brother is a fine man and the King enjoys his company. But he doesn't trust his counsel. It's why he wasn't advanced and you were."

Beauchamp shook his head. "The King could do no less for me than he did for George Boleyn."

Cromwell laughed. "Not at all. If that's all it was, then he would have made your father an earl like he did for Thomas Boleyn. There may have been a precedent, but you earned this. And now your job is to continue to merit it."

Beauchamp stared straight ahead, gloomily. "Easier said than done."

Fascinating. Beauchamp was actually worried about his position, even though he was brother to the Queen. It was really all about power, for everyone. Thomas Cromwell always assumed he would have been less driven if he had not been born a commoner and therefore desperate to escape from the cruelty of life for the low-born. But here was Edward Seymour, a son of the gentry, a viscount whose future was assured, worried that he wasn't taken seriously. *Bah*. How little this boy understood of the world. The court, as cynical as it was, was full of naiveté.

Not Cromwell. He was cunning – and now he was noble. He was a member of the aristocracy, permanently safe. And rich. When he was younger, he would have expected to retire once he had made such a fortune. But how could he walk away from this? The fortune, the influence. He could do and be whatever he wanted, just by giving the King whatever he wanted. The King's threat over Mary's intransigence had just been bluster. It was not the first time the man had yelled at Cromwell. At least this time the King hadn't struck him. The King had these temporary storms then recovered – and his contrition always sweetened the rewards he gave. Like Cromwell's new barony. And the deed to Austin Friars. He would stay, and thrive.

Right now the King needed nothing more, but when he did, Thomas Cromwell would get it for him by aligning their interests. That was the secret to statecraft.

"Just watch me and see what I do. You'll learn quickly."

September 1, 1536 ... 3 p.m.

The red-bricked towers and buttresses of Hunsdon House came into view from the snaking road. Jane had visited there many years ago, and had fallen in love with it. It was built in the rough shape of an *E*, which gave it one of the grandest galleries Jane had seen, and surrounded by a serene, water-filled moat. It inspired confidence and safety, enough that Henry had retired to here in 1527 to escape the sweating sickness. Now it had been designated as Mary's residence, and Jane fully approved of the choice. Of course, anything was better than the Tower of London, which until recently had looked to be the girl's next abode.

Henry turned to Jane and smiled. "We're just about there."

They were on their way to visit Mary for the second time since her formal submission. Because she had not yet returned to court, this was the only way to see her and reconnect. And so they had scheduled a private visit to Hunsdon in the middle of their summer progress – a much pared-down progress compared to last year, more a series of informal hunting trips. Or maybe that was just thanks to Jane's new perspective. It seemed so easy now to travel from one manor house to the next. The accommodations were always ample, the foods always pleasing, and the chaos always hidden. Truth be told, it was heaven. So completely different from how she used to feel about progresses that it made her giggle and cross herself in thanks for this wonderful new life that had been given to her.

"Shall we gallop over to her?" he asked with a hopeful smile on his face.

Jane smiled indulgently and reined in her horse. "You go greet her first. I would like for you to have that time with her."

He blew her a kiss and was off.

Her sister Anne rode up to her. She and Edward had joined Jane and the King on this private visit to Mary. With five servants, the bare minimum. "Your Majesty?"

"I was there the last time, to smooth the way between them," Jane said. "I am not so needed now."

She was also not so hasty now. She was almost four weeks past her expected monthly time, and she had never been this late. Ever. She was already cautiously gentle with herself.

Anne nodded and they resumed their riding. As they neared, Jane watched the King raise Mary from her deep reverence and hug her, tightly, his eyes closed. The raw connection that shone on his face caused Jane's throat to tighten and her heart to warm.

"When will she be returned to court?" Edward asked, and Jane noticed with some satisfaction that his whisper was hoarse as well. For a time he had discouraged her from pressing so hard for Mary's reinstatement, but now that Jane had won he was more respectful. That was an important lesson to learn. For her and him.

"The end of October," she answered. "She will ride with me at my coronation."

Jane felt the glow surround her again and her hand went instinctively to her stomach. She said a quick Gloria Patri and then took a deep breath, willing herself not to make too much of any of these things. To let His will be done, whatever it was. But it was so hard not to feel holy and smug over such a quick reward for doing His work.

Especially since the King did not expect this good news. Last month, he told Chapuys that he felt old and doubted he would have any children by Jane. Jane had cried when Edward passed on that story, she had been so moved. And hopeful that the Lord would help her prove her husband wrong.

The hug had broken; she could join them now. She moved forward to commence the formalities that governed the exchange of greetings even in a private family visit. Deep reverences from Mary were a key part of the symbolism, Jane understood, as were the rich gifts they gave her in return. This time Henry had brought a magnificent horse for her stables, and Jane had chosen new headdresses – richly decorated gable hoods, the new court requirement. Presents to reinforce Mary's position and rank, to reassure, and to please. She really was such a lovely girl; it was so beautiful and blessed to see father and daughter reunited. Jane closed her eyes for a second to mentally cross herself and say the first line of the Ave Maria in praise.

Right then, Jane felt a telltale ache in her abdomen, the cramping that always announced the start of her menstrual flow. A chill settled around her and she tried to calm the breathing she realized was ragged.

Anne was quickly beside her. "Your Majesty?" she asked with a worried look on her face.

Jane put her hand on her sister-in-law's shoulder. Taking a deep breath, she turned to her husband. "Sire, I think I will retire for a short time…I need a moment."

The King broke out into a broad smile. "You need to rest? This is always good news."

Of course he had counted too, even though he had never said anything. Tears rose to Jane's eyes and she gestured to Mary. "No, Sire. This here is the good news."

Mary somehow managed to bow to her and simultaneously signal to her maid to lead the Queen inside. Jane bowed to her husband and Mary before retiring alone with Anne to the manor house.

Once in her own apartments, behind the closed door, Jane pawed frantically at her skirts. When her handkerchief showed red, she sank to the floor. "I have lost the child," she whispered.

Anne ran to the door to order cloths and water while Jane remained prostrate on the floor with her face down. When Anne returned, she stroked Jane's shoulder.

That prompted Jane to sit up, defeated. "How could this be? What kind of timing is this, for the child to be taken from me right at the pinnacle of doing God's work? What does this mean?"

"It means nothing more than that you miscounted."

Jane closed her eyes tightly, not wanting to show her exasperation. Anne was as aware of Jane's regularity as she was of her own. "But why now? Why would He punish me at such a moment?"

Images of the Boleyn flashed in Jane's mind and made her uneasy. The woman had looked so scared and bewildered after she miscarried her son earlier in the year. Jane had not felt compassion then. Just the opposite, since that loss had removed the main obstacle to her own happiness. Now Jane felt deep sympathy, along with real guilt. "You don't think…," she began.

Anne grabbed both Jane's hands into her own. "This is God's way of making sure this moment belongs to Mary. Nothing more. Your own time will come."

September 28, 1536 ... 10 p.m.

Despite the lateness of the hour, Thomas Cromwell sat at his desk in his Austin Friars home, hands cupping a warm cup of cider. He would likely be there for at least another hour, as he loved the quiet hours of the night for tying up the loose ends of the day that inevitably piled up even during what was supposed to be his vacation. He similarly loved the early hours of the morning, before others had risen. It was fortunate that he needed almost no sleep.

The faint sound of galloping in the distance made him pause. It was a single horse, getting closer. At such a time as this, it was likely a message from Windsor. The King and Queen were in residence there instead of on their traditional summer progress, as they wanted to avoid the plague that terrorized the country-side. They had taken only a pared-down complement of servants, since limiting the number of people at court minimized risk – fewer sick people able to come in contact with the royal couple or their inner circle. And Windsor was the perfect refuge: not far from London but completely separate from the surrounding world. The eleventh-century castle sat atop a steep hill, and despite its luxurious decorations was strong enough to withstand any attempted siege, by man or illness.

The horse's hooves clattered on the courtyard's paving stones. The messenger was coming to him. Cromwell rose quickly and hastened down the twenty paces of the hallway to greet him. Cromwell arrived at the front door at the same time as the young page who had recently joined the household. The boy's room was just off the kitchen, a much shorter trip. Not everyone kept Cromwell's hours.

The youth opened the door, letting in a gust of chilled air. "Be sure to close that behind us," Cromwell said to the boy.

The messenger was still atop his horse. He looked to be in his early twenties, strong and straight. A country lad, judging from the round face. Most importantly, he exuded efficiency rather than alarm. "I seek Baron Cromwell," he said.

"You have found him," Cromwell replied.

"Greetings, my Lord," said the man as he dismounted and handed his reins to the page. "Ralph Sadler said you'd be awake when I arrived, Sir. I bring a letter from him."

Cromwell nodded, always happy to be right. "May I offer you shelter, or must you return tonight?"

The messenger smiled. "Mr. Sadler's orders were to get this message to you straightaway and leave it to you to decide on your reply – so whether I return tonight is up to you. I'll water my horse now, and you'll let me know."

Cromwell smiled back, liking the man. "What is your name?"

"Harry. Harry Greenway, Sir."

"I'll remember that, Harry." Good-natured, responsible, and practical. He resolved to have Ralph watch this man. This would be a good opportunity to teach his ward how to recognize and advance talent. "I'll be in my office. There will be food for you in the kitchen. I'll come find you there and let you know."

He opened the seal and squinted his eyes to try to read the letter as he walked back to his office, but it was far too dark in the hallway. Still, he could tell that Ralph hadn't used a cipher, which meant the letter contained no secrets. Always a good sign. Ralph was simply updating him on events, relaying the message or instruction from the King that would have prompted the good Harry Greenway to be dispatched when he was.

Again, Cromwell thanked providence that His Majesty liked Sadler as well as Cromwell did. The King had even appointed Sadler to the Privy Chamber, which kept Cromwell in constant knowledge of the King's thoughts and moods. Thomas Seymour also shared such news, but Ralph was much more reliable. Both were welcome changes from the days of the old queen, when her brother George and Henry Norris had jealously guarded the King's pastimes.

Sitting back at his desk, Cromwell pushed his other papers aside and placed the letter directly in front of him. He grabbed a clean sheet of paper and a pen and put them to the side just in case. Then he began to read. After the greetings and the wishes for health, Ralph quickly recounted a conversation he'd had with the King about the particulars of one of the monasteries. His Majesty did not remember that this one would remain open, and was upset that the dissolution funds had not yet reached his treasury. Cromwell nodded. He needed to address that with the King. Cromwell began to write a note, but decided to wait until he had read the rest. A good choice, as Ralph next got to the meat of the matter:

> After supper, His Majesty returned to his chamber, sent for me, and said he had considered your letters, and seeing how the plague reigned in Westminster, even in the abbey, he was in doubt whether or not to defer the coronation.

Aha. Cromwell had continued to urge that Queen Jane's coronation be postponed for a season. It would be unseemly to mount such a lavish display for this new wife when the old one was still fresh in her grave. Thankfully, luck had given them the ultimate excuse. The plague had reached Westminster Abbey itself – three monks had died there. It would be folly to bring thousands of people to breathe that air. Truly the best approach was to wait a year, until the pestilence was gone and hopefully the Queen was bouncing a son on her knee. That would fully justify such pomp and celebration. And expense.

> He said, therefore, it were good that all his Council were here to consult on it, and bade me write to you that our Lord Admiral, Mr. Comptroller, and the Bishop of Hereford are here, and that you yourself should come hither immediately, and bring with you our Lord Chancellor and the rest of the Privy Council.

The King clearly wanted to deflect any blame for this decision. No surprises there. The Queen might be upset at the thought of her coronation delayed, though that wasn't really her nature. She knew her husband's great fear of sickness, and she was not so reckless as to their own health to go too near the abbey. No, Queen Jane would not be troubled by this. More likely, it was just her brother who was nervous on her behalf. He must have heard – the whole court had – how last week the King had expressed his disappointment over meeting not one but two pretty women "too late to consider wooing them." Beauchamp would want his sister fully anointed, to ensure her protection. As if that had made a difference to Catherine of Aragon or Anne Boleyn.

I said that before you could have word of this summons it would be tomorrow afternoon, and too late to set out, and that next day was Michaelmas Day. "What then?" quoth His Majesty. "Michaelmas Day is not so high a day." Therefore, I perceive, he will expect you on Michaelmas Day, or the next morning, the sooner the better.

God bless Ralph, managing the King like that. Cromwell had taught the boy well – how to set expectations that Cromwell would surely meet and likely exceed. For of course Ralph had sent the messenger immediately rather than waiting until morning, and now Cromwell had an extra day to corral the other gentlemen. He would stop to see each of the Council members tomorrow, to tell them the King expected them, then would leave immediately. It was important that Cromwell reach Windsor first. That way, the extra time it took the others would serve to highlight his own efficiency and loyalty.

Cromwell rose and headed toward the kitchens to tell Harry Greenway to get some sleep. They would leave first thing in the morning.

CHAPTER NINE – 1536

FALL/WINTER

October 3, 1536 ... 1 a.m.

*J*ane sat in bed, sewing, while her husband next to her made notations in the pages of his Ten Articles, the formulary of the faith of the new Church of England. These articles referred to just three sacraments – baptism, penance, and the Eucharist – rather than the usual seven. Jane could understand, when pressed, eliminating confirmation as merely an echo of the moment that had occurred at baptism; but, try as she might, she could not accept that matrimony, last rites, and taking holy orders were not fully sacred moments. Cranmer's doing. And Cromwell's. They pushed her husband far on these points.

The curtains around the giant bed were closed around them, except right next to the headboards to let in light from the candle stands. Her eyes were heavy but she didn't want to nod off. It was so comforting to have Henry there with her, the least she could do was stay awake for the treat. She cherished the moments they spent together in private, which was still most nights when she didn't have her monthly course. And of course this past week she and the King had been together almost every moment, since he had been forced to cancel her coronation. She was happy to be patient given the danger, but it mattered so much to him to celebrate her like that, to show he loved her more than he had loved…before.

The specter she had conjured caused Jane's throat to tighten, and she almost missed the quiet knock at the door. *What was that?* She looked at Henry, who seemed concerned. "Yes?" he called, pulling the curtain to open it.

The door opened and Thomas Cromwell walked in, his mouth a thin line on his ashen face and his eyes only for Henry. "Forgive me, Your Majesty, but I bring important news."

Henry nodded.

"A riot has broken out in Lincolnshire. In Louth."

Henry stiffened. "Didn't we just close the abbey there?"

"Three days ago. After sealing the gate, your representative visited the church next door, St. James, to make a list of its valuables. He was still there with his papers when the villagers arrived for Evensong." Cromwell paused and shifted from one foot to the other. "It is not clear whether the priest incited them, but by the end of the service the entire congregation had taken up arms and threatened attack."

Henry waved an arm. "They should be punished. Send some men and—"

"By the next day, the crowd had swelled to thirty thousand."

Jane was startled to hear Thomas Cromwell interrupt the King, but that was quickly eclipsed by shock at the vastness of the number. Her heart gripped in terror. She put a hand on her husband's arm but he shrugged her off.

"They marched on Lincoln and took possession of the cathedral," Cromwell continued. "They demand the restoration of the abbeys and a return to Rome."

"They demand? By God, those traitors presume too much."

"They specifically claim they are not traitors, that they have no quarrel with Your Majesty. Only your policies. And me."

Relief crept over Jane. This was not truly disloyalty to the King; the situation was not as dangerous as it sounded. Jane snuck a look at her husband. He wasn't comforted. His face was almost purple, and a vein throbbed in his forehead.

"I am my policies," he snarled. "Send men against them."

"The Dukes of Norfolk and Suffolk are in the area right now. They will be able to warn the rebels to disperse or face the royal forces. The good dukes will have their own men; the threat will carry weight. May I so instruct them on your behalf?"

"Why give them warning? Why not send our troops immediately, to make our position clear?"

"We have none right now to send. The ones in the North are brethren of the rebels – we can't chance them joining them. We must bring in troops from elsewhere in the realm."

Henry paused. "That should have been your first action," he said and his voice was flat.

Cromwell lowered his head quickly. He reminded Jane of a dog trying to avoid being struck. "It was, Your Majesty. I sent instructions immediately. But I ordered the troops to assemble first in London, as there is some fear that the rebels will march southwards. Your safety is paramount."

The King drummed his fingers on his papers. "Write to Norfolk and Suffolk. Have them act quickly. And make clear that I will not tolerate rebellion."

"Yes, Sire." Cromwell backed out of the room, bowing the whole way.

The silence was threatening, but Jane was afraid to break it. Instead, she again placed a gentle hand on Henry's arm. This time he stiffened but allowed it. She stayed that way, silently communicating her support, as he continued to fume.

"How dare they?" he suddenly bellowed and bolted out of bed. "Excuse me, Madam. I need to speak further with Cromwell. Perhaps I will write to the rebels, let them hear directly from me."

She sat up. "Shall I find you paper?"

"Nay, I will go to my rooms. I will not return tonight." And just as quickly, he was gone.

Jane sat back, alone in the enormous bed. The fine linen sheets and ermine-trimmed quilts were rumpled beside her, where her husband had left them, and she pulled them up around her against a chill that may well have come from within. The curtains were partially opened and the canopy soared above her, making her feel even smaller and more vulnerable. She knew she should close them, but she didn't want to move.

Rebellion. To restore the abbeys. Rebellion was wrong, but how else were they to get the King to listen to reason?

A timid knock at the door caught her attention. "Yes?"

It was Lady Rochford, her nightclothes rumpled from sleeping on a pallet right outside the bedchamber. "I saw the King leave. Shall I join you now?"

Lady Rochford had recently returned to court, after both Edward and Cromwell had urged Jane to accept her. Not that any pressure was needed, since the woman had always been a friend. Though Jane had felt a twinge of discomfort seeing Lady Rochford's face after...the incidents. But the truth was, if Jane were to avoid all the women who had given testimony against the Boleyn, Jane would lose almost all her household.

She thought a moment. For the first time in a while, she was comforted by the idea that a queen was never left alone unless she wanted to be, that the women around her rushed to be by her side. Of course, it was to their advantage to spend as much time with a ruler as possible, it made it more likely they would be there and participate in any largesse dispensed.

Jane smiled to herself. Henry had taught her to look always for the benefit that a person would gain in any situation; he said that recognizing motive was the most important skill a ruler could have. Lady Rochford's drive was clear, but Jane could not figure out why Cromwell had so quickly named himself as the cause of the rebels' objections. Of course, someone else would have been quick to supply that information. Perhaps he intended it to show his honesty.

Jane made up her mind. "No thank you, Lady Rochford," she said. "Not tonight. But please do rouse me early tomorrow."

Lady Rochford curtsied and left. Jane felt a small pang, but it quickly faded. There was no reason to have the woman stay. Jane wasn't about to talk about the rebellion, or share her thoughts and fears, with such a gossip. Jane didn't even want to be the one to tell Lady Rochford about it. And Jane certainly didn't want to hear the blandishments that Lady Rochford would inevitably offer as comfort.

Squaring her shoulders, Jane left the warmth of her bed to go kneel at her prie-dieu in the corner. Her husband deserved all the help he could get.

October 21, 1536 ... 6 p.m.

Jane had dismissed her ladies after Evensong to enjoy the ebbing of the day by the corner window in her study. The late afternoon prayer service always put her in a contemplative mood and drew her to solitude. Of course, she wasn't completely alone: Edward and Anne had insisted on remaining. They loved quiet time with her. Now that she was queen, anyway.

Edward was speaking, but Jane's ears had closed to his words. He was condemning the good men and women of the North who hoped for reconciliation with Rome. *How could he?*

Jane looked down at the chalice veil she was working, part of a set of altar cloths for the Chapel Royal at Greenwich. Jane planned to complete the veil entirely on her own, while her ladies collaborated on the frontal. This first set was to be for ordinary times, so she had selected a green damask background and relatively standard designs. After almost five months of diligent work, they were far enough along that she was already planning her next series. It would be far grander – gold for Christmas and Easter – and Hans Holbein would create the sketches for her.

Such wonderful plans, all for God's glory. The same thing the rebels were fighting for.

The original uprising had faded, scared off by the King's threats, but another one had arisen in its place, centered in York. This one was better organized, headed by a London barrister, Robert Aske, instead of a monk and a shoemaker. It had a name, the Pilgrimage of Grace, and a banner – a representation of the five wounds of Christ. It also had victories: after occupying the city, it had restored Catholic observances to churches and returned expelled monks and nuns to their houses. Those holy men and women then said hundreds of Masses to pray for the King's good health.

Anger rose in Jane. She could no longer let Edward continue to defend the desecration of Church property in the name of religious reform. He was still talking, but she didn't care. She was Queen of England, and entitled to interrupt anyone but her husband. "But they say they still love the King," Jane said. "It is just his policies they question."

"Question?" Edward asked sharply. "Rebellion is not a way to question policy."

"How else are they to let the King know how they feel? He is surrounded by men who encourage him in this path. No one will tell him the truth."

"What truth would you have them tell? That he should listen to the Bishop of Rome who would have him still married to Aragon? That he should allow corrupt monks to bilk his people of their gold?"

"The abbeys are honest centers of holy life," Jane argued.

"Many are not. You and the rebels forget that."

Jane shook her head. "You are as bad as Cromwell."

Anne broke in. "Thankfully he is not hated as much as Cromwell."

Indeed. Henry's people knew these reforms were all Cromwell's doing. The rebels had made it quite clear they wanted him gone: they seized one of his servants and wrapped him in a bull skin as bait for vicious dogs.

Jane shuddered. "You need to distance yourself from Cromwell," she said.

Edward grimaced. "Distance myself from a true friend? For what? These rebels are traitors who rile people with spiteful inventions. They even claimed that Cromwell wanted to confiscate all the Church plate and impose taxes on weddings and funerals. They deserve death."

"They just want to worship as their consciences tell them."

"They want more than that. They want to change the laws to reinstate Mary."

"But the King is prepared to do that!" Jane exclaimed. "He promised to name her his heir." Although the Second Act of Succession, passed in June, vested the crown in Jane's children, Parliament had also given Henry the radical power to select his own heir if Jane did not produce a son. Henry FitzRoy had died over the summer, some said from consumption, others from a posthumous spell cast by the Boleyn. Either way, his death left Mary as the next rightful heir. Certainly a better choice than the infant Elizabeth. "He could easily assure them of this now."

"I will not be the one to urge any concessions," said Edward. "Not when the threats have been so effective."

"Concessions? Is that what Cromwell calls reason?"

"Cromwell is not leading the King astray, as you seem to think. He is only fulfilling his master's desires. That is why this rebellion is so dangerous. And why it requires such a firm reaction."

Three strikes of the page's stave rapped on the floor. "Your Majesty, the King asks that you join him in the Great Hall."

The Great Hall, not his Presence Chamber. Her husband was living as public a life as he could in these times: he wanted to be among his people so that they could see him and remember their love and loyalty. He had explained last night that he wanted her with him as much as possible, to further burnish his image as a loving sovereign. She had been expecting this summons, and had carefully chosen her gown that morning with this event in mind. He would be wearing a purple and gold coat, so she had chosen a deep red dress with gold embroidery as a counterpoint.

Jane nodded at the page and gave her hand to Edward to lead her. Anne fell in behind them. When they reached the Great Hall, Jane paused at the door to capture the room's attention – a trick Henry had taught her. This also gave her a chance to survey the area. There were about two hundred people in small groups around the edges, and some six hundred more crowded loosely around the center where her husband sat on a raised dais. The lights flickered off the jewels in his clothes, making him glow and giving him an otherworldly authority. A carefully cultivated otherworldly authority.

The room bowed. Jane smiled and nodded back to the corners, another trick that had helped her overcome her old social anxiety. The crowd parted slightly to allow her to join her husband, and she swept through formally, with none of the nervousness that had afflicted her in the early days of her reign. She bowed before mounting the two steps, marveling as always that this wonderful man had picked her among all women to share this life. He nodded back and took her hand to kiss as she sat in her chair of estate next to his.

Without further greeting, he launched back into the conversation that her arrival had interrupted. He had been dissecting the crisis with his courtiers – or pretending to.

"Torch their towns, teach the ruffians a lesson," said one voice.

"Your Majesty has been marvelously patient with the curs," said a second.

"See if their monks will save them as they swing on their ropes," said a third.

Jane groaned inwardly. This was no rounded discussion, this was just a group of people praising their king and sneering at the rebels and their beliefs. Cromwell and Cranmer were maintaining a smug silence, letting others speak for them while her husband nodded self-righteously. This was wrong. These ministers did not understand. She did. She needed to help her husband, help his people. It was what God wanted her to do.

Edward was wrong. This was Cromwell's fault. He pushed the King for religious reforms, even though the country didn't need them. Henry broke with the Church to marry the Boleyn – now that she was gone there was no reason to continue the rift with Rome. Or, fine, continue the separation, but let the people keep their way of life. Churches and abbeys were anchors in a town, they were everything. But how could Henry ever fully understand that, brought up in the isolation of the court?

Jane had been wrong to ask Edward to take charge in this matter. This was her job, no one else's. She needed to do God's work to earn the great blessing that might be growing inside her even now. Helping Mary had not been enough. This was her next challenge.

Her face burned, even her ears were hot, as the excitement rose in her. She took a deep breath and plunged into this new resolve. She stood, turned, and fell to her knees before her husband's chair. "I beg you, Your Majesty, to listen to the rebels," she said, and she was proud that her voice was clear and strong. It would be heard throughout the room. "You have always said that you intended to reform, not destroy, the abbeys. This rebellion can only be God's judgment for closing His holy houses. There is a place for them in England's Church, in your Church. It will heal your country, it will please God."

At the end of her small speech, she sneaked a peek up to see her husband's face. Instead of the gentle smile and quiet indulgence she expected, she saw beady eyes black with rage and thin lips pressed together in contempt. "I will not be instructed by ignorant men. Or women." His words were a contemptuous snarl. "If you wish to avoid Mistress Boleyn's end, Madam, you will cease to meddle in my affairs."

The blood drained from Jane's extremities – her face went

cold, her fingers numbed – and pooled in a knot in her stomach. What had she done? The room dimmed. *You are such a fool,* she thought. *You never could do anything right.* Keeping her eyes low, she gave a deep curtsy with a mumbled apology and tore out of the room.

~

CROMWELL WATCHED HER LEAVE, AGHAST AT HER JUDGMENT BUT relieved that the King had not been swayed. Cromwell looked around at the crowd, a sea of open mouths and downcast eyes. Except the King's. He looked from face to face, lips tight but nostrils flaring with each breath. Suddenly he stood and motioned for Cromwell to follow him before storming out of the Great Hall.

When the two were alone in his study, the King first sat then jumped up to pace. Cromwell quickly fed the King wine to calm him down.

"How dare she," the King spat between sips. "Another woman meddling in my affairs. She needs to be taught a lesson."

Cromwell groaned inwardly and handed the King another goblet. This one was downed immediately then thrown against the wall. "Am I always to be surrounded by harridans?" the King asked. His shoulders slumped as he watched the red liquid drip, and the wildness left him. He slowly took a seat.

"Your Majesty, you are of course perfectly correct," Cromwell agreed, and handed him a new goblet. "That was completely misguided."

The King just held the cup in his hand as he stared off, his lip curled.

Cromwell watched his face, resolving to caution Edward Seymour to keep Jane better in line. To oppose her husband in a time of crisis...the King would calm down this time, but the Queen should not take such chances ever again. Not without a son on her lap.

The King broke the silence with a sigh. "She threw herself on her knees once, she can do so again when she admits her mistake."

Suddenly an idea bloomed in Cromwell's mind and his hands actually trembled. "Sire, forgive me, but it occurs to me that you could use the Queen's error to your advantage."

"Eh?"

"After she apologizes for speaking her mind, you can agree to show forbearance to men who claim to be doing the same thing. You can even agree to listen to their views. Provided, of course, they prove their love and loyalty by dispersing immediately."

"I have already ordered them to disperse."

"But they haven't yet. And we don't have the troops to force the issue. This is even better. We already know that they believe certain lies; you can correct them about everything. All as a favor to your loving wife."

Henry looked at his minister appraisingly. Cromwell held his gaze.

"You would have me be instructed by ignorant men?"

"Nay, Sire. I would merely have you understand that ignorant men are too easily misled. It is your duty as England's prince and pope to guide them back to the obedience they crave."

The King walked over to look out the window and stared for a time. His face softened slowly as his eyebrows unknit and his mouth loosened. Cromwell stood patiently, waiting for the inevitable conclusion.

"It is the perfect feint," the King finally agreed. "She has done me a real service, if this works. Perhaps I should not have been so cruel in my reaction."

Cromwell shrugged. "Such public dissent was wrong. You needed to teach her that."

The King nodded, but his eyes were downcast. He signaled dismissal and turned back to the window.

Cromwell bowed and left the room, almost smug. This was

perfect. The rebels would be comforted by this turn of events, and they would gladly disperse while their leaders fell under the King's spell. It would buy the King all the time he needed. If he needed it. It was brilliant. Again, Cromwell thanked God for Jane Seymour and the solution she had provided. The country trusted her. That more than anything else would reconcile them to the King. And once she birthed a son, they could close every last abbey in the country.

November 1, 1536 ... 11 a.m.

Jane had dismissed her ladies until supper. She didn't want to hear their chatter. Truth be told, she didn't want to hear Anne's or Edward's prattle either, but she had no choice. To dismiss them too would signal that something was wrong, inviting more of the gossip that constantly surrounded her. Especially this week, after her public shaming.

"It is stunning." Anne Seymour Beauchamp looked down at the blood-red ruby ring the King had just given Jane to celebrate the news of the rebels' capitulation and to reiterate his deep and everlasting love. Anne's eyes glittered. "Just stunning."

"Take it, it's yours," Jane declared, trying to pry the band off her finger without success.

Despite the excitement behind his wife's eyes, Edward put a cautionary hand over Jane's. "No, no, Jane. It is yours. It is a magnificent gift from your loving husband. You must wear it proudly to show his forgiveness."

His forgiveness. She was the one who needed to forgive. Her deep regret over her action had quickly ceded to hurt over her husband's outburst – an emotion she couldn't show to him, as it would only inflame him and drive them further apart. Penitence was the only acceptable reaction in this situation.

"I prefer my betrothal ring, a more honest ruby," she said. "This one once belonged to the woman I wronged. It makes my skin crawl."

"The Boleyn never wore such a ring," Anne said, then quickly rushed to add, "And you never wronged her."

"The stone was in a brooch of hers. He had it reset..." Jane's voice trailed off, then rose suddenly with her next words. "Is that how he meant it? As a reminder of his warning?"

"He meant it as an apology," Edward said firmly. "For words he did not mean."

"Didn't he?"

"Stop it. Stop it right now," said Edward. "The King loves you. You are in no danger, you never were. What you did was stupid, not treasonable. Besides, Cromwell turned it around and persuaded the King to show mercy. Because of your plea, lives were saved. You were a blessing."

Edward's words rang hollow. She had heard her husband jest with Cromwell about the foolish rebels who believed his promises of peace. They had used her, nothing more.

She hadn't thought it possible that she would ever resent the man who had transformed her life. Her sovereign lord and husband, God's own anointed. But she did. How could he turn on her so quickly and so brutally?

"I was shamed and threatened."

Edward took a deep breath. "Your public disobedience spurred him to spout ridiculous threats he will never carry through. But there is no reason for you to question the sincerity of his apology now. Especially given how much his people love you."

"That didn't help Catherine of Aragon," Jane answered sullenly.

"But it condemned the Boleyn," Edward replied.

The words struck a chord deep within her, and she lashed out. "I thought treasonous crimes condemned the Boleyn?"

Jane flinched at her harsh sarcasm. She had to stop that, or it would destroy her. Praise God that only Edward and Anne had heard her say that. She dared not suggest that her husband or his minister had manufactured evidence.

"She had to die," Edward said it simply. "The exact charges against her were determined by the lawyers based on what they could prove. For me, they make no difference."

Oh, God, she was right. The Boleyn was not really an evil wanton. Jane willed herself to calm her ragged breathing. She cast down her eyes, fingers pressing a wrinkle on her skirt as if their heat and moisture could iron it out on their own. "You don't think the truth matters."

"Our Lord was able to hold to the truth but look where that got Him. In life we need to weigh evil against the good it does."

Jane couldn't stop a tear from creeping down her cheek. Edward leaned forward and caught it. "Jane," he said gently, "women you know and trust gave honest testimony against her. More than one hundred ancient lords of this country examined the evidence and agreed that the law required them to condemn her to death. This was not the kind of question that provoked a crisis of conscience – there were no martyrs to her cause like Bishop John Fisher or Sir Thomas More. The King was right to do what he did."

Was he? Anne Boleyn's accusing face rose up mutely before Jane. Or was the Boleyn's look one of knowing sympathy for the woman who now stood in her shoes?

"So what will stop him from carrying through with his threat and doing the same thing to me?"

"He'll not harm you."

Edward was speaking the way the old Edward explained things to a sister he considered somewhat slow. He wasn't allowed to do that anymore. She was the Queen. "He needs an heir," she said with full authority. "If I don't give him one, or if I give him a girl, I might be put aside."

Edward was not cowed. "The latest Act of Succession allows the King to choose his own heir. He can father a son anywhere; he does not need to put you aside because of it."

"And that is supposed to comfort me?" she snapped, even though the Act did guarantee her safety.

"Stop thinking that he will treat you the way he treated the Boleyn. He even told the Spanish Ambassador he thought himself unlikely to have more children."

"That was when we were first married. Before I miscarried my first pregnancy. I know how disappointed he is now from how hopeful and expectant he was then."

Edward opened his mouth to answer then shut it just as quickly. "Wait a minute." His eyes glittered. "You said 'first pregnancy'…was there a second?"

Jane flushed and looked away. "No."

"Are you with child now?"

"I don't know."

"How late are you?"

"Not long enough. Two weeks, maybe three."

"She is irregular, don't you remember," added Anne pointedly.

Edward swept down onto his knees. "Your husband loves you, he is committed to you. I beg of you not to endanger the life growing inside you – you must calm your fears."

"She's not like the Boleyn," said Anne. "And this is not like then."

Jane was transported back to January, the day when Anne Boleyn had miscarried after finding Jane on the King's lap. Another horrible thing Jane had done to her. *Oh, God.*

"Of course not," agreed Edward. "But she should take care anyway. There is no excuse for criticizing him in public. She doesn't want to anger him a second time."

"You mean a third," said Jane. "He yelled at me only days after we were married. He was angry with Mary, he wanted to put her on trial for treason – before she had submitted of course – and I defended her. He forgot he was a bridegroom and snarled that I had taken leave of my senses."

Edward shook his head. "Again, you were meddling in state affairs. You must stop doing that."

"But I was right about Mary, and I am right about the abbeys.

Shall I ignore my duty to my conscience, my husband, and my country, and allow him to make grievous mistakes because I am afraid to speak up? God will not forgive me such cowardice."

Edward shook his head. "There are better ways to express your doubts than a public challenge. If you think he is making a grievous mistake, for God's sake do it by questioning him gently in private."

Jane closed her eyes and shook her head. She needed real guidance right now over how exactly she could both satisfy God and placate her husband, but there was no one who could give it to her. She needed a son.

More and more, she needed God's mercy to be revealed in a son.

December 23, 1536 ... 3:30 p.m.

Jane sat alone in her darkened bedchamber at Windsor. The curtains were drawn against the setting sun, and the candles were snuffed. Only the fireplace gave off any light, ghostly tongues of dancing red heat. Jane sat close to it, staring into the flames, with her mother's letter in her hand. It was short, written just to let them know Father had died.

Jane sighed. She looked for grief, but felt only hollow shock. He had been a cruel and demanding parent, a man who cared only about himself. Jane had spent her entire life trying to make him proud of her, but he had been too convinced for too long that she would never amount to anything. One of his meanest comments actually came after her marriage, when he warned her not to congratulate herself unless she birthed a son. Part of her was glad he died before news could reach him that she had miscarried another child. It had happened two weeks ago, the day Mary officially returned to court.

Mary had arrived from Hundson in the afternoon, retiring immediately to her own rooms to prepare for the formal welcome, an occasion that required far more pomp than her travel clothes could offer. Jane and the King had waited for her in Windsor's Great Hall, surrounded by the entire court. After she was announced, the sea of courtiers had parted so that Mary could proceed through their ranks. She curtsied twice, made a sweeping obeisance to the King, then fell on her knees and asked for his blessing. He took her hand, raised her, and presented her to Jane who kissed her and warmly bid her welcome. The applause that broke out caused the King to stare menacingly at his Privy Councilors.

"Some of you wanted me to put this jewel to death," he said.

There was a stunned silence, which Jane broke. "That would have been a great pity, to lose your chiefest jewel of England."

Henry smiled and patted her belly. "Nay, nay, Edward," he laughed. Jane hadn't told him of the possibility – but he clearly knew and had even already named it. She flushed and missed some of the conversation, until Mary asked after her half-sister and whether she could be brought to court as well. Jane didn't answer, not wanting Elizabeth there but not wanting to say it. Jane had felt guilt over her pettiness, but not enough to prompt any kindness toward the little girl whose mother she had supplanted. And then that night the bleeding started.

JANE'S THOUGHTS WERE JOLTED BACK TO THE PRESENT BY A page's unexpected announcement. "The Lady Beauchamp."

Anne appeared at the door, her belly entering before the rest of her. She was big with Edward's child. A constant joy to Jane – and a constant reproach.

"Your Majesty," Anne said immediately. "What are you doing?"

"Sitting," Jane said.

"It is so dark in here," Anne declared, opening the curtains to catch the fading light.

"I would be melancholy over my father's death," Jane answered. "And life."

"Ah." Anne began to close the curtains but just as quickly pulled them back apart. "You still need light, whatever little there is left of it."

Jane shrugged. Anne lumbered over to the chair next to Jane and lowered herself slowly. "This is not the time for melancholy. This is the time for rejoicing. Yesterday should have taught you that."

Jane closed her eyes. Yesterday had indeed been a God-given moment. For the first time in more than twenty years, the Thames had frozen solid, preventing the traditional ceremonial procession of boats that opened the Christmas season. And so Henry, Jane, and Mary went by horseback over the ice from Westminster to the City, warmly wrapped in furs, with the court following behind. The people thronged to see them, enormous crowds of well-wishers. Priests in copes and holding crosiers lined the path to bless them, and soft hymns filled the air. It was one of those magical moments that announces itself as a high-light of life, to be cherished during the experience and forever afterwards. But like so many joys, it had hidden sorrow and regret.

"During that rejoicing, my father lay dead at Wolf Hall."

"We didn't know," said Anne simply. "And I'm glad we didn't, glad that such a perfect moment was not tinged by grief."

Jane cringed at hearing her own guilty thoughts spoken aloud. "But it was, we just didn't know it. Doesn't that make it worse?"

"Just the opposite. More's the blessing."

Jane was not ready to be comforted. "Mother would have wanted us there."

"Your place is here. As is Edward's and mine. You know that, and so does she."

Actually, Mother's letter had stressed how Elizabeth's presence had been a deep blessing during Father's illness. Elizabeth, who would not have been at Wolf Hall had she not betrayed

Jane. That had to be an underhanded rebuke. "I don't know that she does," said Jane.

"It's not as though she is alone. She has Elizabeth. Tom will go. Even Dorothy will likely make the journey. She understands. As your father understood."

More guilt. "I never said goodbye."

"Your last parting was gentle. Take comfort in that."

Jane looked at her sister-in-law, searching for the right words to explain herself. "It was only gentle because I ignored his doubts about me. Now I will never have the chance to dispel them."

There. She'd said it. Jane closed her eyes. She would never be vindicated now. She would never look into his eyes and see contrition, admiration. Even if she birthed a son. Which she might never do.

Anne reached out and took Jane's hand. "I knew this grief was due to far more than your father."

Jane turned away.

"You miscounted," Anne said. "That is all."

"Stop saying that," Jane said, and regretted the sharp edge to her voice. She continued, softer. "You can say it to anyone else, but do not say it to me. I have miscarried twice now since my marriage. I am beginning to think I am cursed."

"You are not cursed; the Boleyn was cursed. She was evil; you are not."

The edge of Jane's anger left her, and her melancholy returned. "You don't understand. In the past, when life went against me, I accepted it. I believed that God was testing me, and was happy to have Him do so. I was ready to bear all the indignities that came my way because I believed in my own essential goodness. I didn't care that others could not see it, I still knew it was there."

"And now?"

"And now I feel God turning from me."

"He is not turning from you, He is smiling on you."

"Is that what you call it? Is that God's favor, to feel your children drain out of your womb, to see people die around you – some because of your very existence?"

Anne shrugged. "I don't know what to say."

"There is nothing to be said. It is why I sit alone in the dark, hoping for some sort of guidance."

"Have you spoken to your confessor about this? Surely he will ease your mind."

"I have spoken to him many times. He has been quick to give me absolution. Unfortunately, I don't trust that he has the power to do so."

At Anne's quizzical look, Jane smiled ruefully. "How ironic is it that I, the great protector and hope of the Catholic faction, do not believe that a priest can intercede with God for me on this issue? This makes me more of a Lutheran than anyone at court."

Anne opened her mouth, but before she could respond, the page returned to announce Lady Rochford.

"Your Majesty," Lady Rochford said, bowing as she swept into the room. "The King begs you to join him in the Presence Chamber to allow the Spanish Ambassador to wait upon you. And Robert Aske and his comrades as well."

The announcement succeeded where Anne had failed. Jane swallowed and let the hope and trust of the previous day's frost fair wash over her. The Spanish Ambassador. Robert Aske and some of the other leaders of the Pilgrimage of Grace. Wanting to wait upon her.

God was indeed smiling on England. He had bestowed grace upon the entire country, and Jane needed to remember that and thank Him for it. Her place was here. She had to be part of the festivities, happily so, for the peace of the realm. Enough of self-pity. "It will be my pleasure," she replied.

Duty would carry her through this time, with its reassuring moral compass. Just as it always did. *Bound to obey and serve, after all.*

February 1, 1537 ... 4 p.m.

Jane's hand rested lightly on her brother's as they strolled down the Long Gallery upstairs at Greenwich Palace. It was just the two of them: Anne had delivered a healthy son and had retired from court. She hadn't gone too far, since Edward had found the perfect location on the south side of the Strand, just off the River Thames. The Strand was the road that joined the Tower of London to the east with the Palace of Whitehall to the west. And the river led to Greenwich Palace, Richmond Palace, and Hampton Court Palace. Edward could go home to Anne every night, knowing he was never more than an hour away from the King or Jane. Even better, he had purchased not just the house but several other buildings, even chapels, around it that he rented out. Eventually he would build a rich residence, but for now the extra income it brought had already almost equaled his initial investment.

Jane was delighted for the two of them, and proud of her brother's cleverness, but her joy was tempered by missing one of the only people with whom she could take off her mask. Anne might be haughty and hard to please to most, but she was fiercely loyal to Jane. Anne had seen Jane through all her crises, taking her side when Edward tried too hard to impose his will. Which was often. Now Jane had no one but Tom to intervene for her. And Tom was not the most helpful or reliable of people.

Not that Jane really needed someone to counterbalance Edward. Nowadays they agreed on most things outside of religion, and she had learned not to discuss that topic with anyone. For herself, she had learned to let her actions, not her mouth, speak for her soul.

She looked out the window at the gardens beyond, and saw the rain driven almost sideways by the wind. They would not venture outside today. No, this was the best way for them to speak privately. Appearances discouraged Jane from being alone in her rooms with Edward. No reason to remind people of her predecessor.

"Elizabeth would like to come back to court," he said. "She is deeply sorry that she hurt you."

Elizabeth wanted to come back. Jane's heart soared, then plummeted as she remembered the hurt of her sister's cruel certainty that the King would never marry Jane. "She said she is sorry?"

"She said she was wrong to doubt you, to allow herself to be ruled by fear."

Jane could hear her sister's voice in those words, and the sound was as comforting as it had always been. She loved her sister, she truly did. But could she trust her? "She was wrong to leave," Jane said firmly.

"She knows that," Edward replied. "She has known that for a long time."

"So why didn't she apologize earlier?"

"She didn't think you would ever forgive her and she couldn't bear your reproach."

Jane turned that over for several paces. People were afraid of displeasing her now. As afraid as they'd once been of displeasing the Boleyn, even though Jane didn't slap people like her predecessor had done. And, after all, Elizabeth had owed a great deal to the Boleyn, enough to justify her fear. Jane had won. And now she could afford to be magnanimous.

"It would be nice to have her," Jane finally said.

"Then may I tell her she is welcome?"

"Yes."

The truth was, she was more than welcome. Jane needed her sister. Desperately. She needed a woman's perspective. Just the other day a disturbing issue had almost sent Jane to visit Anne for advice. It had begun with Will Somers.

"Don't crown her now – she hasn't borne you a son yet. Save your coins lest you change your mind." Those were Somers's actual words, spoken in her husband's chambers, in front of all his men. And according to Tom her husband had guffawed over the joke, as had Sir Nicholas Carew and everyone within earshot.

Somers had next turned to Edward. "Ah, my Lord Beauchamp is not happy with such a jest."

That should have presaged an apology, but his next words were even worse. "You must undoubtedly be thinking of the fate of the brother to the last queen who failed to bear a son."

Such a terrible and mean exchange. Her husband had finally stopped him there, but all he had said was, "Now, now, Will. Enough." No denial, no reassurance.

Tom had sworn that the humor reflected the ridiculousness of the jokes. But Edward had scolded him for telling Jane, and his tightly pressed lips bespoke the truth at their heart.

JANE PUT A HAND ON HER STOMACH AND SIGHED. ANOTHER possibility was growing inside her, another chance at redemption – or downfall. She needed this child. Because winning the King's love was not enough. Just as it hadn't been for the Boleyn. Jane needed to at least carry a child to term, not lose it before it had progressed beyond mere chunks of flesh in her monthly course.

"Do you need to rest?" Edward asked.

Jane snatched her hand away from her belly. "No."

"Elizabeth will be good for you," Edward said.

He was right. Jane needed her sister. Elizabeth would put a calming hand on Jane's belly and bring her steeped herbs to drink. Elizabeth would soothe Jane's fears and turn her mind to happier thoughts.

Yes, Elizabeth would help her be calm for the child's sake and for her own. Fear was deadly. Just ask the Boleyn.

February 25, 1537 … 2:30 p.m.

It was a rare winter day, slightly cold but sunny, and not at all windy. It was the kind of weather that prompted the world to stream outdoors and pretend it was early summer. Indeed, it had spurred an impromptu archery contest for the men of the court, while the Queen and her women looked on and provided appropriate gasps and applause.

It was the King's turn to shoot and he slowly pulled back the bowstring. The arrow found its way to the red center of the target, and the crowd around him burst into hearty appreciation. Courtiers were always so relieved when the King excelled in a competition; it made the world more pleasant. The Duke of Suffolk was up next. Jane saw him squint and adjust his aim a touch lower before shooting. His arrow came in just beneath the King's, barely still in the center, and Jane wondered whether he had done that deliberately. She hoped the thought did not occur to her husband.

"Your Majesty, you have clearly bested me," the Duke said, bowing.

"And I will keep the purse that I wagered," Henry replied. "But I want more of a reward than that." The King turned to his wife. "I shall seek a prize from you, Madam," he said.

Jane smiled. "I made blackwork cuffs for you, Sire. I have been waiting for an occasion to give them to you."

He held up his hand to her. "Lead me to them."

As she placed her hand in his, she looked deep into his eyes. The tenderness she saw there heartened her, but the joy she felt twisted to dismay. He thought she might be with child – she knew from experience that he counted the days as carefully as she did. Was this love for her or for the promise within her, the baby she might too easily lose? What if one day she stopped seeing that look, like Anne Boleyn had after too many miscarriages? Jane cast her eyes down, hopefully before he had read the hurt in them.

Their gentlemen and ladies fell in behind them, chattering among themselves, and they made their way back to the palace where Cromwell awaited them. He quickly approached and whispered into Henry's ear. Jane saw her husband's eyes hood, his lips tighten. He whispered back, and Cromwell nodded solemnly.

"They will feel your wrath," Cromwell said quietly.

Henry looked at Jane. "Come give me my prize," he said. "Leave us," he said to the others.

Jane kept silent until they reached her rooms, understanding that this was what he wanted. Something had happened that he wanted to put aside, and it need not concern her until he was ready to discuss it. She went directly over to the corner cabinet, retrieved the cuffs and handed them to him with both hands and a smile.

She was proud of the work. She had carefully counted the stitches of black silk thread and worked them into the white linen bracelets in a complicated geometric pattern. "It is just the style you prefer."

He looked down at them, unmoved. "It is."

That was a sign that she should press him. They were alone now, he might be receptive. "What's wrong?" Jane asked.

"The rebels are back. Another uprising, this one in Cumberland."

Jane's eyes widened. She had not expected this. How could his people rise again? Jane felt the betrayal personally, as Henry must. The protestors had been pardoned for their treason, they had even been given the chance to speak with their king and express their views with the proper respect. Henry had explained where they were wrong in their thinking, and he had let them convince him to make some changes in his religious policy. Of course, he had also made promises he had no intention of fulfilling, like holding Jane's coronation in Yorkshire, but they didn't know that. Why would they revolt again?

"I'm so sorry," she said.

"This time I will show no mercy. This time my army is ready. And I will tell the Duke of Norfolk to cause dreadful executions. I want him to hang the bastards on trees, quarter them, set the quarters in every town…"

Jane cast her eyes down, nauseated. "That will be a fearful warning."

"Aye," he agreed. "That's what's needed here." He stopped, and his voice turned silky. "But where's your plea for clemency, Madam? Surely you have one."

She looked up at him. His lip was curled and his eyes glinted like the giant ruby reminder she wore on her finger. She shook her head. "Nay."

Some of the anger left him and it left room for pain to enter his voice. "I must stand firm. You have to remove your enemies, not leave them to fester. Forgiveness emboldens a traitor. My father taught me that."

For the first time, Jane understood his side of it. Really understood. Edward had tried to explain this, but it always seemed too pat an explanation. Now, feeling her husband's real regret changed everything. Yes, he had to do this. And yes, God understood.

She took his hand and kissed it with all the reverence she used to offer when kissing the hand of a priest. The rest of his anger dissipated and he took Jane into his arms. "A king can't shy from difficult actions," he said.

"It must be terribly hard to make these decisions and know they are right," she said, meaning it.

His arms tightened and Jane knew she had said the right thing. As they stayed that way, a thought grew in Jane's mind, the bridge between his position and the rebels' misguided actions. Before she spoke, she turned her words over to gauge whether they would anger him and decided to take the chance. "If it were me, I would have to spend my entire life in pilgrimage to reassure myself of God's guidance. When I was younger, I had to make a decision about something or other, and so I visited Hailes. I spent my coin and prayed with the priest and saw the Holy Blood of Christ. It pointed the way for me and comforted me greatly."

Henry raised a single eyebrow and Jane rushed to continue.

"Even now that I know it was fake, I can still remember the grace I felt. It was a comfort to believe that some places are truly holy and some relics can truly bless us. I crave that comfort still."

"I used to go on pilgrimages. Many of them, with Catherine, to beg for a son. I, too, felt comforted, though they certainly didn't make any difference. Of course, I prayed for something that contravened God's laws."

Jane smiled. He had acknowledged the deep emotional appeal of the abbeys. It was a start. And permission for her to continue. "I would love to go on a pilgrimage now, to offer prayers and feel close to God. It's why the abbeys are so important to me, why I begged you to restore them. I do understand that too many are corrupt, that many must be closed so that the righteous ones may flourish. I trust you to find the proper balance. And I'm sure that your people – most of them – do as well."

He was silent but he hugged her tighter. She closed her eyes, finally peaceful. He understood. And accepted.

CHAPTER TEN – 1537
SPRING / SUMMER

March 20, 1537 ... 11 a.m.

*J*ane sat up in her bed, clutching at the bowl in her hands, and retched again. Her ladies paused their sewing to watch her struggle.

The wave passed, and she lay back weakly.

"May we bring you something?" called the Duchess of Suffolk.

"No," Jane replied, wishing she didn't have to speak. The effort worsened her nausea, and she wished they would just trust her to ask if she wanted something instead of trying to prove their concern and efficiency.

The page rapped on the floor to announce a guest. Jane ignored it.

"Yes?" asked the Duchess, as if she had read Jane's mind.

"The Lady Ughtred."

Elizabeth. Her sister was back.

Her sickness forgotten, Jane sat up quickly in bed and turned toward the door where Elizabeth stood, waiting. She had lines on her face that were not there a year ago. She looked older, more careworn. She walked in, eyes wide and shoulders hunched, before bowing formally and low. "Thank you, Your Majesty, for having me," she said. "I am honored."

Elizabeth looked so contrite and humble that it hurt and soothed Jane's heart at the same time. She jumped out of bed to raise and hug her. "I am so glad you are here."

Elizabeth clasped Jane hard but pulled away quickly. "Your Majesty, go back to bed. There is no reason for you to be up and about right now."

Jane let herself be led back and allowed the other ladies to greet and hug her sister. Elizabeth had always been a favorite, and none of them had seen her since their days together in the Boleyn's household.

Jane watched from the bed, listening to the gossip, which did not require anything more than a smile. Such a blessing. Jane was happy to see the color return to Elizabeth's face along with her easy attitude. *Her sister was back.*

Suddenly the prattling annoyed Jane, it impinged on her own time with Elizabeth. "And now, ladies, you may be excused so that I may hear some family news. I shall not need you until after supper."

"What shall we have sent in for you?" asked Lady Rochford.

Jane closed her eyes. How could she stand this for another month, this horrible sensitivity not just to food but even to odors? "Chicken. Maybe a sirrop of quinces. No bread." The smell of seared meat was fine, but a crust of bread secreted in a maid's pocket went straight to her stomach. And felt just like fear.

She turned to Elizabeth and patted the bed beside her. "Sit with me. You make me feel better just by being here. It is good to have you back."

"It is good to be back. I was wrong to leave. I just—"

Jane cut her off. "You did what you thought was right at the time, as did I," she said. "All is done."

"Thank you for understanding."

The plaintive note in her voice touched Jane and made it easier to let some of her veils fall. "I need you. I cannot be truly myself with anyone here, except Edward. And even him…"

Elizabeth giggled. "Well, I am glad to bring you comfort. Though I am glad you don't seem as sick as Edward warned me you were."

"Ah, but you have made me better."

Elizabeth reached out and patted Jane's knee, a soothing gesture that would have been condescending from Edward.

"Is it so terrible?" Elizabeth asked.

Jane shrugged. Women were given such sickness to atone for their original sin, so to a certain extent the misery reassured Jane. Though the theory conjured up Catherine of Aragon with her haircloth shirt mortifying her flesh so that God would give her a son. Which hadn't helped her.

"Truth be told, I am relieved that I have finally been given such a chance," she said. "And afraid that it will be taken from me."

Another pat from Elizabeth, more comforting than any words.

"And it's really not so bad," Jane continued, "just terribly unpleasant. If I keep absolutely still, sometimes I can trick the nausea into going away."

"That is indeed a good trick when it works."

"Was it this bad for you?" Jane asked.

"Yes," Elizabeth admitted with a smile in her voice. "But you will forget all about it once you bounce a happy, healthy baby on your lap."

That scared Jane. It was too close to hubris. The child still had not moved, what if it never did? What if it was already dead in her womb and this sickness was just her body trying to push it out? "Stop. You'll bring the Devil's eye onto me."

Elizabeth flinched. "I'm sorry, sister. I will be more careful. But you know that this sickness is a good sign, don't you? It means the baby is strong inside of you."

The old wives' wisdom calmed Jane. She took a deep breath and closed her eyes. That was all that mattered, that the baby be strong inside her. Praise God for this blessing. The pause let her pull her thoughts back. Trust in God, that was all she could do.

She retched again.

"Poor sister," said Elizabeth.

"I would have preferred to keep this secret until the baby quickened. But one moment I was speaking with the Duchess of Suffolk at a public supper and the next I was turning my head to vomit behind me." Jane shook her head at the memory. "The entire room fell silent. It was far beyond embarrassment. I had no idea what to say or do – and then they all broke into applause."

Elizabeth laughed. "I can well imagine."

"My husband most of all. First he called for the Archbishop of Canterbury to lead us all in prayer for me, then announced a celebratory masque for that evening. So much for discretion."

"There is no discretion possible with such a blessed occasion," Elizabeth said calmly. "The world wants to share your joy with you."

Again the prospect of happiness brought Jane's fears running. "What if joy turns to sorrow? Any failure now will be equally public, and then they will question my legitimacy, my—"

"Jane," Elizabeth interrupted her, reaching a hand to caress Jane's forehead, or perhaps test for fever.

How ironic that Elizabeth had left court because she didn't believe Jane would ever be Queen of England, and now that she had returned, would not resurrect any of her old doubts as to Jane's true destiny.

"I'm afraid. I don't feel worthy."

"Oh, Jane," Elizabeth hugged her and hushed her. "You of all people? You are the only one who is actually worthy of this – partly because you think you're not. You are the Queen of England doing her duty, and no one is better than you at fully committing to service."

Jane closed her eyes. "I need a son."

Elizabeth shook her head. "You don't need anything. It would be a blessing to give England an heir, but Edward says Parliament has ruled that one could come from anywhere."

Cromwell's doing. He had legislation passed that allowed her husband to father a son by any number of women and have him inherit despite his illegitimacy. It was supposed to reassure Jane, and indeed there was a part of her that appreciated the gesture, but the idea itself was devastating. Again she wondered whether Henry had strayed yet, as he had with Catherine and Anne Boleyn during their pregnancies.

Edward thought not. He said the King would be faithful until the child was born, out of superstition, but that Jane should not expect more than that. Jane already knew that, much as she prayed otherwise. The thing was, if she had a son her husband would love and honor her above anyone else. Forever. That would make it easier to tolerate his inevitable transgressions.

The soothsayers had predicted a son, but they had predicted a son every time any of the King's women had found herself with child. It would be stupid to do otherwise – they were rewarded for telling a happy King what he wanted so desperately to hear and would have been treated as knaves for suggesting that the baby might be a girl or die in the womb. Her women, too, said she carried a boy, because an old wives' tale claimed that girls stole your beauty and Jane's face had not changed. Jane constantly bit her tongue to keep from mentioning how until quite recently no one had ever believed that she had beauty in the first place.

But she liked the predictions; it was reassuring that everyone was filled with goodwill as if it were still Yuletide. The whole world seemed happier now, filled with hope. The rebels had been dispersed, and while the leaders would die for their mistake, thousands more had been pardoned. The King had determined to restore four of the seven sacraments that had been omitted from the Ten Articles, and he had told his bishops to draft the changes to the *Bishop's Book*. He was returning to the true faith, slowly but surely. That had to further her case with God. *Lord, give me a son and I'll save your abbeys.*

Jane winced at her attempted bargain with the savior who had shown Himself so impervious to her actions, and the movement made her retch again. Elizabeth put a hand to help hold the bowl but Jane motioned her away and lowered it, empty, when the wave passed.

"Not the best welcome for you," she said.

Before Elizabeth could answer, the page announced Edward and Tom.

Edward first nodded to Jane then turned to Elizabeth. "We heard you'd arrived and thought to greet you and our queen at the same time."

Tom did the opposite, nodding at Elizabeth before turning to Jane. "Also to bring your husband's apologies for countermanding your request for chicken."

"What?"

"You know how you said you craved quail?" Tom asked. "Well, your husband canvassed all of Christendom and finally found some. He received a box load this morning from an envoy from – Edward, was it Venice, or Flanders?"

"Does it matter?"

"I suppose not. Anyway, they are reserved for you alone, and your first batch will be in your room momentarily. He would have come to tell you himself but he is with the French Ambassador. Who sends his affection and congratulations by the way."

Quail! For the first time in days, Jane's stomach looked forward to a meal. "How wonderful! Though I have already gotten Lady Lisle to promise to send me some from Calais – in exchange for my promise to take one of her daughters into my service." Jane leaned back on her cushions.

"The ones she has been trying to place at court for the last ten years?" asked Edward. "She has sent rich gifts to every noble lady in England, probably France too."

"Well, perhaps she should have promised quail earlier," answered Jane.

"You're only taking one of the girls?" asked Tom. "Which one?"

"I told her I would take whichever one is more sober, sad, wise, discreet, and obedient. The other will join the household of the Duchess of Suffolk."

They all laughed. As always, the joy sobered Jane. "I am so grateful for all these gifts," she said, "and at the great care you are all taking of me. You too, Elizabeth, I am so glad you are here."

Another wave of nausea came over Jane, and she looked down, her mouth twisted into a grimace.

"Again?"

Jane closed her eyes and nodded.

"This phase will be over soon," Elizabeth said. "And then you will rise like the phoenix you are. Soon."

April 10, 1537 ... 2 p.m.

Thomas Cromwell kept his hands tight on the horse's reins to make sure its pace stayed slow and smooth on the path. He closed his eyes for a moment to let the sun shine warmly on his face and took a deep breath of the clean, Kentish air. He looked around at the small riding group and exulted again in his good fortune.

They were on a tiny, two-week progress to allow the King and Queen to inspect a newly-constructed pier at Dover, an important addition to the strengthening system of coastal fortifications. The trip also gave them an excuse to get away from London where the plague claimed ever more victims – and an opportunity to have the servants scrub the royal residences yet again.

The traveling group was just twelve carefully chosen people and some servants, since this was being treated as a private retreat rather than an official visit. The King and Queen rode ahead, setting a slow, comfortable pace while everyone else followed. Because he had overseen the construction of the pier, Thomas Cromwell had made the King's list, along with Thomas Seymour and Ralph Sadler, and even Cromwell's eighteen-year-old son, Gregory, who was riding next to the Queen's company, her sister Elizabeth. She and Gregory were engrossed in conversation and laughing quietly together. What a perfect match they made. How had Cromwell never thought of that before? What a triumph that would be, marrying his son into the extended royal family.

Would Beauchamp agree to the match? Yes. Even if the man hadn't owed his entire current success to Thomas Cromwell, the heir to a barony was a step up from the girl's last husband, and Cromwell would not demand a rich dowry. Still, Cromwell should bait the trap. He could get Beauchamp elected to the Privy Council, a position he coveted. That would do it. Cromwell filed away the information for later use and turned his attention back to the King.

Henry VIII was clearly glad to be in the country. The King was terrified of the plague, more terrified than he wanted to let on. When someone near him coughed, he flinched and his eyes flickered toward the source of the noise. If the man looked at all sick, he would be sent from court. Even if the man looked well, Henry would still have him watched to catch the first signs of deterioration. Henry had always hated sickness, and his discomfort was growing.

Cromwell had used the Queen's pregnancy as an excuse for Henry to minimize the physical exertion that would be required. The King had gratefully agreed to limit the daily riding time and keep a slow pace "for Her Majesty's sake" even though he was actually more infirm now than his wife. The fall from his horse back in January 1536, the one that knocked him unconscious for two hours, had unleashed something in his leg. He had always had occasional muscle spasms in his left calf, but they had become much more frequent and intense since the accident. And now both legs were subject to occasional ulcers that healed for a time only to reopen and bother him again. He had spent the last couple of months indoors, eschewing the hunts that once consumed entire days for him. Cromwell had suggested a carriage, but the King had insisted he didn't need one. He was ready to resume activity, he said. Slowly, of course.

THE KING SUDDENLY STOPPED AND CIRCLED HIS HORSE AROUND to face the people behind him. "That should be Sittingbourne up ahead of us," he declared, pointing to a church tower that rose up through a clump of trees.

"Are we going straight there?" Jane's smile was teasing, and the King and Cromwell exchanged puzzled glances.

"Why not?" asked the King. "It is today's destination."

Jane burst out laughing. "I know you too well, husband. This trip takes us right past the tomb of St. Thomas à Becket. You announced it only two days after I told you how I longed to go on a pilgrimage. You are so wonderful to me."

Cromwell had to work hard to keep a casual expression on his face. *Oh, God.* Not only was this not part of the plan, but the most valuable of the votive offerings to the dead saint already sat in the King's treasury for "safekeeping." Cromwell silently cursed the Queen's soft heart and Catholic leanings. This could ruin everything.

With only a single missed beat, the King agreed with his happy wife. "You do know me too well, sweetheart. But right now our path actually does lead to Sittingbourne." Turning to Cromwell with eyes laden with warning, or perhaps his own fear, the King continued. "Crum, when do we visit the tomb?"

"Your Majesty, it had been my plan to sneak away from you when we arrived to make sure the monks would be ready for us tomorrow…or the next day."

The Queen smiled smugly. The King exhaled deeply, clearly

in relief, and smiled back at her. Cromwell continued. "Er, now that the secret has been revealed, perhaps you would give me leave to go now to prepare the way for you?"

"Shall I accompany you, Father?" Gregory asked.

"Thank you, but I would take Sadler with me, if the King will spare him." Sadler had been the head of the group entrusted with bringing back the chief valuables of Beckett's shrine.

"Of course," the King agreed, waving his arm expansively before turning to ride on with his wife. Gregory turned back a last time to check on his father, who waved them on with a set smile.

Once the group was far enough away that he knew he could not be overheard, Cromwell, his heart racing, whirled around to Ralph. "How obvious is it that jewels are missing?"

Ralph's eyes crinkled. "Calm your mind, my Lord. Not at all. Becket's coffin is beautifully wrought of gold and silver and marvelously adorned with precious gems. We left it intact, and just took the gifts attached to hanging draperies or placed on pedestals nearby – which was where the greater value lay."

"So it appears untouched?"

"Praise God, yes. With no dissolution orders signed for it, we were careful not to take any steps that could not be undone. Or easily noticed."

Praise God. Praise God for this mercy. If Thomas Cromwell had been Catholic, he would have ordered a thousand Masses to be said in thanks for this reprieve. Henry VIII could not have borne the reproachful eyes of his beloved wife if she had been faced with a shrine that had been visibly desecrated. Such an experience might well have made him decide to halt further dissolutions and ruin the careful pace of reform that Cromwell was implementing. The King found it easy to order destruction but shunned its aftermath. It was how he could plot against the Boleyn for months: he knew he would never have to face her after she'd discovered his intentions.

"You are a good man," Cromwell said to his ward.

"You taught me well," Ralph replied.

Cromwell gripped the bridle to signal his horse. The men rode in silence. Cromwell was lost in thought, trying to strategize the royal visit to minimize the popish appeal. That would not be easy – especially since the Queen pursued the opposite goal. They would never be able to catch the monks in idleness or sin. Better to use this opportunity to further his latest plan, a semi-royal bride for his son.

May 27, 1537 ... 10 a.m.

The court had returned to Hampton Court, which had truly become the main royal residence in London. Greenwich of course was still a mainstay, but as it had been Anne Boleyn's favorite palace, Jane preferred to minimize their time there. No need to torture herself.

Jane had dismissed her other ladies, leaving the sisters alone in her library. Jane smiled at Elizabeth and said, "I felt it."

Elizabeth looked at her quizzically, then her eyes widened in sudden comprehension. "The baby? It quickened? Just now?"

"At Mass." Jane put her hand on her belly. "God smiled at me. It was a sign."

"And on Trinity Sunday! Let us tell the King, he will have Te Deums sung throughout the land on this glorious day."

Jane took a deep breath. "I know it will give him great joy, I know the world will rejoice with us, but there is a part of me that doesn't want to share this quite yet."

Elizabeth gave an automatic look around to make sure no one, maid or guard, was left in the room, then grabbed Jane's shoulders to give them a quick shake. "Stop it. All is well. There is nothing to fear."

Jane disengaged herself. "Nay, Elizabeth. This is different. I felt it move inside of me. And I felt such an urge to protect it as I have never known."

"You must stop allowing yourself to be overcome by fear."

"You don't understand. I am not. This is not about me, this is about my child."

Elizabeth looked confused. "So…"

"So I am afraid to celebrate the happy moments. I am afraid God will punish such arrogance."

"Ah, Jane," Elizabeth replied softly. "Whatever happens in the future, you are blessed now. Enjoy the grace of God while it is given to you, at least allow yourself to be grateful for this time. I loved my first husband, and as devastated as I was when he was taken from me, it would have been worse if I had not savored every moment with him while he was alive."

Jane looked over at her sister's gentle face and hugged her. She was right.

"And just as I loved my first husband, so will I love my second…"

Jane pulled back and looked at her quizzically. "What did you say?"

Elizabeth smiled and a tinge of pink spread across her cheeks. "Edward and Cromwell have discussed a match between me and Gregory."

Jane shrieked and hugged Elizabeth all the harder. Jane only stopped to wipe away a tear that trickled down her face. "I am so glad to hear this," she said. "It has been obvious for some time how the two of you have a great deal of respect for each other. When did this happen?"

"Edward told me this morning," Elizabeth said. "He also mentioned that the terms proposed were excellent," she added, a twinkle in her eye. Trust Edward to focus on matters like that.

Just then the baby moved again, and Jane gasped. She looked up, eyes shining. "This is a good sign. A sign that we should enjoy every moment of beauty and grace and hope. I am so happy for you. For all of us."

July 1, 1537 ... 11 p.m.

Jane practically purred with contentment. Her husband was rubbing her feet and hitting the sensitive spot at the top of the arch. It was just the two of them, in her bed with the curtains drawn around them.

"Your poor feet, so swollen."

"Everything is swollen. They say it happens to most women..."

"Are you sure this doesn't hurt?"

"Just the opposite. It is marvelous."

She closed her eyes. Emotion welled up in her. Fear and ecstasy at the same time and in the same measure, as if the fear was the price of the pleasure. The two together presented a tidal wave of intense emotion, both good and bad, neither good nor bad.

This could be the harbinger of a life lived in such joy – or it could be the taunting memory of something never to be enjoyed again. It was both and neither. And that was the answer. The only way to live with uncertainty was to embrace it. If these months were to be the last time she would enjoy such contentment in her life, so be it. Elizabeth was right: a far better attitude was to thank God every minute for giving her this time rather than squandering such a wonderful gift. By worrying, she would deprive herself of it all. She would end up afterwards with her life destroyed and no memories of what God's grace could look like to succor her.

The insight gave her a sudden need for action; she would jump out of her skin if she continued to just lie back and receive. "Let me at least have your feet at the same time," she urged, reaching for him. "Please."

"I should refuse...but I would enjoy it."

They soothed each other for a time, and Jane was thankful for the peace that enveloped her...at least until she saw a tear on her husband's cheek. "Henry? What's wrong?"

He started, then looked at her. "I am so very blessed right now, and so afraid for the future. I have come from darkness to light, and I am afraid that I was so long in the darkness as to ever be denied my heart's deepest desire."

It was the first time she had seen the terror in him, a terror that matched and even exceeded her own. "But you—"

"You center me, Jane. You calm me and bring me to a place of purity where God blesses me."

She reached to hug him, and rather than breaking away he pulled her to lie beside him in his arms. "It is through your name, your goodness, that I earn the right to petition God for a son. If this child is a girl, it will be my fault. If this child dies, it will be God's judgment of me. I chose two women who were denied to me by scripture. I made a mistake in ignorance but repeated it in full knowledge. You are the gift He has given me, you are my grace. And I accept all that comes with that."

Just then Jane felt a kick, as if the life inside her had heard the words. She took her husband's hand and put it on her stomach to comfort them all. *Surrender to grace,* she reminded herself and smiled.

CHAPTER ELEVEN – 1537
EDWARD

September 16, 1537 ... 7 p.m.

*C*romwell reined in his horse and turned on the white cobblestones. The King had paused yet again to wave at his wife's face in the receding window. The sun glinted off the distinctive red bricks for which Hampton Court was famous, making them glow with an otherworldly sheen.

Judgment was near.

With the estimated birth date of the royal baby exactly a month away, Queen Jane had "taken to her chamber." She had established her own residence at Hampton Court, where she would stay with none but her ladies while the King lodged with his men at Eltham Palace, his boyhood haven. It was close enough that he could be by her side within ten minutes. The King would maintain the official royal seat separately for an entire month, removed from the birthing process, the screams and the blood. He would not see his wife again until after the baby was born, after Jane had been bathed and robed and moved to the bed of estate from which she would receive the world's congratulations.

This was all part of the detailed protocol put into place by Henry's terrifying grandmother, Margaret Beaufort. The woman who had catapulted from an illegitimate branch of Edward III's descendants to matriarch of the Tudor dynasty when her son had, against all odds, seized the English crown. While history might give formal credit to Henry VII's military victory at the Battle of Bosworth, Cromwell knew it was Lady Beaufort's scheming and personal force that made it all possible. And once her son was on the throne she had worked so hard to secure for him, she turned her full attention to the rituals that would burnish his image and keep him there. The rich decorations, the pomp and formalities. Everything to stress the high office they held. It was a brilliant strategy, and a lesson that Cromwell kept ever in mind.

The King and Queen had enjoyed their last quiet meal together with their attendants before reciting Vespers in the chapel. Henry had brought Jane to the Great Chamber with all expected pomp, as if he hadn't done this so many times in the past – or been cheated of this experience because a babe had died early. Still, the King's face had been tight and Cromwell wondered whether he felt the room mock him with ghostly laughter. It would explain the abrupt departure, which was followed now by endless stops to catch a final glimpse of Jane until the great looming question was answered: boy or girl?

Cromwell was sanguine, as much as it was possible to be under the circumstances. It would be what it would be. If an heir was not born now, they would get one elsewhere. But it would be such a miracle to get it now. It would soothe the entire country, reassure them that God loved their king. And it was time, after all. Even the worst run in dice eventually produces a winning roll.

The King waved one last time. He clicked his cheeks at his horse and turned around to ride off. He didn't look back again. Cromwell didn't either. It was back to work now, to keep the kingdom safe regardless of what happened with the women. As always.

October 12, 1537 ... 1 a.m.

Jane tossed and turned in her great bed, unable to find relief. The red streaks of pain were worse than any she had ever known. They gripped the very core of her being and she could hear the hiss of their threats to never leave her. Over the past three days and three nights Jane had known only momentary respites between pangs. It had never occurred to her that someone could suffer like this and still live.

Her ladies could do nothing for her. They mopped her face and purred soothing words but they could no longer penetrate the pain that separated her from the world like a suit of armor. The room was no help. The rich draping over all the walls and windows, the cloth of Arras that was meant to be regal and comforting, was oppressive. It made Jane feel as if the walls were closing in on her.

Some of her ladies, like her sister Elizabeth, had been through this themselves, and their eyes were filled with under-standing tears; some, like the Lady Mary, were new to this, and their eyes betrayed their panic. Jane had considered sending Mary away but feared that the gesture would be misunderstood. Besides, protocol required her presence, and there was safety and comfort in following the rules.

Jane heard the bells again, pealing from every church in the city. The King had sent the royal heralds to London with the news of her labor, and the churches had delivered their ringing response. It was comforting to hear their different timbres, faint and far off at times. When the pain subsided, she imagined that she heard the murmurs of the thousands of supplicants at the Masses she knew were being said for her safe delivery. So many people were praying for her. The hopes of an entire country were centered on her now. Surely God would be merciful, for their sakes.

"Good job, Madam. You are almost done." Elizabeth's voice was gentle as she laid a cool cloth on Jane's forehead.

"Ye'll be ready to push soon. It's just a short time now," said the almost toothless midwife. She was a thin old woman with stooped shoulders. Her skin was heavily lined but her gnarled hands were strong and her brusque ways inspired confidence. Her daughter had been the one Jane had hired, a gentle lady, plump and soft, who had tended the Queen from the first twinges to the gut-wrenching grips these thirty or so hours later. But after such a prolonged labor, Jane had stopped responding to gentling, and the hag had emerged from the shadows by the fire. Her peppery voice gave sharp orders the ladies all scrambled to fulfill.

Jane moaned again, and Elizabeth rubbed the furrows in the Queen's brow, trying to calm her. "You're almost there."

"*Dominus vobcisum,* Thy will be done," Jane panted. "*Dominus vobcisum. Dominus vobcisum, dominus vobcisum.*" When the next pains hit, she opened her mouth to scream but no sound came out. Through her agony she could see Elizabeth bite her lip and flinch.

"Tell me," Jane gasped when it had passed. "Was it this bad for you?"

"My own labor was shorter. I was not so tired as you."

Jane closed her eyes and nodded.

"But I have forgotten all the pain already. I felt relief the second the babe was out, so much so that my body longs for a younger brother for my son. As will yours, sweet sister. It is only a small time yet until yours will too."

"A son." Jane whispered the words, her eyes still closed. Terror that this pain was part of her punishment and not the price of exaltation intensified each spasm.

Another contraction. Her innards were on fire and she gripped at her stomach.

"Push, Yer Majesty. Push as hard as you can."

Jane tried to do as she was told, but the old hag just kept yelling at her. "Push. Push, I say. Harder."

And then the gnarled hands were on her stomach, pressing on it as if she would force the child out herself.

The pain passed and the toothless face was in hers. "Ye'll have to push harder."

Jane had pushed with all the strength she had. How much more was needed? *Dominus vobcisum.*

"Ye'll have to push even harder if you want the babe to come out. He's in there good."

Jane moaned by way of response. Even that took all the strength she had right then.

"She'll not last through this."

Jane heard the old hag's voice as if through a fog, as if Jane were floating.

"She's too weak," said another voice.

"Her hips are too small."

Maybe this was her punishment. To die in childbirth and never hold the sweet thing who had kicked and hiccupped inside of her. Never touch its tiny cheek, never look on its face, never find out whether it was a boy or a girl. Was this what God had in store for her?

Was this her test? Again she asked herself whether this was ultimate punishment or sweet mercy. Visions of her signature circled around her, whether like guards or attackers she could not be sure. "Jane the Quene" she had signed on hundreds of birth announcements. The first few were blotchy, her letters unsure and crooked, and she had discarded those before anyone else had seen them. She made Edward hold her hand to guide her through the shapes, and pride had replaced shame once she had gotten the knack of it. Of course, that same pride ceded to panic after he left, when she looked at the pile and remembered a similar stack in Queen Anne's bedchamber just before the birth of Elizabeth. Card after card announcing the birth of a prince, card after card that had to be changed. This time, the scribes had left themselves room to add two esses, and Jane had wondered whether she was the only person who noticed the taunting power of the empty space, the challenge to keep it blank and the doubt that she would.

Sweet Jesu! Another pain, but not so bad as before, or maybe she just didn't care. What did it matter? Boy or girl, pain or death. Whatever happened would expiate her sin and set her free, praise God.

"Push, Yer Majesty."

She heard the voices but barely understood them. What did they want? Why were they bothering her?

"Push harder."

She felt the hands on her stomach, pushing and prodding.

"Wake up, Yer Majesty. Wake up and try to help us."

She would help soon. Just a little sleep first.

Then a new pain, sharper than the rest, pulled her out of her trance.

"You must do this," she heard from a great distance. "Push."

Her mind fuzzy, she summoned every bit of the nonexistent strength left in her reserves to push the air from her lungs, push the blood to her hands and feet, and push the child out of her womb. The relief was immediate, but she didn't have time to thank God for it.

She had already passed out.

October 12, 1537 ... 2 a.m.

Cromwell handed the King the next of the documents to be signed.

"This is your approval of the fees of the deputy wardens of the East and Middle Marches, and the annuities of the pensioners," he said. "Half of these are to be paid now."

The King grunted. He was exhausted, they all were, but too anxious to sleep. To keep his sovereign calm, Cromwell pushed the King through his paperwork. A practical solution, plus it had the tinge of virtue. If you had a plea for God as they did, it helped to cloak yourself in honor.

"The next installment will be paid at Christmastime," Cromwell continued.

The King lifted his hand to sign the paper, but the clattering of horse hooves in the distance stopped them both and they looked out the tall window to the left. It was the final quarter of the moon and cloudy, so they could only see a dark blob approaching. But it came from the direction of Hampton Court.

Cromwell looked over at the King, his quill frozen in midair. A messenger had arrived every hour since the Queen's labor began three days ago, to update them on her progress. This one seemed early. Very early. Or was it just that they hadn't noticed the last one was late? The bells that marked the hour stopped after midnight, so he wasn't sure. He looked at the candles. They had not burned anywhere near enough for it to have been an hour. This was it.

They watched, riveted, as the horse stopped in the courtyard. The hood on the messenger's cloak hid his face. He leaped off his mount, threw his reins to a page and took off into the castle. No different from any page before him, but Cromwell felt a tingling down his spine. Judgment was imminent.

The same thoughts must have been going through the King's mind because he pushed out his chair and sank to his knees. Cromwell quickly imitated the King's stance, and the two men bent their heads over clasped hands and whispered fervent prayers until the messenger's footfalls were heard in the hall.

"Out of my way, fool," they heard in the doorway. "The King has been awaiting this news for nigh on thirty years."

The two men crossed themselves before pushing up to standing. The King lifted his head to wait, like Julius Caesar staring down Brutus. Only his hands betrayed his turmoil, trembling on the desk in front of him.

The messenger burst in without waiting to be announced, throwing himself on his knees without taking his eyes off the King's face. "Your Majesty, the Queen is delivered of her child." His voice shook but his face glowed. "A boy."

Cromwell felt grace envelop him. *Praise God.* He could rest now, England was safe. *Praise God.*

The King blinked, but otherwise remained immobile. Meanwhile, Will Somers and Edward Seymour came running into the room, eyes wild and mouths slightly ajar.

"You have a son, Your Majesty," the messenger repeated. "God save the little prince and God save Your Majesties."

The King turned his gaze to the sky. "I have a son," he whispered with wonder in his voice and tears in his eyes. The humility passed quickly, and he raised triumphant fists into the air. "I have a son!" he yelled.

More men tumbled into the room, not just the King's gentlemen but pages and servants who couldn't help themselves and needed to celebrate such an event. This was a blessed day for the entire country.

"God save Your Majesty," someone called, which led to cheers and hugs all around.

Taking his arm from around Cromwell's shoulders, the King detached a small velvet purse from his waist and tossed it to the man in green. "Thank you for the tidings. You have earned this."

"The world will rejoice with you," said Somers.

"Here, here," the men repeated. Then one broke in, "When do we repair to Hampton Court?"

Cromwell cursed silently that his joy had distracted him from his duty. There were a thousand things to take care of now that the child was born. All his lists and papers relating to the birth and the resulting celebrations were there, at Hampton Court, waiting for him. He turned to the King. "We should go now," Cromwell said.

The King needed no urging and took off down the hallway. Edward Seymour followed after him.

Cromwell raced over to the window, and yelled out to one of the pages below. "The King needs a horse. We all need horses. Work quickly, man, for the love of God."

He turned to the messenger. "Go find the Lord Chamberlain

and tell him the news. The King may choose to sleep at Hampton Court tonight, and many of his men may want to do the same."

"The quarters were prepared at the Queen's first pains," said a voice behind him. Cromwell whirled around and saw the Lord Chamberlain had just arrived, a broad smile on his face. "All of them," he continued. "And there will be a fire in the King's rooms by the time he arrives. The servants all have their instructions."

"I'm going over as well, and will not return. I have my important papers there but I will still want everything on my desk. And the King's."

"I have prepared for that too."

"Good job, my Lord," Cromwell said and clapped the man on his shoulder. Then Cromwell dashed out of the room to follow the King. Cromwell didn't want to miss this. He had earned the right to stand beside the King at this moment.

When Cromwell got to the courtyard, he saw that the King and Beauchamp had just mounted their horses. The King spurred his on but Beauchamp courteously waited for Cromwell to leap onto his mount. They caught up easily, though kept a length behind for protocol and respect.

The quiet respite and rhythmic pace gave Cromwell a chance to think. And to fret. The entire country would see this heir as the divine seal of approval. What if he was sickly? What if he died? The messenger's demeanor hadn't suggested that, but what if he was sent too soon? Cromwell found himself needing to see the tiny boy, to be comforted by strength and vitality. And life. *Please God, let it be so.*

The ride was short enough that no one else caught up to them before they arrived at Hampton Court and found the pages there waiting expectedly, cheering as the men approached. "God bless Your Majesty," they said as the King dismounted.

"God bless us all," the King answered, starting to run. "And God bless the Queen," he hollered to anyone who listened.

Cromwell found himself out of breath, and Edward too

panted, but they still managed to keep up even though the King never slowed his pace. "My son! Where's my son?" he bellowed as he went.

The doors to the Queen's chamber were wide open, and the ladies milled about, laughing and looking at the King full in the face. Cromwell had never seen that before – he had only ever seen people shrink from their news, or stutter with terror over it. This was no fairy tale, this was the prince they'd been waiting for.

One of the ladies held up the lad, swaddled already in cloth of gold to meet his father. His face was round and full, with cheeks ruddy like the King's. His eyes were closed, but you could see his features were regular and strong. *Praise God.*

In three giant and hurried strides, the King crossed to the foot of Jane's bed, where she lay arrayed to greet audiences. Her lady thrust the precious bundle into the King's arms. He staggered slightly from the weight of the tiny baby and froze again as he had when he'd first heard the news.

His shoulders began to shake. He turned to face Jane, tears streaming from his eyes. "My son," he whispered.

"Our son," she answered with a smile, stretching out a hand as a sign to draw near.

A woman came to take the child, but the King motioned her away and instead made the sign of the cross over the tiny forehead and kissed it. The sudden touch startled the boy, who broke out into strong, lusty sobs that warmed Cromwell's heart. The entire room, King included, smiled indulgently at the imperiousness of the young prince. The King called the woman back and handed over the precious bundle to be fed and cosseted.

The King looked empty as his son was taken away, but then recovered and turned his attention to his wife. He staggered to the side of her bed and sank to his knees to lay his head on her chest and sob his thanks.

Elizabeth took Edward by the hand but motioned for the ladies to withdraw. Cromwell took his cue and slowly backed out the door, glad to have seen this holy moment. And the healthy child.

Now the awe overtook him. It was done. Cromwell had kept such a tight rein on his hopes, hadn't let himself truly believe this would happen. And now it had. He could relax now. All his contingency plans, spurred by fear, could be put away in his cupboards. England had an heir.

A new sense of purpose rose inside him and he rubbed his hands together. Now the real work would begin. He smiled to himself. The Lord Chamberlain was not the only one who had prepared for this moment.

Cromwell strode off.

October 13, 1537 ... Midnight

Cromwell stood at the closed door of the Queen's bedchamber, waiting to be announced at this most intimate and yet most formal of occasions. He was stopping by to greet the King and the Queen before the christening of the long-awaited heir to the throne, since they would not attend the ceremony. Protocol afforded the young prince the chance to shine with full precedence, something that was only possible if his parents were not present. Even kings and queens were provided such a kindness: Henry had not gone to his father's funeral, and had remained hidden at Anne Boleyn's coronation. He would remain hidden at Jane's coronation, which had now been well earned.

And this young boy would one day not attend his father's funeral.

Cromwell bit his lip. *Careful.* Imagining the death of the King was treason. It was one thing to think it, but God forbid he should voice such a thought. At least there was no one there he would have said it to – he had carefully arrived before the rest of the court. Most importantly, he had arrived before Norfolk.

"Ah, Cromwell," he heard. "Come."

He walked into the room. The Queen was in the great bed in

which she would receive the world for the next ten days. Her long blond hair was carefully arranged to flow loose over the crimson mantle, edged with ermine, she had chosen for this occasion. The King sat in a chair of estate next to her, holding her hand. The beam on his face had not left since the child's birth and showed no signs of waning yet.

"Your Majesties, it is my great honor and joy to attend you on this most blessed occasion," Cromwell said, bowing deeply.

The King came over and embraced him. He held him for several moments before releasing him, nodding. "We are indeed blessed."

"Praise God," said Jane in a small voice.

Her face, always pale, was chalky white from her three days of labor. She was tired, but she held herself tightly upright. The rich gown made her look worse, in a dramatic twist from her usual pattern, where opulent trappings drew out her beauty.

"Just to let you know, Sire, I have eliminated those people from the guest list tonight."

"Good," the King said before turning to whisper an explanation to his wife.

They had prepared a list of invitees well in advance, but when the prince was born, Henry cut it by fifty guests and hundreds more attendants – a duke was allowed only six guests to accompany him, while a marquess was limited to five, an earl to four, a baron to three, and a squire to two. While the world deserved to rejoice, too many people were showing signs of sickness of late. The fewer people near the prince the better – nothing must touch the boy.

Not wanting to interrupt a private moment, Cromwell looked around to check the room again. It was ready for the festivities; thanks to Margaret Beaufort's rules, it had been ready since Jane first took to her chamber a month ago. Tonight was the most public celebration, the christening. Tomorrow would be the investiture, where the boy's rank as heir to the throne would be formalized through important titles. Right after that, the Seymour brothers would receive their own rewards – an earldom for Edward and a title for Tom – for the fertility of their proudest member. It had been Cromwell's idea to elevate them all at the same time and impress the Queen with her husband's thoughtfulness. He had made the suggestion without hinting at the ease with which such plans could be canceled, as they had been when Elizabeth was born. He knew the King had heard the unspoken words.

Cromwell let his mind open to all the possibilities this birth had opened up. It was a blessed first step to have an undisputable heir. Once the Queen provided a second son, the King's illegitimate daughters might be reinstated. That would make the girls powerful diplomatic tools, especially Mary who was currently of marriageable age. The signal was already given: both of them were being treated with the honor due to them as royal princesses. Yes, England's future had changed now. Thank God.

"God bless, sister, on such an occasion," Cromwell heard Edward Seymour's voice, heartfelt, intense.

The Queen held out her hand. Her brother walked over to her and let her pull his face close to hers before he rose to hug the King. While it was technically a violation of precedence, on this occasion it was right for him to use his unique position to congratulate the Queen before the King. Brilliant move.

Edward then turned to Cromwell and embraced him too, comrades. This was the culmination of everything. They had been successful, fully successful, at the one thing that mattered in life. Jane Seymour had birthed a son.

Again, the King and Queen turned to each other, whispering in blessed private moments, and so Cromwell and Edward did as they had always done: enjoyed each other's company while Their Majesties were otherwise occupied.

"Your sister is immortal, Viscount Beauchamp. Which I say reluctantly, wanting to call you by the title that awaits you, Earl of Hertford."

"I am happy to wait for that honor until the morrow. And I

thank you deeply, as I well know how much you were involved in the planning. I particularly appreciate your linking my elevation with my nephew's. It puts me in a better place to protect him and I know that you have conveyed to His Majesty how proud I am to take on this lifelong duty."

Well said. If Cromwell hadn't conveyed those thoughts to the King, that fine rhetoric would have prompted him to do so. Well done.

"His Majesty knew that long before I told him," Cromwell said, reassuring Edward on both fronts.

"I am beginning to tire of the bells, though."

Cromwell started, then saw the wry grin on Seymour's face and laughed, delighted. Every church within fifty leagues of the City continued the nonstop ringing that had begun at Jane's first labor pains.

"They will continue through the elevations, and several days after that, until we get the word back that every part of the country has heard the news. This is too important to stop the trumpeting too early."

"Good point," said Edward. "As long as the wine continues to accompany it."

Companion to the bells since the birth, wine flowed through every conduit in the seven parishes around the City. Why not fully celebrate the event that would cause the English people to set aside all resistance to the royal judgment? More than two thousand rounds of ammunition had been shot from the Tower within an hour of the birth, and an army of heralds had been dispatched before dawn to every part of the country to share the tidings. Five hundred announcements had left his office that morning, headed by the words "We be Delivered of a Prince," and laboriously signed well before the fact by a superstitiously reluctant "Jane the Quene," along with gifts to ambassadors and foreign rulers based on a carefully crafted list. Cromwell had, after all, planned this for years.

A vague commotion could be heard from the hall. People

were arriving. Two of the Queen's ladies rushed in from the side door, curtsying quickly to see if the Queen wanted any last-minute upkeep to her carefully arranged hair, or her pillows plumped, or anything else private before people arrived. Then one page introduced the Duke of Suffolk and the Archbishop of Canterbury, and a second page waited at his elbow to announce still more guests. The wave had begun. Some thirty people were expected to assemble in the Queen's apartments, after which the group would form a formal procession to the Chapel Royal. After the ceremony, they would all return to celebrate, but in the interim the Queen would have a chance to rest a bit, maybe even sleep. That would be good for her; it was clearly an effort for her to keep her eyes open. Poor thing, she needed to conserve some strength.

October 13, 1537 ... 2 a.m.

A gentle kiss on her lips penetrated Jane's consciousness. The touch was cool, a sharp contrast with the heat of her body. She opened her eyes slowly; Henry's face was only inches away. She smiled, happy.

"The ceremony is over," he whispered. "They're proceeding down the hall now. Can you hear the singing?"

She could, and she immediately stirred, panic gripping her.

He kissed her again and rose, offering her an arm to pull herself up to a straighter sitting position.

She gratefully accepted, and forced herself to wake even though she craved more sleep. The world would arrive momentarily to publicly celebrate her moment of triumph, and she had to be ready. "I should stand to receive them," she said.

"No, you shouldn't," he said. "They'll bring our son to me, then to you. There is no reason for you to stand for any of that."

He was right. No need to push herself. "Thank you," she said.

His face spread back into the smile that hadn't left him since he burst into her room, arms outstretched, an impossibly short time after she had sent the messenger to give the King the news of his son's birth. Every hour since then, he had whispered the name "Edward" to her, and kissed her hand.

They had settled on that name after he had said it to her belly on the night Mary had formally returned to court. It was the right choice. They didn't want another Henry; there had been too many others with sad ends. The son that Catherine had borne in 1512, who died after only 59 days of life. A second one, who had lasted less than an hour. And, of course, Henry FitzRoy. Truly, "Edward" was a better choice, especially since he had been born on the eve of the feast of St. Edward. Another divine sign. It was also nice that Jane's brother shared the name of the future King of England. His nephew. It cemented the Seymour role.

Cemented the Seymour role. Jane was struck again by how far she had come in only two years. From Edward threatening to send her from court for her failure to marry well, to making the best match of all. And bringing her family along. Triumph hummed in her, together with a profound gratitude that her ultimate wishes had been fulfilled.

THE HONOR GUARD SOON APPEARED, BEARING THE YOUNG prince. Her son. The rest of the revelers poured into the room after him, in order of carefully crafted precedence. First Mary and Elizabeth – King's daughters for all that they had been named bastards. Mary was godmother to the boy and Elizabeth carried the chrism, earning their places ahead of the Dukes and Duchesses of Norfolk and Suffolk, the Marchioness of Exeter, and Jane's own brothers, Edward and Tom. Jane stopped tracking the rest of the guests when Henry's daughters reached her side and began the bows and greetings of court ritual. Shouts of laughter and joy were everywhere, and the general glee sapped her energy more than she could ever have guessed. Mary and

Elizabeth knelt formally to the King and Queen, but beamed from the certainty of their father's good mood.

Jane was momentarily surprised at how practiced Elizabeth was at court etiquette. Here she was, only four years old yet a mature and engaging child whose bright eyes missed nothing. There had been talk around the time of Anne Boleyn's trial that Norris might have fathered her, or even Smeaton. But to look at her was to see a miniature version of the King, all red hair and white skin. And the same imperious mouth with its thin lips and tight smile. The child was clearly no proof of Anne's adultery, if it existed.

Jane rubbed her eyes to clear her mind. The sight of Elizabeth always managed to trouble her in the end. The child was a constant reminder, a living accusation, a…

"Is anything amiss, love?" Henry asked.

"Nay, nay," she answered, shaking her head and forcing a smile.

Henry cocked his head to one side but shook off his unspoken question, and turned his head to the rest of the guests to be received. Jane smiled and nodded in a gentle fog, until the sight of the Earl of Wiltshire, chosen to carry the taper, brought back the gnawing discomfort to her soul. The position was an important formal role, and a mark of special royal favor. He was laughing at something someone said, but it sounded forced and his smile seemed tight. Or maybe that was just what she expected from the father of the dead woman Jane had supplanted. He had seemed completely genuine when he thanked them for this honor. Though the choice still seemed contrived to Jane, a way of forcing him to bear mute testimony to the justice of the sentences against his beloved children. At least he'd been spared from serving on the jury that declared them guilty.

It was getting warm in the room, and that fed her utter exhaustion. Jane closed her eyes and rubbed her temples to dull the ache that gripped her head and made her see everyone in double. All she wanted to do was shut her eyes. If only she were not the center of this celebration, if only she could keep her eyes closed with no one noticing. It wouldn't dampen her enjoyment of the celebration, she would still listen and peek on occasion, but it would make it so much easier to bear. How ironic that she had spent her entire life pushing herself to keep working long after those around her had paused, her stamina fueled by guilt over undone tasks and fear of people's judgment. Now that all guilt was gone and she was finally ready to be replenished by rest, she couldn't. This was still part of her job, one that was larger than her.

"God save the King and his noble son, Prince Edward," someone called, probably Jane's brother Tom. The sudden noise broke Jane out of her reverie. The failed unison of the room's response was touching: some struggled with the unfamiliar formulation while others defaulted to the easier "God save Their Majesties." Good-meaning people all. Jane smiled and thanked them, and allowed her eyes to close while she breathed another prayer of thanks to the Lord for blessing her and the country with His grace.

October 18, 1537 ... 10 a.m.

Sunlight streamed through the giant windows whose curtains were deliberately opened wide to signal the successful end of the Queen's travails. Cromwell watched as the Duke of Suffolk approached the Queen to take the young prince from her. Suffolk had been the one chosen to hold the infant during the investiture ceremony, which would take place here, in the Queen's chamber, so that she could attend without leaving her bed. The boy would be created Prince of Wales, Duke of Cornwall, and Earl of Carnavon. Right after this, Jane's brothers would be elevated and the Seymour family's triumph would be complete.

The ceremony was brief, the time filled mainly with Archbishop Cranmer's prayers for the candidates. Applause broke out after the gentle touch of the King's sword on the men's shoulders, and the courtiers drew in round Their Majesties and the new peers. Cromwell kept his distance. They could all have this time. He didn't need it and didn't begrudge them. Eustace Chapuys was one of the first to congratulate the King and Queen, and one of the first to move away after making his reverences. He came to join Cromwell in a toast to the new world order. "Ah, Lord Cromwell, I congratulate you and your master on this day."

Chapuys' smile was genuine; he looked truly happy for them. Of course, it was prompted by gratitude over how well Mary was honored, but genuine nonetheless. It was one of the reasons Cromwell so respected Chapuys. You knew where you stood with him. Everything was personal but nothing was. They were both servants, after all, Cromwell and Chapuys, and viewed everything through the lens of that service.

"I tell you," Chapuys continued, "I was worried the Lord had turned his face from you. There were whispers that the Queen might not live through the ordeal, that her strength was not up to it. She was in labor for what, three days?"

"About that, yes," said Cromwell. His spies had reported the same whispers. As well as the rumors that the King had given orders to save the babe whatever happened to the Queen. Whether this was true or not, for once he really couldn't say. Though given how things turned out, it didn't matter.

"I am surprised that she can participate in all these celebrations after such exertion," Chapuys continued. "Is that wise?"

"She was insistent," Cromwell said off-handedly. "Wouldn't anyone be? It would be a shame to miss such triumph."

"Well, at least she is taking rest when she needs it."

Cromwell looked over at the Queen. Her eyes were closed and her mouth was slightly open. His first thought was to send a lady over to rouse her, but Chapuys' words stopped him. That and the dark smudges under her eyes that contrasted sharply with her ghostly pallor. She clearly needed this rest. She certainly deserved it. Let her have it.

October 20, 1537 … 7 p.m.

Jane opened her eyes. After rallying to near-full strength two days ago, she had slid deep into sickness, alternating between fever, diarrhea, and pain. And sometimes all three.

A cough gripped her and the pain in her abdomen redoubled. She moaned softly, praying for peace.

Another mixture. How many draughts had been pushed into her hands and onto her lips these past few days? How many times had she been wrapped in red flannel to break her fever and then sweat it away? They needed to accept the fact that nothing was helping her. Nothing would help her.

"Please, Jane," Elizabeth urged, wrapping Jane's fingers around the cup and guiding it to her mouth.

Jane sniffed and smiled. Fennel. She was transported back to the garden at Wolf Hall, the day her whole life had changed. *I toss fennel into everything.*

"Your husband spoke to your doctors, he insisted you have this."

Jane didn't bother telling her sister that she had already figured that out. She sipped the warm drink and felt comforted. Her fingers were close to her eyes for the first time in days and their red color drew her attention.

"My hands are so swollen." Even with all the sweating she'd done.

"Ah, but you've been in bed this whole time. I swelled up too after both my children. It will go away, Jane. Don't worry about it."

"The fennel will help," she mumbled and the effort exhausted her. Her arm felt heavy and she pushed the cup back to Elizabeth. "I am tired," she said, closing her eyes.

"You should drink more," said Elizabeth. "To gain strength."

Jane smiled. *Silly girl, to think that would happen.* "If only."

"Jane…"

The wave of exhaustion passed as her thoughts came back to her. She opened her eyes and looked around. "Who else is here?"

"We are alone."

"Mary?" The girl had been almost as loyal as Elizabeth, keeping vigil at Jane's side. But there were some things she should not be privy to…

"Mary went off to rest," said Elizabeth.

This was Jane's chance. Who knew when it would come again. "I am going to die," she said.

"No, Jane. You—"

"I will not recover," Jane said, not wanting Elizabeth to argue. There was no arguing. It had been eight days, and Jane was only getting worse. She had seen this before. Childbed fever. "I need you." Pain racked her, and she took a breath before continuing. "Be a mother to my son."

"You can mother your son. You just have to fight. You cannot die. Your son needs you. We all need you."

Jane shook her head.

Elizabeth pushed the cup at her. "Drink some more and fight harder."

Fight? How? Should she let herself sleep as much as she could in the hope that her body might regain its strength? Or should she fight to wake from a fever that threatened to never end? What was it to fight when just breathing was a struggle?

Unable to articulate her pain, Jane looked at Elizabeth. She had to make her sister understand. She had to make them all understand. This was God's decision, not a fight for Jane to wage. They had to accept His will. "God is merciful. He is calling me."

"God is merciful, He will let you live. You were almost recovered once, you can do it again. But you have to fight. Like you did to birth Edward. You had to rally at the end to push him out, now you need to rally to cast off the sickness. It is still possible, the doctors say."

The doctors had no idea how Jane felt inside. She had been

sick before, but never like this. This was different and Jane knew it.

But Jane also accepted it. God had blessed her with a son. She was immortal now, her son would rule England. She would die in triumph.

But how to express that when she didn't have the strength to speak more than a few words at a time?

She shook her head.

"Drink," Elizabeth insisted.

Looking at her sweet sister's worried face, Jane knew that Elizabeth would never accept the truth until Jane breathed her last. Poor thing. The best course was just to humor her. While she was awake, anyway. "One sip."

October 20, 1537 ... 11 p.m.

"Jane?"

Jane heard her husband's voice from a great distance, and opened her eyes. It was darker in the room, though that could be her eyes rather than the hour. "I am here," she said as she looked over at him and smiled.

He smiled back, but the expression did not reach his moist eyes.

"How long have you been here?" she asked.

"I only just arrived, but you were stirring. You seemed...aware."

"Yes," she breathed.

"I am so glad to see that." His voice was raw and he dropped to his knees to bring his face close beside her. "Jane. You need to live. You cannot die. You must fight this. I lost my mother like this. I cannot lose you too."

His mother. Another queen sacrificed to the realm by childbed fever. The motto Jane had chosen for her own queen-ship filled her mind. "Obey and serve," she said.

More pleading words from her husband, but she couldn't

quite understand them. It was too much effort to try, and she had something else she wanted to say. She tried to straighten out her jumbled thoughts. She might not have such a moment again. "Pray for me," she finally said. "Masses for my soul. Monks. Promise me."

"No, Jane, don't leave me. Please don't leave me."

Poor man. She felt his hands cup her cheeks and she smiled.

She closed her eyes again and shook her head. Sometime later, she couldn't tell how long, she heard sobs. Her husband was still there, at her side, head down and shoulders heaving. He held her hand against his cheek, mumbling something like, "You, Brandon, Carew...such a long line of people as have borne my punishments for me..."

What guilt was this? He saw her as one of his whipping boys, those designated friends in his youth who were beaten when he misbehaved, since of course a royal prince could not be punished like an ordinary child. He had told her, she couldn't remember when, how hard it was to watch them crying and screaming and writhing and know that he was the cause of that suffering. As it must be hard now.

But he needn't feel that way. It wasn't like that. It was simply her inescapable fate. She had spent the first twenty-eight years of her life undervalued, watching every good thing snatched away from her. It had all changed when Henry saved her from certain spinsterhood, but even then she had feared that the pattern would return. Her miscarriages had spooked her, suggesting she was being punished for the undue temerity of happiness. Or for stealing a husband away from another woman. For months she had worried that something terrible was looming. This outcome had not occurred to her, but truly, it was not so terrible. This was not punishment – God had given her a son. Yes, she would die, but everyone died. She had been given the gift of a good end. That was eternal.

She tried to rally to explain to him that she was blessed, that they were blessed, but instead felt herself slipping back into unconsciousness.

October 24, 1537 ... 10 p.m.

Cromwell looked across at his King, then down at the Queen. To look at her was to know she would die at any time. Indeed, she had already received Extreme Unction, though she had not been conscious enough to make any of the responses. Four days ago was the last time Jane had truly been with them, enough to say the goodbyes that they refused to accept, and to share the deathbed wishes they insisted she would live to fulfill herself. Since then, she had stirred a few times as if to try to say something more – but her eyes never fully opened and her mumblings made no sense. Now she was at a point where even delirium could not rouse her from her coma. She was also at a point where her breathing sounded wet, though they kept denying it was the death rattle. They still all hoped for a miracle, kept trying anything they could do to get one. Poultices, warm and cold, remained a constant fixture on her forehead, neck and chest; and she lived in a red flannel wrap. An entire country prayed for her, and scores of monks chanted and blessed any item brought into the room or used near her. But still she weakened.

Cromwell looked around at the six of them draped around her bed, a bedraggled bunch after their lengthy vigil. Even Cromwell, though he had not been with them much – he knew that being unkempt was a badge of respect. The King had claimed the right-hand side to which he was entitled, and Cromwell stood behind His Majesty's elbow. Elizabeth had the left side of the bed, close to its head, when the doctors weren't ministering to the Queen, and farther down when they were. Mary, Anne, Edward, and Tom shared the foot of the bed. Not a lot of room for them, but no one cared. When the King and Cromwell left, the women would take that side. And the King didn't come in all that often now: there was no point other than to torture himself. Not something he was known to do.

What horrible irony, that God had finally granted him the son he needed but took his perfect wife. Cromwell should have seen this coming – it was divine retribution, after all. The circumstances had always shielded Henry from real judgment. Catherine had been aged, so he would have had to leave her for someone – why not his heart's choice? Anne had to be sacrificed to the realm like Empson and Dudley, so the King needed to choose a third wife. But there was a price to pay. One he could not dispute when his ultimate prayer had been granted by the Lord. Such irony.

Tragedy too, of course. Even for Cromwell. There was his curse. His own divine judgment, equally fair. The next wife, the next wife's family, would not owe Cromwell a debt of gratitude like this one. Cromwell had been set. Now he had to do it again.

He took a deep breath. *Stop.* Everything was fine. This was not about dead or alive, boy or girl. It was about redemption. Jane Seymour had redeemed her son from the sins of his father. Edward would be an even better ally now. And after all, they were family now that Elizabeth had married Gregory.

What to do now? That was the only question. This one son was important, but not enough to secure the dynasty. He could still die, whether after two months like the tiny Henry all those years ago, or after sixteen years like FitzRoy. England needed another heir. The King needed another wife. And Cromwell needed to be the one the King turned to in the search.

This would be the perfect chance for a political marriage. Spain maybe? Cristina of Milan, Charles V's niece, was much praised for her beauty and her charm. It was too awkward for England to actually broach the subject, given Henry's treatment of the Emperor's aunt...but surely Cromwell could manipulate Chapuys to think of the suggestion himself.

Of course, the King was not yet ready to remarry. But Cromwell needed to suggest it immediately. That would make the topic easier to broach. It would also allow the King to engage when he was ready, knowing that sooner was better than later, knowing that he would not be judged. Part of the secret of dealing with kings.

"You shall have something to remember her by, Mary," the King said, out of the silence.

"No, Your Majesty, don't talk like that," Mary answered.

"She'll not live. Just as my mother didn't live," he said. Then his face twisted, and he practically spat his next words. "You shall have Beckett's amethyst. God owes me the stone for taking my wife's life. I'll wager the king who left it didn't see his prayers answered either. He's no martyr, just a false saint misleading my people. He should be exhumed and burned for his sins."

Cromwell kept his face impassive, though he could see the others were less successful. Mary and Elizabeth looked horrified, the others just seemed stunned by the viciousness. Did they really not understand their king?

Truly, Cromwell tried not to smile at this clear political turn. The monasteries would never survive now. Except perhaps one. Jane had extracted from the King a promise to found a Benedictine abbey where monks would forever say prayers for her soul. No matter what Henry might do with the rest of the monasteries, there was one that would be saved forever. Assuming he followed through.

"She is our Moses," the King declared. "She earned her great triumph – she ascended Mount Nebo and saw the holy Land of Israel...but like Moses she will not make it back down." Tears streamed from his eyes, and he brought Jane's limp hand to his lips to kiss it. "She is like the blessed phoenix symbol she chose, though she did not have its long life."

The mythical bird that died to give a new one life, as she had with her son. Jane Seymour had chosen her badge well. Of course, she had seen it as representing the love rising from the shambles of the King's failed marriage to the Boleyn. Edward had told Cromwell about that reasoning, inadvertently admitting that Jane had thought of it herself. The woman understood image. Better even than Margaret Beaufort.

Henry nodded and stood. "That should be her epitaph. 'A phoenix who died in giving another phoenix birth.' I want to add 'let her be mourned, for birds like that are rare indeed.'"

He looked over at Cromwell, who nodded. He would remember. And take care of it.

Henry cast his eyes down, and made a silent sign of the cross over Jane. He turned and walked out of the room without looking back.

Thomas Cromwell looked around at the group that remained. He looked at Jane, her face in morbid shadows. Such a sad end for a woman at the pinnacle of achievement. Still, she would die a queen – something neither Catherine of Aragon nor Anne Boleyn had done. Jane would be buried as one too, with a funeral that displayed all the pomp and formality of the coronation she never had. Cromwell would see to it that every detail was perfect, he owed that to her. England owed that to her.

"I will have more candles sent in," he said. "Enough to light the room as if it were day. Maybe that might confuse the Grim Reaper." He bowed to the others and left for the last time.

READ ON

THE PATH TO SOMERSET

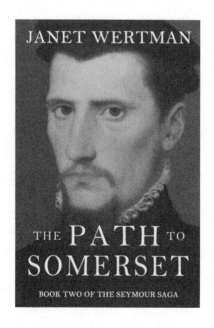

CHAPTER ONE

March 3, 1539—Tower Hill

London was a city of contrasts. It was England's expansive soul, the center where some twenty small rivers came to nourish the majestic River Thames, that main thoroughfare whose banks were dotted with the glorious manors and expansive gardens of its noblest citizens. It was also England's warped mind, a maze of twisted streets and lanes where rickety houses stopped the light from shining on the faces of the poor.

Today, more than three thousand people crowded Tower Hill, the intersection of the two Londons, the grisly site where the King's justice was meted out to the high born. The Tower itself, its white stones glinting ghostly bright against the dismal gray sky, had just disgorged another prisoner to his fate, and now a murmur of anticipation was rippling through the assembly.

Edward Seymour, Earl of Hertford and brother-in-law to King Henry VIII, swallowed to relieve his dry throat as his onetime mentor, Sir Nicholas Carew, mounted the three steps to the scaffold. Edward held his breath when Carew turned around to look at the section where Edward sat with the rest of the King's Privy Council. Thankfully the death stare never reached him. Instead Carew's lip curled when his gaze fell upon Thomas Cromwell, the man responsible for this moment, and then Carew's eyes turned back to the distance above the crowd.

Edward looked down at his hands. His long thin fingers were carefully interlaced in his lap, their pallor stark against the peplum of the black silk doublet that covered his hosed thighs. He didn't want to be here, but the presence of the Council confirmed the legitimacy of the sentence; they had little choice but to attend.

Carew began his speech, his eyes blank. "Good Christian people, I am come hither to die, condemned by the law against which I will speak nothing."

Carew's thin voice faltered with the uncertainty of a man shocked by his fate. He had failed to bring treason to light, had claimed to be unaware of the treachery when he corresponded with the traitors, but his excuses were riddles that could be taken several ways. That was all it had taken to plunge from power to death, despite his closeness to the King.

"Instead I will urge you to study the Gospel, all of you, to keep your minds on what is good and true, for I fell because of my false views."

Interesting turnaround for the conservative Carew, given that his quest to restore Roman Catholicism and roll back religious reforms had given credibility to the charges against him. Men said surprising things on the scaffold.

"And thus I take my leave of the world and of you all, and I heartily desire you all to pray for me."

Carew handed the executioner a small bag of coins – a bribe to do his job well – then knelt before the block and spread his arms. Edward felt a shattering rush of life as the axe rose, glinting in the light, then a sudden void when the weapon struck with a dull thud. He hid his flinch by scratching at an itch in his beard, trimmed to match the King's. Edward kept his thinning hair almost shaved, as well, since the King himself was bald.

"So perish all the King's enemies," said Thomas Cromwell.

The other Councilors kept their eyes downcast as they rose to pass through the crowd, parted for them by the guards.

Edward walked down to the Thames for the ride back to Whitehall Palace. The water had been blue and calm this morning, but it was gray and angry now. A sign from God? Perhaps, but whether it was wrath for a traitor's crime or outrage over false witness was not clear.

Edward wondered again whether Cromwell had taken advantage of the King's anger. Carew had refused His Majesty's request to trade some lands and had insulted him after a game of bowls. Had Cromwell manipulated the evidence, as some claimed? It would not have been the first time.

As Edward scanned the dock for a boat for hire, a quiet voice behind him asked, "Would you like to share mine?"

Edward looked over his shoulder. Cromwell's black eyes were uncertain, almost nervous. He had lost many allies over his prosecution of Carew. Edward made his choice and nodded at his friend. They walked over to the small shallop whose hull displayed the arms of Cromwell's three-year-old barony. The crewman handed them cushions; they, too, trumpeted Cromwell's title.

They sat, and Edward fixed his eyes on the rough waters. Blessedly, Cromwell held his tongue so Edward could indulge in the moment's natural melancholy. Only the slap of the oars punctuated the silence.

Once the boat docked at Whitehall Palace, the two men went directly to Mass in Henry's private oratory, a sanctuary whose wood-paneled walls exhaled incense even when none was being burned. Reverence was required, though business was welcome. This was the King's favorite time to get things done – though he frowned on others attending to any needs other than divine or royal ones. Attention could be diverted from God to the King but no further.

Edward joined the King for Mass every day. Favor and fortune came from proximity to the throne, and Edward was determined to remind the King in a thousand small ways that they were still brothers, that he deserved to be advanced. Edward's younger sister, Jane, had succumbed to childbed fever after giving birth to Henry's heir three years ago. Had she lived, Edward would surely be a duke by now. After all, it had been the quest for a male heir that led the King to destroy two wives and tear asunder his realm's religion. Edward had been appointed to the Privy Council when the King took an interest in Jane, was named Viscount at their marriage, and was elevated to his earldom at Prince Edward's birth. A second son would have completed the trajectory, but Jane's death made her brother's influence uncertain. He needed to work hard now.

Edward and Cromwell waited at the door until the priest turned a page in the Psalter, then took their seats. The King's eyes flickered at their entrance, and they bowed their heads in ostensible prayer. They had arrived during the readings. Edward usually arrived early so he could speak with the King before the service; Cromwell usually came late and spoke with the King afterwards. Cromwell's lateness was calculated, though Edward could not tell whether it was meant to signal industry or disdain for traditional Catholic practices.

Such an interesting man, Cromwell. Unlike Edward and most other highborn courtiers, Cromwell's black hair was long and his face was beardless. Cromwell downplayed any physical similarities to the King – a backhanded way for a commoner to demonstrate loyalty. Another example of the insight that had earned him a barony and three of the most important posts in the land: Lord Privy Seal, Principal Secretary, and Chancellor of the Exchequer. He was a good ally and a true friend, albeit one whose outspoken dedication to religious reform, among other things, had earned him numerous enemies.

The Eucharistic prayers were beginning; Edward knelt. He was enough of a reformist to no longer believe in the host as actual body and blood, but he did hold it sacred. Not that he discussed this with the King: denying the Real Presence was dangerous. Only Cromwell and the Archbishop of Canterbury, Thomas Cranmer, dared broach this issue, and even they tempered their arguments to avoid angering the monarch whose only real quarrel with Roman Catholicism was the Pope himself.

Mass over, the King stood and called to the page in the corner, "Have some food sent to the library."

In the months after Jane's death, Henry had shut himself in his rooms, emerging only to worry about his son and impose rules to protect him from pestilence and assassins and whatever new evils came into the King's increasingly suspicious mind. Food became his only solace, and he had steadily expanded until his arms were larger than an average man's thighs, and his pages had taken to opening both sides of the double doors when he passed through. He had resumed hunting and other active pastimes; these seemed to keep further expansion in check but made him more ravenous than ever.

The page bowed with a flourish and ran out.

"Now then," said the King, leaving the chapel for the library.

The room had been rearranged to accommodate the King's latest conceit, a new illuminated manuscript he'd had commissioned, and which stood open on a tall lectern. Four of his other favorite texts graced stands of complementary heights. The King was obsessed with the beauty of this art, and only commissions truly indulged his obsession. The thousands of other manuscripts he had acquired from the dissolution of the monasteries tended to be of modest quality – like the men who had peopled the houses – and would not do.

The King chose a chair and settled in. Edward poured him a cup of wine.

"You were late today," the King said to Edward.

"Sir Nicholas Carew departed the earth this morning."

The King took a breath and his eyes flashed to Cromwell. "It is a sad thing when men turn traitor."

Cromwell nodded. "He redeemed himself at the last and recognized his false views."

The King sniffed. "Why is it that men's eyes only seem to open when death is imminent?"

"The certainty of their eternal sentence turns many men to the truth," Cromwell replied.

"Amen," said Edward, even though Carew might simply have been trying to protect his wife from further retaliation. The King would brook no criticism of his Church, which he created when the Pope refused to annul Henry's twenty-year marriage to his brother's barren widow so he could marry Anne Boleyn. The Church of England was guided by the King's own conscience; only fools believed he would abandon it just because he had turned on Anne.

The King looked out the window.

The silence was broken by a familiar voice from the hall. "Prepare for a feast," it called, and suddenly Edward's brother Tom was bowing melodramatically and waving in a parade of pages. Each carried a large tray heavily laden with food: meats on one, custards and savory pies on a second, desserts on a third.

"Ah, thank you, Tom," the King said. "Of all my men, you know my appetites best."

Tom smiled and tucked his reddish hair behind his ears. He was well suited as a gentleman of the Privy Chamber. Tom had inherited the Seymour ambition but not the Seymour talent; he was all show, no substance. Edward prided himself that those traits were reversed in him even as he secretly envied Tom's *bonhomie*.

The King lumbered over to the table and took generous portions, then gestured to the men to join him. Edward and Cromwell piled their plates to match the King's, but Tom took only some baked pears with scraped cheese and a small marzipan subtlety. The men were quiet for a time, as the King smacked his lips and licked his fingers.

A knock came at the door, then a page's face appeared. "Doctor Butts asks leave to attend you."

"I saw him in the hallway," said Tom to the King. "I told him to give you some time."

The King clapped Tom on the shoulder. "This is as good a time as any. Better to be distracted, eh?"

The three men bleated their agreement, and Butts entered, his black and scarlet robe billowing behind him. Two assistants followed with his supplies. The King pushed his chair sideways and stuck out his leg. "Well, how does it look today?"

Butts crooked his finger, and one of the assistants set a footstool on which the other placed the King's leg. Butts started to remove the bandages that began just below the knee and went all the way up the King's thigh. The inner layers were stained yellow and brown; a putrid odor crept into the air as the ulcerated sores came into view. Edward quietly pushed his plate away.

The King had injured his leg three years ago from a bad fall during a joust, and the wounds had plagued him since. On good days he hid his pain well enough, but on bad ones he could not hunt or even walk comfortably. Such a sad state for the man who had once been the golden prince of Christendom. And probably one of the reasons he hadn't remarried. Not that Edward wanted to push a new wife. He was quite happy being the brother of the King's one true love. Indeed, Edward dreaded the day when some other brother would come along to take his special place...

End of Excerpt

AUTHOR'S NOTE

There is not a lot written about Jane Seymour. She never said or did much publicly, and she signed only one document, the one announcing the birth of her son (she signed it "Jane the Quene" - hence this book's title). Historians largely ignore her, and most people dislike her (as they dislike all the Seymours). That's why I had to write this book – and begin the Seymour Saga.

Admittedly, Jane's story is not an easy one: she married Henry just ten days after Anne Boleyn was executed for crimes she did not commit. But Jane was known to be devout in this time when the fear of God was paramount, so the way she justified it all became central to the narrative...this and the fear that must have dogged her. We know she had at least one miscarriage because of the incident where Henry places his hand on her stomach and says "Edward, Edward." I gave her a second one, just to spook her.

I also gave her a confidante that did not exist. Jane did have a sister Elizabeth, but I gave the two women more of a relationship than they likely had. Elizabeth had left court during Anne's reign and did not return until just a few months before Edward's birth (she was with her children in York) – but I needed to get Jane out of her own head and Anne Seymour was not the right person for this supporting role (besides, Anne had retired from court to have her own children).

I hope you appreciate the choices I made – and I hope you love the book! Please consider leaving a short review (even just a star rating) on Amazon or Goodreads (or Barnes & Noble, or Kobo, or iBooks – or your library's website!) to help other readers discover it. It really does make a difference and it would mean the world to me!

Made in the USA
Monee, IL
27 February 2022